Seaborn Series Book 1

Athlanmara

J.M. Burrows

Visit Seabornseries.com

DEDICATION

To my wonderful children, Dan, Jake, Grace and Truman.

You taught me the meaning of love.

CONTENTS

Prologue   Pg 1

1   Birthday Presents   Pg 5

2   "I Love Sailing!"   Pg 14

3   Bad Business   Pg 25

4   The Song   Pg 30

5   The Seals   Pg 41

6   The Seunach   Pg 52

7   "Forget About It"   Pg 61

8   Introductions   Pg 66

9   The Search   Pg 76

10 The Island   Pg 81

11 Guardians   Pg 89

12 Blue Lagoon   Pg 92

13 The Colony   Pg 112

14 Best Friends   Pg 114

15 Revelations   Pg 120

16 Search and Rescue   Pg 135

17 A Whole New World   Pg 147

18 Monsters   Pg 156

19 Heroes   Pg 166

20 Savages   Pg 176

21 One Mind   Pg 188

22 "Humans Scare Me!"   Pg 196

23 Best Day, Worst Day   Pg 210

24 Covert Plans   Pg 223

25 Kilts in the Keys   Pg 230

26 A Big Mistake   Pg 251

27 "911"   Pg 261

28 Lies   Pg 274

29 Hunters   Pg 287

30 The Coming Storm   Pg 294

31 Villains   Pg 304

32 Video Games Pay Off   Pg 318

33 I Need A Hero   Pg 326

34 After the Rain Has Fallen   Pg 340

35 New Beginnings   Pg 347

    Epilogue   Pg 353

    A Note To My Readers   Pg 356

ACKNOWLEDGMENTS

This book could not have been written without the invaluable help of my four children. Thank you Dan for the series title. Thank you Jake for being excited about talking about the nitty gritty of story. Thank you Grace for being the first reader and telling me like it is, you can't have four bad guys in the first book! Thank you Truman for listening and offering your words of wisdom, the best advice being the force is cool, midichlorians are dumb. Also, thanks for finding my entire manuscript on the computer when I thought I lost it.

I also want to thank my amazing beta readers, Jolene, Dennis, Mary, Steven, Ann, Irietys, Ellie, Emma, Alyssa and Rebecca. It is so true, "faithful are the wounds of a friend". You helped turn my fun visions into something readable and I am so grateful.

Finally, I would like to thank my mom and dad, Irietys and Roger, for introducing me to books and always telling me that I could do anything.

PROLOGUE

The Russian cargo ship Kasimov churned through the frigid Baltic waters, it's bow cutting through the early morning fog. The rusting metal hulk hugged the coast of Sweden staying far away from the customary shipping lanes. Arctic gusts made the ship's lights dance on frozen wires and played a eerie melody through the rigging.

Dr. James Gordon entered the bridge shaking the ice from his mackintosh. He was a tall man, distinguished looking, though not handsome. He had a long clean shaven face, piercing sky blue eyes and his light brown hair was beginning to turn grey. At the moment he had a trace of a smile on his thin lips. After devoting thirteen years and most of his fortune in his quest, he had finally captured the creature he was searching for.

"How long till we reach Aberdeen?" he asked the captain anxiously, his cultured British accent revealing his breeding and education.

"Depends on weather," the captain answered, in a thick Russian accent.

Gordon walked to the window, he looked out into the darkness of the early morning and hoped for smooth sailing. Even though his specimen was bound and drugged, he was worried. He couldn't rest easy until he had it back in his secure lab in Scotland.

Gordon began to pace. He could hardly keep his hands from shaking. His mind was racing, thinking of the scientific breakthroughs this new creature could unleash and the myriad of benefits it could bring to mankind, not to mention the difference it would make in his own life.

He couldn't decide if he should return to the tank where the glowing creature was floating unconscious or if he could make the boat go faster by harassing the captain. Suddenly, the frigid air was filled with the blaring sound of a warning horn.

Gordon froze. "No!" he whispered. He whirled around. "What is happening?" he barked at the captain.

The captain immediately got on the intercom yelling orders in Russian but his pale face told Gordon all he needed to know. Gordon ran out onto the bridge deck. He looked down. He could barely see the silhouettes of the guards as they ran through the thick fog on the Kasimov's lower deck, their Uzis waving in tandem with their arms.

He heard a scream directly below him. A guard stumbled into view, a large knife sticking out of his chest. The next moment two naked boys ran out of the passageway. One was tall and muscular with dark hair. He was being supported by another teen whose light brown hair was hiding his face. Blood ran down onto the deck from the taller boys leg. He was still bleeding from where he'd been speared by Gordon's men.

 The young rescuer tossed his bleeding friend over the side of the ship just as the guards surrounded him. The boy held up his hands in surrender. The guards seemed frozen, unsure of opening fire on an unarmed youth. There was a moment of tension, Gordon couldn't breathe, he could barely process the drama below. The boy slowly lowered his hands. Then he quickly leapt over the side of the boat, a hail of gunfire following him.

"Hold your fire!" Gordon yelled, "Prekratit ogon! Prekratit ogon!"

The gunfire stopped. Gordon looked at the empty sea. Just like that his prize was gone.

Grimly, Gordon climbed down the steps to the deck, in the span of three minutes all of his plans had been ruined. Malcolm Stewart walked up to Gordon, he was a large man, bald, with dark beady eyes and a sharp nose.

He rubbed the stubble on his chin. "Why'd ya stop them from shootin' doc?" he growled in his thick cockney accent, "A dead one's better than nothin'!"

Malcolm walked up to the screaming and bleeding guard and yanked the knife out of his chest. He grinned, revealing his tobacco stained teeth. With his greasy handkerchief he wiped the blood off the knife and handed it to Gordon.

Dr. Gordon shuddered. He almost regretted hiring Malcolm and his crew but his scientific mission wasn't exactly the type that would be written up in National Geographic magazine. He knew some scientists would question his methods, but Gordon was willing to risk anything and use whatever methods it took to realize his goals. That meant he had to work with some people who were comfortable with doing things that were not technically legal.

Dr. Gordon looked at the knife in his hands. He turned it over, studying the intricate Celtic carvings on the handle. He wasn't surprised at the discovery.

Gordon walked along the deck until he came to a seagrass rope dangling from the side of the ship.

A man dressed in a blue hazmat suit, holding his bleeding head approached him. "I'm sorry sir, I don't know what happened," he said.

Gordon didn't look up from his perusal of the rope. "Tell me you inserted the tracking beacon before a teenage fish attacked you," he said, cooly.

The man looked at the ground. "Yes sir, I did."

1 BIRTHDAY PRESENTS

The intense Florida sun beat down on Brooke Williams as she walked up to the front entrance of Marathon High school. She was a tiny, pale figure with freckles on her nose and shoulders. The strong wind blew her strawberry blonde hair around her head like a crazy halo. She tried to smooth her hair with her hands. Brooke pulled up the straps on her dress for the thousandth time, wishing she hadn't listened to Zoe.

Zoe had thought it would be so fun if she and Brooke dressed up for the last day of school. Brooke had reluctantly agreed, after all it was a special day, not only was it that last day of school but it was her sixteenth birthday.

She sighed and looked up at the perfect blue sky. The gulls were making random patterns in the air calling to one another. Brooke hunched her shoulders. She felt like they were mocking her as she clomped up the walk in the new wedge shoes Zoe insisted she wear with her borrowed dress.

Brooke took a deep breath and opened the school doors. Instantly, she was assailed by the smell of dead fish. "Oh, crap!"

She knew exactly where the smell was coming from, her science experiment. Brooke had been working on an experiment that dealt with the effects of a low oxygen environment on fish populations. Her teacher had given her permission to continue the project after school got out, but something must have gone wrong.

Brooke hurried through the halls past her fellow students who were holding their noses and making faces at the revolting smell. She was glad they were too distracted by the stench to notice her.

She walked into the Biology classroom and the smell almost knocked her over. There, floating belly up in the fish tank, was all her important research. Brooke had no idea what could have gone wrong. She inspected the filters and carbon dioxide infusers on the tank and discovered that the main filter had been unplugged.

"Dang it!" she exclaimed.

How could this have happened, she wondered. It was probably Reehan, he's always doing something mean to torture me, she thought. He's just jealous that I won the spot on the science decathlon team. Brooke almost laughed at the thought of someone being jealous of her. No, I'm sure some stupid kid just pulled the plug out to charge their phone.

Brooke looked sadly at her ruined experiment. She had put months into her project and she had hopes that her data could make a difference for the oceanic environment. She took a deep breath and swallowed the lump in her throat.

Come on, Brooke, pull yourself together. Did Rosalind Franklin give up on discovering DNA? No, no she did not!

Brooke looked around for something to put the dead fish in. I can at least take the fish to my dad's lab and get some tissue samples read, she thought. Brooke was no quitter, especially when it came to her science experiments.

She found an old garbage bag and gingerly removed the rotting fish from the tank. Brooke realized she couldn't just put the fish in her locker so she made her way to the front of the school. She would have to try to make it home and back to school before first period started. It's no big deal, she assured herself, it's not like we're doing anything in class today but signing yearbooks.

Brooke had gotten to school early to avoid walking through crowded halls in her irregular state of dress but it had taken her so long to clean up her experiment that now the halls were crawling with excited students. She walked quickly through the halls. Brooke kept her head down hoping not to attract any attention but the big black garbage bag she held, dripping malodorous goo made that impossible.

"Oh my gosh!" a girl exclaimed, "What is that disgusting smell?" She and her friends gave Brooke dirty looks.

Brooke tried to walk faster. She hated people looking at her, which normally was not a problem. Brooke was used to being the 'invisible girl' at school. No one ever gave her a second glance. She looked up, only thirty feet to the front door. Come on Brooke, you can do this!

At that moment, Chris DeLuca and his friends walked in the front doors. Brooke's heart sank. Chris DeLuca was the cutest guy in school and the captain of the football team. She realized he probably didn't even know that she existed but she of course knew everything about him. Brooke froze in her tracks desperately trying to come up with an escape plan, but it was too late.

"Dude!" Chris said to his friends. "What is that rank smell?" They all turned to stare at Brooke and her dripping garbage bag. Chris looked her up and down and grinned. "Going on a hot date with your fish?" he sneered.

All his friends burst out laughing. Brooke felt her cheeks burning. She knew her pale face was flaming red. She willed her body to move but for some reason it wasn't responding.

A crowd, attracted by the laughter, surrounded Brooke. She felt like a trapped animal. Brooke turned on her heels to flee but as she had been frozen in place a large puddle of slime had accumulated at her feet. When she turned to run her feet slipped out from under her and she fell hard on her backside, splashing fish goop all over herself and the closest observers.

Students screamed; some with disgust, others with laughter. Brooke tried to get up but slipped again in her unaccustomed footwear. Frantically, she pulled off her shoes and ran for the door barefoot leaving all of her work in a pile on the floor. She didn't stop running until she reached her bike in the school parking lot.

Sobbing, she jumped on her bike but her foot slipped off the pedal. "Come on!" she yelled. The interminable flock of seagulls, drawn by the smell, began to dive and screech at Brooke. "Shut up and leave me alone!" she cried.

Brooke finally got her ancient bike moving. She tore out of the parking lot with the absolute intention of never coming back.

The sounds of the Overseas Highway dimmed as Brooke turned down her little side street. She headed for the tiny yellow house near the end of the street where the pavement faded into the Atlantic Ocean. Brooke ran in the front door and slammed it behind her.

She stumbled into the bathroom and saw mascara rivers running down her cheeks. She let out a sob and started to wash the makeup off her face. Why did I let Zoe talk me into this? She's always making me do things I don't want to do!

Brooke dried off her face and went to her room. She took off her dress and threw it in the corner. She could still hear the laughter in her head. Brooke pulled on her tank top and shorts, put her hair up into her usual messy ponytail and sat down on the floor. She started to chew on her nails. Brooke was mad at herself for overreacting to the stupid kids at school.

Normally, school was tolerable for Brooke. She concentrated on her studies and biology experiments, keeping herself away from social situations as much as possible. Science was easy to understand, people were not. She wished she had someone to talk to. She wished for the millionth time she could feel her mother's arms around her and hear her say it was going to be alright.

Eleven years ago Brooke's mom, Nina, had left. She hadn't even said goodbye. It was like her mother was there one minute and gone the next. She remembered waking up the day after her fifth birthday and feeling like there was a big hole in her heart. She sensed her mother was gone even before her dad had told her.

She knew her dad kept hoping that her mom would come back someday but every year that passed she could see his hope fading. Her dad began to throw himself more and more into his research. Now he was hardly home at all and Brooke's birthday tradition was sitting home alone feeling sorry for herself.

Enough of this! There are people way worse off than me, she told herself. Brooke wiped her eyes. She grabbed a science textbook off the floor and opened it. Who cares about high school? I'm sure some Kardashian will have another baby soon and they will forget all about my spectacular performance today. Brooke stared at the words on the page but she kept seeing the faces of her laughing classmates.

All at once, she became aware of the faintest sound of singing. Brooke held her breath, straining to hear. It sounded like a chorus of women's voices far away. The music was very beautiful and haunting.

Brooke was fascinated. She got up and went to her window, thinking the sound was coming from outside. Yet, standing at her window, she realized the sound was coming from inside her house. Her heart started to pound with fear but she felt compelled to find the source of the beautiful song.

She walked out into the hall and the music became louder. She followed the song to her father's room. She put her hand on the doorknob then hesitated, she knew her dad didn't like her going into his room.

Brooke had childhood memories of playing with all sorts of interesting curios from her parents travels but when her mother left her father had collected everything and thrown it all in an old trunk in his room. It was like he was trying to erase her. Brooke's hand trembled but she felt compelled by the melody. She turned the doorknob and opened the door.

"Brooke!" a voice yelled from the other room.

Brooke was startled so badly she almost fell to the floor. Guiltily, she pulled the door shut and dashed into the living room. There stood Jackson Hale, his curly brown hair clinging to his sweaty temples, his baby face red from exertion. He was holding a smashed cake box out to her.

"I brought you somthin' for...your...birthday!" he said between gasps. Brooke took the cake box, not knowing whether to laugh or to cry.

Jackson had been Brooke's friend since kindergarten. They had gravitated to each other as they had both been little outcasts, Brooke was too shy to talk to other kids and Jackson would never shut up.

She opened the cake box. Inside was a cake with pink frosting and the words, 'Happy Birthday Bro..' written on top. She realized that it was supposed to say 'Brooke' but it looked like the box had been dropped and one side of the cake was smashed.

"My mom made it!" he said. Then he noticed that Brooke was about to cry. Jackson's face fell. "Yeah, sorry about that. It was hard to ride my bike and hold the box," he said.

Brooke put the cake down and gave Jackson a hug. "No, I love it," she said and sniffed, trying not to cry again. "Thanks."

Jackson plopped his lanky frame onto the couch, still breathing hard from his bike trip. He had never been into doing anything physical. All his skills were related to video games and playing Dungeons and Dragons.

Brooke sat down next to him. "Aren't you supposed to be making up your Algebra final right now?" she asked.

Jackson snorted. "Whatever, even if I fail it I will still get a 'C' in the class," he said, nonchalantly.

She knew that Jackson's parents were giving him trouble about his grades but he had risked all that to cheer her up. She punched him in the arm. "Dork!" Brooke said, smiling.

Jackson grabbed his arm. "Ow!" he exclaimed. Then he punched Brooke back. "Nerd!"

They both started laughing but inside Brooke was wishing she had two parents who got on her case about anything. Jackson's dad was the Coast Guard Master Chief and his mom stayed home taking care of Jackson and his three sisters. They seemed like the perfect family.

She sighed. Jackson glanced at Brooke. He nervously bit his lip and tried to come up with another plan to keep her mind off the school fiasco. He knew what had happened. Marathon High was a small school and news traveled fast.

"Hey!" he exclaimed, overly enthusiastically, "Let's go sailing!"

She looked at him and lifted her eyebrows. "You, want to go sailing?" she asked.

None of the other kids in town liked to sail and Brooke knew that Jackson didn't need any help being unpopular. He also hated everything to do with the ocean, much to the disappointment of his father.

"Sure!" he said. "It's officially summer and you told me you'd teach me how to sail this summer and we better get started 'cause it's probably gonna take the whole three months for me to learn."

Brooke laughed. "Fine! I'll get my shoes."

Brooke loved sailing, she spent as much time as she could on the ocean. She had spent her early life sailing the world with her father and mother as they traveled wherever their research took them. Her first steps were on the deck of a boat and she knew how to sail one by the time she was four.

Ironically, though she was thoroughly at home on the water, she was terrified of being in the water. When Brooke was a child she had almost drowned, so her dad told her. She couldn't really remember the incident. She just always felt this deep dread of the ocean, like it was a creature that wanted to swallow her whole.

Her father seemed to dread the ocean even more than Brooke.

Since her mother left he had never again set foot on their sailboat, The Sea Witch. He also wasn't happy that Brooke went out on her little racing sailboat.

As Brooke walked down the hall towards her room, she paused as she passed her father's door. There were no voices now. Did I dream the whole thing, she wondered.

Brooke still felt drawn to open the door. She had a distinct feeling that her dad was hiding something. She looked over her shoulder nervously, but she could hear Jackson rummaging around in the kitchen looking for something to eat. She turned the handle and opened the door a crack.

"Brooke, come on!" Jackson yelled from the kitchen.

Brooke closed the door with a sigh. "I'm coming!" she yelled.

2 "I LOVE SAILING!"

Four hours later they were still on the bay at the Marathon Boat Club sitting in Brooke's tiny racing sailboat. The boat was only fifteen feet long and made for short races with one or two sailors. The boom sail swung to one side or another depending on which way you wanted to turn. This arrangement caught the wind and propelled the craft forward or in left and right angles. Brooke had taken down the forward jib sail so all Jackson had to do was turn the boat with the tiller and swing the boom to one side or another but he just couldn't get the hang of it.

"No, don't point the bow straight into the wind! You see, we are stalling again," Brooke said.

Jackson fumbled with the lines trying to swing the boom around to catch the wind but it was too late. The boat came to a complete stop. Jackson dropped the lines, "Dang it!" he exclaimed.

Brooke moved to the back of the little boat. "Here, switch with me again. I'm sure it's my fault, maybe I'm just a terrible teacher."

Jackson shook his head. "Yeah, right, that's why you get paid $25 an hour to teach bored retirees how to sail. I'm just a loser."

"Hey, losers! Thought I would find you out here!" Zoe yelled at them from the dock. "Get over here and pick me up and I'll show you how to sail," she bragged.

Brooke grinned. "Sit down, we'll be there in an hour," she yelled back at Zoe.

Zoe snorted and plopped down on the dock, letting her long, tan legs swing on the edge. She pushed her thick, wavy black hair off her shoulders and pulled out her cell phone.

Zoe Moreno was the girl that every boy had a crush on and every girl hated. After Brooke's mom left, the Moreno family had practically adopted Brooke and her father and she and Zoe had grown up like sisters. Brooke had taught Zoe how to sail, even though the popular activity in Marathon was spearfishing. Zoe had tried to teach Brooke how to flirt with boys, but Brooke was hopelessly awkward at interacting with the opposite sex and feared she always would be.

As Brooke turned back to work the sails she glanced at Jackson and saw that red patches had formed on his brown cheeks. She realized he didn't want to look stupid in front of Zoe. Brooke tried to suppress her laughter as he leaned back on the edge of the boat trying to look cool. Both girls knew he'd had a crush on Zoe since the seventh grade.

Brooke maneuvered the boat and finally bumped up against the dock.

Jackson stood up and bowed with a geekish smile towards Zoe. "My lady, your chariot awaits."

Zoe laughed as the boat began to tip over.

"Jackson sit down!" Brooke yelled as she grabbed the back of his life jacket and pulled him down.

Zoe hopped in easily. "Let's do this girl!" she said. Zoe put her hand up to give Brooke a high five.

Brooke placed her hands on her hips. "What happened to the end of school yacht cruise with stupid Chris 'My Dad Owns the Whole Town' DeLuca?" Brooke demanded.

Zoe raised her eyebrows. "Chris who?" she asked innocently.

"What?" Brooke's face brightened. "You broke up with him already?"

Zoe looked down and grabbed a lifejacket. "He's a total jerk!"

She had found out what Chris had said to Brooke earlier. The girls exchanged a glance. They had been friends for so long Brooke could see in Zoe's eyes that she had broken up with Chris for her.

"Come on let's go!" Zoe said, trying to change the subject.

Jackson was grinning from ear to ear and gazing at Zoe with a moony look on his face. Brooke knew he was wondering how he could orchestrate them getting lost on a deserted island so he could make his move on Zoe.

"Hey, space boy!" Zoe yelled. She snapped her fingers in Jackson's face breaking him out of his romantic trance. "You're in the middle, move it!"

Jackson quickly got out of Zoe's way. He put up his hand for a high five. "Yes! Let's do this!" he yelled. Zoe just glared at him.

Brooke took the tiller, Zoe the jib sail, the two girls working together flawlessly. Brooke was a technically smart sailor and Zoe took chances, which was why they won the Florida Sailing Association Youth Regatta three years in a row. Jackson tried to stay out of the way. He sat in the middle of the boat staring at Zoe.

Out past the bay the wind picked up. It was so strong the side of the fifteen foot boat began to rise up out of the water. Brooke moved to the uphill side of the boat to try to balance it. She stretched her body out over the water holding the boom sail taunt as it captured the force of the wind.

Brooke loved the feeling of flying over the water. She felt so free, yet totally in control. Her problems receded from her mind as quickly as the shore, until a huge gust of wind hit the boat almost capsizing it. "Come out here Jackson, I need your weight!" she yelled.

Jackson clawed his way to the uphill edge of the boat next to Brooke. The little boat was almost perpendicular in the water. Zoe threw her body next to Brooke and Jackson to keep the boat from heeling over. The three of them leaned out over the water. The ocean sprayed in their faces, but Brooke wouldn't let up.

All of a sudden, they were surrounded by a pod of dolphins, their noses pushing into the wave off the bow. A dolphin breached directly under the teens spraying them. They all laughed joyously.

"I love sailing!" Jackson screamed into the wind.

The wind was so strong the three of them together could barely keep the boat in contact with the water. Brooke realized they had better go back to a more sheltered area. She nodded to Zoe, the two of them almost reading each other's minds. As one, Brooke and Zoe ducked under the boom pole to turn the boat. Unfortunately, they had forgotten about Jackson. The swinging boom hit him square in the chest knocking him into the water.

Jackson came up out of the water sputtering. "Hey! Help!" he yelled. The girls couldn't help but laugh.

"See ya Jackson! The swim back will do you good!" Zoe called back to him.

The speed of the boat had taken it about fifty yards from Jackson and the girls knew it would take them a while to maneuver back to pick him up.

"Hang tight, we are turning around!" Brooke yelled as she grabbed the tiller.

Zoe leaned out to yell at Jackson again, that's when she saw it; something was in the water behind him. "Jackson behind you!" Zoe screamed.

Jackson turned around and saw a shape coming towards him. It looked like the body of a woman with hair trailing over her face. "Ahhhhh!" Jackson screamed. He swam faster than Brooke had ever seen him swim before.

The girls expertly maneuvered the boat and in seconds they were near enough for Zoe to lean out and grab Jackson's hand. She pulled, he kicked and he flopped into the boat on top of Zoe.

"Get off of me!" Zoe yelled, shoving him to the bottom of the boat.

"I'm sorry!" Jackson gasped, trying to get out of Zoe's way. "What is that thing?" he cried, his eyes wide with terror.

"It looks like a woman's body," Brooke said quietly, peering out over the water. Brooke subconsciously tightened the strap on her life jacket. The irrational dread she'd always had about drowning swept over her again. The two girls slowly brought the boat closer to the floating shape.

"Maybe it's a dead mermaid," Zoe joked, trying to lighten the mood.

As the boat got closer they could see that what they had thought was hair was actually a pile of seaweed and sticking up out of the water behind the seaweed was a fin.

"Shark!" Jackson yelled.

Zoe snorted. "That's no shark fin you idiot, it's a dolphin."

Zoe was right. Brooke used an oar to move the seaweed and unfortunately what they saw was a dead dolphin. The three of them peered over the side to get a closer look at the poor animal. They could see the dolphin was covered with lesions. Probably lobomycosis, Brooke thought. It was a yeast infection that affected dolphins in polluted waters, she had seen it before.

"Poor thing!" Zoe exclaimed.

She put her hand out to touch the bumpy skin. Suddenly, the dolphin opened it's eye and made a weak splash with its tail. Zoe screamed and fell back onto Jackson. For a moment their faces were inches from each other, Jackson smiled. Zoe struggled to get up but Jackson, trying to be a gentleman, kept grabbing her arms trying to help, which made it impossible.

"Get off of me!" she snarled.

"Sorry!" Jackson cried, desperate to accommodate Zoe.

Brooke felt like she couldn't breathe. She had seen so many sick sea creatures lately. Just last month over two-hundred sea turtles had beached themselves. Brooke had been one of the volunteers who spent days trying to nurse the poor turtles back to health at the Turtle Hospital in Marathon. Most of them didn't make it.

Brooke couldn't handle another animal dying in front of her but she didn't know what to do. Her heart was pounding, she was on the verge of hyperventilating. Brooke wanted to run away. I have to get out of here, she thought, panic rising in her throat.

Zoe finally pulled herself up, looked at the dolphin again, then looked at Brooke. Zoe knew what was going on in Brooke's head.

Zoe gave her a smile. "It's gonna be okay," she said.

Brooke took a deep breath and nodded, her eyes wide.

Zoe pointed at Brooke. "You call your dad and the Dolphin Research Center, tell them to meet us at the dock." Zoe turned to Jackson, "Give me your lifejacket. We can make a sort of sling and drag the dolphin back to the dock."

With all the drama Jackson was terrified of letting go of his life jacket but he wanted to look mature and brave in front of Zoe. "Do you think it's really gonna make it?" he asked, slowly taking off his last shred of safety.

Zoe grabbed his jacket. "Shut up! It's going to be fine!" she exclaimed. Zoe glared at Jackson and tilted her head towards Brooke.

He got the message. "Yeah, of course," he said, smiling encouragingly at Brooke.

Brooke huddled in the boat, listening to her dad's phone ring. It went to voicemail. Of course, she thought, that's my dad, always unavailable. She called the DRC and they assured her they would have a boat at the dock soon.

"The DRC will be at the dock," she said to Zoe.

"Great!" Zoe said.

Brooke was glad Zoe didn't ask about her dad. She watched as Zoe tied her life jacket to Jackson's, making a rough sling. Brooke wished she could be strong and brave like Zoe.

"Okay, now I'll just slip this under the dolphin and we'll drag him back to the dock," Zoe said, but she hesitated to jump into the water with a wild dolphin.

Zoe and Jackson looked at Brooke. Brooke knew what they were thinking. She had always been the one who had a special bond with animals. Maybe it was because of her quietness, but Brooke was always able to calm any agitated creature and wherever she went animals sought her out.

Zoe smiled at Brooke encouragingly, she knew that Brooke was terrified of going in the water. "You got your life jacket and I'll go with you," Zoe said.

Brooke knew she needed to do this. She had to try and save the poor, sick animal. She nodded at Zoe as she slowly moved to the edge of the boat. Zoe got into the water and Brooke, hands shaking, slowly dropped into the water beside her. The two girls swam carefully towards the sick dolphin. Zoe let Brooke approach the wild animal first.

"It's okay buddy," Brooke said quietly as she reached out and gently stroked the dolphin's side.

The dolphin didn't react which worried Brooke, she could feel him slipping away. Brooke kept talking softly to the dolphin while Zoe slipped the jacket sling under the dolphin's belly and tied the other two straps together. Zoe signaled to Jackson and he threw her a rope. She tied it to the jacket sling.

Brooke kept up her soothing voice. "You're gonna be fine, I promise. We just gotta get you some medicine," Brooke whispered to the dolphin. This time it made a pitiful whistling sound, almost like a human cry.

Zoe motioned to Brooke and the girls quickly swam back to the boat and leapt into it.

"Let's go! You hold the line Jackson," Zoe commanded as the two girls got the boat going at a steady clip.

Jackson strained to hold the line. "Okay, but if this turns out like that pelican rescue you organized, I am not going to jail this time!"

When they got close to the dock they could see the Dolphin Research Center team was ready. They had a sling in the water and their boat waiting to transfer the dolphin to their facility in Grass Key. Steve McRae, a friend of Brooke's father and a marine biologist, was already in the water.

Steve was tan and young looking even though his sandy blonde hair had some grey in it. For a while he and her father had worked closely together on projects for Florida Atlantic University. He was always coming over to their house and Brooke loved the stories he would tell about her dad.

Steve would tell stories of the adventures the two of them had together all around the world before her dad had met her mom. He even had some stories to tell about her mother, but always when her dad wasn't around.

As the boat floated closer, Steve swam over. With the help of his trained crew they maneuvered the dolphin into their sling. They carefully lifted the animal onto a foam pad on the back of the DRC boat. Brooke and Zoe got their sailboat alongside the DRC cutter and Brooke jumped over. She and Steve knelt next to the still dolphin.

"Where'd you find this guy, Brooke?" Steve asked, as he ran his hand along the dolphin's side.

"Just out beyond the bay in the open water. He looks like he's got lobomycosis."

"Yep," Steve grimaced, "Man, this is really bad."

Out of the water they could see that the dolphin was almost entirely covered with lesions from the yeast infection. It's eyes were just slits and the animal was having trouble breathing. Steve took out his stethoscope and listened.

He looked at Brooke with concern. "I don't think he's gonna make it Brooke."

Brooke's breath caught in her throat. "But you can give him antifungals right? He just needs some time to get better," Brooke pleaded, with tears in her eyes.

She so wanted to be able to save this beautiful creature. Steve was about to speak when the dolphin let out a big breath and rolled to its side.

Brooke tried to roll it back up. "Someone get some water, maybe if he feels water he'll breathe!" she said frantically. The other team members looked away.

Steve put an arm around Brooke. "Honey, he's gone. You did your best, it happens."

Brooke felt stupid for crying over a dolphin she had just found but she couldn't stop her tears.

Steve patted her back. "We'll take him to the center and do an autopsy, see if we can find out anything useful," he said reassuringly.

Brooke heard yelling further down the dock. She turned to see Zoe trying to maneuver the boat alone.

"Jackson!" Zoe yelled.

"Sorry! I'm just trying to help!" Jackson exclaimed, but the more he tried to help the more he got in Zoe's way.

Brooke took a deep breath and tried to wipe her tears away. She jumped up onto the dock. What good is crying going to do, she said to herself.

"Thanks Steve," she murmured.

"Hey, how's your dad been?" Steve asked, "I haven't seen him around for awhile."

"Me neither," Brooke said. She walked off down the dock.

3 BAD BUSINESS

Ten miles down the Overseas Highway, tucked away behind the DeLuca Yacht Sales and Marine Center, a group of fishermen were toiling in the late afternoon sun. The rough looking men were loading fifty-five gallon drums onto a decrepit commercial fishing boat. Paul DeLuca, a short pudgy man in his fifties, watched them. He glanced at the notepad he was holding and nervously chewed on the end of his pen.

He ran his hand through his thinning grey hair. "Eddy!" Paul yelled.

A short, slender man with a tightly cropped afro, ambled over to Paul. "What dya want?" he said through pursed lips, while lighting a cigarette.

"You gotta get all these dumped tonight, ya hear me?" Paul said, gesturing at the drums in front of the warehouse behind him.

Eddy laughed. "No way man, it takes us four hours just ta get out far enough from shore."

Paul gritted his teeth. "Then load more on the boat!" he growled.

Eddy blew a cloud of smoke towards Paul, his dark weathered features veiling his contempt. "I'm takin an awful big risk already, man," he griped.

Paul wiped the sweat from his forehead. "That's why I'm paying you the big bucks, now get moving!" he yelled.

Paul stormed off. His phone buzzed, he glanced at the caller and his heart skipped a beat; it was Lombardi. Paul knew he would be calling to hassle him about more shipments coming down from Jersey. He declined the call.

Paul walked through the shipyard where crippled vessels were propped up on keel blocks waiting to be revived. He entered the Marine Center's showroom and walked past the sleek, expensive yachts. The crisp, cool air conditioning helped to calm his frayed nerves.

"Evening, Mr. DeLuca!" his salesman said.

Paul ignored him and stormed into his office. He collapsed into his chair. Paul took a deep breath and reached for his accounts book, knocking his family picture off the desk.

He cursed. Paul hated that he was so clumsy. He picked up the picture and paused, looking at his beautiful wife Ava and his handsome son Chris. Unfortunately, his daughter Caitlin took after him. He was so proud of his son. Chris was everything Paul never was, handsome, athletic and popular.

"See, money can buy you anything," Paul muttered to himself.

He placed the picture back on his desk and reached into a drawer to pull out a bottle of scotch, he poured himself a drink. He thumbed through the pages of his account book. Paul wanted to be doubly sure before he confronted Dennis. Paul was no accountant but he didn't get to own a multi-million dollar business by being stupid. It was easy to see where Dennis had been fudging the numbers.

"Crook!" he muttered.

There was a tentative knock on the door. Paul reached into his desk drawer. This time he pulled out a small handgun. He put the gun in his waistband under his jacket. "Come in!" he yelled.

Dennis Reynolds nervously walked into the room. He was a tan, slim man in his forties. He looked more like a tennis coach than an accountant. "Hey, Paul!" Dennis said, trying to sound nonchalant, but Paul could hear the tremor in his voice.

He started to sit down but Paul stood abruptly. "Let's go for a walk," he said.

The two men walked out of the office, past the lustrous yachts, out through the graveyard of boats and into a desolate warehouse. With every step Dennis grew more and more agitated. Paul stopped by a stack of barrels that smelled of sulfur.

"Look Mr. DeLuca, I think there's been some mistake," Dennis blurted out.

"Oh, so it's 'Mr. DeLuca' now?" Paul's voice was hard. "And there's no mistake."

Dennis' face went pale. He glanced around, there were only a couple of Paul's lowlife crew loading barrels onto pallets to take out to the boat.

Dennis held up his hands. "Mr. DeLuca, it was only a few thousand dollars, my kid, she's...she's got medical problems," he stammered.

"Your family issues aren't my problem Dennis! You take food out of my kids mouths, after all I've done for you?" Paul yelled. He pulled out his gun.

Dennis took a step back. "Whoa! Wait a minute! I have copies of the records in a safe deposit box. If you kill me everyone will find out about your years of dirty dealings with East Coast Chemical Disposal!" he threatened.

Paul snorted. He reached behind a barrel and pulled out a safety deposit box and dropped it on the cement floor with a bang. "This box?" he yelled.

Dennis got down on his knees, almost crying. "Please Paul," he begged, "our families have spent holidays together."

"I know," Paul replied coldly. He aimed the gun at Dennis' head. "I trusted you." Paul pulled the trigger, there was a click. Dennis looked up, fear and shock on his face.

Paul grabbed Dennis by the shirt and pulled him to his feet. "If you ever cross me again, I will stuff your body into one of these barrels, you understand me?" he growled.

Dennis nodded, tears running down his face. Paul threw him to the ground, put away his gun and walked out of the warehouse. He was so distracted by the confrontation with Dennis that he almost ran into Chris.

"Oh, hey, buddy! I thought you were going out on the yacht today with that Chloe girl."

Chris looked at the ground. "Her name is Zoe," he mumbled. "And she stood me up."

Paul tried to pat Chris on the shoulder but he pulled away. Paul looked at his son confused. "Well, don't worry about it. Here," He pulled out his wallet and started shoving bills in Chris' hand. "You just go buy her something nice. She won't be able to resist that!"

Chris just shrugged his shoulders, refusing to look at his father. "I guess," he said sullenly, taking the bills.

"That's my boy!" Paul said, smiling at his son. As Chris started to walk away Paul called, "Hey, how bout having some dinner with your old man?"

Chris paused. "Nah, I'm..I'm gonna go over to Jordan's," he stammered.

Paul nodded his head over enthusiastically. "Sure, sure! You go have fun with your friends!" he said, hiding his disappointment. Chris nodded then almost ran out of the shipyard.

4 THE SONG

A gloomy cloud mountain advanced on the Florida Keys creating two bizarre worlds; one of sun the other of darkness. It wasn't unusual for storms to come out of nowhere and turn the tranquil island paradise into a treacherous environment. Brooke unlocked her back door and tiptoed into the kitchen. She hated coming home to a dark, empty house. She felt scared and lonely.

Brooke took out her cell phone and tried to call her dad again. She heard a buzzing sound coming from the living room. Of course, she said to herself. She walked to the living room and saw her dad's phone on the coffee table, half buried under his research papers.

It was obvious her dad had fallen asleep on the couch again while he was reading last night and just got up in the morning and left. Brooke nervously straightened her dad's papers, then decided to get herself some dinner and eat alone as usual. As she was walking to the kitchen a huge clap of thunder startled her so badly she almost screamed.

"Brooke!"

She heard a woman's voice call her name. It sounded far away, like it was coming from outside. Terrified, Brooke peered out the window. She didn't see anyone. I'm sure it was just an auditory hallucination brought about by stress, Brooke reassured herself.

"Brooke!"

She heard the voice again, her heart started to pound. Brooke ran to the back door and locked it. There was a flash of lightning followed immediately by a clap of thunder, the storm was on top of her now. Shaking, Brooke turned on every light in the house. She sat on the couch and tried to start her summer reading assignment, but she couldn't concentrate. She felt like she was waiting for something or someone. Rain started to pour down on the house, like thousands of fingers drumming on the roof.

Then Brooke heard the music again. The same song she heard before Jackson interrupted her. For some reason this time the music didn't scare her, in fact it seemed to calm her. The music was soft at first, then it became more definitive, more powerful. It sounded like a chorus of women's voices rising and falling. She walked softly down the hall, her bare feet making no sound on the cool tiles.

Brooke opened the door to her father's room. Almost in a daze she was drawn to a small trunk in the closet. She wasn't one to pry into other people's things, but she couldn't help herself. It was like some other power was directing her movements.

When she opened the trunk she felt surrounded by the voices, it wasn't that the voices got louder, rather it was as if she had become part of the melody. Brooke dug around in the trunk searching for the source of the music. She found a small pottery statue of a lion with wings, a gold coin with what looked like a bee on it, a metal statue of a dragon and lots of old maps and papers. Her parents had traveled all over the world as marine biologists, however she knew very little about their travels. Her dad never talked with her about it but apparently they had collected some interesting artifacts.

When Brooke reached the bottom of the trunk she felt something hard and square, she pulled it out. It was a beautiful silver box about the size of an orange. The edge of the box had intricate Celtic knot patterns all around it, and carved in the center of the lid was the figure of a woman, a seal and a dolphin, all swimming around in a circle. It looked very ancient.

The voices became more intense and though she couldn't understand the words of the mysterious song she felt like it was commanding her. She was conscious of a strong desire to open the box but she was also filled with fear, as if she stood upon a precipice. If she went over the edge there was no turning back.

Brooke held her breath and opened the box, instantly the voices ceased. Inside the box, on a bed of purple velvet, was an exquisite, gold bracelet. She picked up the beautiful piece and when she held it in her hand it seemed like the whole world went silent. All Brooke could hear was her own heartbeat pounding in her ears.

The bracelet was solid gold, she could tell because it was heavy for its delicate form. She examined the piece and saw that it was carved in the shape of a mermaid, the tail of the mythical creature curving around to meet the head. There was some ancient writing on the inside of the bracelet that she didn't recognize.

Without thinking Brooke slipped the bracelet onto her wrist. She was surprised that it felt warm, not the cold metal feeling she had expected, and it seemed to form itself to her arm. Brooke liked it. She could feel the warmth travel up her arm and surround her, almost like a hug. The sensation also terrified her.

Brooke and her mother had been intimately connected. She had felt so safe and cherished as a child. But after her mother left, she had never felt close to anyone. She knew her dad loved her, and

Zoe and Jackson were great, but every time someone tried to get close to her she pulled away. She couldn't risk getting hurt so deeply again. The bracelet seemed to open up that giant wound of emptiness in her heart and it was overwhelming.

"Brooke"

This time the woman's voice sounded close, and full of love. Brooke whirled around expecting to see someone behind her, but she was standing alone in her room. Suddenly, Brooke laughed out loud, the sound startled her. What am I feeling, she asked herself.

Brooke closed her eyes and took a deep breath. "I feel strong!"

Her voice echoed in the silent room. Brooke opened her eyes. There was such power in the words that Brooke wondered if they came from her or from somewhere else. She laughed again. I want to run up and down the beach, no I want to punch someone, no I want to sail my boat to nowhere! Wait, she thought, is this some sort of mania induced by anxiety? You *were* hearing things, Brooke. She tried to methodically run through her symptoms in her head but her mind was racing, she couldn't concentrate. She also couldn't stop giggling. I feel so good, I don't care!

Brooke shoved everything back into her father's trunk except for the silver box. She took the box to her room and hid it in her underwear drawer. Another bolt of lightning lit up the sky outside her window and thunder shook the house. Brooke laughed again, grabbed her rain jacket and ran out the door.

The storm clouds made the evening sky look threatening. Chris DeLuca felt the darkness adding to the emotional weight he carried as he walked up to the door of the Moreno house. At least there's a break in the rain, he thought. He could hear voices inside the house yelling in Spanish. It always seems like Zoe's family is fighting, he thought, but least they talk to each other.

Chris started to get sick to his stomach again as he remembered what he had seen at his dad's warehouse; his own father standing over his accountant with a gun. Chris' hand trembled as he started to knock on the door but then the voices seemed to get louder and faster. He lowered his hand and turned to walked away.

I don't need this hassle! But Zoe is hot, and I've already dated every other girl at school.

Chris didn't want to admit that what he really needed was someone to talk to. The day's events had really shaken him.

Chris worked up his courage and knocked loudly on the door. The door flung open and Mrs. Moreno stood there looking at him. She was shorter than Zoe and, though in her fifties, her beauty was still intimidating.

"What?" she asked in a thick Spanish accent.

"Uh, is Zoe here?" Chris stammered.

"Zoe! Mr. Bigshot, he is here!" Tina Moreno yelled as she turned and left Chris standing at the door, his face turning red.

Zoe walked towards the door having a heated exchange in Spanish with her mother, including lots of hand gesturing. "What do you want?" Zoe said standing at the door with her arms folded.

"Uh, I thought we were going to hang out today, you never showed," Chris said in his sweetest voice that he reserved for manipulating girls.

Zoe snorted. "Did you think I wouldn't find out what you said to my best friend?"

"Is that what you're mad about?" he laughed, "What I said to fish girl?"

Zoe poked Chris in the chest with her finger. "Don't call her that! It wasn't her fault that her experiment stank up the whole school!" Chris had to back up as he absorbed Zoe's jabs. "You just think you're so much better than everyone!" she yelled.

Chris thought about ditching the whole attempt at making up with Zoe but she even looked sexy when she was mad.

He tried another tactic. "I'm sorry babe," he said sweetly. He pulled out a small jewelry box. "I got you this."

Zoe hesitated, she took the box and opened it. Inside was a beautiful pair of diamond stud earrings. Chris knew he had this in the bag; girls were suckers for jewelry. He had seen it work for his dad a million times.

Zoe closed the box and looked at Chris. "You think you can buy me off," she said quietly.

She threw the box at Chris and started yelling. "You are the most self-centered, lowdown, jerkface, moron,..." at that point Zoe started to yell at him in Spanish.

Chris picked up the box. "Jeez, you are so not worth it," he said.

Zoe pushed him off the front steps. "Get out of here! I never want to see you again!" she yelled.

She went in the house and slammed the door. Chris stood holding the box. A clap of thunder rang in his ears and the clouds opened up like a waterfall over his head.

"Perfect," he said.

The rain poured down so hard that Brooke could hardly see where she was going on her decrepit bike. She'd been on the gravel road so many times however, she had no trouble navigating to her dad's lab. Lab, hah, she thought. It's just an empty old warehouse.

Her dad, Dr. Tom Williams, used to work at the beautiful facility at the Harbor Branch of Florida Pacific University. That was until he decided not to care about anything anymore, including the research he was paid to do. Now they survived on whatever grant money he could scrounge up. There was only one thing he seemed to care about anymore, his crabs.

They weren't even useful crabs, like the ones you could eat, these crabs were some species of Yeti Crab; small, pale, hairy crabs that lived deep on the ocean floor by volcanic sea vents. Scientists discovered that the Yeti crab colonies survive by eating the bacteria that collect on their hairy legs. However, these particular Yeti crabs were starting to be found in other places, far from the sea vents and they were behaving in strange predatory ways.

Brooke pulled open the creaky metal door to her dad's lab. There he was, hunched over a microscope looking at his beloved crabs. He didn't even notice when Brooke walked in.

"Crab for dinner again?" she asked sarcastically as she shook the rain from her jacket.

Tom looked up, his blue eyes bloodshot. As he ran a hand through his black hair, Brooke noticed the grey at his temples. "Oh shoot, what time is it?" he asked, dazed.

Brooke plopping down on a stool next to a jar full of dead crabs. "Way past dinner time."

Tom rubbed his eyes and stood up. He stretched his over six foot frame and groaned. "Sorry honey, lost track of time again. Should we go pick up a burger or something?"

Brooke let out a sigh. "Oh my gosh dad! You know I don't eat beef, I barely eat fish!"

Tom walked over to Brooke and tried to give her a hug, Brooke pulled away.

"I know, I know, I'm just not thinking right now," Tom said, not noticing Brooke's mood. "This crab puzzle is really giving me grief." He pointed at the jar next to Brooke, "Would you look at the size of this one!"

Brooke glanced at the jar. There seemed to be crabs of all different sizes. She rolled her eyes. "So what?"

Tom went on, ignoring her uncharacteristically nasty attitude. "Normally yeti crabs are around six inches, but this one is twice that size!" He tapped the glass for emphasis. "Why are they getting so big? I think they are growing abnormally large because they are moving to shallow areas that are warmer and have less pressure. But why are they migrating? Also, we know that the yeti crabs function in groups but they've actually been observed hunting in a manner similar to…"

"I'm sick of hearing about boring crabs!" Brooke exclaimed.

"Right, sorry honey, I'm focused now." Tom grabbed a folder, "How was your day?" he asked his eyes on the pages.

Brooke clenched her jaw to stop the tears. I could say I blew up the school and he would probably just say, 'That's nice'.

Brooke got up from the stool and started pacing. "Oh, not great, I only made a fool of myself in front of the entire school and tried to save a horribly poisoned dolphin which died. Miss any phone calls today?"

Tom looked up, his face fell. He patted his pockets, obviously not remembering where he left his cell phone. "I'm sorry Brooke, I must have left my cell at home. Did you call Steve?"

Brooke turned her back on her dad and walked to the door. "Of course I did and of course he came." Brooke opened the door to leave.

Tom rushed across the room and grabbed her arm. "Brooke wait!" He looked down and saw the bracelet on her wrist. Tom dropped her arm like it burned him. "Where did you get that?" he said with fear in his eyes.

Brooke's heart started to pound with fear and guilt. She had forgotten to take the bracelet off when she left home. "I...I found it, in a box," she stammered.

"Take it off now!" Tom yelled at her.

Brooke was shocked, her dad never yelled. "Why?" Brooke asked quietly.

"Just take it off! It doesn't belong to you!" Tom reached for the bracelet. Brooke pulled her arm out of his reach.

Anger washed over her. "No! I want it!"

"Brooke, you don't understand," he pleaded, "Just do what I tell you."

Brooke took a step towards her dad. "Do what I'm told? That's all I ever do!" she yelled. "I do my homework, I clean the house, I do all the cooking, I work a part time job. I'm sixteen now, maybe I'm old enough to do what I want!"

Tom stared at her wide eyed. Brooke continued her tirade. "Yeah, it's my sixteenth birthday, which I'm sure you forgot!"

Tom looked at the floor. "Brooke, honey, I'm sorry, it's just…"

"You know," Brooke said, "I've always felt sorry for you, thinking, 'Oh poor dad, mean mom left him with this little kid to raise'. Well maybe she left for a reason! Maybe she left because you were a terrible husband because you sure are a terrible father!"

Brooke knocked over a stool and stormed out the door. Tom ran out the door but Brooke jumped on her bike and sped away.

"Brooke!" he yelled fruitlessly, the rain soaking him in seconds.

He ran back into the lab and started searching for his keys. He looked under pile after pile of notes but came up with nothing.

"Dang it!" he cried, knocking over a pile of papers. Tom sank to the floor and put his head in his hands. "Nina," he mumbled.

He took a deep breath then stood up. He grabbed his coat and slowly walked out the door.

The wind was starting to pick up by the time Brooke got home. It felt good, the wild weather mimicking her wild feelings. She slammed the door as she walked into the house. For a moment she paused, the guilt about what she said to her dad catching up to her. Brooke had never talked back to her dad in her life.

Brooke looked around the room. How many nights have I spent in this house alone? Loneliness smothered her like a blanket. All the horrible feelings she had, seemed to cascade down on her at once; the dead dolphin, her dread of facing the kids at school, her dad's indifference and the aching hole inside her heart.

I have to get out of here! The thought was pounding in her brain. A flash of lightning lit up the ocean outside the window. She saw the outline of her father's sailboat. Brooke ran to her room, grabbed her backpack and started shoving things into it. She ran to the back door and threw it open, letting the rain splash onto the worn kitchen tiles.

She turned and yelled into the empty house. "And I'm never coming back!" Brooke slammed the door shut.

5 THE SEALS

As the sun rose over the Atlantic, the sky grew lighter but the wind was still driving dark clouds before it like a celestial sheep dog. Brooke, straining at the wheel of her father's sailboat, could hardly keep her eyes open. She had been sailing all night. She was exhausted but she didn't care as long as her sailboat was skimming across the water like it had a mind of its own. Anywhere but home is where she was headed.

"Come in Sea Witch! Brooke get back here now!" the radio crackled. It was her dad again, his pleading had changed to threats. "The weather report is getting worse and so is your punishment!"

Brooke switched off the radio. She realized it wasn't a smart thing to do. The dark clouds up ahead were getting bigger and the waves were starting to swell but she needed the freedom of the open sea. Tears were streaming down her cheeks, a combination of the wind and her own self-pity. She angrily wiped them away. It wasn't the first time she and her dad had fought but this time something was different, Brooke felt like she had the power, that she wasn't a child anymore. But why was I so cruel, she chided herself, it's not like me.

The wild storm was starting to scare her but she didn't want to go back, she was still angry. Maybe I'll just head up the coast and spend the summer with Uncle Jimmy in Boston. The idea made her laugh. Wouldn't he be surprised to see me. She quickly calculated the trip. It would probably take all week, she thought.

Brooke bit her lip. It's not like me to be so irresponsible. I'm the girl who calls my dad to let him know I got to Zoe's house safe. What's wrong with me?

Brooke looked out at the angry waves and suddenly she felt as empty as the sea. She let out a deep breath and her anger seemed to blow away in the blustery wind. I just want to go home.

All at once, a line snapped. Brooke hadn't realized how strong the winds had become. She glanced at the GPS. Her stomach dropped. She had never been out this far alone, and in her father's boat. She began to regret her rash decision.

Sailing her father's thirty-five foot sailboat in a storm was proving to be too much for her. Brooke edged the boat out of the gale-like winds and started to turn back towards shore. As she turned the wheel to head for home, the boom sail whipped towards her unexpectedly in an angry gust. Brooke dove for the deck and just missed being knocked overboard. Her heart pounded with adrenaline.

"That was close," she gasped.

A sick feeling began to grow in her stomach. There was no one to save her out here. As she got up from the deck she glanced out over the rolling waves and noticed a group of seals, their heads just barely sticking up out of the waves. They stared at her with large expressive eyes.

Great, now I'm having visual hallucinations. Seals don't swim around in the middle of the ocean. Not to mention, there are no

seals in the Caribbean. Brooke, pull yourself together! She took a
deep breath and focused on getting the boat under control.

Under the rolling surface of the storm tossed waves, four sleek
figures swam in unison, not seal shaped as Brooke had supposed
but shaped like men, at least from the waist up. From the waist
down the creatures had what looked like a tail which they used,
dolphin like, to propel themselves forward in the water. Their arms
were at their sides as they swam, with only small movements of
their webbed hands needed to change course, which they did
quickly and often as they jostled one another to remain in the lead.
One solitary figure swam after the the jovial group.

The creatures had sleek hair only on their heads as the rest of their
bodies were finely muscled and hairless. They gazed on the sea
with large soulful eyes and their pale skin glowed as they swam.
One creature, larger than the rest, with huge muscles and dark
hair, broke from the group and shot up towards the bottom of the
heaving sailboat. He slapped it hard making a hollow thumping
sound. He looked down at the others and grinned.

He rejoined the rest of the group. *Told you I would do it, Kai!* Maksim
said, silently.

The creatures, though they had the ability to make sound, were
able to communicate telepathically when in close proximity to each
other. Kai was small but quick, his almost black hair contrasted
with his pale skin and glowing blue eyes. He saw Maksim's guard
was down and rammed him in the chest with his shoulder.

Glogach! Kai sneered.

Maksim set on Kai, wrapping his strong tail around his body and pinning his arms to his sides. Zale and Sevan came to Kai's defense but the two of them together couldn't pry off Maksim.

The lone figure observed the struggle but didn't intervene. He was large and muscular, though not as big as Maksim. He had brown hair, pale skin and striking hazel green eyes. What set him apart from the others were the intricate glowing patterns on his skin. He circled under the tormented boat, fascinated.

Adrian! Kai yelled at his brother. Adrian continued to ignore the others and gaze at the bobbing craft.

Why did humans come out on the dangerous sea, he wondered. He knew they took fish and other creatures from the sea to eat and he knew that they transported items and people from one place to another. Yet, sometimes humans just sailed out on the sea for no reason.

Adrian wanted to know more. He had been taught by his father, Bronte, that all humans were evil creatures. They made killing a sport and poisoned everything in the sea. But Adrian had found human books, some from the ships that went down and some he had stolen from the Builder.

He had deciphered the words and discovered a different story about humans. The humans in the books protected the weak and punished evil, some were kind to each other and they had something called love that they were willing to die for.

A profound and secret mystery, Adrian said to himself, repeating a quote from a human book as he gazed up at the floundering sailboat.

Adrian! Kai screamed in his head.

Adrian looked down at his brother impassively, still struggling in Maksim's grip. Maksim looked like he wasn't trying at all. Adrian knew the only threat to Kai was a bruised ego.

Let 'im go, Adrian said, in the Scottish twang he had picked up from his father.

Maksim loosed his grip and Kai slapped him in the face with his tail as he and his friends retreated to a safe distance.

Maksim swam up to Adrian and looked at the boat. *Leave it alone. You know your father will be angry with you if he knows you were even this close to a human.*

 Kai came back and circled them both. *Everyone knows he's a human lover,* Kai sneered. Zale and Sevan laughed.

Adrian swiped his tail at Kai but he was too quick. Kai took every chance he could to bait his brother. Adrian knew it was just his way of desperately trying to prove himself. Every male Athlanmaran was supposed to travel the world on their own during their sixteenth year. If they returned they would be accepted into the tribe as an adult, many however, never returned.

It was on Adrian's journey that he had seen Maksim captured and had rescued him. Bronte however, refused to let Kai go on his journey because of his sickness. Kai would frequently have fits of tremors, no one knew why.

Adrian looked at Kai sadly. *Let's be off, Mak.*

The two friends slowly moved down to deeper, calmer water. Kai watched them go still stewing over his humiliation with Maksim and hating the pity in his brother's gaze.

Zale and Sevan began to follow the older boys but Kai stopped them. *Let's have some fun before we go back.*

Zale and Sevan looked at each other. *I don't want to get in anymore trouble,* Zale muttered.

Kai swiped his tail at Zale knocking him into Sevan. *You're such a leanabh!* Kai mocked, *I just want ta knock over one stupid boat in the middle of nowhere. No human will notice this time. Come on!*

Zale and Sevan followed Kai reluctantly. They positioned themselves below the floundering boat, pointing their strong tails upward and began to wave them back and forth. Their skin began to glow brighter.

On the surface of the ocean the storm was getting worse. Brooke struggled to pull the sails down. It was a hard job to do alone. Finally, she got them down and stowed good enough. She went back to the tiller to start the engine and head for home.

Abruptly, everything around her seemed quiet. There was no shriek of the wind in the rigging, though the ocean was still acting like a deranged roller coaster. Gripping the wheel she gazed out at the silent sea feeling small and alone as she had never felt before on the ocean.

She noticed a glow in the water to port. Brooke felt a wave of fear wash over her as big as the waves washing over the deck. She punched the engine button. The engine choked for a moment then died. She frantically punched the button again, nothing.

Brooke glanced at her control panel. Every dial was going crazy. She looked out at the waves. The glow in the water was intensifying. Her heart was pounding. All she could hear was her own shallow breathing.

 All at once, the boat dropped out from under her like a elevator that snapped its cables. One minute she was bobbing up and down the next moment she was in a free fall, like a hole had opened up in the ocean.

Brooke looked up. For a split second she was surrounded on all sides by walls of water, then the water collapsed in on her like a brick wall. She was pinned to the deck of the sailboat under the weight of the water. Her entire world became pressure, rushing noise and water. The boat flipped. Brooke, released from the drag, kicked away from the craft fighting for her life.

Instinctively, she followed her air bubbles. Brooke strained for the surface but she was yanked backwards. She looked down and saw that her foot was caught in the poorly stored rigging. She reached down and clawed at the tangled lines trying not to let panic rise up in her throat. Brooke managed to get her foot free. She made a desperate attempt for the surface, her whole body screaming for air.

She could see the light dancing on the waves. Come on, Brooke, you're almost there! A large swell beat against the floundering vessel. The boat rolled towards Brooke, the top of the mast came down hard on her head. Brooke saw stars. She gulped in sea water.

I'm going to drown. I always knew I would drown. Strange thoughts swirled around in her mind as she lost consciousness. I never got to go to college. College would have been so much better than high school. And I never kissed a boy, I always wanted to. Oh, shoot! I left my clothes in the washing machine, then darkness.

As Adrian and Maksim were making their way down to calmer waters, Adrian wondered about the human on the boat.

Maksim looked at his friend. *I know what you are thinking*, he said.

Adrian kept swimming trying to avoid Mak's gaze. *What are ya talking about?*

You know, you are always getting yourself into trouble, Maksim said, swimming in front of Adrian to stop him. *Why do you care about the land walkers? They are worse than sharks! They will destroy you!*

Adrian swam around Maksim. *Not every human's like the ones that took ya. I'm sure there's bad humans and good humans just like they're bad Athlanmara and good Athlanmara.* Adrian kept swimming serenely.

Maksim followed, scowling at Adrian. *Your father doesn't think so. Bronte knows that all of our problems come from the landwalk...the humans. Where are the good ones when half the sea is dying?* Mak asked.

Adrian was about to answer Maksim when Kai and his friends came shooting by them. They were jostling and laughing.

Did you see it's face? Zale shouted.

Sevan spun around them in circles. *Yeah, and there were only three of us!* he bragged.

Kai looked slyly at Adrian. *One less ta bother the Athlanmara,* he sneered. Then the three of them disappeared in the gathering gloom of the deeper water.

Adrian felt sick, he knew what Kai had done. He glanced guiltily at Maksim, then sped toward the surface.

Adrian, no! Maksim yelled, but it was too late.

He knew he had to follow Adrian, it was his duty. Adrian had saved his life two years ago and he had promised to always have Adrian's back. The huge boy let out a groan of bubbles and followed.

Adrian could see the outline of the sinking boat against the surface of the water. He slowed down as he came closer, not wanting to risk being seen. He carefully searched the wreckage. Adrian came upon an unconscious human girl. He reached out to touch her.

Maksim came up behind him and pulled him back. *No Adrian! They are dangerous!* he pleaded.

Adrian shook him off. *She isn't dangerous!* he protested.

Maksim grabbed his arm again. *Just let her die, they drown all the time. It just happens.*

Adrian looked at Maksim with anger in his eyes. *It didn't just happen, Kai made it happen. He's the one who killed her! Who's bad now?* Adrian yelled. Maksim backed away from Adrian.

Adrian looked at the dead girl. She was beautiful, but not like the female Athlanmara that he had seen. The suire, as they were called, were beautiful but it was a fierce, dangerous beauty. This girl was so...innocent.

Her strawberry blonde hair was floating around her face, her pale skin shone. Adrian looked at the little brown spots on her nose. He had never seen freckles before. I wonder what color her eyes were, Adrian thought.

Suddenly, the girl opened her eyes and choked out a few bubbles. Startled, Adrian flew backwards bumping into Maksim. Mak took off in a panic like a fleet of sharks were after him.

Adrian quickly recovered himself. He knew he had a chance to save this girl. He grabbed her hand and began to drag her to the surface as quickly as he could. As Adrian glanced back at her limp body, to his surprise he noticed that the hand he was touching was glowing. The strange glow was moving up her arm.

Before he could even wonder about that his head broke the surface of the rolling ocean. He pulled the girl's head out of the water but she still wasn't opening her mouth to breathe. He knew humans could only breathe through their mouths. Maksim popped above the surface about twenty yards away.

"How do I make her breathe?" Adrian yelled at Maksim.

Mak just scowled and shook his head. Adrian took a breath with his mouth and tried to think of what to do. As he breathed out he had an idea. He would force her to breathe with his breath.

Adrian opened her mouth and breathed into it. He looked at her face, her skin was so pale, she still looked dead. He tried again and again. All of a sudden, she coughed up water and gasped for air on her own. Adrian sighed in relief. Maksim circled the pair ready to wade into the fray if Adrian needed his help against the dangerous human.

Brooke opened her eyes and looked at Adrian. He marveled at how blue her eyes were, like the blue of the reef water.

"The seals saved me," she said. Then her eyes rolled back into her head and she lost consciousness. Adrian laughed, just glad she was alive.

Maksim risked coming up behind Adrian. "Humans are stupid," he muttered over Adrian's shoulder. The two boys looked at each other. "Well, what are you going to do with her now?" Mak asked.

Adrian hadn't thought about that. He had saved the girl's life and for some reason he felt fiercely protective towards her. Maybe it was because she was so helpless and lost, a human girl alone in the middle of the ocean.

He thought for a moment, while Maksim circled impatiently. It was getting harder and harder to keep her head above water in the rough waves. He knew they couldn't put her in their vessel. The bata was designed for Athlanmarans and was full of water not air.

At last, Adrian had an idea. "We'll take her ta the hidden island!" he yelled at Maksim over the sound of the wind. "It's not too far."

Adrian began swimming furiously through the waves on his back, holding the girl up out of the water as best he could. He was worried she still might die, her body was so limp.

Maksim followed at a distance. "You know that is forbidden!" he yelled, but Adrian just kept swimming. "I won't be around when your father finds out!"

Maksim slapped the water with his tail, furious at the whole situation. But being committed to his friend and terrified of being left alone, he had no choice but to follow.

6 THE SEUNACH

The storm clouds began to disperse as the sun rose higher over the modest city of Marathon, Florida. The bright rays did nothing to cheer Tom as he sat on the couch in his living room, his head in his hands. He was living a parents worst nightmare.

Reynaldo Moreno, Zoe's father, a slight, greying man, sat morosely on a chair at the table watching his wife putter around the William's kitchen. Tina Moreno finished making the coffee and walked over to Tom.

Tina put her hand on his shoulder. "Here, drink this. This, it will warm you up."

She handed him a cup of strong espresso with milk. The Moreno's had been at the William's house since they found out Brooke was missing.

Tom took a sip. "Thank you," he said. He put the coffee down on the table and put his head in his hands again. "This is all my fault."

Tina sat down next to him. "No! Now you be stopping that right now!" she said emphatically. Tom looked at her bleary eyed. "This, this is no one's fault. Kids, they do stupid things all the time.

You trust me! I have the five of them!" she said, patting Tom's arm. "You know, the Coast Guard, they is out looking and they will find her. Coast Guard Mr. Hale, he is out looking and he will not give up." Tom nodded. He had to hope. The thought of losing his only daughter was too horrible to comprehend.

There was a knock at the door, Mr. Moreno went to open it. Paul DeLuca stepped into the William's tiny home. He stood by the door awkwardly trying not to drip all over the tile floor.

"Tom, I heard about your daughter, I'm so sorry, is there anything I can do?" Paul asked.

Tom got up and walked over to shake his hand. "Thanks for coming by Mayor DeLuca," Tom said.

"Now, it's Paul, Tom," he said patting Tom on the shoulder. "Have you heard anything yet?"

Tom started aimlessly pacing. "No, it's only been light for a few hours, so we're hoping to hear something soon."

"Oh, I'm sure you will. From what my son tells me, your daughter is a good sailor!" Paul plastered a smile on his face.

Tina snorted. Paul looked uncomfortable for a moment. "Wow, that coffee smells good!" he exclaimed.

Tina sat on the couch with her arms folded glaring at Paul. "Yes, it does," she said.

Paul got the hint. He put his arm on Tom's shoulder and angled him away from Tina's prying eyes. "You know I've been thinking about you working away in that run down old warehouse next to my boat yard, and I remembered a property I own on this side of town," Paul said quietly. "It would be perfect for a lab! It's closer to your house, it's got all the amenities you'd need, we could work out a great deal. What do you think?"

Tom rubbed his head. "I don't know. I can't even think about that right now," Tom mumbled. "What would you even want with that old building?"

"My business is expanding and look Tom," Paul lowered his voice even more, "I see the lights on in your building till late at night. Seems to me you should be spending more time at home, then things like this could be avoided." Tom stared at Paul, pain in his eyes.

Tina jumped off the couch and pushed Paul towards the door. "That's it! You...you get out of here!" she yelled. Mr. Moreno got up and silently opened the door to aid his wife. Tina pushed Paul out the door.

He stuck his head back in. "I'm just trying to help Tom, to keep you closer to home. You never know what dangers are out there," Paul warned, his voice becoming harsh.

The tropical storm seemed to follow the two tiny figures moving slowly through the bright Atlantic waters. Adrian's strong tail was making a trough through the rough waves but he was beginning to tire. It was no easy task swimming backwards and holding a limp body up out of the water.

He was also worried about the girl. She hadn't stirred since her comment about the seals and her body felt cold on his chest. He knew humans had to be on land to be warm. If he could only get her to the island in time. Thankfully, he knew they were close, even with the wild winds he could smell the rich scent of land.

Maksim swam underneath the waves to his right. Every time Adrian looked over he could see him glaring. Finally, Adrian heard the crash of waves on rock.

He put his cheek next to the girl's ear. "We're almost there lassie, keep breath'n," he whispered.

Maksim's head broke the surface next to Adrian. "I hate this," Maksim said, scowling at the island.

"I know," Adrian grinned.

It was a small island just over the edge of the Bermuda Triangle. From the water it looked like any of the thousands of palm tree and brush covered islands that dotted the area. The two boys swam around the rocks into a small protected bay where the water was calmer, and they made their way towards the shore. As the water became shallower, Adrian arched his back. He felt the familiar white hot pain shoot through his body as the skin on his tail began to split and two legs appeared.

Adrian's feet hit the white sand of the beach and he stood up. He lifted the girl out of the water and carried her to the tree line. He laid her gently on the sand. Maksim also transformed however, when his feet hit the sand he fell over, cursing. He struggled into the unfamiliar upright position and ended up hopping out of the water, his feet together.

Adrian laughed. "You're supposed ta use them one at a time, ya glogach!" he yelled.

While Maksim was struggling to put one foot in front of the other Adrian turned his attention to the girl. He had never been able to examine a human this close before, well, not one that was alive.

He put his face next to hers to check that she was still breathing. Thankfully, she was, but she still seemed so cold. He pulled off her wet windbreaker and saw that she had more clothes on underneath. He also noticed a strange gold bracelet on her arm shaped like a suire. Adrian took in a quick breath in surprise. He recognized the bracelet as a seunach, a powerful magical amulet worn by dangerous suire.

Maksim stumbled up next to him. "Why do they have so many coverings?" he sneered. Adrian threw the jacket aside. Suddenly, Maksim noticed the bracelet, his face went pale. "She's going to kill us," he whispered. He grabbed Adrian's arm and tried to drag him away. "Hurry, let's go before she wakes up!"

Adrian pulled his arm away from Maksim. "She's no suire, she was drownin, remember?" Adrian knelt down next to the girl. He picked up her arm and examined the bracelet closely.

Maksim peered over his shoulder anxiously. "Well, if she's no suire then she's even more dangerous. You know you have to kill a suire to get a seunach," Maksim said, his eyes wide with fear.

"Not necessarily," Adrian replied, deep in thought.

He was trying to remember all the legends he knew of the capabilities of the seunach. Each one had different powers, he knew that. Some had power to control minds, some could be used as a deadly weapon, some, he remembered, had the power to heal disease.

If I could get this seunach for myself maybe I could heal Kai and the other Athlanmarans that are suffering, he thought. For a moment he let himself imagine the look on his father's face when he returned to the colony with the seunach on his arm. He would be proud of me for once, Adrian mused.

Adrian looked down at the helpless human girl. Maksim was right, the seunach could only be removed from someone who was dead, or if the person willingly gave it to you. But who would do that, he wondered. Wait, she's not a suire, she's a human. Adrian thought he might have a chance. Maybe she doesn't even know what it is.

He grabbed the girl's arm tightly and pulled on the bracelet. It didn't budge. He tried to bend the ends with his fingers but it seemed to be physically part of her body.

Maksim shook his head. "I told you," he said stubbornly, "You should have let her die."

Adrian stood up. He didn't know what to do. He knew his father would be furious that he had saved a human, even just one; his father wanted them all dead. He had never disobeyed his father. On top of that, bringing the girl to the hidden island was putting the whole colony at risk.

Protect the colony at all costs had been drilled into his head from childhood. Adrian looked out over the stormy bay. Humans are destructive, soulless, murderers, that's what his father had always told him. Maybe I should have let her die.

Adrian knelt down beside the girl and looked into her face. She was so fragile, so helpless. He could stop her breathing right now just by putting his hand over her mouth. He brushed a strand of damp hair from her face. Adrian touched the small brown dots on her nose and cheeks. He put his hand over her lips, he could feel her warm breath. The girl groaned softly and turned toward Adrian. His heart was pounding, he couldn't do it.

Adrian stood up and looked at Maksim. "I saved her life, maybe she'll just give it ta me," he said hopefully.

Maksim scowled. "I'll do it," he said and moved towards the girl.

"No!" Adrian yelled and pushed Maksim away.

Maksim looked at Adrian like he'd gone crazy. Adrian looked down, ashamed of his feelings. What's wrong with me, he wondered, what does one human life matter? He looked back at the girl. It matters to me.

Adrian put his shoulders back and squared off to Maksim. "I saved her, she'll help us." Maksim sighed, and backed off.

Mak looked at the girl. "She might still die," he said hopefully.

Maksim was right. Adrian could see that the girl was shaking uncontrollably and her lips were almost blue.

"These wet things aren't help'n her ta be warm," Adrian said.

Adrian knelt down and pulled off Brooke's shoes. He tried to pull off her shorts but, not knowing how to unbutton the wet jeans, they wouldn't budge.

Mak looked at Adrian and shook his head. "Are you sure that isn't part of her body too?" He wondered if Adrian knew as much about humans as he claimed.

Adrian picked up Brooke's limp arm, he wasn't sure how to get her tank top off. Not wanting to look foolish in front of Maksim he decided to leave it on. As he put Brooke's arm down he noticed that she had bumps all over her arm with little hairs sticking up. He ran his warm hand across the bumps and they went away. That gave him an idea. Adrian lay down next to Brooke and put his arms around her body and his legs around her legs.

"What are you doing?" Mak exclaimed.

"I'm makin her warm," Adrian said, his cheeks turning red. "She has ta be warm ta live."

Maksim sat down on the sand awkwardly.

He sniffed the air. "Well, at least she doesn't stink like most humans."

It was true Adrian thought. Most humans smelled like sweat and dirt and chemicals, at least the ones he could smell from boats and whenever he got close to land.

Adrian laid his head on the sand next to the girl and breathed in her scent. She smelled like plants or trees, like something warm and alive in the sun. Adrian couldn't quite figure it out but somehow it reminded him of his mother.

The girl's body began to relax as she warmed up. She sighed and turned toward Adrian. He had never been this physically close to anyone, other than wrestling his friends. The Athlanmara in general were not affectionate, the highest value in their culture was loyalty to the tribe. Adrian's father had behaved toward his sons like a drill sergeant, always pushing them. His mother had been the only being he had ever felt close to, but he barely remembered his mother. Adrian was six when she died.

Unconsciously, the girl snuggled closer to Adrian's warmth. He looked down at her childlike face. He had saved this girl from death, she needed him. Adrian had never felt needed before, the colony merely tolerated his presence. If it wasn't for his father's high standing he would probably have been driven away by now.

The Athlanmara were all connected, it was called, the aonachd, the unity. When in a group the Athlanmara were able to act as one, even their movements were perfectly coordinated. It was necessary for their survival. But Adrian had never been connected, he had never felt the aonachd. His father was ashamed of him and the other Athlanmara treated him like an outcast. No matter how hard he fought, no matter how much he did for the colony, he would never be accepted. To protect himself from the pain of that rejection Adrian had built up walls around his heart.

Yet, as Adrian lay on the sand holding the helpless girl in his arms something changed inside of him, like a muscle that had been clenched his whole life relaxing for the first time. Adrian looked down at the girl, her long lashes brushing her cheeks, the strange little brown spots, her full lips, something inside him felt warm. Maksim glanced over at Adrian and saw the look on his face.

He put his head in his hands. "This is not good," Mak muttered.

The girl groaned, her eyes fluttered, suddenly, Adrian was terrified. It was one thing to hold an unconscious human but what was she going to do when she woke up? What if Maksim was right and she was dangerous? Adrian carefully untangled himself from the girl trying not to wake her. He stood up. Maksim struggled to get to his feet. The girl groaned again and put a hand to her head.

Maksim grabbed Adrian's arm. "Let's go now, before she wakes up! If she doesn't see us we won't be in so much trouble!"

Adrian pulled his arm away. Maybe Maksim was right, they should just leave her here.

The girl rolled over. "The seals…" she mumbled.

That was too much for Maksim. He hopped away as fast as he could and dove into some nearby bushes. Adrian backed away from the girl but he couldn't run. His heart was pounding, he felt himself standing at a crossroads. He could choose to do what was best for the colony, to kill the girl and take the seunach, or he could abandon everything he'd been taught and let her live. Adrian took a deep breath and held his ground. For some reason he felt his life would never be the same.

7 "FORGET ABOUT IT"

With the storm clouds gone, the tropical sun beat down unhindered and the damp ground sent up waves of steaming heat. Anthony Lombardi walked down the steps to Paul DeLuca's dock feeling like he was in some deep African jungle.

Lombardi looked completely out of place in the lush surroundings. He was pale and overweight. He was wearing tan shorts with black socks, loafers and a garish Hawaiian shirt. He kept removing his straw hat and wiping his sweating forehead with a silk handkerchief. He wished he was back in Jersey.

The Italian businessman was followed by two large men wearing the same ridiculous garb, the only difference being they had handguns sticking out of their shorts.

Paul reluctantly followed behind. "Mr. Lombardi, you really didn't have to come all this way," he said.

Lombardi paused and looked back at Paul. "I guess I did, since ya never take my calls," he said and continued to plod towards the yacht. Paul tried to keep a smile pasted on his face but a deep dread was growing inside of him. "You two stay here," Lombardi said to his lumbering doppelgangers.

Paul helped Mr. Lombardi struggle onto the bobbing boat and jumped aboard himself. He looked up to see Chris running down the steps of the boat house.

"Dad, I wanted to use the yacht today!" Chris whined at his father.

Embarrassed by his son, Paul glanced at his unwanted guest who was removing his straw hat to wipe his brow with his handkerchief for the second time in as many minutes.

Paul quickly jumped up to intercept his son. "Chris, Mr. Lombardi stopped by today and we need to talk some business in private. Here," Paul pulled out his wallet and began to shove bills in Chris' hand, "take this and go have a good time. Take your girlfriend to a movie or something, have some fun!" Paul chuckled awkwardly. Chris looked down at the bills in his hand then at his dad. He had never seen his dad act so nervous.

Chris scowled and looked at the ground. "She broke up with me."

Paul turned to Lombardi and forced a laugh. "Well, I just can't keep up, you've had so many girlfriends." Chris glared at his dad then slowly walked away. Paul turned to get some drinks from the minibar still wearing his smile. "Sorry, about that Mr. Lombardi."

"Kids today, they just wanna play around with those crazy video games, am I right?" Lombardi laughed.

Paul forced a laugh. "You're right!" he said, "Can I get you a drink?"

"Nah, let's take this boat out a little and talk some business 'fore I melt."

"Absolutely," Paul said, quickly putting down his own drink.

Paul took the yacht out to sea wondering why Lombardi even

wanted to be on the boat. The storm had passed but the water was still choppy. The old Italian just hunched down, clutching his hat against the wind with one hand and the arm of his chair with the other. As the sea got rougher, he looked like he was going to throw up.

Finally, he held up his hand. "Okay, okay, this is good enough, stop this roller coaster ride!" he cried.

Paul cut the engine. "You sure you don't want a drink, Mr. Lombardi?" he asked. Lombardi just sat there looking pale and panting.

He started to fan himself with his straw hat again. "Nah, nah. It's Africa hot down here, am I right?" Lombardi asked, cheerfully.

"Yeah…" Paul was wondering when he would get to the point, "So, you wanted to talk business?" he asked, "I hope that my services have been satisfactory."

"Oh, sure, sure," Lombardi said, then stopped his fanning, "Of course, there is this one little problem of you refusing that last shipment."

Paul became as pale as Lombardi. "Mr. Lombardi, my warehouse is full, I explained that to Tony Junior. My boats are going out twice a week now. I can't do anymore, people would get suspicious."

Lombardi held up his hand. "Yeah, yeah, people don't notice as much as ya think they do. Your warehouse is full eh, so, you buy another warehouse, come on, you got enough money." Lombardi laughed, then his eyes got hard. "I seen your big house, you got this beautiful boat, huh? So, you get more room to put the barrels in, you get another friggin' boat to take em out." Lombardi got up out of his chair and walked over to Paul. He patted him on the cheek. "It's business," he said smiling.

Paul began to get a sick feeling in his stomach. "Look, Mr. Lombardi, I've tried to get more space. This is a tiny island, there's a limited amount of land, I just can't do it," he said, trying to keep his voice from wavering.

Lombardi walked over to the edge of the yacht and looked out over the water. "So much water, it looks like it never ends," he turned back to Paul and smiled, "Am I right?"

Paul nodded silently. "Mr. Lombardi, I'm a respected businessman around here and…"

Lombardi held up his hand chuckling. "I know, I know, that's what makes you such a valuable contractor for East Coast Chemicals and Waste." Lombardi walked up to Paul and put a hand on his shoulder. "I get it, you need help, don't worry about it. My sisters kid, Raffe, he's had some trouble but he's a good kid. I'll send him down here to help you out. Kind of keep an eye on things for you, right?"

Paul backed up, he didn't like to be bullied, he was the one to bully people. "Mr. Lombardi, I have my own people, and as I said I'm at my limit," he said tersely.

Lombardi walked back to the edge of the boat. "There ain't no limit!" he yelled out over the ocean. Lombardi held out his arms, "Look at all this, who cares how many barrels you throw down there." Lombardi laughed staring into the water. "Nick would love this, he's always lookin' for somewhere to drop a body."

Lombardi turned back to face Paul. "That's a nice boy you got," he said, his face hard. Paul could feel the threat, as real as the heartbeat in his throat. "Kid looks like he's got a bright future, eh? Family's important, am I right?" Paul just stood there frozen.

Lombardi sat back down in the chair and started to fan himself again. "Come on, let's get back, I'm meltin." Paul started up the engine without saying a word. Lombardi started to chuckle. "Limit…" he muttered, "forget about it."

8 INTRODUCTIONS

Brooke opened her eyes, she saw palm trees blowing crazily in the wind. She lay still for a moment taking in deep breaths, trying to get her bearings. Where am I, she wondered. Slowly, she became aware of her body being soaking wet, her ankle throbbing. All at once, she remembered, the boat! Brooke sat bolt upright, instantly regretting it as searing pain shot through her head.

Brooke lay back down, holding her aching head. "I drowned, no I'm alive, I think." Brooke closed her eyes, her head throbbing. When she opened them again there was a face inches from her own.

Brooke screamed and sat up so fast she knocked her head into the person peering down at her. Brooke grabbed her head and looked up, her heart pounding with adrenaline. There standing in front of her, holding his forehead, was a naked man.

"Ahhhhhhh!!!!!! Get away from me!" she screamed.

Brooke jumped to her feet and stumbled away from the man, crying out again as the pain from her ankle reached her brain. She fell on her butt, grabbed a palm branch and held it out in front of her. The boy, for she could see now that he wasn't much older than herself, held out his hands and spoke to her with the strangest accent, like he was from Scotland.

"I mean ya no harm, I saved ya," he said, smiling at her encouragingly.

Brooke sat there open mouthed in shock. The boy was tall and fair skinned, finely muscled with light brown hair. But his eyes, Brooke was mesmerized, she had never seen eyes so green, so luminous, yet they looked somehow familiar.

The boy took a step towards her. "Are ya alright?" he asked.

Brooke realized she was staring, she turned beet red and looked away. "Uh, you're naked," Brooke waved her hand up and down indicating his body, while keeping her eyes on the sand, "No clothes! Where are your clothes?"

Out of the corner of her eye she saw the boy look down at himself then look around helplessly as if he had never heard of something called clothes. He finally noticed her windbreaker on the sand where Brooke had been lying. He ran over picked up the jacket and turned it around and around.

Brooke gave up trying not to look, as his behavior was so strange. She began to relax as the boy looked so confused and helpless, he didn't seem like much of a threat.

Brooke finally dropped her branch and stood up. "Put it around your waist, like this," she said, miming with her hands going around her waist.

The boy tried, he would put the sleeves around his waist but not knowing how to tie the arms together, the jacket kept falling to the ground. The situation became so funny that Brooke actually laughed. The boy looked up and grinned. When their eyes met Brooke felt a warmth, like the two of them were already friends.

He held out the jacket to her. "I'm hopeless," he said with a twinkle in his eye.

Brooke limped over to him and took the jacket. Averting her eyes, she put the body of the jacket in front of him and reached around to tie the sleeves in the back. She couldn't help but feel how warm his body was.

"There!" She took a step back and held out her hand, "I'm Brooke, what's your name?"

The boy looked at her hand and copied her, holding his hand out. "My name's Adrian," he replied.

Brooke grabbed his hand and shook it which seemed to startle Adrian, but he went along with it. "Nice to meet you Adrian and thank you, I guess, for saving me," Brooke said. Adrian smiled and kept shaking Brooke's hand until she pulled it free. "Now, what the heck happened to my boat? And why were you swimming naked in the middle of the ocean and where are you from? Are you an illegal immigrant? And where are we?"

Adrian looked scared and took a few steps back. There was a rustling in the underbrush behind him then out jumped another naked boy. This boy was at least a foot taller than Adrian with black hair, darker skin and huge muscles. He came jumping at Brooke, his legs pinned together like he was in a potato sack race with no potato sack.

Brooke screamed and ran as well as she could on her bruised ankle to the tree line. She grabbed her palm frond again and turned to fight. She saw that Adrian had grabbed the arm of the strange naked giant and they were both gesturing wildly. It was like they were having a heated argument, though their lips didn't move and they were making no sound at all.

Adrian seemed to have convinced the other boy that he was in no danger and then he started to gesture at the boy's nakedness showing him how he had covered up. They both looked around fruitlessly for something to cover him up. Then Adrian seemed to get an idea. He ran into the brush and came back with a vine-like plant with large leaves. The two of them managed to wrap it around his body until his friend was covered sufficiently.

Adrian waved at Brooke. "Brilliant, ya can come back now," he yelled.

Brooke took a few steps towards the boys but didn't drop her weapon. "Who's that? He looks dangerous," she said, gesturing at Maksim. He was glaring at Brooke, his dark brows knit together.

Adrian pushed the other boy behind him a bit. "Tis just Mak, he's my mate. He'll not cause ya any harm."

Brooke's head and ankle were throbbing, she had no idea what had happened to her or really what was happening right now. She sank to the ground and started to shake. Storm clouds were still overhead and the strong wind blowing on her wet clothes chilled her, but it was the shock of the accident and her adrenaline that put her over the edge.

Adrian started to edge towards her like he was approaching a wounded animal that he thought might bolt. "Tis alright, you're safe now," he said softly.

Brooke looked up at the strange boy hesitantly. His eyes are so captivating, she thought, it's hard to think when I'm looking at them. Brooke hugged her knees to her chest trying to stay warm. I guess he seems like a decent guy, after all he did save me from drowning. I kind of feel safe around him but there's also something about him that's…, Brooke tried to analyze what she was feeling; there's something about him that's wild, she thought.

Adrian slowly sat down next to her. His body blocked the wind and seemed to radiate heat but Brooke scooted away from him. She still had no idea who these strange naked boys were or where they came from. Maksim sat down where he was, his brown eyes looking at Brooke with distrust.

The three of them sat there awkwardly for a few minutes till Brooke got up the courage to speak. "So where's *your* boat?" she asked. She could see the entire bay, there was no boat in sight.

Adrian shifted uncomfortably. "I don't have a boat," he said.

Brooke looked at the two of them and her mouth dropped open. "So, wait a minute, you guys are stranded here?" Brooke smacked her own forehead, which did nothing to help her headache. "Oh, duh! You were in a storm, lost everything including your clothes. Great! Just great! Now I'm here and there's just one more person who needs to be rescued!" Maksim looked at Adrian and rolled his eyes.

Adrian plastered a smile on his face. "Why were ya out on the sea alone?" he asked. Adrian looked tense, like he was about to run at any sign of danger.

He probably thinks I'm a crazy person, Brooke thought. She took a deep breath. "My dad and I had a big fight," she said.

Adrian looked shocked. "Your father beat ya?" he asked.

Brooke had to laugh. "No, I mean we had an argument, with words," she explained. Adrian nodded. "He...he never, he's just never there for me and my mom left us and I'm always alone and...now I'll probably never see him again! I said such terrible things to him!"

Brooke started to wail. Adrian jumped up and ran over to Maksim who had also jumped up at the sound of Brooke's sobs. Mak motioned to Adrian to put his hands over his ears. Adrian quickly clapped his hands over his ears. They stood there, two half naked boys with their hands over their ears looking at Brooke in terror.

After a few minutes of hysterical sobbing Brooke looked over at them. Her sobs turned into hysterical laughter, they looked so ridiculous. Adrian took a look at Mak, then quickly put his hands down, his face turning red. He tried to get Maksim to do the same but the scowling giant refused. He stubbornly held onto his ears and looked at Brooke warily.

Adrian slowly walked back to sit by Brooke, who was trying to get control of herself. Brooke pulled up her tank top to wipe her nose. Adrian leaned in closely, staring at her face.

"What?" Brooke asked, "Do I have a big booger on my face?"

Adrian reached out his hand and touched her face, gently wiping a tear off her cheek. He tasted it. "Salt!" Adrian grinned. "Saltwater's comin' out your eyes!"

Brooke sniffed, wiping her cheeks. "Uh, yeah, tears are salty," she said. It was her turn to stare at Adrian. "Who are you?"

Adrian looked at Maksim. His friend shook his head angrily. Before Brooke could confront Adrian on his strange behavior, it started to pour. Brooke jumped up and looked around for some sort of shelter. She couldn't just sit there forever on the beach in the pouring rain. Strangely, Adrian and Maksim didn't even seem to notice the weather. They just sat there soaking wet and slightly steaming.

Brooke was irritated. "You have any shelter on this island? I want to get out of this rain!"

Adrian jumped up excited. "Aye, shelter, like a house, I have one!" he proclaimed proudly.

Adrian started off towards the part of the island with the thickest vegetation. Brooke followed slowly, trying not to put weight on her bruised ankle. Maksim followed behind her at a distance, like a rear guard in case she tried anything on Adrian.

In a moment Adrian realized that Brooke wasn't behind him. He ran back to her and saw her injured ankle. He picked her up easily and started to carry her in his arms.

"Hey! I can walk!" Brooke protested.

Adrian just laughed. "No worries, I'm brilliant at walking," he bragged.

Brooke wasn't sure how to react to that statement. Was he being funny? Or has he gone crazy from being on this island for years, she wondered. The thought scared her. Her next thought was even more disturbing. How long will I be on this island with two apparently crazy guys? Adrian looked at her and grinned.

After pushing through some underbrush they came into an area that looked like a cultivated orchard. She recognized orange and lime trees as anyone who grew up in Florida would. She also saw banana trees, plum trees and something she assumed was a giant mango tree. In the middle of the little orchard was a house, or what Adrian had called a house. It was really just a frame of small branches with a roof of palm fronds and more palm fronds arranged on three sides. Adrian set her down in front of it and gestured proudly.

"Yeah, it's great," Brooke said, trying to look impressed.

The two of them had to crouch to get into it. Adrian went first to brush debris and a few hermit crabs aside. Brooke followed, surprised that the rickety structure did keep out most of the rain.

"There ya are," Adrian patted the dry sand, "tis a grand place ta rest."

Brooke sat down gently, trying to keep her ankle elevated. She was so tired and hungry. She had been up all night and hadn't eaten anything since the day before. She figured it must be getting close to noon even though it was impossible to tell because of the storm.

Adrian looked at her ankle with concern. "It hurts much?" he asked.

"I'll be fine, it's just bruised," Brooke said. She tried to scoot into a place that wasn't dripping. "Got anything to eat around here?" she asked, trying to make the best of the awkward situation.

Adrian smiled and ran out to the orchard. While he was gone Brooke spied a broken knife in a corner of the hut. She grabbed it and hid it in her shorts. I can't be too careful, she thought.

Adrian returned with his arms full of various fruits. "I've grown all these myself!" he said, smiling. He dumped the fruit on the sand by Brooke.

She grabbed an orange and peeled it. "This is really good!" she said, with juice running down her chin.

It was like Adrian had won the lottery, he was beside himself with pride. He grinned and looked over at Mak, who was still standing in the rain outside the shelter. Mak just scowled and walked away, ripping off his leaf covering as he went.

"What's his problem?" Brooke asked as she was peeling a banana.

Adrian paused and looked around as if trying to find an answer. "He's Russian!" Adrian said, smiling and nodding.

"Yeah, I got that from his accent," Brooke mumbled with half a banana in her mouth, "I guess that explains a lot." She stopped chewing. "No, that doesn't explain anything. What are a Russian guy and a, I guess Scottish guy...," she waved in Adrian's direction hoping to get some clarity, "doing naked on an island in the middle of who knows where?"

Adrian looked uncomfortable. "It's difficult ta explain," he said simply.

With food in her stomach, Brooke's aching body was craving sleep. She lay down on the sand, hardly able to keep her eyes open anymore. "Well, I guess we'll have plenty of time for stories later. If you two haven't been rescued by now, I don't have much of a chance." She closed her eyes, the pressure of the knife giving her some feeling of safety in the crazy world she'd found herself in.

Adrian sat and watched as Brooke's breathing slowed. When he was sure she was asleep he took off the jacket from around his waist and put it over Brooke to keep her warm. He walked out of the hut, Maksim was nowhere in sight. He walked to the beach and saw Mak sitting on the sand. Adrian sat down next to him.

"What are you doing, Adrian?" Maksim growled, "You're just going to wait till she decides to give you the seunach?" Adrian sighed, picked up a rock and threw it at the waves. "You know the Athlanmara will find her and then what?" Mak continued, "They will kill her Adrian, or worse she will kill them!"

Adrian dug his feet into the wet sand. "I know, but I couldn't kill her." He turned to Mak, "There's a kindness about her. Maybe if I ask, she'll give me the seunach. Or maybe she knows a way to help our people."

Maksim just shook his head. "Well, what now?" he asked Adrian, "You can't even take her back to land, we left the bata behind, remember?"

Adrian was starting to realize what a dire predicament they were in. They couldn't go home or take the girl back to land without the bata, their underwater vehicle, and they couldn't get another one without messaging someone in the colony. If someone came they would find the girl and kill her, seunach or no seunach. That was the supreme law of the colony, if a human saw an Athlanmaran, they had to die.

"Maybe there's some way ta get the seunach and get her back ta land," Adrian said hopefully.

Mak just scowled. Adrian picked up a rock and threw it as hard as he could at the waves. He wished he could just stay on this island and have everyone leave him alone. He felt like the island was the only place he belonged.

Adrian took a deep breath. What am I doing, he wondered. I'm risking death, or worse for a human? Maybe the girl had put a spell on him.

Adrian got up. "Come on," he said, "We need ta get some coverings. Ya gotta help me dig a hole."

Maksim reluctantly got up and followed Adrian. "Sure, that will solve all our problems," he growled.

9 THE SEARCH

"Well, I've really dug myself into a hole," Jackson sighed and tossed his phone on his bed. "My dad isn't even answering me now."

Zoe had been camped out at the Hale house since she heard that Brooke was missing. Jackson's family had a radio which could keep track of the Coast Guard's search for Brooke.

Zoe got up from her chair and started pacing again. "I told you to stop texting an hour ago!" she said, wringing her hands. "I'm sure they will tell us if they find any…." Zoe broke off, trying not to cry. She slumped down on the bed.

Jackson sat down next to her and handed her a tissue. "Brooke is a great sailor, we all know that," Jackson said reassuringly, "She probably pulled into some little bay somewhere and is riding the storm out just fine. I can see her now with her little chess board, beating herself in chess and laughing to think that we are all worried about her."

Zoe laughed. They had both teased Brooke about playing herself in chess because she couldn't find anyone smart enough to play. Zoe couldn't stand the thought of never seeing Brooke again.

She choked back more tears and blew her nose on the tissue. "Yeah, I am going to be so mad at her when she gets back!" Zoe grinned through her tears, "I'm gonna kick her butt!"

"That's the spirit!" Jackson said, "Keep those positive thoughts going!"

Jackson wished he had the guts to put his arm around Zoe. He hated to see her cry. He was terrified for Brooke too, he felt so helpless, he had to do something.

Jackson got up, it was his turn to start pacing. "Can't we just go out on your boat and start looking ourselves?" he asked miserably, "I'm sick of just sitting here!" He kicked his chair.

Zoe snorted. "My little Seacraft boat? In this weather? Yeah, right! Besides it's almost dark now."

"I suppose you're right," Jackson said, slumping back down in his chair. "But what about tomorrow, as soon as it gets light?" he asked hopefully. "The weather is supposed to get better tomorrow."

Zoe sighed. "Fine, I promise we'll go out tomorrow," Zoe paused, "But I'm sure they'll find her safe and sound before then."

Jackson forced a smile. "Yeah, of course!" he said with enthusiasm, "Her dad is probably chewing her out right now."

Zoe looked from Jackson to her hands twisting the tissue. "Her poor dad," she murmured, "He was almost crying when he called me this morning."

Jackson walked over and sat down on the bed next to Zoe. He tried to put his arm around her, but ended up just patting her shoulder awkwardly. He picked up his phone and looked at it for the millionth time. "Dad's do worry," he muttered. The two of them sat slumped on the bed in silence.

Deep below the tossing waves the bata made another circle, looking more like a creature of the sea than a machine. The sleek metallic blue hull slipped through the water with only a slight thump of the turbine engines to give it away. The top of the bata was clear and extended out from the body of the craft allowing a faint light to shine into the blackness of the deep ocean. The glow came from three grim faces peering into the gloom.

"We are almost to the coordinates Kai gave us, Bronte," said Nereus.

Nereus, Bronte's top lieutenant, was small for an Athlanmaran, he hailed from the Salasku tribe near Indonesia. They were known to be a fierce and ruthless clan. His sharp dark eyes peered into the depths, missing nothing. Gursel, a large Athlanmaran with fair hair, sat in the front of the bata. He glanced at Bronte and thought it best to say nothing.

Bronte didn't answer Nereus, he just continued to stare into the sea. He was a handsome Athlanmaran, with a strong jaw, aquiline nose and eyes that glowed with the same unearthly green color as his son. His striking features were marred however, by a long scar that extended from his left temple down to his chin.

Bronte's scowl deepened as he tried to hide his worry. On the way back from the boat incident Kai and his friends had run into a swarm of Guardians, they had barely escaped with their lives. The Athlanmara had named the small white crabs Guardians for they huddled around the deep underwater vents where the Athlanmaran colony drew the energy they needed to survive. But lately, even these innocuous crustaceans had become treacherous.

Why were the Guardians acting strangely ferocious, Bronte wondered. He was sure it had something to do with the humans, every crisis in the sea could be traced back to them. Bronte felt there was a war between the Athlanmara and the humans, and his people were losing. Now his eldest son was missing.

Why did Adrian have to behave so foolishly! He was the son of Bronte, of the clan of Muirrigh. It was probably the fault of that stupid giant, Maksim, that Adrian had picked up on his journey two years ago. Why he spent time with that leth-chu, Bronte couldn't fathom. He and his sons were the noblest family in the colony.

True, some in the colony didn't give them the honor they were due. After the fall of his family in Alba, Bronte was forced to come begging at the colony for protection. He couldn't survive on his own with two small sons to look after. But he had worked his way up to head of security and now he was feared and respected.

Before he had come, the colony had no organized security force to protect them and if there was one thing Bronte was good at, it was inspiring young Athlanmara to follow him. He had built up a strong force of Athlanmarans that would follow any order Bronte gave them. With a little help, he mused, fingering the silver band on his wrist. I can inspire everyone but my own son, he thought bitterly.

Kai was an eager learner, but as he grew older his fits became more and more frequent. Bronte began to distance himself from Kai knowing he would soon die as other Athlanmara with the same symptoms had died. Adrian was his only hope for an heir, but he had never become part of the aonachd. Adrian was an outsider and a dreamer, always asking questions, always off on some fanciful adventure when he should be learning battle strategy or hand to hand combat. How could he be so like his mother when he barely knew her?

Einin, just thinking her name was like a knife in Bronte's chest. He looked down at his wrist, the silver band was engraved with a bird in flight, a Scottish Lapwing.

"Einin, my little bird," he whispered.

For a moment he could see her coal black hair blowing in the wind and hear her plaintive song. Bronte gripped his spear until his knuckles turned white. I will not let memories make me weak, he told himself. The sea is becoming poison, the Guardians have turned against us, something needs to be done and it's up to me to do it.

Nereus glanced at Bronte, he was loath to speak to him when he looked so grim. "We are at the coordinates now," Nereus said quietly, hoping not to incur the wrath of his commander. Bronte made a motion to Gursel and he brought the craft to a stop.

The three glowing faces looked up and saw the outline of a sailboat on it's side, barely floating in the water. There was no sign of Adrian's bata. The figures sat silent in their craft watching and listening.

Bronte decided it was safe to take a look. He opened the hatch at the bottom of their craft and silently Bronte and Nereus entered the sea. They made a wide circle around the drowned sailboat. They could see no signs of any humans or Athlanmarans.

Suddenly, bright lights swept over the craft from above, Bronte could hear the pounding sounds of some human flying machine. Nereus and Bronte fled back to the bata. Gursel had them moving straight down just as a human diver splashed into the sea.

10 THE ISLAND

Warm breezes caressed the tiny island nestled in the open sea. The morning sunlight cheerfully filtered through the palm fronds as if the storm the day before had been only an illusion. Brooke, in her exhausted state, had slept through half a day and all through the night.

The rays of the sun danced on Brooke's eyelids until they waked her. Brooke yawned and opened her eyes, for a moment she thought she was at home in her own bed. She looked at the palm fronds on the roof of the hut moving gently in the breeze and tried to get her bearings. She felt a warm body behind her. Her heart skipped a beat, as the memories of the last twenty-four hours washed over her.

She turned her head slowly and saw that Adrian was lying on his back behind her fast asleep. Brooke carefully scooted away from him and sat up. She made the most of the moment to examine this strange boy, without those startling eyes to distract her. She was glad to see that he was wearing some sort of swim trunks now. They were fluorescent green and yellow, like something from the 80's and they looked like they were about to fall apart from age.

Adrian was tall, she remembered that, and muscular like one of those Olympic swimmers she had seen on T.V. last year. I suppose that makes sense, she said to herself, living on a deserted island for who knows how long. What didn't make sense to her was how pale his skin was. Shouldn't he be really tan, she wondered.

She looked at his face. He had a straight nose, full lips and a strong jaw but there wasn't anything remarkable about his face. It's just when he looks at me with those vivid green-blue eyes, I can't think straight, she mused.

Brooke scooted closer and saw dim blue patterns on Adrian's skin, almost like faint tattoos. The tattoo on his upper right arm was shaped like two discs connected in the middle with a backwards 'Z' going through them. On his chest she noticed the faint outline of what looked like a wolf. Down Adrian's left shoulder was a light brown birthmark about the size of her hand. It was oddly shaped, though it seemed almost like an upside down heart.

Brooke saw that he had thin line scars all over his body. Could they be from a knife she wondered. Looking closer, she also saw a scar on Adrian's abdomen, actually it was many little scars. She leaned in closer to get a better look. The scars ran down his stomach in a curved line. All at once she realized that it was a scar from a shark bite.

Brooke shivered. It was dangerous to be alone on an island far from any help. Adrian's brown hair had fallen over his forehead and his smooth face made him look almost like a child. Shouldn't he have some sort of facial hair, she wondered, he seems old enough.

Brooke quietly got to her feet, testing her swollen ankle. It didn't hurt too much. She was relieved, you obviously had to be fit to survive on this island. Brooke found her shoes outside the hut and put them on.

It was a beautiful day. The storm had passed and the sun had been up for a few hours. She saw some fish hanging on the side of the hut and a weapon she recognized as a Hawaiian sling. It was a metal pole about three feet long with a barb on the end, there was a loop of rubber attached to the bottom of the pole that, when extended, made the pole shoot towards the fish you were aiming at.

She also saw a battered old suitcase lying open on the ground and some moldy clothing items strewn about. Guess that explains the swim trunks. But it was all very strange and confusing. Who were these boys? How did they end up on this island?

Brooke saw a rain barrel and went and got a drink from it. She didn't see any sign of Maksim. She was glad. She didn't trust him, he always looked at her like he hated her.

Brooke took a deep breath and looked all around the little clearing. Suddenly, she wondered why she wasn't afraid. Brooke grinned. I'm shipwrecked on an island with two strange boys and I don't ever remember feeling so serene.

Brooke turned back to the hut and saw a small shelf she hadn't noticed yesterday. She walked over to it quietly. There were a few books on it and some strange odds and ends, an empty Coke bottle, a plastic toy dog, a tattered baseball and ironically a set of car keys. Brooke couldn't help but giggle quietly. Those will get us nowhere, she said to herself.

She picked up one of the books, it felt damp and had a musty smell like it had been in a cellar too long. The cover was too damaged to tell what the title was but as she opened the pages and started to read she realized it was the *Tale of Two Cities* by Charles Dickens. Brooke had read it last year in school and loved it. She stood there in the sun for a moment transported away from her own troubles into another world.

Brooke sighed and looked up, Adrian was watching her. His eyes looked hard, his entire body was tense. For a split second she thought he looked like a cat about to pounce. Brooke's heart started to pound, she took in a breath, ready to run.

Then Adrian relaxed, sat up and smiled at her. "How's it like being you?" he asked.

Brooke furrowed her brow. "Uh...you mean how am I?" she clarified, once again wondering if she was on an island with crazy people.

"Aye, how am I," he repeated.

Brooke gave up on the grammar lesson. "Well, my ankle is better, thanks!"

Adrian stood up, walked over to Brooke and touched her hair. "Your hair, tis dry," he said, smiling down at Brooke. Her heart started to pound for a different reason.

Brooke's face turned red. "Yep, it's all dry now," she said awkwardly. She tried to take a step backwards but her feet got tangled and she fell on her butt. Brooke was mortified. Adrian took a step towards Brooke, grabbed her hand and helped her up.

"Thanks, I'm such a klutz," she said, trying to laugh it off. You are an idiot, she chided herself. Adrian didn't let go of her hand.

He touched her bracelet. "Where'd you get this?" he asked quietly.

His touch and those intense eyes made it hard for Brooke to collect her thoughts. "Uh...my dad, I think, he found it somewhere on his travels." She pulled her hand away from Adrian, she hoped nonchalantly. Brooke pointed at the bracelet. "It's a mermaid. I don't know what the writing is though." Brooke pretended to be engrossed in the bracelet to avoid Adrian's intense gaze.

"Aye, mermaid." Adrian chuckled at the term some humans used for the Athlanmara. He moved closer to Brooke and stared into her eyes. "Can I see it, maybe I can read the writin?"

Adrian's words were casual but Brooke could feel his tension, she felt like she was in danger. "No!" she said loudly. Adrian looked disappointed. Brooke was horrified at her reaction, she never talked to anyone like that. "I'm, I'm really sorry, it's just that...it really belongs to my dad and...I...I'm really hungry, are you gonna cook those fish?" Brooke stammered trying to change the subject.

Adrian looked surprised. "Ya can't eat the fish how they are?" he asked. He grabbed a smelly fish and held it out to her smiling hopefully.

Brooke wrinkled her nose. "Well...I guess I could, if I was desperate. You've never made a fire here?" No wonder they haven't been rescued she thought.

Adrian dropped the fish, disappointed. "We could make a small fire I suppose and then put it out directly," he said. Adrian walked out of the hut and began to search the ground at the edge of the clearing.

Brooke followed him. "But if we made a big fire with lots of smoke, someone could see it from far away and come rescue us," she said hopefully.

Adrian looked at Brooke aghast. "No, we can't do that!" he cried.

Brooke furrowed her brow. "But why? Don't you want to get rescued?"

"Because..." Adrian bit his lip, trying to think of a reason, "Because there are wicked humans who will find us."

Brooke's jaw dropped. "What are you talking about? Wicked humans...like pirates?"

Adrian looked relieved. "Aye, pirates!" he nodded his head enthusiastically.

"Right, pirates of the Caribbean, huh?" she asked sarcastically. Adrian kept nodding his head. Brooke decided to let the issue drop. After all, she thought, I don't know what these guys have been through. Who knows, maybe they were attacked by pirates. Great, there's another thing to worry about. Well, at least I'm not at the bottom of the ocean. She tried to think positive thoughts. Adrian found the spot he was looking for and began to dig.

Brooke forced a smile. "Now we're looking for buried treasure?" she asked.

Adrian ignored her sarcasm and kept digging. In a few moments he triumphantly pulled out a little box covered in tin foil. He carefully pulled off the foil, opened the box and pulled out a wooden match. "These are matches!" he said to Brooke, like she needed an explanation.

"Yay!" Brooke pretended to cheer, "Now let's make a fire and eat."

"Only a small fire," Adrian reminded her.

After twenty minutes of watching Adrian try to light wet sticks Brooke realized she was going to have to be in charge of making the fire. She pulled down some of the dried palm fronds from the inside ceiling of the hut. She walked through the orchard and pulled off some semi dry branches from the trees, everything that was on the ground was soaking wet.

Brooke found an open spot in the clearing by the hut. She made a shallow impression in the sand then made a nest of the driest part of the palm fronds. She lit them with a match and blew on them until the flame caught. She carefully added small sticks until a decent flame was going. Adrian had watched the whole process fascinated, to him it seemed like magic.

Brooke gestured to the tiny flames. "Ta da!" she said.

Adrian looked at Brooke absolutely impressed. "Brilliant!" he exclaimed.

Brooke laughed, jumped up and started to dance around the flames singing nonsensical words. At first, Adrian looked shocked, then he burst out laughing. Brooke ran over and grabbed his arm and pulled him around the fire with her. Adrian tried to dance and he looked even more ridiculous than Brooke. They both fell down on the sand laughing so hard they could barely breathe.

Maksim walked into the clearing, shocked anger on his face. He dropped the armful of scallops he had gathered, ran over to the fire and started to kick sand on it.

Both Brooke and Adrian jumped up. "No!" they yelled in unison. Adrian grabbed Maksim and Brooke worked on saving the tiny flame.

"What are you doing?" Maksim screamed. "They will find us!"

Adrian glared into Maksim's face. "No! They won't!" he yelled. Brooke was scared, whoever 'they' were seemed to terrify the huge boy. Adrian looked over at Brooke then back at Maksim. "Eist do bheul!" he said quietly to the shaking giant. I guess there are pirates after all, Brooke thought.

The cooked fish was delicious. Brooke and Adrian enjoyed it immensely. Maksim just stood there with his arms crossed wearing a ridiculous Hawaiian shirt kilt, obviously the only thing from the old suitcase that fit him. He stubbornly refused to eat any of it. The smell of charred flesh disgusted him. He wondered how Adrian could shove the disgusting food into his mouth and act like he enjoyed it. Maksim stood over them glowering like an Easter Island statue. He wouldn't relax until Brooke had covered the fire with a layer of sand.

Brooke stood up and stretched. She leaned over and tried to run her fingers through her tangled hair. Adrian watched her, enchanted by her golden hair with shimmers of red, her perfect skin, her slender limbs and the way she moved so gracefully on land. He had never seen anyone so beautiful. Even Maksim stopped scowling for a moment and watched in appreciation.

Brooke sighed and gave up on her hair. Ugh, I must look so gross she thought.

"Well…" said Brooke, turning to the boys. The three youths stood looking at each other awkwardly. "Why don't you guys tell me how you ended up on this island?" she asked. Adrian and Maksim looked at each other in dismay.

"I'm keen for a swim!" Adrian said over enthusiastically.

Brooke was annoyed. She could tell they were deliberately not telling her anything about their past. She really wanted to find out the story behind these strange boys. Maybe they had some traumatic boat disaster and they watched their whole family be eaten by sharks or something, or maybe they were captured by pirates and marooned here. She sighed, well I guess they'll warm up to me in a month or so, she thought.

"Sure! Let's go swimming!" Brooke said with the same artificial enthusiasm.

11 GUARDIANS

Miles away from the tiny island, the bright Caribbean sun filtered down through the crystal blue waters and made dappled patterns on a remote reef. Cahal, his silver hair floating serenely, looked out over his group of young Athlanmarans. They ranged in age from nine to thirteen, the youngest was little Alana.

Cahal looked over at Alana. The other students had spread out around the reef, but Alana always stayed close to him. He had never had a little suire in his group before, there were many things in the colony that were new and different from the long held traditions of the Athlanmara.

Traditionally, young children stayed with their mother until they were five years of age. At five, the males were turned over to their father never to see their mother again. The suire have nothing to do with their fathers at all, they spend their entire lives among other suire and only leave for a short time to find a mate.

Here in the colony, the Builder encouraged male and female couples to live together with their offspring. Cahal had been training young Athlanmara for many years and he could tell that the children of the colony were different, better, than the children of the clans.

There were things that males and females could learn from one another he admitted. The Builder had also encouraged the

Athlanmara to learn from the humans, which was a part of today's lesson as each of his six pupils were struggling to master the Hawaiian sling.

He glanced over just in time to see Alana almost spear her own tail. Cahal quickly swam up to her and showed her how to keep the sling out away from her body while she aimed. Alana held out the weapon and shot it straight. She looked up at Cahal with pride and affection.

For a moment Cahal felt his chest tighten. He thought of his own daughter, Thera. Years ago, when he had been part of starting the new colony of Athlanmara far away from the old clan wars, he had searched out Tehgan his mate and begged her to come with him. She had laughed at him and called his idea foolish dreaming. Little Thera had come up to him shyly and took his hand. She had looked up at him and smiled. He would never forget her beautiful brown eyes.

Cahal was brought back to the present by a sharp cry of danger. Some of the older boys were fleeing towards him with terror on their faces. Behind them was a sight that made Cahal's blood run cold; Guardians. The pale, hairy crustaceans were lifting off the reef like an army of deadly dirigibles. They were everywhere, the tiny group of Athlanmara was surrounded. Cahal was frozen in shock for a moment. How had I not seen them, he asked himself uselessly.

The floating crabs were becoming more active. The blind predators seemed to sense the warmth and movement of their prey. They began swimming about and concentrating into large groups, hunting groups.

Terror filled Cahal, he repeated the high pitched danger cry. He tried to herd the young ones towards the bata, towing little Alana by the hand. The clouds of Guardians were surrounding them now. There were just too many of them. When he swatted a few away from Alana twenty more creatures took their place. The children screamed in fear as the sharp claws ripped into their limbs.

Cahal ignored his own pain, he pulled little Alana close and tried to shield her from the hellish talons. Pools of blood began to cloud the water which seemed to send the beasts into a frenzy. Cahal looked down at Alana, her huge hazel eyes looked back at him with complete trust. With a last massive effort of his torn body Cahal reached the bata and pushed the children through the hatch, trying to pull the creatures off their bodies. Alana refused to let go of him. She clutched at Cahal's fishing bag.

Cahal quickly slipped off the bag and pulled the hatch shut from the outside. As the Guardians overwhelmed him Cahal's body went numb. A smile spread over his face. The last thought in his mind was Thera's shining brown eyes.

Through the window the whimpering children saw the flush of blood float up amidst the ghastly mass of colorless bodies. Alana looked down, in her hands was Cahal's sea grass fishing bag. As the older boys rapidly turned the bata towards the colony, Alana's piercing scream filled the vessel.

12 BLUE LAGOON

Gentle waves caressed the peaceful shore as Brooke, Adrian and Maksim walked onto the small beach. It was a typical gorgeous Bahaman cay with white sand and unearthly, crystal clear turquoise water. The sun was high in the sky and it was getting hot.

The water looked cool and beautiful to Brooke but she felt the familiar pit of fear in her stomach as she thought about swimming out into the ocean. Adrian and Maksim were standing on the beach staring at Brooke like they were waiting for a show. They had never actually seen a human swim and they couldn't wait to see what Brooke was going to do.

Brooke felt the pressure of her audience. She stood on the beach biting her nails. They are going to think I'm a total freak if I don't get in the water. After all, I was sailing in the middle of the ocean. Stop being so stupid Brooke, it's not like you can't swim!

Brooke was mad at herself. She had no idea why she was so afraid of drowning. It made no logical sense and Brooke loved logical sense. She chewed harder on her nails as she concentrated on remembering the facts.

Okay, statistically, most drowning's occur in the age group one to fourteen, so, I'm good there. Also, eighty percent of people who die from drowning are male, so that helps. I am not swimming alone.

It doesn't look like there is any undertow. And my odds of getting killed by a shark are one in eight million. Brooke paused and realized she was chewing on her nails.

"Dang it!" she murmured.

She took a deep breath and walked towards the water. Nervously, she glanced at the boys. Brooke was a modest girl, she didn't like to parade around in just her bikini like the other high school girls in Marathon. Maybe I should just swim in my jean shorts and tank top, she thought. No, it's taken forever for them to dry, I don't want to be walking around all day in wet jean shorts.

Brooke took another look at the boys then unbuttoned her shorts and pulled them off.

Adrian shoved Maksim with his shoulder. "Told ya!" he said, triumphantly. Maksim just glared at Adrian.

Brooke took off her tank top and dropped it on the sand with her shorts. She stood there for a moment in her blue flowered bikini trying to ignore the boys, then she started to wade into the gentle surf. Adrian looked slightly disappointed.

Maksim groaned. *They even swim with coverings on!* he complained to Adrian.

Adrian walked over and picked up Brooke's jean shorts. He studied the zipper and button on the shorts, fastening and unfastening them.

Maksim walked up behind him. "What are you doing now?"

"I might need ta know how ta work these things some day," Adrian explained.

Maksim just shook his head. "All you need to figure out is how to get the seunach from the human," he said, with disgust.

Brooke was up to her waist in the water, she turned back to the boys. "Aren't you guys coming in?" she asked. Adrian smiled and started to take off his swim trunks. "No!" Brooke yelled, "Leave your swim trunks on!"

Maksim laughed at Adrian, who sheepishly pulled his trunks back on.

Adrian waded up next to Brooke, trying to adjust his uncomfortable shorts. "So ya can swim?" he asked.

"Shut up!" Brooke said. Adrian was shocked for a moment. Then he saw that Brooke was smiling. "Of course I can swim!" she said, though she didn't feel as confident as she portrayed. Adrian raised his eyebrow skeptically.

Brooke dove into the water and swam a few yards in an awkward freestyle. She stood up and looked back at Adrian. He was standing in the water with his mouth open. Maksim was on the beach laughing so hard he had to sit down.

"What's wrong?" Brooke demanded.

Adrian wasn't sure what to say. He had never seen a creature move through the water with so much flailing about. "Uh...aye, that was swimming," he said, lamely.

Brooke was offended. "Well, let's see you swim!" she taunted.

Adrian dove into the water and with two powerful dolphin kicks he came up next to Brooke, barely disturbing the water. Adrian stood up in front of Brooke grinning. She couldn't help but admire the view. Now I know how he gets those awesome abs, she thought.

"Yeah, you're a pretty good swimmer, I guess," she teased, smiling at Adrian, "What about you?" she yelled at Maksim, "Can you swim?" Maksim just shook his head, still laughing.

"Never mind that glogach," Adrian said, "Do ya want ta see the reef?" he asked tentatively.

Brooke smiled and nodded. Adrian gently took Brooke's hand and led her towards the deeper water. Brooke's heart fluttered at his touch. It was more than the fact that his hands were so manly and strong, there was an electric connection she felt. His energy was like a cool breeze blowing away all of her fear. Swimming out to a strange reef on a deserted island suddenly seemed like no big deal to her. Brooke realized she couldn't stop smiling. I'd probably follow him into a burning building right now, she thought.

As the water got deeper Adrian let go of Brooke's hand. He started swimming smoothly with his strong dolphin kick looking back to make sure Brooke was following. Brooke swam after him, self consciously trying not to splash too much with her freestyle kick.

As they approached the reef Brooke couldn't believe how beautiful it was. She had done a bit of snorkeling with her dad off the reefs in Florida, but she had never seen anything like this.

The coral was pristine and brilliantly colored. There was star coral, mushroom coral, pillar coral and even the endangered Elkhorn coral everywhere she looked. Clownfish and Angelfish swam around them in colorful clouds. Brooke saw a nurse shark resting on the sandy bottom, she knew she was in no danger from the nocturnal feeder. Brooke wished she had some fins or at least a snorkel. She was in good shape and could hold her breath for a while but she was annoyed at having to surface every few minutes.

Brooke was impressed with how long Adrian could hold his breath, he seemed to hardly surface at all. At least the visibility is good, thought Brooke, there is so much to see. She had always had good eyesight underwater and she rarely wore goggles when she snorkeled. They were always fogging up. She found she could see better without them.

A stingray glided through the water below them. Brooke tried to follow after it for a few feet. She looked over at Adrian and smiled. He easily outpaced the ray and swimming in front of it, he tried to herd it back towards Brooke but the shy creature picked up it's pace and disappeared.

They had reached a deeper part of the reef when Brooke saw something she had never seen before, a rare Leatherback turtle. She was so excited she almost screamed underwater. She waved at Adrian and pointed frantically at the turtle, he nodded his head. It was a juvenile Leatherback, probably five feet long and weighing five hundred pounds Brooke estimated. She knew adult Leatherbacks can be seven feet long and weigh over one-thousand pounds. They followed the turtle for a while but Adrian could see that Brooke was getting tired.

The next time she surfaced he came up beside her. "We can sit on those rocks for a while," he said, pointing at the rocky edge of the bay.

Brooke nodded. Adrian swam to the rocks in a flash and pulled himself up with no trouble. Brooke followed glad to be taking a break, she was getting a little cold.

Adrian was surprised with Brooke's reaction to the creatures in the sea. He wasn't sure what to expect from a human. All he'd been taught was that humans took what they wanted from his home and then treated it like a dumping ground.

But Brooke acted like she loved the sea. She reminded Adrian of a curious young seal, taking a breath then diving down to investigate the next thing that caught her attention. While they were swimming, he could barely take his eyes off of her shining face. It was all he could do to keep himself from grabbing her hand. In his mind he could still feel the touch of her tiny hand in his. It was more than just a physical feeling, her touch seemed to bring light and warmth into the cold depths of his soul.

"Can you believe we saw a Leatherback!" Brooke exclaimed as Adrian easily pulled her up onto the rocks beside him.

Adrian laughed. "Leatherback? Is that what ya call them?" he exclaimed, "There's loads of them around here." Brooke tried to wring some water out of her hair. She shivered. She had goose bumps on her arms and legs again. Adrian resisted the urge to run his hand along her slender legs. "Why do ya get those bumps when you're cold?" he asked her.

"They're goosebumps," she said.

Adrian laughed again. "Goose...bumps," he repeated like it was the stupidest thing in the world.

"Yeah," Brooke laughed, "it is a stupid name," she said looking at Adrian strangely. "You've never gotten goosebumps?"

"Oh aye, we just call them something else," he said, awkwardly trying to cover his slip.

"Oh yeah," said Brooke, "what do you call them?"

"Uh…" Adrian racked his brain, "people bumps!" Brooke burst out laughing, Adrian joined her. Then he became serious, he looked into Brooke's face with his luminous eyes. "You love the ocean?" he asked her quietly.

Brooke felt the intensity behind the question, this wasn't small talk.

"Yeah, I really do," she answered. "I've been around the ocean all my life, we even lived on a boat when I was little, but it's more than just being familiar with it." Brooke pulled her knees up to her chin to get warmer, she tilted her head and looked up at Adrian. "There's just something about it that feels like," Brooke paused, "like it's part of me."

Adrian's heart beat faster. Looking at Brooke, her strawberry blonde hair blowing around her face, her blue eyes reflecting the sunlight on the water, those tiny brown spots on her nose and cheeks, it all made his heart hurt for some reason, and it made him scared.

Adrian knew that he was betraying his people just by bringing Brooke to this place, and if she found out what he really is, Adrian didn't want to think about the consequences of that. But maybe what he had been taught about humans all his life wasn't true.

Brooke wasn't a murderer, she seemed to care about things in the ocean. What if his father was wrong? Adrian put all thoughts of his father out of his mind and scooted closer behind Brooke trying to block some of the ocean breeze.

Brooke felt like leaning into Adrian. What was it about this place that made her feel so safe? She tried to remember a time when she felt as peaceful as she felt right now, she couldn't think of anything. Was it Adrian who made her feel safe? She tried to remind herself that though this boy had saved her life, she really didn't know anything about him. Take it easy Brooke, she told herself, let's not go all 'Blue Lagoon' in a day.

They sat for a while warming in the sun, listening to the waves on the rocks.

Adrian saw that Brooke's goosebumps were gone. "Do ya want ta see somethin' special?" he asked.

Brooke had no idea what Adrian could think was special. In the last hour she had seen multiple endangered species. Was this some sort of place that time forgot, she wondered. Brooke looked up at Adrian, his hair had flopped over his forehead, his eyes were twinkling, he was smiling his crooked grin. Brooke sighed. She couldn't find any words, she just smiled and nodded her head.

Adrian swam around the edge of the rock entrance to the bay, he was towing Brooke by the arm, the current of the incoming water was too strong for her to make any headway. She had tried to help by kicking but that only seemed to annoy Adrian so she just let him drag her. She couldn't believe he was strong enough to pull them both through the opening against the current.

When they got into the open ocean Brooke was able to propel herself on her own. The water was much rougher than the calm bay but for some reason Brooke wasn't scared at all. She felt like nothing could happen to her with Adrian around.

Brooke swam with her head out of the water, there wasn't much to see as they had left the teeming reef behind them. Adrian stayed close to Brooke and was constantly going below the surface to scan the ocean around them, he knew the dangers of the open sea.

They had only been swimming a few minutes when Brooke heard what sounded like loud growling. Adrian heard it too, he surfaced and looked at Brooke.

Her eyes were wide with disbelief. "No...way.." she said.

Adrian grinned. They came around a bend in the rock and there on a thin sandy beach was a small group of Caribbean Monk seals. One of the males on the shore was making a low loud growling sound.

"That can't be what I think it is!" Brooke said. She was beside herself with amazement. "No one has seen a Monk seal around here since the 50's!" Brooke started to tear up.

Adrian was at her side in an instant. "Are ya hurt?" he asked her with concern.

Brooke sputtered in the water. "No," she choked out a laugh, "I'm just happy." Adrian was confused, she cried when she was sad and now she's crying because she's happy? Humans are very strange, he thought.

The seals spied the people in the water, in a moment a few of the curious young seals were swimming around them. Brooke dove underwater to watch their antics. The seals were amazingly agile in the water for how bulky and awkward they looked on land.

One young seal spun around Adrian and came right up to Brooke. He stared at her with his huge brown eyes. She resisted the urge to reach out and touch his soft fur. She knew this was a wild animal, not some cute pet, though they did remind her of frisky dogs.

She watched as Adrian playfully chased another seal. He would swim after the seal, then the seal would turn around and chase after Adrian. She was impressed with how agile Adrian was under the water. He was holding his own in their bizarre game of tag. All I can do is float here like a lump, Brooke thought.

Adrian looked over at Brooke, she was floating in the water her golden hair spread out like a fan around her head, eyes sparkling and a huge smile on her face. He thought she was more beautiful than any suire he had ever seen. Brooke floated to the surface to breathe. Adrian swam up to her, they were both laughing with joy .

They dove down again, Adrian was just below her when a seal

swam by Brooke so close it brushed her hand. The next moment Adrian kicked her hard in the leg knocking her to the side. Before she could even react a huge, nine foot Bull Shark zoomed past her. It's rough skin scraped her upper thigh.

Brooke was in pain and terrified. One in eight million, one in eight million, she repeated in her brain as she struggled to the surface. The seals on the shore began barking at the disturbance. Brooke's heart was pounding. The only thought in her brain was, I'm going to die. Instinctively, she struggled towards the thin bit of sand hoping she could make it before she felt razor sharp teeth tear into her leg and drag her down.

Adrian had seen the Bull Shark's drive out of the corner of his eye and had reacted in an instant that saved Brooke's life. He could see that she was swimming excruciatingly slowly towards the small beach. Adrian quickly scanned the area for the shark and noticed another Bull Shark closing in on Brooke.

Adrian had no time to think. He swam towards the huge predator as fast as he could and rammed it with his shoulder. The shark swam off quickly, not too interested in prey that fights back. The first shark that missed Brooke found a young seal easy prey. It grabbed the seal and pulled it under. The little seal thrashed and managed to free itself, however now the water was filled with blood.

Brooke could barely breathe. She could hear the thrashing behind her and the cries of the poor seal. She swam with all her might towards the shore but the closer she got to the rocks around the beach, the more the strong sideways current pulled her away from it. Brooke just didn't have the strength to fight against it. She was exhausted from her accident the day before, the hours of swimming she had done earlier and her terror.

She was slowly being drug back towards the opening of the bay.

Where is Adrian, she wondered. A sob broke through her lips at the thought of his blood mingling with that of the seal. Brooke was in a panic. I have to get out of here, she thought. Brooke gave in and swam with the current towards the bay.

Brooke was swept into the little bay. She managed to pull herself up onto the first rocks she could grab hold of. She got to her feet and looked back, trying to catch a glimpse of Adrian. She couldn't see anything because of the curve of the island.

Brooke sat down on the rocks, hugged her knees and cried. She was ashamed of fleeing and only thinking of saving her own skin. You are such a coward, she chided herself, but what could I do? I'm not strong enough to fight a shark. Maksim; the thought hit her like a ton of bricks.

Brooke jumped to her feet and scanned the distant beach for Maksim. The beach was empty. Then she saw him in the water near the reef, swimming. She screamed his name as loud as she could but with the wind and his head being underwater he had no chance of hearing her.

Then she had an idea. Brooke grabbed a loose rock. She thrust it under the water line and started banging on the side of the rock she was sitting on. Three quick strikes, three slow strikes, three quick strikes, over and over again. She didn't know if Maksim would know the Morse code for S.O.S. but at least it would get his attention.

It had the desired effect. Maksim's head popped up out of the water and he looked towards Brooke. She stood up. "Help, Adrian!" she yelled.

Maksim's head went down and all was silence. She peered into the bay trying to see him swimming towards her but she saw nothing. She listened, holding her breath, she heard nothing. Frantically, she picked up the rock and started banging it again. Maybe he didn't understand her. It was no use, she looked all around, there was no sign of Mak or Adrian. There was no sound except the sound of the waves and the seabirds in the sky.

What if they both get killed by sharks and I'm left on this island alone, she thought. Fear rose in her throat. Then another worse thought came to her. What if Adrian gets killed and I'm left on this island alone with Maksim? Brooke shuddered, then sat down, buried her face in her arms and bawled.

In a few minutes there was a gentle splash near the rock. Adrian pulled himself out of the water. She lifted up her head startled.

Adrian saw the terrified look on Brooke's face, he saw her red scrapped thigh, he felt terrible. Why did I put her in such danger, he chided himself, she'll probably hate me now. He sat down slowly next to Brooke. He braced himself for her anger. The two teens sat there looking at each other for a moment. Then Brooke grabbed Adrian around the neck and started crying harder than ever. Adrian didn't know what to do. Was this a happy cry or a sad cry, maybe it's a mad cry, he thought. It was all very confusing with humans.

He just decided to pat her back softly. "Tis alright, lassie, you're safe now," he said.

Maksim poked his head up out of the water, scowling as usual. "They're gone," he said. Then he disappeared under the water.

Brooke sat up, she became aware that she was crying all over Adrian's chest. Aghast, she tried to wipe her tears off his chest then realizing what she was doing, she turned beet red. Adrian looked entirely amused. Brooke glanced down and saw that Adrian had a huge gash on the top of his foot. Blood was oozing down onto the rock.

"Oh no! You're hurt!" she cried.

"Tis only a scratch. Kicked a little too close to somebody's mouth," Adrian said, grinning.

Brooke reached down and touched the top of Adrian's foot. Suddenly, she felt a strong warmth travel down her arm towards the hand on his foot. For a moment Brooke's hand was so hot it felt like she was touching a burning stove. She jerked her hand away from Adrian and looked up at him, wondering if he had felt the heat.

Adrian made no sign that he had noticed anything unusual. She looked back at his foot, the wound was gone. She sat there with her mouth open for a moment in total confusion.

Adrian quickly wiped the remaining blood off his foot. "See, told ya it was only a scratch," he said quickly.

Brooke nodded her head, slowly. "Yeah, that's right, little scratches can bleed a lot sometimes," she said. She wasn't sure if she was convincing Adrian or herself.

The adrenaline Brooke had been running on suddenly crashed. She started shaking so hard her teeth chattered. Adrian put an arm around Brooke to steady her.

Then he jumped into the water and held out his hand to Brooke. "Come on, I'll take ya back," he said.

Brooke jumped into the water. Adrian wrapped his warm arms around her, holding her with her back on his chest. He swam backwards towards the shore. Brooke was too exhausted to protest. It felt good to have his strong arms around her.

When they got to the shore Maksim was already there chomping down his latest pile of raw seafood. Brooke was disgusted. How can he just eat everything raw, she wondered. Brooke sat down on the warm sand.

Adrian walked over to Maksim. "Brooke needs something ta eat, she's done in," he said.

Maksim rolled his eyes and tossed a bloody squid onto Brookes lap. The slimy tentacles hit her bare legs and one bloody eye stared up at her. Brooke screamed and jumped up. Maksim laughed hysterically. Brooke glared at him. Even Adrian was trying not to laugh.

Brooke started toward Maksim, her arm raised. "You big jerk!" she yelled. Maksim just kept laughing.

Adrian stepped between them. "Hey, now, we've had enough fightin for today." Adrian patted Brooke's shoulder, "I'll get ya some nice fish."

As Adrian went to pick up the Hawaiian sling, he shoved the still laughing Maksim with his shoulder. "And you can go pick some fruit," he growled.

Maksim stopped laughing. He glared at Adrian, then strode off towards the orchard with his usual scowl.

As Adrian waded into the warm waters of the little bay his heart was pounding. He had just found out two very important things, the suenach can heal and Brooke had no idea what it does. But how can I get it away from her, he wondered. He knew if she found out it's power she would never give it away and the other option, Brooke's death, was beginning to become unthinkable.

Adrian swam slowly through the crystal water, his mind racing. If only I could think of a way to trick her into giving it to me. Maybe if I offer her something beautiful she will trade with me, he thought. He had heard stories of the suire loving beautiful things, though he had no personal experience with the females of his race.

He knew there were some wonderful treasures hoarded in the colony, but that in itself was a problem. He couldn't just take a treasure without someone noticing, there would be questions and that could be disastrous. The thought crossed Adrian's mind to confess everything to the Builder and ask for his help but Adrian couldn't be sure of his reaction.

The Builder was the Athlanmaran who created the colony on the bottom of the sea. It was his use of human technology that allowed their settlement to thrive far away from the old clans. No one knew where he came from, he never claimed any certain clan as his own, but he did have an immense knowledge of machinery and he used that knowledge to improve the lives of the Athlanmara.

Adrian was drawn to the Builder as he seemed to understand everything about humans and also because he was almost an outcast like Adrian. The other Athlanmara, though they benefited from his expertise, didn't trust him.

Adrian believed that the Builder truly cared about the colony, but there were some things about the him that made Adrian uneasy. To create all of the machinery that made the colony run, the Builder sank human ships. He seemed to have an uncanny ability to know which ships had the items that he needed, and he had no qualms about doing whatever it took to acquire them. Adrian had heard stories about hundreds of human sailors being drug to the depths to drown. His father had been part of the attacks.

No, Adrian thought, he couldn't risk the Builder finding out about Brooke. He speared another fish without thinking and added it to his string. The cool water had calmed him after his brush with the sharks and distancing himself from Brooke helped clear his mind.

Why should I care so much about some human girl, he wondered. I should care more about my people, my family.

Yet, even though he tried to stop them, strange emotions were welling up inside of Adrian. Things he had never felt before. I want to touch her, to feel that warmth again. I want to protect Brooke from everything. Adrian shot his spear into the sand in frustration. What is wrong with me?

Oblivious to Adrian's struggle, Brooke lay down on the white sand trying to get warm. She was almost asleep when she heard a blood curdling scream. Brooke sat bolt upright, her heart pounding. She heard a crashing in the underbrush and Maksim came barreling out onto the beach.

Brooke jumped to her feet. "Did you hear a woman scream?" she asked him.

Maksim's face turned red, he looked at the ground. "I screamed," he admitted sheepishly.

"What?" Brooke demanded. Her fear turned to anger. Was this some prank he thought was funny, but she looked at Maksim and he seemed genuinely afraid.

He started gesturing to the orchard. "There was a monster in the trees, all hair and yellow teeth and a tail like a sea snake!" Maksim mimed the terrifying creature that attacked him.

Brooke looked out towards the water, Adrian was still out fishing.

She had a pretty good idea what this creature was, the 'tail like a sea snake' part gave it away. It was probably some sort of Caribbean wood rat. She had seen plenty of them in Florida. They weren't dangerous, they just ate fruit and leaves in the trees. Obviously, Maksim didn't know much about the local fauna and she saw her chance to have some fun with Mr. Big Muscles.

Brooke got a serious look on her face. "Oh no! That's a neotoma floridana. They shoot acid out of their eyes and can strip the flesh off a man in thirty seconds!" she told Maksim. His face went pale. "If we don't kill it now," she continued, "it will lay hundreds of eggs and this whole island will be overrun in a matter of days!" Maksim looked out towards the bay, hoping to see Adrian coming back.

Brooke tried not to smile. "You're not scared are you?" she asked, innocently.

The scowl came back to Maksim's pale face. "No!" he protested loudly.

"Then let's go get it!" she said.

Brooke led the way to the orchard, walking stealthily through the underbrush, Maksim following as quietly as his huge body would allow. When they got to the orchard, Brooke turned to Maksim and put a finger on her lips. He nodded, his eyes wide.

She picked up a large branch from the ground and tiptoed through the trees looking for the rat. She saw the huge, brown, ugly thing up on a branch in a plum tree, it's body alone was at least two feet long and it looked quite well fed. Brooke knew that the rat would jump to the ground and run if frightened so she motioned for Maksim to go ahead. Then she mimed knocking it on the head with her branch.

He nodded and walked slowly toward the tree. It was hard for him to walk because he kept covering his eyes to protect them from the spraying acid. Brooke shook with suppressed laughter. She couldn't believe he was actually falling for her prank and she couldn't believe she actually had the guts to pull it off.

This is the kind of thing I think about two days after I have the chance to do it, she thought. In fact I am doing a lot of things I 'never' do. For a moment Brooke felt a pang of fear, she wondered at this sudden change in her personality, but then she smiled. I like this Brooke, she said to herself.

As soon as Maksim got too close the rat jumped to the ground. Maksim yelped and covered his eyes. Brooke was on the rat in an instant and knocked it senseless with one blow.

"Did you get it?" Maksim asked still afraid to uncover his eyes.

"I think so…" Brooke answered hesitantly.

She waited till the animal stopped twitching then she picked it up, held it to her throat and started to scream. Maksim pulled his hand from his eyes and stared in horror at Brooke writhing on the ground with the terrible creature at her neck. For a split second Maksim thought of running to the beach to get Adrian but the principle of never abandoning a comrade in danger was so ingrained in him that he couldn't leave Brooke to her terrible fate.

Maksim scanned the ground and found a branch twice as big as Brooke's. He lifted the branch over his head and ran towards Brooke screaming at the top of his lungs.

Brooke leaped up. "No!" she yelled, dropping the dead rat. Maksim stopped in his tracks. He looked at Brooke, then at the dead rat. Brooke started laughing. "It's just a rat." Maksim dropped the stick confused. Brooke continued to crack up. "They just eat fruit and plants, they don't shoot acid," she giggled.

Maksim started to understand the trick Brooke had played on him. He walked over to the rat and kicked it with his foot. Brooke kept giggling. He scowled at her and then he started to laugh. He picked up a rotted plum from the ground and threw it at her. She screamed and dodged it. Still laughing she grabbed a plum and threw it at Maksim.

Adrian walked out of the water with a string of reef fish and two big crabs. He thought it would be enough for Brooke to eat. He had eaten his fill while he was fishing and Maksim could catch his own fish.

He scanned the beach, there was no sign of Brooke or Maksim. Then he heard Brooke scream. Adrian dropped his catch and ran towards the sound. He cursed himself for leaving Brooke alone with Maksim. Mak must be trying to get the seunach from her. The thought filled him with anger.

Adrian burst into the orchard clearing panting for breath and couldn't believe what he saw. There were Brooke and Maksim giggling and throwing fruit at each other. He was immediately filled with relief, but as he watched the two of them smiling and laughing at each other, another emotion rose up.

Maksim had maneuvered himself behind a tree but Brooke kept changing her position, she was much better at dodging missiles than he was. Maksim finally had enough, he made a mad dash grabbed Brooke around the waist and carried her out of the trees both of them laughing.

Then they saw Adrian. Maksim instantly dropped Brooke on the ground.

"Ow!" she yelped as she fell hard on her butt.

They both looked at Adrian guiltily. Adrian stood there clenching his fists, his eyes were filled with anger and locked on Maksim.

Brooke jumped up. "I was just playing a trick on Mak," she said quickly. She could feel the tension between the boys.

Adrian was breathing hard. I'm going to kill Maksim, he thought. The intensity of the feeling shocked him. He had never felt this way before. Mak was his best and only friend. They had been on adventures and saved each other lives numerous times.

But as Adrian looked at Brooke, feelings of protecting her overwhelmed him. She needs me, not Mak! I'm the one who saved her, he would have let her die.

The two boys stood there frozen, staring at each other. Finally, Adrian took a deep breath and tried to calm his emotions. Mak visibly relaxed.

He walked past Adrian quickly without looking at him. "I'm going fishing," he murmured.

13 THE COLONY

Deep under the rolling surface of the Bermuda Triangle a faint glow came from hundreds of domes on the ocean floor. The structures were connected to each other by a network of tunnels, batas slipped in and out among the domes like schools of silvery fish. In the center of the cluster of domes was one that was larger than the rest. Flashes of light pierced the ocean gloom from the edifice as if from a localized lightning storm.

Bronte burst through the doors of the workshop. The Builder glanced up from his welding project, his dark glasses making him look like a shrivelled beatle.

Bronte threw a fishing bag onto the ground. "This is all that's left of Cahal, and he wasn't anywhere near the vents. And now my son is missing!" Bronte was shaking with anger.

The Builder sighed and got up from his workbench. He was short for an Athlanmaran and bent with age, though his blue eyes were still bright and fierce. His most notable feature was his scraggly beard which was unheard of for their race. He slowly walked over to Bronte, bent down and picked up the fishing bag, his hands shaking.

He took a deep breath then rubbed his hairy chin with a calloused hand. "Why are the Guardians behaving this way?" he murmured to himself.

Bronte leaned down. "We both know the answer to that. It is the humans, they must be destroyed before we all end up like Cahal!"

The Builder chuckled. "Destroy the humans?" He painfully got up, Bronte offering no assistance. "You will never be able to destroy the humans, they are much too powerful." The Builder walked back to his bench.

Bronte followed him. "Then we must beat them back from our shores ta keep their poisons out of our water!" he cried and slammed his hand on the workbench.

"No," the Builder said, picking up his project again, "If we attack the humans they will hunt us down until they find us. We would all be destroyed. The only way to survive is to hide as our people have for thousands of years," he said, wearily.

Bronte paced the room. "So we will hide and die one by one from the Guardians and sickness, until not one of us is left?" he exclaimed. He glared at the Builder, working away on his project, ignoring him. Bronte fingered the silver seunach on his arm. "What we need to do is attack the humans while we still can." Bronte's voice had the slightest tremor in it, like the echo of a plucked string.

The Builder looked up at Bronte and chuckled. "You know your tricks don't work on me, you must be desperate."

Furious, Bronte strode to the workbench and in one sweep of his arm knocked the tools and spare parts to the ground. "What good are your trinkets and machines if we are all dead!" he yelled. The Builder calmly looked at Bronte and remained silent. They held each other's eyes for a moment. "The council will side with me this time Old One, watch and see," Bronte threatened. Then he strode from the room.

14 BEST FRIENDS

Paul DeLuca stood on the gravel road in the darkness. He took another drag on his cigarette, the burning embers lighting up his face with an eerie orange glow. Paul threw the cigarette down and ground it out with his shoe. He was disgusted with himself, he had worked so hard to quit smoking two years ago and now he was back at it.

He ran his fingers through his thinning hair and started pacing back and forth in front of the chain link gate that led to his warehouse. Paul stopped pacing when he heard the trucks approaching. He quickly opened the gate to let in the two flatbed trucks packed with barrels. Following the trucks was a black Cadillac Escalade which came to a stop next to Paul.

The driver rolled down the window. "You DeLuca?"

Paul stared at Raffe Rossi. He was just what he had been expecting, a hoodlum. Raffe sat there with a sneer on his face, wearing a tank top to show off his ridiculous tattoos. His dark curly hair was slicked back and a garish gold cross hung around his neck.

"Yeah," Paul answered.

Raffe grinned. "Guess we're gonna be best friends." Paul gritted his teeth and said nothing.

Adrian and Brooke lay on the beach. The sky was brilliant with stars, the air was warm and the waves played a soothing melody. Mak was nowhere to be found. Brooke was glad after that awkward moment in the orchard. She gazed up at the beautiful night sky. The stars were so bright, she felt like she could reach out and touch them.

I can't believe I feel so happy she said to herself. I've been shipwrecked with two strange guys, attacked by a shark and have no hope of a rescue but I can't remember when I've felt so... light. She sighed and glanced over at Adrian. I also can't believe I am lying here next to this gorgeous guy, she thought, maybe that's why I don't care if I ever get rescued.

Brooke had a thousand questions running through her mind. I really don't want to break the stillness of this moment, she thought, I'll just lay here quietly.

Two minutes later she sat up and turned to Adrian. "So how did you and Mak meet?"

Adrian looked uncomfortable. "Well," he began, "a couple years ago, I was...travelin." Adrian remembered she had talked of her father's travels. "Mak got into some...trouble with these...fishermen." Brooke nodded, encouraging him to continue. "They'd captured him and who knows what they were gonna do ta him."

Adrian sat up, he was getting into the story now. "I climbed up the side of the boat in the dark, I snuck along the deck and went down inta the depths of the boat. I had to avoid the ah... fishermen in the small tunnels. When I got ta Mak he was all tied up and terrified out of his wits. I used my knife ta cut him free. We were sneaking back ta the deck when a fisherman spied us. We made a run for it, but Mak was barely able to walk. We finally made it ta the deck. I pushed Mak overboard and was jumping myself when ah...fisherman shot me in the back."

Adrian turned and showed Brooke the long red scar along his left shoulder blade. Brooke had noticed the scar but had no idea the dramatic story behind it.

"Oh my gosh!" she exclaimed, "You were shot by a fisherman! That's crazy!"

Adrian was pleased with her reaction. "From then on Mak swore he'd always be my mate and try ta pay me back one day."

"Wow, you're really brave," Brooke said. Adrian grinned and sat up straighter. Brooke pondered Adrian's dramatic story for a moment. Man, the best thing I've ever done for Zoe was help her write a paper in Language Arts.

Adrian noticed a small scar on Brooke's knee. "What happened to ya?" he pointed to her knee.

Brooke turned red. "Uh...I fell off my bike when I was eight," she said, lamely. Adrian laughed, Brooke joined in. Then she got serious. "It was really kind of traumatic for me, I mean I didn't get shot or anything, but..."

Adrian could sense she was trying to hold back tears. "What happened?" he asked quietly.

"Oh, it's stupid!" Brooke tried to laugh it off.

Adrian looked into her eyes intently. "No, it's not," he said.

Brooke looked down at her hands. "Well, I fell off my bike onto a really sharp rock, I was by myself of course, there was blood everywhere, and blood really freaks me out. Anyway, I limped home and called my dad. He told me to put a Band-Aid on it, like he didn't even listen to me, as usual. So, I lay down on the kitchen floor, cause I didn't want to get blood all over the house, and I waited."

Brooke dug her toes in the sand, trying not to cry. "When my dad finally got home, hours and hours later, he found me on the floor in a pool of blood. He didn't say he was sorry for not listening. He just acted mad at me then he called his friend Steve to come over and give me stitches. He wouldn't even take the time to take me to the doctor." Brooke quickly wiped a tear off her cheek hoping Adrian didn't notice.

She laughed and put on a smile. "So that's my dad! Quite the sob story, huh?"

Adrian furrowed his brow. "He should have taken care of you."

Brooke had spent so many years making excuses for her dad that Adrian's comment took her by surprise. "Well, he was so busy and he didn't know…"

"He should have taken care of you," Adrian repeated. His gaze never left Brooke's eyes. There was something about Adrian that was so guileless, so pure, she couldn't argue with him.

Brooke took a deep breath. "You're right, he should have taken care of me."

As she said those words she felt even lighter, like a piece of lead had melted out of her heart and drained into the sand. Brooke smiled a real smile. Adrian kept looking at her. Brooke blushed. She lay back down on the sand and looked up at the stars. Brooke started laughing.

Adrian lay down beside her. "What?" he asked.

"I was just remembering this little star projector light I had in my bedroom as a kid. My mom would come in at night and we would make up silly stories about the stars."

Adrian smiled and looked at the sky. "My mother told me stories about the stars too."

Adrian hadn't thought about his mother for years. What was it about this girl, that was stirring up memories and emotions he had never felt before? Maybe it was the power of the seunach.

 Adrian glanced over at Brooke, their eyes met for a moment, she quickly looked away. He studied Brooke, she was so beautiful, so fragile. Adrian turned away. Stay focused, he told himself, you just want to get the seunach to help the Athlanmara.

But that wasn't true. He wanted to know what it was like to ride a bike, or ride in a car, or fly in an airplane. He wanted to know what human families were like. He wanted to hold Brooke close and let her warmth fill up the empty places deep inside.

Adrian wished they could stay on the island forever. He wished that he never had to go back to his isolated existence. Adrian sighed, it was a fools dream. He knew his father would keep searching for him. Bronte was clever and persistent, it probably wouldn't take him long to figure out what happened.

Adrian knew that every moment that passed put Brooke in more danger. He was torn between his desire to experience intimacy and his desire to protect Brooke at all costs. Adrian turned his face towards Brooke. He caught her staring at him, this time she blushed but didn't turn away. He reached out and took her tiny hand in his own. He again felt emotions rise up inside his chest. He didn't even know how to express what he was feeling, but it was good.

15 REVELATIONS

Sunlight began to filter down into the depths as the silent bata made sweep after sweep of the chosen area.

The signal is getting stronger, Gursel reported to Bronte.

Abruptly, the outline of a drifting bata came into focus. It was clear the craft was empty. Bronte clenched his jaw. After scanning the area for danger he slid the bottom hatch open and entered the sea with Nereus.

They cautiously approached the abandoned bata however, they found no signs of a struggle. The bags and spears belonging to the boys were left in their places. The bata was in neutral and there were no telltale scratches on the surface that would point to the Guardians. It was as if his son had just swam away.

Bronte's scowl deepened as he turned over the events in his mind, Kai sinking the human boat, Adrian and Maksim missing but abandoning their bata. Why would Adrian leave the bata behind? In a flash, the answer came to him. Bronte slammed his spear on the outside of the empty vessel startling Nereus.

We are going to the island, bring this bata, Bronte commanded. Nereus obeyed without question.

The crash of scallops hitting the ground woke Brooke and Adrian. She looked over and saw Mak sit down on the ground next to his pile of shellfish and begin to pry them open with his knife. She looked back at Adrian lying on the sand, he was staring intently at her. Brooke felt tingly all over just looking at him.

"Good morning," she said, her face turning red.

Adrian sat up, leaned on his arm and smiled down at Brooke. "Good morning, lassie," he said softly, repeating her greeting.

Brooke giggled. What is wrong with me, she wondered. It had only been a day since she met Adrian but so much had happened. Brooke felt like she had known Adrian all her life. The two teens gazed at each other.

Maksim made a sound between a growl and a snort. They looked over at him and laughed. Maksim scowled at them both. He had hardly ever seen Adrian smile not to mention laugh. He didn't like it.

After a breakfast of fruit and raw scallops, which took Brooke quite a while to choke down, Adrian took Brooke's hand and started to walk towards the beach.

She stopped. "Uh, why...why don't we stay on land today," Brooke stammered, "You could show me the rest of the island!" she suggested.

Brooke had had enough of sea adventures for a while. Adrian smiled. Maksim just rolled his eyes, sat down and started to pry open more scallops.

The island wasn't that big. The clearing where they started out from was the lowest part so whatever direction they went was uphill. The center of the island was open and cultivated but, the rest of the island was covered with low growing brush.

Adrian and Brooke pushed straight through the brush, there weren't any trails. As they got close to the north edge of the island the vegetation got so thick and tangled they could barely move.

Brooke tapped Adrian on the shoulder. "I get it, this way is a dead end, we can go back now."

Adrian shrugged his shoulders and led Brooke south towards the widest part of the heart shaped island. As the elevation increased, the ground became rockier and easier to navigate. By the time they were almost at the highpoint of the island, the sun was directly overhead and it was getting hot.

Weather in the Bahamas is unpredictable and can go from cool rain to blazing heat in a day. Brooke was getting thirsty and she could feel her nose getting burned. She could tell the heat was getting to Adrian too, his pace began to slow.

"Hey," Brooke came to a stop, "is there any water around here? I'm dying of thirst."

Adrian spun around. "You're dyin!" he exclaimed.

Brooke giggled. "No, I'm not dying, it's an expression. I just need some water."

Adrian smiled, getting the joke. "There's water up ahead," he said grinning.

Brooke could tell that he was keeping some sort of secret. Brooke smiled, she couldn't help it. I probably shouldn't be having so much fun being shipwrecked on an island she thought.

The climb got steeper and Brooke could hear the echoing sound of water trickling. Adrian stopped and as she came up beside him to see what he was looking at he grabbed her by the waist. Brooke gasped. They were both standing on the precipice of a huge sinkhole. Adrian had stopped her from falling six stories down.

The sinkhole was on the limestone cliffs at the edge of the island. Time and water had eroded a huge hole from the top of the cliff down to the ocean below. Brooke held on to Adrian and peered over the edge. It was beautiful. She could see ocean water flowing in and out at the bottom of the sixty foot hole. The water was a startling bright blue and the light reflecting off the sides of the rock made the entire cavern sparkle.

"It's beautiful!" exclaimed Brooke.

Adrian grinned and then his smile softened. "The water is the color of your eyes," he said quietly.

Brooke looked down, her cheeks were burning and not from the sun. She let go of Adrian and took a step back from the edge. She wasn't sure what to do, she wasn't used to attention from boys. The boys in Marathon pretty much ignored her. Maybe it's because I'm always standing next to Zoe, she thought. Well, there's no competition here, Brooke smiled.

Adrian stood looking at Brooke awkwardly. He also wasn't sure how to interact with the opposite sex. In Athlanmaran culture males and females had little to do with each other. In the colony he had always avoided the suire. They were beautiful, but dangerous. He had heard stories of them putting spells on males with their voices and dragging them down to the depths to do who knows what.

He watched Brooke walk over to the little stream and get a drink.

She was different from any female he had ever observed. For one thing she actually looks at me, he thought.

Adrian loved the way that Brooke looked at him. She looks at me like I'm worth something. She needs me. The thought filled Adrian with something he was unfamiliar with, purpose.

Brooke knelt down beside the brook and cupped the water with her hands. Adrian wanted to take Brooke in his arms, he wanted to feel her body close to his, but he wasn't sure how she would react. Should I just try it? Maybe she would stab me, he thought. Adrian knew she still had the broken knife hidden in her shorts.

What does she think of me, he wondered. Adrian had a sinking feeling in his stomach. She thinks I'm human, he said to himself. What would she do if she found out what I am?

Brooke walked around the sinkhole and stood on the highest edge of the cliff. From that vantage point she could see the entire island. To her right she could look down on the small bay that was the indented part of the heart. She could see the lower middle of the island and noticed a large pond behind the cultivated area that Adrian hadn't shown her yet. She could also see how isolated the island was. In every direction there was only open ocean.

Brooke's heart sank. She wondered what her father was doing. He probably thinks I'm dead by now. Will I ever see him again? Brooke wiped away a tear.

Well, you're not dead so stop crying and make the best of it, she told herself. She looked back at Adrian. At least I'm not alone. She couldn't help but smile when she looked at her rescuer.

Adrian's face lit up when he saw her smile. He walked over to Brooke. "Shall we go back?" he asked her with a grin.

"Sure…" Brooke answered hesitantly.

Adrian had that impish look on his face again. He grabbed her hand and pulled her to the edge of the sinkhole. He tilted his head toward the hole.

Brooke pulled her hand away from his. "What? You want me to jump into that hole?"

Adrian laughed. "It's not lethal, I've done it loads of times," he bragged.

Brooke peered over the edge again. It was literally six stories down to the water. "We could just walk back," she said hopefully.

Adrian moved closer to Brooke. "I'm tired of walkin." He took her hand in his strong grip. "Come with me," he said.

Brooke wasn't sure if it was a question or a command. Her heart was saying, yes, I'll follow you anywhere but her head chimed in with, hey, this guy is crazy remember?

She peered down into the cavern again. "What the heck!" Brooke laughed. She grabbed Adrian's hand with both of hers. "On three okay?" she said. Adrian nodded.

Together they said, "One.."

"Wait!" Brooke shouted, she looked at Adrian with pleading eyes, "I'm not going to die, right?"

Adrian brushed his fingers over Brooke's cheek. "I won't let ya die," he said quietly.

Brooke's heart melted. "Okay, let's do this!" she squealed.

They started the countdown again. "One…two…three!" Adrian and Brooke leapt into the void. Brooke's scream echoed on the walls of the cavern. The fall seemed to last forever.

They hit the water, after being so hot the cool water shocked Brooke. For a moment she panicked, she wasn't sure which way was up. Then Brooke felt strong arms around her and in two seconds her head was above the surface. The two teens floated in the water laughing.

"Oh my gosh! That was crazy!" Brooke yelled.

"Aye, crazy!" Adrian repeated, grinning from ear to ear.

Brooke gazed around the cavern. She could see tunnels and smaller caves. "This is amazing! But how do we get out of here?" she asked.

"I know the way."

Adrian moved slowly towards a brightly lit tunnel. Brooke swam past him. Adrian started laughing and grabbed her foot as she went by.

Brooke stopped and turned around. "What?" She saw that Adrian couldn't stop laughing. "Stop making fun of my swimming!" she said, trying to look mad.

"Your legs...it's like you're tryin to walk in the water!" he laughed.

Brooke pretended to be offended. She splashed water in Adrian's face then swam down the tunnel as fast as she could, giggling. Adrian smirked. It took him half a second to swim under Brooke, come up in front of her and splash her back. She tried to splash him again but he grabbed both her arms.

"Hey!" she cried, pretending to struggle. She looked down and saw that Adrian was almost lifting them both out of the water with his strong dolphin kick. "Okay, okay, I give up!" she laughed.

Adrian let her hands go but drew her body close to him. Their faces were inches from each other. His eyes grew serious. Brooke was barely breathing, she had never kissed a boy. I think I'm going to faint, she said to herself.

Adrian pulled Brooke tighter to his body. He never wanted to let her go. Then he heard it, a faint thumping sound. He pushed Brooke away and dove under the water to hear better. Brooke had no idea what just happened.

"Adrian?" her voice echoed in the empty cavern. What, am I that repulsive, she wondered.

Adrian's head shot up out of the water. "Cac!" he exclaimed, "They've come!"

Without waiting for a response, Adrian grabbed Brooke with both his arms and dove under water. Brooke couldn't breathe, she couldn't see. Adrian was swimming so fast she felt like she was being drug behind a jet ski. Brooke was just about to run out of air when they broke the surface of the water in the little bay.

Brooke gasped her, lungs aching. "What is going on!" she sputtered.

Adrian was already dragging her to the shore. "You're not safe, ya have ta hide!" he said urgently.

Brooke could tell that Adrian was terrified. She was about to ask about the pirates when she glanced back and saw a huge fish tail in the water. Brooke screamed. Adrian paused, his face went pale.

Brooke gasped, "What is…" Then she looked at Adrian and realized it was attached to him. Her eyes widened. "Oh, my gosh…oh, my gosh…" She could hardly breathe.

She looked at his arms around her. His hands were webbed and at the end of each finger was a sharp claw. She cried out and tried to break free. Adrian's face hardened, he tightened his grip on Brooke and picked up speed.

They were at the shore in moments. Brooke stumbled onto the sand. She turned back and watched Adrian walk out of the water on two legs, without the swim trunks. "But you're human...now..."

"There's no time ta explain!" Adrian exclaimed. Adrian cupped his hands around his mouth and made a piercing cry. He looked at Brooke. "Ya have ta hide, they'll kill ya," he said quietly.

Brooke was having trouble collecting her thoughts. "Who? The pirates or...mermen?" she started to cry, "What is going on? What are you?"

Maksim came tearing out of the jungle, a knife in his hand. "They've come?" he asked, his whole body shaking. Adrian nodded. "I told you we should have let her die!" Maksim bellowed, "Maybe if we kill her now, we won't be fed to the Guardians!"

He ran towards Brooke, holding the knife high. Brooke was frozen in shock.

"No!" Adrian screamed. He tackled Maksim to the ground. "Run!" he yelled at Brooke, "Hide!"

Brooke took off running as fast as she could towards the clearing. Maksim pushed Adrian off, both boys stood up. They could see the outline of two batas entering the bay. They looked at each other in fear and ran for the clearing.

The boys entered the clearing just as Brooke had decided her only option was to hide in a tree. She scrambled up into the mango tree, adrenaline giving her extra speed. Adrian and Maksim couldn't have been more surprised if she had sprouted wings and flown away. They had never thought of the possibility of climbing a tree.

Maksim ripped off his shirt covering. He ran to the hut and grabbed Brooke's jacket. He furiously started to dig a hole in the sand with his hands. "We have to hide the human things!" he cried.

Adrian stood there motionless for a moment. Then he grabbed the jacket off the ground. Maksim stuffed the shirt in his hole and tried to grab the jacket from Adrian.

"No!" Adrian yelled at him, "We need it! He'll smell her." Maksim kept frantically pulling on the jacket. "Mak!" Adrian yelled.

He put a hand on the terrified boy's shoulder and looked into his eyes. Maksim made a choking sound, then he let go of the jacket and turned to fill in the hole he had dug. From her vantage point Brooke could see the entire clearing but she hoped she would still remain hidden by the thick leaves of the tree.

Just as Maksim stood up three naked men walked into the clearing. I'm gonna need therapy when I get home Brooke thought. Each of the men held a long spear with barbs on the end. They didn't look like fishing spears, unless the fish was as big as a whale, she noted.

The tallest man in the middle had a long scar on his face. All three of the men had multiple scars all over their bodies, to Brooke they looked terrifyingly fierce. The man with the scar was wearing some sort of necklace, it looked like a string with a green jewel in it. His face was twisted with rage.

He strode up to Adrian. "What have ya done?" his voice shook with anger. Adrian said nothing. "Where is the human?" Bronte was screaming now.

Adrian was remarkably calm. "There's no human, I just took a few things from the boat." Adrian held out Brooke's jacket.

Bronte grabbed the jacket and threw it on the ground. "Don't lie ta me, this whole place reeks of human stench!" Bronte began to pace back and forth in front of the boys. Nereus and Gursel stood as still as statues. Brooke could see that Maksim's hands were shaking. "Why did ya leave your bata behind if ya just took a few things from a boat?"

Bronte's words were cold and calculated. Maksim started to open his mouth. Adrian glared at him, imperceptibly shaking his head, but it was too late. "We lost the bata in the storm," Maksim said loudly.

Bronte whirled around. "Was I talking ta you leth-chu?" he growled. Bronte hurled his spear at Maksim's chest, but Adrian pushed his friend to the ground.

It all happened so fast Brooke could hardly comprehend it. There was Adrian, blood gushing from a deep wound in his arm and a spear vibrating in the trunk of the mango tree below her. Nereus and Gursel didn't move a muscle.

Brooke put her hand over her mouth to keep from crying out. Her brain was reeling. What should I do? If I come down from the tree they will only get in worse trouble and I know they'll kill me, but I just can't sit here and watch Adrian die.

Maksim scrambled to his feet. Adrian grabbed his arm and tried to stop the bleeding.

Bronte walked over to Adrian and looked him in the eye. "There's no honor in that wound," he sneered.

Bronte held his arm out for the spear, still glaring at Adrian. Gursel ran and pulled the spear from the tree trunk. He looked up into the branches for a moment. Then he spun around and ran to give Bronte his spear.

Bronte searched the ground. He found the remains of their tiny fire. He stabbed his spear into the dead coals and flames jumped up six feet in the air.

He turned to Nereus and Gursel. "Burn it all."

Nereus and Gursel ran to the hut and grabbed everything Adrian had collected and threw it on the fire. The pages of the books curled up in smoke, the little dog melted in moments, the suitcase and moldy clothes caught fire like they were doused in gasoline.

Brooke could see Adrian clench his fist but other than that the boys stood like they were made of stone. Bronte kept his spear in the flames until the tip was glowing red. He walked up to the boys, holding the spear in front of their faces. They didn't flinch.

He passed them and thrust his spear into the roof of the hut. It burst into flames immediately. He motioned to Nereus and Gursel, they followed Bronte as he walked towards the beach. Brooke could see Adrian and Maksim finally relax.

Bronte called back over his shoulder. "Clean up this mess and bring the bata back. You are forbidden ta come to this island again."

The boys stood absolutely still. Brooke held her breath up in the tree, watching blood drip down Adrian's leg.

Maksim finally broke the silence. "Adrian...I..I," he stammered.

"No worries, Mak, tis only a scratch," Adrian said with forced cheerfulness. Maksim looked down at the stain of blood on the sand. "Go see if they've gone," Adrian whispered to Mak.

Mak trotted off towards the beach. Adrian sat down hard on the sand. He heard a rustling in the tree branches behind him. He painfully turned around and held up his hand to stop Brooke from coming down. He had to make sure they were gone.

In a few minutes Maksim returned dripping wet and panting. "They've gone. I checked the whole bay and out around the rocks," he said. Adrian let out a sigh of relief.

Brooke dropped softly to the ground. She ran over to Adrian and knelt beside him. "Oh my gosh! I thought they were going to kill you!" she cried, tears running down her face, "Who was that horrible guy?" she asked.

Adrian chuckled. "That 'guy' was my father," he said grimly. Brooke's eyes widened, she didn't know what to say.

She took a deep breath and tried to stop crying. "Let me see your arm," she said to Adrian.

He removed his hand gingerly from the wound, immediately it started bleeding heavily. Brooke felt faint, though she had considerable experience curing wounded sea creatures, she hated the sight of blood. No time for that now you baby, she told herself.

"That's really bad Adrian, I don't suppose you have any medical supplies around here." She looked at the dying fire and the smoking remains of the hut. Not likely she thought.

"Nah, I'll be ta rights in a few days."

He tried to sound brave but she could see that his face was drawn with pain and even paler than normal.

Brooke pulled off her tank top and began to rip it into strips. Adrian and Maksim gazed at Brooke in her bikini top then looked at each other and grinned. She glanced up at them and saw the goofy looks on their faces. She shook her head. Boys, she thought, they are all the same, even mermen, I guess.

Her stomach felt queasy at the thought of Adrian's fish tail. I can't think of that now, Adrian is bleeding to death, she told herself.

Brooke began to wrap the strips around Adrian's arm, trying to get the edges of the wound to press together. The bandaging stopped the bleeding. Maksim looked relieved. Adrian struggled to get to his feet. Maksim pulled him up and held him steady.

Brooke jumped up. "I think you should rest," she told him, "you've lost a lot of blood."

"No worries, ya done a grand job," Adrian said. He wondered why the power of the seunach didn't heal his wound. He looked down at Brooke. "I need ta get ya back safe."

Adrian reached out to touch Brooke's shoulder, but she took a step back and looked at the ground. Adrian dropped his hand awkwardly. Now he understood. She has to want to heal me, he thought. What did you expect, he asked himself, she thinks of you as a sea monster now. The tightness in his chest hurt more than his throbbing arm.

Brooke started to tear up again. "Yeah, I just really want to go home," she sniffed. I don't even have my tank top to wipe my nose anymore, she thought. Maksim lit up with the prospect of getting rid of Brooke.

Then his face fell. "We have the bata but how is she going to breathe in it!" Mak said exasperated. They had seemed so close to being done with this terrible mess.

Adrian put on a strained smile. "Already have a plan for that. We can put air in the forward compartment, it should last long enough ta get her close ta land," he explained. Maksim just looked confused, Brooke wasn't paying much attention, she just liked hearing the word, 'plan'. "Just go ta the pond and grab the big water barrel Mak, I'll show ya how we'll do it."

Maksim ran off. Brooke and Adrian stood there for a moment,

each of them trying hard not to look at the other.

"So…" Brooke broke the awkward silence, "you're a merman."

Adrian kicked some sand on the last of the coals. "We call ourselves, the Athlanmara," he said quietly, not looking at Brooke.

"You can breathe under water then?" she asked. Adrian nodded. "And you can have a fishtail whenever you want?" He nodded again, still not looking at Brooke.

Brooke couldn't believe this was actually happening. She started to giggle, then she laughed out loud. Adrian looked at her strangely. Brooke couldn't seem to stop laughing, the whole experience she'd had over the last two days seemed utterly ridiculous.

She saw the confused look on Adrian's face. "I was just thinking about…" she gasped between bouts of laughter, "how I'm going to explain any of this to my dad."

Adrian walked towards Brooke slowly, his green eyes flashing. "Ya can never tell anyone about us," he said, menacingly, "Never!"

Brooke stopped laughing and gulped. She suddenly saw a resemblance between Adrian and his father.

16 SEARCH AND RESCUE

Jackson sat on the warm pier, his legs dangling over the edge. He nervously whirled a set of keys around his finger. He watched as a group of pelicans swooped by, their wings almost touching the shining water. He looked at his phone, it was almost ten am.

Jackson and Zoe had spent the entire day before in her sailboat searching for Brooke. They didn't get far in her tiny boat so the two teens had come up with a reckless plan to find their friend.

Jackson looked around anxiously. He wondered what he would do if someone started to walk towards him down the pier. Oh, hello Mr. DeLuca, you're looking fine this beautiful morning, no that's lame. No hablo Ingles, ha, that won't work. Ah, my appendix, call 911! Jackson smiled at his foolproof plan.

He looked at this phone again. Dang it! Zoe is always getting these crazy ideas, he thought, and I'm the one who gets in trouble. Well, maybe I am done doing what she tells me. Jackson got up and started to walk back towards the house.

Zoe came tearing around the corner. "Run!" Zoe yelled.

Jackson immediately turned and started running back down the dock. "I don't know if I can," he panted as Zoe caught up with him, "I think I might throw up after what I just saw."

"Oh, grow up!" Zoe snapped. She grabbed the boat keys from Jackson's hand in mid stride. "How else were we going to steal the keys from Chris?" They reached the yacht.

Jackson jumped aboard while Zoe cast off the lines. "Well, I thought by 'distraction,'" Jackson made air quotes with his hands, "you were going to fall down a flight of stairs or something, not get into a twenty minute make-out session," he said sarcastically. "Really, it only took me five minutes to find the keys," he added. Zoe just glared at him.

She jumped aboard and started the engine. "I'm willing to do whatever it takes to find my friend," she yelled over the powerful engine. Jackson was about to answer but Zoe gunned the throttle and he fell backwards onto the deck. The beautiful fifty foot craft leapt out into the open ocean.

Chris DeLuca watched from the window as Zoe took off in his father's yacht. He realized he'd been played. Zoe waved at him, her hair flying in the wind.

Chris grabbed his cell phone to call the police. He started to dial, then stopped. Maybe if I don't tell on her Zoe would get back together with me, he thought.

"Ahhh!" he yelled, throwing his cell phone across the room. He sank down on the couch. What is it about that girl that is driving me crazy, he wondered.

Jackson picked himself up off the deck and sat at the small table that was next to the driver's seat. "Hmmmm, nice, genuine leather," he said, patting the seats. He turned to Zoe, "Well I guess we'll get a lot more area covered with this Cadillac of the sea than with your sailboat, but how long do you think I'll be in jail?"

Zoe rolled her eyes at Jackson. "Oh, stop being so dramatic! We're only borrowing it for a rescue mission for heaven's sake. No one's going to jail! We're going to find Brooke, I know she's out there!" she said emphatically.

"Yeah," Jackson said with less enthusiasm, "She's gotta be out there somewhere."

A warm gentle breeze swept over the serene ocean giving no evidence of the drama playing out below the surface. Brooke was trying not to panic. She was stuck in a small space with a bubble of air around her and fifty feet of ocean above her.

Adrian and Maksim had wanted to take the bata deeper but Brooke had warned them that she could get decompression sickness if they went too deep. Adrian was running the bata as fast as he could. Both boys were wary of attracting human attention at such a shallow depth.

They had decided before they started out to head straight for the Keys, and as soon as they saw a smaller boat, Brooke should swim out and call for help. Brooke felt like she had been trapped in her bubble prison for hours but there was no way to tell the passage of time. There was only the gentle thumping of the engine and the unearthly glow of the two creatures in the next compartment.

She looked back at Adrian and Maksim. They were floating in water, their skin glowing with a blue-green light. Their large eyes constantly scanned the ocean around them while their tails remained motionless in the confines of the craft.

Tails, she said to herself. Brooke still couldn't believe any of this was real. Seriously, I must be unconscious somewhere dreaming this all up, she told herself. Yes, that makes the most logical sense.

Adrian glanced at Brooke, she immediately looked away. Her heart was pounding. Figures, she said to herself, if I dreamed I was in love it would have to be ruined by the guy being a merman. That is just my luck. Brooke squeezed her eyes shut. I just want to get home, or wake up, whatever. I just want to see my dad again.

Her hands started to shake. She took a deep breath. You can not panic now, she chided herself, you don't have enough air. Brooke dug her fingernails into her palms, closed her eyes and focused on repeating the scientific name of every sea creature she could remember.

Adrian looked at tiny Brooke huddled in the front compartment. His heart felt like a stone in his chest. He wished he had never gone near Brooke's boat. He had put the entire colony at risk, and for what, he asked himself. He hadn't even got the seunach from her. There would be no hero's welcome for Adrian when he got back to the colony, just more shame and suspicion.

Adrian was used to that existence. The connection he felt with Brooke was over, he knew he would never be able to see Brooke again. Not that she would want to see me anyway, he brooded, she thinks I'm a disgusting monster.

Suddenly, there was a tiny thump on the window of Brooke's compartment. Startled, she glanced over and saw a small, white creature on the glass. She looked closer, it was just like the little Yeti crabs her dad studied. That's strange she thought, why would it be in such shallow water?

Then another one hit the craft, and another, and another. She looked back at Adrian. His eyes were wide with terror. In moments the windows of the bata were covered with the crawling crabs. Some were three feet in diameter.

The crabs started to attack the ship. The noise of thousands of claws scraping against the hull was deafening. Terrified, Brooke looked back at Adrian again. He and Maksim seemed paralyzed with fear.

"What do we do?" she yelled at them over the din.

Then she heard a crack. She looked up, a tiny line appeared on the glass of her compartment. She could see little air bubbles escaping into the water above; her air. Brooke frantically pounded on the glass separating her from the boys.

"Go to the surface! I'm going to drown!" she pleaded. Adrian seemed like he was in a daze. "Adrian!" Brooke screamed.

Adrian had heard stories of the Guardians, horrible stories, of lives and limbs lost. Brooke pounded on the separation again. Adrian looked at Brooke then back at Maksim. The large boy gazed at him with fear and trust in his eyes. Adrian had another choice to make. Should he surface the bata to save Brooke when it would put himself and Maksim in danger of being seen by humans? Their exposure could endanger the entire colony.

Adrian could see a tiny stream of water cascading into Brooke's compartment. She stared at Adrian, her blue eyes pleading, her breathing space getting smaller and smaller. Adrian pointed the bata towards the surface.

As the water filled her compartment Brooke was forced closer and closer to the glass and the seething crabs. It seemed to Brooke as if her nightmares were coming true. Not only would she drown in sight of the surface, she may be torn to pieces by monsters. Just as the bata finally broke the surface the glass cracked and claws snapped in Brooke's face. She screamed.

Come on Adrian! Maksim yelled. He grabbed the lower hatch door wanting to bolt.

No! Adrian stopped him. *We'd never make it, they're everywhere!* As the water receded, Adrian and Maksim recovered their legs.

"Adrian!" Brooke screamed.

She was trying to use her shoe to stop up the crack with little success. Adrian opened the door between them. He grabbed her other shoe and pushed it up on the glass. He looked at Brooke sadly. Adrian's defeated attitude terrified Brooke. He fought off sharks single handedly, if he's afraid...

"What are they?" Brooke gasped.

"Guardians," he replied.

"Isn't there anything that will stop them?" she asked frantically.

"No," Adrian said quietly, resigned to his fate.

Brooke racked her brain. She thought of her father's lab. The crabs in jars, the equipment, then it hit her.

"Do you have a battery?" she asked Adrian. He looked at her quizzically. "How does this ship run? What powers it?" she yelled.

"Aye, the power box, it's under there." Adrian pointed to a small hatch door on the floor.

She handed her shoe to Adrian. "You hold them!"

Brooke opened the small hatch and found what she was looking for, a very large marine battery. She dug in the compartment looking for cables and found some that would work. Adrian could barely hold back the crabs. They were making the hole in the glass bigger. Razor sharp claws began to slice through the flimsy shoes Adrian was holding.

"Mak!" he yelled.

Maksim had been cowering in the corner. He saw what was happening to Adrian and finally went into action. He ripped off part of the inner metal sheathing of the bata with his bare hands. He shoved it up towards the hole. Adrian looked at him and grinned.

Brooke had attached the cables to the battery. She turned towards Adrian and Maksim, a cable in each hand. "I hope this doesn't kill us," she said. She touched the cables to the hull of the ship. There was a spark. Adrian and Maksim fell to the ground immediately.

"Adrian!" Brooke screamed.

She could feel a charge in the water she was standing in, but it was bearable to her. For some reason her bracelet began to glow. She paid little attention to that and kept holding the cables to the hull. She could see the movements of the crabs slowing, they were dropping off the ship.

Brooke looked down at Adrian and Maksim. They were laying in the shallow water twitching. She was terrified she was killing them, yet terrified to let go and have crabs pour into the ship and rip them all to shreds.

In a few moments, the crabs had cleared the glass. She quickly unhooked the cables knelt down and pulled Adrian's head up on her knees. Brooke looked for a pulse on his neck. She breathed a sigh of relief when she felt Adrian's heart beating. She couldn't tell if he was breathing. There was no air coming out of his mouth and nose, but she figured he could breathe through his skin in the shallow water.

Brooke brushed his hair from his forehead. "Adrian," she said softly.

Adrian's eyes fluttered, he looked up and her. "Lassie," he said groggily. He glanced around, and saw the crabs were gone. "Ya saved us."

Mak sat up slowly, holding his aching head. He glared at Brooke. "You almost killed us!" he growled.

Adrian and Brooke looked at each other and laughed. Maksim stood up painfully. Brooke took Adrian's arm and helped him to his feet. He looked down at Brooke's hand on his arm. She saw where he was looking and quickly pulled her hand away. Adrian clenched his jaw and looked at Brooke with sadness in his eyes.

Brooke's mind was filled with turmoil. I've never met anyone as amazing as Adrian, she thought, but what am I supposed to do, date a merman? She looked at Maksim. He was glaring at her like he wished her at the bottom of the sea.

And what about Adrian's charming dad, she asked herself. If he thought Adrian had even spoken to her, she shuddered at the thought of what he would do to Adrian. No, this whole thing is ridiculous and I need to just be honest with him.

Brooke took a deep breath. "Adrian, I...", she was interrupted by the sound of a boat approaching.

"Cac!" Mak exclaimed.

Adrian grabbed Brooke by the shoulders. "Ya have ta go!" he said. Brooke looked at the hatch then at Adrian, her eyes wide with fear. "It's alright, lassie, they've gone," he assured her. She nodded her head but made no move towards the hatch. Adrian took Brooke's hand. "I'll go with ya," he said.

"Adrian!" Mak yelled. It sounded like the boat was almost on top of them now.

"Mak, take it down!" Adrian commanded, as he opened the hatch. He took Brooke in his arms and entered the sea.

The bata disappeared from view as their heads broke the surface. Brooke could see a yacht about five hundred yards away coming straight for them.

She turned to Adrian who was still holding her. "Adrian I…I..." she stammered. The boat was getting closer. Adrian, I love you, is what Brooke wanted to say. The pair floated in the water, Adrian's arms around her waist.

She stared into his luminous eyes wanting to memorize every detail of his face. I'm never going to see him again. The sound of the boat engine grew louder. Adrian's lips were inches from Brooke's.

She could feel his breath on her face. "Adrian, I love you," Brooke whispered. Adrian's eyes grew wide. A surge of heat swept through his entire body, his arm immediately stopped throbbing. Brooke pulled away and started to swim towards the boat.

Adrian was in shock. He knew he should be diving out of sight but he just couldn't move. She loves me, he thought. Adrian wasn't sure what that meant. He had read of love in human books and the word had always confused him. He was sure of one thing however, it was good.

A smile spread over Adrian's face as he sank below the surface. He looked up and watched as Brooke swam awkwardly towards the approaching boat. He wouldn't leave until he was sure she was safe on board. She loves me, he repeated to himself. A warm feeling spread through his chest.

Jackson sat on the bow of the yacht, binoculars pressed to his face.

"Well?" Zoe yelled at him through the window.

"I don't know," he said, "it was there one minute then it was gone."

Zoe cut the engine and came out to the bow. "Give me those!" She grabbed the binoculars from around Jackson's neck, almost choking him. She put the binoculars up to her eyes and scanned the ocean. "I don't see anything."

"Well, it had to be something!" Jackson insisted, "It was like a flash of sun off of something shiny."

Zoe put down the binoculars and sighed. "It was probably just some trash," she said.

She slumped down next to Jackson. They had been scanning the empty ocean for hours and Zoe was losing her fragile faith that Brooke was alive.

Jackson glanced over at Zoe. He could tell she was losing it. "Come on now," he said cheerfully "You're the positive one, I get to be the sarcastic cynic, remember?"

Zoe looked at Jackson and tried to smile with tears in her eyes. "We might as well…"

"Wait!" Jackson interrupted her, "I heard something!" They both sat up on the bow tense, straining their eyes and ears for any sign of hope.

"Help!" came the faint cry again.

Zoe and Jackson looked at each other in shock. They both jumped up at the same time and ran to the back of the boat where the cry was coming from. There was Brooke swimming toward the boat.

"Brooke!" Jackson yelled as he leapt into the water.

"You're alive!" Zoe choked out, then she started to bawl hysterically. Jackson swam awkwardly to Brooke and grabbed her around the neck. They both went under.

Brooke kicked him off and they both surfaced choking. "What? Are you trying to kill me!" Brooke sputtered.

"I'm just so happy to see you alive!" Jackson yelled.

Brooke laughed and swam past Jackson to the ladder Zoe had put off the back of the boat. She climbed up the ladder and was immediately engulfed by a weeping Zoe. Jackson clambered up the ladder and joined the weeping and laughing girls.

"We thought you were dead!" Zoe said, when she could talk again.

"Yeah, I totally knew you were dead!" Jackson added with enthusiasm.

Brooke just smiled. She was so happy to see her friends she couldn't think of any words to say. Zoe wrapped Brooke in a towel, Jackson helped her to sit down. They both kept staring at her like she was going to disappear.

"So, when did you get a new boat?" she asked trying to lighten the mood.

"We totally stole it from Chris DeLuca!" Jackson said triumphantly. Then he looked serious. "My dad is probably going to lock me in the brig for months."

Zoe hit herself on the forehead. "Your dad!" she exclaimed. She ran to the radio. "PAN, PAN, Coast Guard come in. This is the Bama Breeze, we found Brooke Williams!"

17 A WHOLE NEW WORLD

Deep under the surface of the ocean, the crushing black depths were pushed back by the gentle glow of the tiny colony. The faint light attracted the creatures of the abyss which harmlessly swarmed around the dwellings of the Athlanmara.

Agitated, Bronte swam back and forth in the small confines of his dome. Kai floated nearby still shuddering from his latest attack. He knew Kai was getting worse. The strange attacks were becoming more frequent. Bronte was afraid it wouldn't be long before Kai was dead.

For a moment the lights flickered and went dark. Bronte paused listening for the generators. In a moment they came back on. He knew the methane seep they were using for power was almost empty. Someone from the colony would have to locate a new source.

Bronte gritted his teeth, they couldn't afford to lose anymore of their people. What used to be the normal rhythms of their society had become a suicide mission because of the Guardians. None of their people understood why four years ago, the previously harmless creatures had invaded new territory and grown to be ferocious predators.

Adrian swam slowly into the dome. He picked up on his father's mood and avoided his gaze. Bronte saw the bandage on his arm made of human clothing. He swam up to Adrian in a flash and ripped it off his arm.

What do you think you're doing? he yelled in Adrian's head, *Do you want the whole colony to know what you've done?* Adrian's blood ran cold. He knew his father would see his healed wound and figure out everything. But Bronte was so distraught, he just continued his tirade. *It's bad enough you won't be one with the Athlanmara but this obsession with humans is dangerous for all of us.*

Adrian looked down ashamed. It was true. All the Athlamara had a psychic bond, they understood each other, they had a knowing that helped them to work together as a group. But not Adrian.

Adrian didn't know why he couldn't connect, even Kai with his sickness was one with the Athlanmara. Many in the colony were suspicious of Adrian already because they couldn't connect with him and his obsession with all things human made it worse.

I've tried father, I'm sorry, Adrian said quietly.

Bronte ignored him. *Look at your brother! Look at what your precious humans have done to him!* Bronte swam up to Adrian forcing him to look him in the eyes. *If you care about your people, if you care about your brother, you will help me destroy the humans once and for all.* Bronte stormed from the dome. Adrian swam slowly up to Kai and touched him on the arm.

Kai opened his eyes and tried to smile at Adrian. *Told you so.*

Even in his suffering, Kai tried to stick it to Adrian. For some reason this made Adrian's heart ache for his brother even more.

Adrian grinned at his brother. *You're gonna get better Kai, I know it!*

Kai shook his head and chuckled. *We both know I'm gonna die, ya lebnah,* Kai said, weakly. *And there's nothing you can do about it.*

Adrian's throat tightened. There was something he could have done. If he had let Brooke die his brother would be healed right now.

Nereus entered the dome. *You must come before the council,* he announced. Adrian nodded, he squeezed Kai's hand and followed Nereus out of the dome.

Brooke sat on the couch in her jammies, wrapped in her fuzzy blanket drinking the hot cocoa her dad had made. She felt warm and comfy but it was something more than the hot cocoa could supply, it was something deeper. She felt happy and peaceful, she wasn't sure why.

Brooke glanced over at her dad. He wouldn't stop staring at her. "Dad! Stop staring at me, you're making me feel weird!" she said.

"Sorry honey," he said and tried to look at the papers he was holding. Brooke sighed, at least he let go of my hand, she thought.

Tom put down the papers he was pretending to look at. "Brooke, I just want you to know that things are going to be different. Steve and Mrs. Moreno had an intervention with me," he chuckled, "I promise I'm going to be home every night at five sharp and I'm not even going back to the lab until you feel up to going to work at the marina." Brooke nodded and smiled at her dad. She sipped her cocoa and stared out the window watching the sunlight fade on the ocean.

Out of the corner of her eye Brooke saw her dad staring again. She could tell he wanted to say something but then stopped himself. She had a feeling it was about the bracelet. Brooke had kept wearing it and her dad hadn't mentioned anything about it since she got back, but she knew it made him nervous. I'm sure he's afraid of upsetting me, she thought.

Brooke sighed again. Things are certainly going to be different. She felt like a different person, she had been through so much in the last two days. Two days? It feels more like a lifetime. And after what I've learned about Adrian it seems like a completely different world, she mused.

Brooke had always known the ocean was teeming with life but human type life? It was still hard for her to wrap her mind around the idea. Brooke closed her eyes and remembered Adrian's intense eyes staring into her own. She remembered the scars on his muscular body, the strength of his arms around her, his fearless honesty.

Then she remembered his webbed hands with wicked claws and how hard his eyes looked when he warned her to keep quiet. She opened her eyes and shuddered. Brooke wondered for the millionth time if she had been dreaming the whole thing, but she had a big bruise on her leg where Adrian kicked her and she looked at her hands again. They had cuts on them where the Yeti crab claws had poked through her shoes.

Thinking about the crabs, or Guardians as Adrian called them, made her heart start to pound again. I escaped from them because of my knowledge of electrical engineering but what about Adrian and his people? How can they protect themselves from those aberrations of nature, she wondered, their weapons are useless.

Brooke stared off into space and started to chew her nails. What causes an organism to abandon their specific environment? It had to have something to do with food, shelter or fear. Food is a big driver but why the change, why now? Her dad was trying to find the answer. Adrian, whatever he was, had saved her life and she owed it to him to find a way to help.

She looked over at her dad who quickly looked away, pretending that he hadn't been staring at her again. "So, dad, I was wondering, could I go with you to the lab tomorrow?" she asked, "I want to learn more about your crabs."

The ebbing sun sent orange tongues of fire across the tropical sky. Chris DeLuca stomped through the rivers of light pouring in the expansive windows of his beautiful mansion. His only thoughts were of his miserable love life. He opened the door of the exercise room.

"Crap!" he said under his breath. There was Raffe, shirtless and sweating all over his private gym equipment.

Raffe racked the weights he was lifting and sat up. "Yo, Chris, there you are," he said wiping sweat out of his eyes with Chris' towel. Chris just stood in the doorway and said nothing. Raffe got up. "Chris, buddy, you don't remember me?" he asked.

Chris was mad when his dad had told him some relation of his business partner was staying with them but now the guy was acting like they were best friends. It was annoying.

"No," Chris said.

Raffe walked up to Chris and punched him playfully in the stomach. "You know, your cousin Nicky's birthday party two summers ago in Jersey," he looked at Chris expectantly, "Your Aunt Rita is cousins with my Uncle Dom, you know, the Moretti's."

Chris did have some memory of his Aunt Rita but he had met like a million distant relatives that summer. How does this guy expect him to remember any of them? He just decided it would be easier to go with it.

"Oh, yeah, now I remember," Chris said, deadpan.

Raffe ignored his attitude and looked around the room. "This is some sweet setup you got here bro!" Raffe looked Chris up and down. "You rolling in the dough, looking like some tan Hollister model. I bet you got all the babes in this itty bitty town drooling for you, am I right?"

Chris was beginning to like Raffe. "Yeah, that's right," Chris grinned.

"Who's the babe of the day then, show me a picture!" Chris pulled out his phone and showed Raffe a picture of Zoe. "Whoa, she is hot!" Raffe exclaimed, "She got an older sister you could hook me up with?"

"Nah." Chris put his phone away and picked up some free weights. "She's not that great anyway," he said.

Raffe walked over and stopped Chris from lifting the weights. "Bro, I am sensing some trouble in paradise," he said seriously.

"Yeah, well, she broke up with me for no reason."

"What?" Raffe yelled, "is she mentally insane?"

"She's just kind of a brat" Chris said. It was nice to have someone he could talk to about Zoe, his dad never listened.

"Right, okay bro, all you gotta do is win her back, then dump her like yesterday's trash," Raffe said, as he sat down on the bench and started to lift again.

"I tried that," Chris whined.

"Did you buy her some nice jewelry?"

"I bought her diamond earrings and she threw them in my face!"

Raffe racked the weights and sat bolt upright. "You're kidding me."

"No," Chris said.

"Oh, so she's one of those 'don't try to buy me off' harpies?" Raffe said in a mocking voice. Chris was impressed with Raffe, he really got what was going on.

"Yeah!" Chris exclaimed.

"Okay bro, all we gotta do is find some way to make you the hero." Raffe went back to lifting. "When you got her eating out of your hand, you dump her. Don't worry about it, Raffe's on the job."

Chris smiled for the first time in a week. "Thanks dude," he said, "By the way, what kind of work are you doing for my dad?"

Raffe got up and walked over to Chris. "I don't work for your dad bro," Raffe patted Chris on the cheek, "He works for me."

Adrian and Mak swam out of the council room.

Three weeks working the vents! Mak exclaimed. Adrian ignored Mak and kept on swimming. Mak grabbed Adrian's arm. *I can't stand going down there,* Mak said his eyes wide with fear. *I'm still having nightmares about them crawling all over the bata.*

Adrian looked at Mak like he just noticed him. *Uh, no worries, Mak,* he said, swimming off slowly.

Mak got in front of him. *No worries!* He shoved Adrian. *This is all your fault! If you hadn't saved Brooke, I mean that human, none of this would have happened!*

Quick as lightning Adrian had Mak in a choke hold. *Eist do bheul!* he said quietly in Maksim's head. Adrian let go, Mak glared at him and rubbed his neck. Adrian looked around cautiously. *Ya know what they would do ta us if they found out.*

Mak shook his head. *To us, or you?* Adrian looked down ashamed. Mak pushed past him and swam away.

He's right Adrian thought, everything is my fault. I disobeyed every law of the colony and forced Mak to be a part of it. What's wrong with me, he asked himself. All I can think about is that girl, the way her hair moved in the wind, her blue eyes.

Adrian swam slowly through the dim glowing tunnels. He was always surrounded by other Althlanmara but never in his whole life had he felt close to anyone like he felt when he was with Brooke. When they touched he had felt such a strong connection. Is that what the aonachd is like, he wondered. She said, she loved me, what does that mean?

He shook his head trying to dislodge the memories. Being on the island with Brooke was another world, completely foreign from the world of the Athlanmara. This is my world, he told himself emphatically, I will be loyal to my people, I will save Kai. Adrian clenched his jaw, his eyes grew hard. Whatever it takes.

Adrian knew he had to get the seunach from Brooke, but how will I find her, he wondered. The Builder had showed Adrian maps of the land and told him that humans used numbers to find certain places. If he could find the numbers where Brooke was he could find her. Adrian had an idea, he looked around cautiously and headed for the nearest bata portal.

18 MONSTERS

Brooke was flying, no there was something all around her, like air but more viscous. She felt so free and powerful. She looked up and could see light. I'm swimming, she realized.

Above her she could see the outline of a boat. She swam into the boat and looked around. There were items floating everywhere but she knew what she was looking for.

She made her way to a certain drawer and pulled out the boat registration. She looked down at the soggy paper and saw the hands that were holding it. They were powerful, scarred hands, with sharp claws.

Brooke sat up in bed gasping. She looked around her room confused. The dream was so real that she looked down at her hands and expected to see the ones from the dream. All she saw were her tiny pale hands with rope callouses from sailing. The late morning sun was shining in her window, the blowing palm branches making patterns on the tile floor. She jumped out of bed and ran to look at herself in the mirror.

"Am I going crazy?" she asked her reflection.

She had been having all sorts of strange dreams about swimming underwater but they were different from her previous drowning nightmares. In these dreams she felt totally at home under the water but detached like she was seeing through someone else's eyes. It was exhilarating and at the same time terrifying. She took a deep breath and tried to calm herself.

"Brooke!" Zoe yelled as she barged into Brooke's bedroom.

"Ahhh!" Brooke screamed and almost fell to the floor in fright.

"Geez, Brooke, what is your problem lately?" Zoe exclaimed.

"What...what do you mean?" she stammered as she sat on her bed shaking like a leaf.

Zoe folded her arms and gave Brooke a scrutinizing look. "Uh, well for one thing, you are always looking over your shoulder like someone is after you," she began, "And then I catch you sighing and looking all moony eyed like you just lost Prince Charming," Zoe sat down on the bed next to Brooke and put her arm around her. "Come on, I know you too well, what is going on?"

Brooke felt like there was a hundred pound weight on her chest. She looked at Zoe longingly. She so wanted to tell her friend everything. Then she remembered how terrifying Adrian looked when he warned her not to say anything. She couldn't put her friends, or her dad, in danger.

Brooke looked down at her hands. "It's nothing, I...I'm just still scared from the shipwreck," she lied.

Zoe's eyes narrowed. "Humpf, I know that's not it, but whatever, you can tell me when you're ready." Zoe jumped up. "Now let's talk about me!" she said, looking at herself in the mirror, "I'm so bored! Why don't we go get Jackson and take him out on your boat and laugh at him!"

"Zoe!" Brooke exclaimed, "That's not nice!"

"Oh, you know I'm just kidding," Zoe giggled. "Seriously though, I am going to go crazy this summer, if some cute guy doesn't show up soon!"

"I'm sure some poor, helpless guy will fall into your trap shortly," Brooke said. She got up off the bed and sighed sadly.

Zoe rolled her eyes. "There you go again, sheesh, you're acting like it's the end of the world." She grabbed Brooke's arm. "Let's go do something fun on your one day off Ophelia, don't drown yourself yet!"

The piercing sound spread quickly through the aqueous tunnels. Bronte was awake in an instant. He knew the distress cry well, it had become a persistent part of life in the colony. Bronte glanced around his dome, there was still no sign of Adrian. Kai was awake and looking at his father hopefully. Bronte turned away, he could never count on Kai for help. He could never know when a fit would come upon him.

Bronte left his dome and swam quickly through the tunnels to join the other security forces. Where was Adrian, he mused. He and Maksim were supposed to leave to work on the pipes but then Adrian had disappeared. Normally, he wouldn't have thought anything about it, young male Athlanmarans frequently went exploring for weeks. But with the recent dangers Bronte was worried for his son's safety.

As Bronte traveled through the colony he saw his people huddled in groups, their faces drawn, eyes wide with fear. Anger rose up inside his heart. Has our proud race been reduced to these frightened masses, he asked himself. Our kind have ruled the sea for eons, why is it turning against us now? He had no trouble coming up with an answer, the humans.

The humans used to be no problem for his race, they stayed on land, the Athlanmara stayed in the sea. However, a few hundred years ago things began to change. Their boats got bigger and more destructive. Their insatiable appetite severely depleted the only sustenance available for the Athlanmara. And then there were the poisons. The trash and chemicals dumped into their home was the final straw, Bronte wasn't sure if the Athlanmara had a future.

The distress cries became more insistent. Bronte picked up his pace and was joined by other warriors as he went. The security force was met by fleeing colonists with terror on their faces. The mob of colonists were all talking at once in Bronte's head.

Guardians! The Guardians had breached an outer dome!

Bronte glanced at Nereus and Gursel, his trusted lieutenants. They looked at their commander with faces like flint. They knew they could do nothing to defeat the Guardians. Most likely they were going to their death.

As the rescuers traveled down the narrow tunnel to the outer dome, they came upon an appalling sight. The Athlanmara who made it out of the dome had locked the access port to the tunnel from the outside. The few that were left inside the dome were literally being torn to bits by pale clouds of voracious hellions.

Bronte looked through the portal window at the grisly scene. Suddenly, a hand clawed at the glass. The face of a suire appeared, hardly recognizable as her torn flesh hung from her skull in ribbons.

She pushed her child up to the portal, a little suire unconscious from blood loss. *Open the door!* she pleaded, *Save my baby, open the door!* Bronte felt sick. He put his hand on the lever.

Don't open the door! The Builder spoke with surprising strength and authority. Bronte whirled around to see him swim slowly up to the paralyzed fighters. *You would put the whole colony in danger!*

Bronte locked eyes with the Builder and pushed up on the lever. The Builder was on him in a flash. His sharp claws dug into Bronte's hand and forced the lever back down. Their heads were filled with a horrific scream.

Bronte turned back to the window to see a blush of red fill the glass. The only sound left was the sound of clicking claws.

There was nothing you could have done, the Builder sighed as he turned away slowly.

Bronte slammed his spear impotently on the metal door. *I won't stand by while you do nothing!* he cried.

The Builder whirled around. *I am in charge of this colony,* he said, his voice like ice. *I will decide what you do and when you do it.*

Bronte swam up to the Builder. *You know the humans are the cause of these abominations. We must attack the humans before we all are dead!* Bronte raged.

The Builder eyed him calmly. *I am doing what I can. You can't attack the humans. You have no idea what you are dealing with!* The Builder swam closer until his face was inches from Bronte. *You are free to leave this colony, but if you stay, don't ever disobey my command again!* He held Bronte's gaze for what seemed like an eternity, then he swam away.

Bronte turned to his dejected troops. *We cannot live like this, I will do something, I will find a way to destroy the humans.* Bronte fingered his knife. *And I won't let anyone get in my way,* he said, grimly.

The Athlanmara slowly floated down the tunnel away from the tragedy. The eerie wailing of the mourning suire filled their heads.

Gursel cautiously dropped back from the group and quickly headed for his bata.

The air over Marathon, Florida rested on the tiny town like a steaming blanket. It was nine at night and the broken-down warehouse where Brooke and Tom were working still felt like an oven after baking in the sun all day. There was no air conditioning in the flimsy building and even if there was Tom couldn't afford to run it.

Brooke wiped the sweat off her forehead as she peered through the microscope at the forty-fifth crab of the day. Looking for bacteria on crab legs was a tedious job and she had been at it for weeks, but if Brooke was anything, she was determined.

"None on this one either dad."

Brooke gingerly picked up the crab and tossed it on the pile on the table. It was hard for her to handle the crabs after what she had been through. The memory of their sharp claws inches from her face was never far from her mind. Other memories also haunted her, of sparkling hazel eyes and a crooked smile. Brooke sighed.

Tom sat hunched over his computer reading reports. "Hmmmm, what was that honey?"

"I said, that crab doesn't have any bacteria on it either." Brooke walked over to her dad. "More spectrometry reports?" she asked.

Tom looked up. "Yeah, it's weird though. All markers point to these crabs being the same species as the crabs found deep in the ocean by the methane vents. They just don't seem to be behaving the same. They are growing at an enormous rate and not relying on bacteria as their food source."

Brooke moved a pile of food containers off the chair next to her dad and sat down. "So what would make them suddenly move from their ecosystem and act completely different?" she asked.

Tom rubbed his eyes and laughed. "I guess that's what I get paid the big bucks to find out."

Brooke didn't laugh, she was worried. Her dad had a grant from some environmental group to study the crab phenomenon. She knew the money wouldn't last much longer and he didn't seem to be getting any closer to finding the cause of the crabs strange behavior.

She started to absentmindedly chew her on fingernails. Their financial problems weren't her only worry. Brooke knew that the Athlanmara were in danger from these 'Guardians' as they called them. The same Athlanmara who included her rescuer Adrian. He had risked his life and his whole world to save her. She had to do something to help him and time was running out.

"Dad, what can I do to help?" Brooke said her voice cracking. She felt tears spring to her eyes a the thought of Adrian being ripped to shreds.

Tom glanced at his daughter. A tear was slipping down her cheek. She had dark circles under her eyes and her clothes were disheveled. She had been working at the sail club every day then coming to the lab every night and helping him. Tom's heart sank.

She's beginning to look like me he thought guiltily. "Hey now honey," Tom put his arms around Brooke, "it's gonna be okay. We'll figure this out," He looked into Brooke's eyes, "Let's just take a break now. We can go home and watch a movie or something."

Brooke hastily wiped her eyes. She sat up straighter and grabbed another crab. "No! I want to be here, I want to help you dad. I need to know why they're hurting...I mean why they're acting so strange."

Tom could see that look come over Brooke's face, the flash in her eyes, the set of her jaw. It pierced his heart like a knife. She looked so like her mother.

He knew it was useless to argue. "Okay, okay, but we're not staying past ten tonight."

Brooke hugged her dad. "Thanks, daddy!"

Tom almost got tears in his eyes. I wish she would stay my little girl forever he thought. He glanced at Brooke's arm, the sight of Nina's bracelet made fear rise up in his heart. He hadn't pushed the issue since Brooke came back. After all, Brooke was home safe and she seemed to be back to her old self. I'm sure everything will be fine. He took a deep breath trying to ignore his nagging fears.

He grabbed his laptop and handed it to Brooke. "Here, you can look through all the data from the Kilroy network ORCA sent us."

Brooke opened the computer and looked at the thousands of lines of data. "Oh yeah, those are the water sensors they have everywhere. Will they pick up any chemical traces?" she asked.

Tom turned back to his spectrometer reports. "They should, it's making sense of all the data that's the hard part."

Brooke peered intently at the data. "Well, we know that the crabs live off the chemosynthetic bacteria and when the bacteria convert methane to energy the by products are sulfur and sulfur compounds, so....." Brooke was racing through the data as fast as she could, "we....just...need to find....sulfur." She jumped up and shoved the laptop at her dad. "Look at this!"

Tom peered at the data. "Hmmmm, that's weird, those are super high readings." He pulled up a nautical map on his computer. "And that's just outside of the territorial zone." Tom smiled at Brooke. "Good work honey!" Brooke beamed.

"We might be able to catch some of these monsters in action!" Tom exclaimed.

Raffe slammed the chain link gate shut as the last truck drove through.

Paul strode up to him. "Where do you think I'm gonna put those?" he said through gritted teeth, "The warehouse is overflowing!"

Raffe sneered. "Not my problem DeLuca," Raffe said, "Your job is to get rid of the stuff, my job is to make sure it keeps comin'."

Paul's face started to turn red. "Look around you, there is nowhere for it to go!"

Raffe glanced around. The warehouse was packed to the rafters and the workers were piling barrels in the gravel yard. He walked across the yard and stopped at the fence.

He pointed to the lights on in Tom's lab. "What about that place?" he asked.

Paul rubbed his eyes. "I tried to get that stupid egghead to give up his lease, he wouldn't do it. I tried to go around him. I talked to the owners but they can't kick him out until his lease runs out next spring." Paul sighed, "I've run out of options!" he said, trying to stay calm.

Raffe laughed. "That's it?" he asked incredulous, "You think that's all you can do?" Raffe chuckled as he pulled on the chain link fence and eyed the ramshackle building. "Don't worry DeLuca," Raffe said grinning, "I got a plan to kick the loser out of that warehouse."

Raffe turned to face Paul. Paul just stood there glaring at him. "You think I won't?" he yelled, "Just watch me!" Raffe pushed past Paul and stormed off.

Paul thought Raffe was just a low life hoodlum when he showed up weeks ago but now he was beginning to think he had some sort of drug problem.

Raffe had intense mood swings that put Paul on edge and he was always catching him popping pills. He was beginning to think that Lombardi just sent his nephew down here to get rid of him.

Paul wished he could send Raffe away too. He hated that Raffe and Chris were spending time together. He cursed himself for not making Chris go on that trip to Europe with his mother and sister.

Paul stood in the gravel yard of the business he had worked so hard to build. Everything was getting out of control. He had just wanted to make some extra money, to give his family all the nice things they deserved. Now he was in over his head and he saw no way out. Paul sighed and walked through the sweltering heat to his car.

19 HEROES

The twinkling tropical stars shone down on the tiny yellow house. The stillness of the tranquil night was broken by a shriek.

"Get out!" Zoe pushed Brooke off her own bed, "I can't believe any of this!"

Brooke crawled back up on the bed. "I swear Zoe, if you do that one more time I won't tell you anything."

"You have been back for over a month and you are just telling me now that you were on a secret island with a merman!" Zoe yelled.

"Keep your voice down!" Brooke said in a hoarse whisper, "Gosh, I never should have told you! You are freaking out."

"Uh, duh!" Zoe lowered her voice, "Why wouldn't I freak out, your story is crazy! I mean, I knew something was up, but mermen!" Zoe tried to calm herself, she took Brooke's hand in hers. "Are you sure you didn't just imagine the whole thing sweetie, you know, while you were floating for days in the ocean."

Brooke pulled her hand away from Zoe. "No! I showed you the bruises and the cuts from the Guardians, I mean crabs, when I got back. And really, how could I survive that long floating in the ocean?"

Zoe thought for a minute. "You have been acting really different since you came back."

Brooke laughed "Maybe almost dying a bunch of times is good for me."

Zoe shook her head. "No, it's like…" she tipped her head and looked at Brooke intently. "It's like you're so calm, or confident or something."

Brooke knew Zoe was right. She had changed. She had no idea why but she didn't feel the normal pressure of constant fear and the emptiness inside of her wasn't as strong.

Zoe snapped out of her seriousness and started bouncing up and down on the bed again. "Oh my gosh! A merman in love with you! That is so romantic!" she gushed.

"Really?" Brooke said dryly, "It's more like a tragedy. Fish girl in love with a fish, just my luck," Brooke sighed, "I'll never see him again."

Zoe patted Brooke on the shoulder. "Oh cheer up! Maybe you'll see him again."

Brooke rolled her eyes. "Uh, do you remember the part about his dad almost killing him because he thought he had even talked to a human?"

Zoe looked sad. "Oh yeah, that part does stink," she said.

Brooke sighed. "Adrian saved my life, I just want to do something to help him and his people. My dad has been showing me all the stuff he's learned about the yeti crabs. They are chemosynthetic creatures that feed off of bacteria that use chemical reactions for energy instead of sunlight. It's like they're drawn to certain chemicals such as hydrogen sulfide. My dad thinks they are getting so big and acting weird because of pollution of some sort. If we can figure out a specific chemical compound that is affecting them we might be able to trace where it's coming from. Lot's of chemicals like hexachlorobenzene, carbon tetrachloride,... "

Zoe mimed talking with her hand. "Blah, blah, blah,.. you're sounding just like your dad! I want to hear more about those gorgeous guys!"

"Zoe! This is serious! People...the Athlanmara...whatever, they're in danger!" Brooke said, her voice starting to crack. Brooke looked like she was about to cry.

Zoe grabbed her hand. "I know sweetie, and you want to save them, like you always do." Zoe was getting all bouncy again. "But it's so exciting! You could finally have something to post on your Facebook page other than links to the FAU Harbor branch videos."

Brooke grabbed Zoe by the shoulders and looked hard into her eyes. "Zoe, you can't...tell...anyone. I only told you because I was going crazy, I had to tell someone."

"Oh, of course! My lips are sealed," Zoe mimed zipping her lips. "If scary merman dad himself walked through that door he couldn't beat it out of me."

The door to Brooke's room burst open.

"Ladies!" Jackson said loudly. Brooke and Zoe screamed at the top of their lungs. Jackson fell to the floor like he'd been shot. "My ears!" he cried, writhing on the floor.

Brooke and Zoe threw pillows at Jackson.

"Are you trying to scare us half to death!" Zoe yelled at him.

Jackson got up. "What? I think I lost my hearing for life," he said loudly. He picked up a pillow off the floor and smiled at Zoe. "But are we having a pillow fight?" For a moment Jackson thought his wildest dreams were coming true.

Zoe grabbed her pillow from Jackson. "Oh, shut up!" she said.

Brooke glared at Jackson. "What are you doing here, in my bedroom, at midnight? We are trying to have a girl sleepover."

Jackson sat on the bed. "I know!" he said, "It sounded like so much fun I had to stop by!"

Brooke and Zoe looked at each other and both pushed Jackson off the bed.

"Owww!" he whined, "I was just on my way home from work and wanted to see how you're doing. Gosh! I haven't seen you for days. Unlike some people…" Jackson looked at Zoe, "I have to work off my life of crime."

Zoe groaned. "Oh you big baby, like it's so hard to take a nap in DeLuca's air conditioned showroom."

"Well it's still scary and not fair," Jackson exclaimed, "You get grounded for a week and I have to work as a security guard at Mr. DeLuca's creepy shipyard until I pay off the gas that *you* burned up stealing his yacht!" Jackson quickly turned to Brooke. "It was totally worth it though, cause you're home safe and all." He turned back to Zoe, "Just wish the consequences were spread more evenly."

Zoe stood up in front of Jackson, her arms folded. "If I remember right, it was your dad's idea for you to work it off. Don't blame me! Now, get out of here," Zoe said, pushing Jackson out the door, " we are having girl talk, Brooke has a new boyfriend!"

"Zoe!" Brooke yelled.

Zoe spun around and faced Brooke, her eyes big. "Oops!" she yelped covering her mouth.

Jackson pushed back into the room. "What? A boyfriend? How did you get a boyfriend? See, I've missed everything!" Jackson sat back down on the bed.

Brooke pushed Jackson onto the floor again. "I do not have a boyfriend!" she said through clenched teeth, glaring at Zoe.

Zoe looked pained. She drug Jackson up from the floor and started pushing him out the door again. "Of course she doesn't have a boyfriend! I was just kidding! Where would she find a boyfriend, the middle of the ocean?" Zoe forced a laugh.

Jackson grabbed the door jam and stuck his head back in the room. "You guys are weird. I don't care about your girlie games, anyway. Sailing tomorrow?"

"Get out!" the girls yelled in unison.

Deep under the surface of the ocean, in the darkness and the crushing weight, Adrian and Maksim struggled to lift a heavy pipe.

Ahhhh! Maksim cried out as another tiny crab skittered across his arm. He dropped the pipe for the third time.

Cac! Adrian swore, *If ya do that one more time, I swear, I'll leave ya down here alone ta die!*

Mak looked at Adrian. His eyes were sunk deep into their sockets from the intense pressure, his skin was pressed so tightly against the bone that he looked like a living skull. The only light in the total darkness was coming from the bluish glow of their own skin. Adrian couldn't tell if Mak was mad or terrified but his heart sank, he knew this was all his fault.

Sorry Mak, no worries, we'll get this done in no time, Adrian said, trying to reassure his friend.

Mak didn't answer he just slowly grabbed the pipe again. All of the boy's movements were painfully slow as they worked under 250 atmospheres of pressure.

Working the vents was miserable work but necessary for the survival of the colony. The colony was only able to thrive because of the energy they harvested from the methane seeps and hydrothermal vents deep on the ocean floor.

The Builder had come up with the system that had allowed the Athlanmara to live in an area that had never before been colonized, which in turn freed them from the clan wars of old. The Athlanmara had only been living in the Bermuda Triangle area about a hundred years but their particular colony had made such advances in technology and societal stability that it was beginning to draw attention from the other clans.

The weeks Adrian and Mak had spent working the vents had given Adrian time to think. Why was I so foolish, he asked himself for the thousandth time. I had the seunach within my reach and basically threw it away. I could have helped the colony, saved my brother's life, maybe even made my father proud. What is wrong with me? Some human girl looks at me and I lose my mind?

Adrian slowly connected the last pipe in the line to the generator. Against his will images of Brooke entered his mind, her deep blue eyes, the little brown dots on her nose, her body pressed close to his chest.

Then the dream images started coming again, of rooms and cars and crabs, images he barely understood. It was like he was seeing through someone else's eyes. The waking dreams had been plaguing him for weeks.

Ahhhhh! Adrian growled, squeezing his eyes shut trying to block out the disturbing pictures.

Mak turned to Adrian. *Guardians?* he cried, his eyes wide with fear.

No, sorry Mak, it's nothin'.

Adrian opened the valve on the tank to clear the pipes of water so the methane gas could enter the combustion chamber. Mak slowly swam up next to Adrian, he couldn't wait to be done with this.

First, they had spent weeks slowly exploring the ocean floor trying to locate new methane seeps close enough to the generators to run pipe to them. Then they had spent more days wrangling the heavy pipes. Every moment Maksim felt as if tiny sharp claws were inches from his back ready to tear him to pieces. He put his hand on the start button.

Adrian was deep in thought. I am going to find the girl and take the seunach, no matter what. He had the paper with the numbers on it that he found in the girl's boat before the humans towed it away. He knew he could find out where she was from the maps the Builder had.

I'm just gonna go up to her and ask for the seunach, he said to himself. If she doesn't give it to me, I'll...I'll threaten her, and then...

Adrian bit his lip. He felt a knot form in his stomach. He glanced over at Mak and saw that he was about to push the start button on the generator.

Mak no! Adrian yelled, knocking Mak's hand away from the button.

Mak looked at Adrian shocked. *Let's just start it, I want to get out of here!* Mak yelled back.

Adrian shook his head. *If ya start it while the valve is open it'll cause an explosion all down the pipe and maybe spread to every methane seep in the whole area!* Bubbles replaced the water flowing out of the open valve. Adrian shut off the valve and went over to the generator controls. *Ya could'a blown us all ta pieces and even started an earthquake ya lebnah!*

Adrian fiddled with the controls then pushed the start button. They heard the generator hum to life.

Mak let out a sigh of relief. *Let's go back to the colony!* he said, starting for the bata, *I'm starving!*

Adrian followed slowly. *Not yet Mak, I gotta plan,* Adrian said.

Mak groaned. *No! No more of your ideas.* Mak stopped swimming and folded his arms. *That's what got us down here in the first place!*

Adrian smiled slyly. *Ah, come on, this plan will make us heroes!*

"That's when your dad decided to be a hero!" Steve McRae said laughing.

Steve, Brooke and Tom were sitting around a fire in the backyard of the Williams house. Brooke loved when Steve came over, she had no relatives nearby so besides her dad he was her only family.

"He jumped in the water, swam through a hail of bullets and started to cut the seal free," Steve continued.

Brooke almost laughed to think of her dad as heroic. The dad she knew was a quiet scientist who was always distracted and could never find a clean shirt.

"What did you do?" she asked.

"Me?" Steve laughed, "I was trying not to pee my pants! But I grabbed my wallet and held up my Florida driver's license and yelled 'Polizia' as loud as I could." Brooke and Steve started laughing, even Tom joined in.

"The fishermen stopped shooting long enough for your dad to free the seal but as we turned our boat around I kept thinking they were gonna shoot us in the back."

"Oh, come on!" Tom protested, "It wasn't that dramatic, they wouldn't have shot us."

"Well," Steve argued, "That whole area back then was pretty volatile, after all, Nina got shot."

Brooke was shocked. "My mom was shot?" she exclaimed. Tom glared at Steve.

Steve quickly tried to change the subject. "This Hefeweizen is great! You got any more?" he asked.

Tom got up. "I'll get you another, but it's about time you got to bed Brooke," he said. Tom went into the house.

Brooke scooted closer to Steve. "What happened to my mom?" she whispered when her dad was out of earshot.

Steve looked uncomfortable. "I don't really know, when we found your mom she had a bullet wound." He looked up to make sure Tom wasn't coming. "It was your dad that saved her."

"I thought you were the one with the medical knowledge," Brooke said. Brooke wasn't sure if Steve's stories were true or just tall tales.

Steve leaned closer to Brooke and whispered. "Yeah, but all he did was…"

"Brooke!" Tom said loudly. Brooke nearly jumped out of her skin. "Time for bed! You have lessons in the morning." Steve looked away guiltily.

Brooke jumped up. "Okay, night Steve!"

Brooke gave Steve a quick hug and went into the house. Tom sat down next to Steve silently.

He stared out at the water. "I don't want you talking to Brooke about Nina," he said.

Steve took a swig of his beer. "Tom, it's not fair to Brooke that she doesn't know anything about her mom."

"I don't want her to be hurt!" Tom retorted. Steve was about to answer but Tom cut him off. "You know what's out there! I can't risk it, I can't lose Brooke too!"

Steve looked at Tom and nodded.

20 SAVAGES

August had come to the Florida Keys bringing the tropical storms that were typical of the season. The days were hot and so were the nights, but the ocean breezes made the heat bearable.

Brooke, Zoe and Jackson were walking down the street on a lazy Saturday evening. The sun was setting, causing the latest storm clouds to glow like they were roasting over a fire. The palm trees were swaying in the gentle breeze and the three friends were feasting on huge waffle cones. Everything should be perfect, Brooke thought, but it wasn't. She just couldn't get Adrian out of her mind.

"This is the best therapy ever!" Zoe exclaimed.

"Therapy?" Jackson asked, "I thought we were just eating ice cream." Brooke glared at Zoe, who gave her a guilty look.

"I just mean, ice cream makes everything better," Zoe said quickly.

Brooke took another bite of ice cream and sighed. She knew Zoe was trying to cheer her up. She had been dragging around lately feeling sorry for herself. How will I ever recover from being with Adrian, she wondered. Every other boy seems so disappointing compared with him.

A big black Escalade SUV came screeching to a stop next to the teens. Zoe was so startled she almost dropped her ice cream.

"Hey!" she yelled. The passenger window rolled down.

Chris DeLuca leaned out. "Hey Zoe," he said, trying to act nonchalant, "Where ya been, I haven't seen you around."

Zoe rolled her eyes and kept eating. "Duh, I've been working at my Aunt's coffee place," she said irritably. Brooke and Jackson just stood on the sidewalk.

Chris purposefully ignored them. "Well, are you gonna come to my birthday party next week?" he asked, only looking at Zoe.

Raffe leaned over from the driver's side. "It's gonna be sick! My friend is coming down from Miami to DJ."

Zoe sneered at Raffe. "Like I care," she said, and started to walk away.

Brooke and Jackson followed her. Raffe drove the car along slowly, pursuing the group.

He yelled out the window. "Hey! Why do you have to be such a jerk?!"

Chris tried to keep him quiet. "Just come, okay?" he yelled at Zoe as Raffe gunned the car and sped down the street, tires squealing.

"What an idiot!" Zoe exclaimed.

"Yeah, that guy scares me," Jackson said, his eyes big.

"You know him?" Brooke asked.

Jackson took a big bite of ice cream. "Yeah, I was at DeLuca's shipyard and he kicks me, wakes me up and tells me I'm fired!"

"Sleeping on the job, huh?" Zoe snorted.

"Well, Mr. DeLuca didn't care, he told me I could sleep, but that Raffe guy," Jackson shuddered. "After he wakes me up he pulls out a gun and tells me to never come back. I thought he was going to kill me!"

"That's weird," Brooke said, wrinkling her forehead, "Why would Mr. DeLuca have some guy like that working for him?"

Jackson took another big bite. "I dunno," he said with his mouth full, "But weird things are going on over there and I'm glad I'm fired."

"What kind of weird things?" Brooke asked.

"Well, they have trucks coming in all the time at night and people working," Jackson said between bites. Zoe looked at Jackson, he had chocolate all over his face.

She shook her head and handed him a napkin. "Okay, thanks for all the info Sherlock," she said sarcastically. Jackson's face turned red as he wiped his mouth.

As the three walked by a trash can Zoe threw away the rest of her cone. Brooke and Jackson looked at her shocked.

"I need stronger therapy after that brush with idiocy!" Zoe growled, glaring down the street where the Escalade had disappeared. "And you know what that means," she said looking at Brooke. Brooke nodded, smiling. Jackson started walking backwards away from the girls.

"Taylor Swift sing-along!" the girls yelled simultaneously.

Jackson stared at them in fear. "Okay...well I have a zombie hoard to deal with at home!" He started walking quickly in the opposite direction. "See you guys later!"

The water of the little inlet was perfectly calm reflecting the stars like a mirror. Two sleek heads popped up breaking the counterfeit image. Two sets of eyes scanned the boats lining the canal.

How much longer are we going to do this Adrian? Mak asked between bites of raw fish. They had been searching for Brooke's house for two nights with no luck.

Adrian furrowed his brow. *I thought it would be easy ta find with the numbers,* he said.

Adrian had been all fired up to confront Brooke but now he was getting frustrated. There were so many houses and so many boats and so many people, and he and Mak had to be very careful not to let anyone see them. They swam along slowly when they noticed a fire on the shore with people around it.

Mak grabbed Adrian's arm, and started to pull him under. *Come on Adrian, we can't let them see us.*

Wait! Adrian exclaimed. He swam closer to the edge and peered at the boat that was docked nearby. *The Seawitch, it's her!* he said, excitedly.

As the aquatic creatures swam closer they could hear music. They peeked out of the water and saw two figures dancing around a fire. One of the figures passed behind the fire. It was Brooke. Adrian's heart started to pound. It's now or never, he told himself.

Let's go! he said to Mak. With a groan Mak followed.

Brooke and Zoe collapsed into their camp chairs laughing hysterically.

"See! This is just what you needed!" Zoe gasped, "You can't spend the whole summer being depressed about some guy you will never see again."

Brooke could hardly stop laughing. "You're right, Zoe!" Brooke jumped to her feet, grabbed her red Solo cup full of root beer and held it up. "Forget him and all guys!" she yelled. Brooke took a drink.

Zoe laughed. "Your neighbors are going to think we're drunk, Brooke!" she giggled.

Brooke took another swig. "Who cares! I gotta stop caring about what people think!" Brooke held her cup high. "This is a toast to all the girls who've gotten their hearts broken by beautiful, unattainable guys," she said, grandly. "May their green eyes and gorgeous muscles be forgotten forever more!"

Behind Brooke, two muscular men holding short spears walked into the firelight. Zoe screamed like she had never screamed before. Brooke whirled around so fast she fell to the ground. She looked up and saw Adrian and Mak.

Brooke covered her eyes and joined Zoe in her never ending scream. She recognized Adrian and Mak but to see them standing naked in her backyard looking like fierce wild men was too much for her frazzled nerves.

Zoe tried to scramble out of her chair but fell over backwards. Brooke was scuttling away as fast as she could on her hands and knees across the yard. Zoe, being the fighter that she was, jumped up and threw her camp chair with all her might at the intruders. It fell harmlessly at their feet. Then she pulled Brooke to her feet and they both ran, still screaming, into the house and slammed the door.

When the screaming started both Adrian and Mak were paralyzed with fear. With the girls gone they just stood looking at each other in bewilderment. Suddenly, they heard another door slam and a woman's voice yelling.

"Brooke Williams!"

This new threat got them moving. The two boys ran to the side of Brooke's house and pressed themselves against the wall. They heard the woman's steps getting closer. They frantically looked around for a place to hide. Adrian noticed an opening in the house, he motioned to Mak and they both dived through the window as the woman reached the house.

The woman pounded on the front door. "Brooke Williams, you open up right now!"

Adrian and Maksim found themselves in a dark, square room. Adrian knew right away it was Brooke's room by the scent. The boys had no trouble looking around in the darkness as their eyes were used to the lightless depths under the surface of the ocean. To Adrian it somehow seemed familiar.

Adrian found Brooke's closet and couldn't believe how many coverings she had all hung up in a row. He went to her bed, her scent was strongest there. He moved her blankets around wondering why she had so many.

Mak came up behind him. *Why are humans always covering themselves?* he said, wrinkling his nose in disgust.

Adrian didn't answer, his mind was back on the island remembering the way the light danced in Brooke's blue eyes. He looked at how big Brooke's room was and felt embarrassed when he remembered how proud he had been to show her his palm shack. The memories of the intimacy shared with Brooke on the island began to destroy his resolve to hate the human girl.

Adrian moved towards Brooke's dresser, suddenly he saw two figures. He lifted his spear ready to fight, but then he realized it was only he and Mak's reflection. He moved closer and peered at himself in the mirror.

His pupils were wide in the dim light, his hair tousled, in one muscular arm he gripped his spear. There were scars all over his body and his hands still had claws at the end of each finger. Suddenly, all his hopes stirred by the memories of the island were dashed.

This is what Brooke sees, he said to himself. The reflection brought back the pain in his chest. Adrian remembered when Brooke said 'I love you' but he also remembered the fear in her eyes when he tried to touch her arm. I'm just some wild sea creature to her, he thought bitterly.

Being confined in the room was making Mak nervous. *Adrian, come on! Let's get the seunach and get out of here!*

Adrian nodded, gripped his spear and moved towards the bedroom door.

While Adrian and Mak were exploring, Mrs. Kowalski had not let up on the front door.

Brooke finally cracked the door open, her eyes still wide with fear. "Hey, Mm..mm...Mrs. Kowalski," Brooke stammered.

Mrs. Kowalski stood on the porch in her robe, her arms folded, bright orange hair poking out of the scarf on her head. "Now

Brooke, you know I don't mind you and Zoe having a little fun and playing your music but all the screaming is just too much!"

"I'm sorry, Mrs. Kowalski," Brooke said.

Mrs. Kowalski tried to look past Brooke. "What is going on? It sounded like you were being attacked by savages!"

Brooke stifled a gasp. "No, no, it was...Zoe just... got a bug in her hair."

Mrs. Kowalski frowned. "Well of course, with that fire you're attracting every crazy creature in the neighborhood!" She sniffed at Brooke suspiciously. "You girls haven't been drinking have you?"

Zoe jumped up off the couch where she had been huddled. "Of course not, Mrs. Kowalski!" Zoe said pushing the door closed, "We're fine now, thanks!" The girls leaned against the closed door, breathing hard.

"What the heck is going on Brooke!" Zoe said, in the quietest whisper she could manage in her terrified state, "I'm assuming that was Mr. Merman and his buddy?" Brooke just nodded. "Oh...my...gosh!" Zoe continued, "I know you told me all about them and I believed you, I really did, but...they're real?"

Zoe started pacing. "What are we going to do? What do they want? They had weapons, are they here to kill you? Should we call the police? Oh my gosh! What are you going to tell your dad?"

Zoe talked a lot when she was freaked out, Brooke was frozen in shock. It was like a dream had come to life and she couldn't seem to think of what to do.

Zoe was just taking a breath to launch into more questions when they were both grabbed from behind. Mak had Zoe, one hand on her mouth to stop the screaming, he had learned his lesson, Adrian had Brooke. She knew it was him even before his arms were around her. She felt like she had seen him walk up behind her.

Adrian held her tightly suddenly wondering what to do. All of his plans to intimidate Brooke left his head. He just stood there holding her and breathing in her sweet, earthy smell. Mak's cry snapped Adrian out of his momentary insanity.

Zoe had no intention of being a victim. She bit Mak's hand hard. When he pulled away she whirled around punched him in the throat and kicked him in the groin. Mak sunk to the floor groaning.

Zoe dashed to the kitchen and grabbed a knife. Adrian saw her coming. He let go of Brooke immediately, holding up his hands in surrender.

Brooke stepped in front of Adrian. "Zoe stop!" Brooke yelled.

Zoe, her adrenaline flowing, started swearing at the boys in Spanish and brandishing her knife. Brooke held back Zoe while Adrian helped Mak to his feet. Mak glared at Zoe, it wasn't so much that he was hurt, he was mortified that some human girl had got the jump on him. Brooke finally got Zoe to calm down.

"So," Brooke turned to Adrian trying to sound nonchalant, "What are you doing here...at my house...at night?"

Adrian's mind was racing, should I threaten her, he wondered. All his plans seemed really stupid to him now, standing in Brooke's house looking at her calmly waiting for an answer. "I, wanted ta see ya," he said lamely. Mak rolled his eyes, exasperated.

Zoe didn't wait for Brooke to answer, she was still mad and scared. "So you come here and have fish boy attack us!" she yelled pointing her knife at Mak.

Adrian narrowed his eyes at Brooke. "Ya told her?"

It was Brooke's turn to be nervous. "I..I had to tell someone, I'm sorry," Brooke looked down.

Adrian took a step towards her. "I told ya not to tell anyone!"

Mak smiled.

"Well, you have Mak, I have Zoe, she's my best friend and she won't say anything to anyone!" Brooke said, her hands starting to shake.

Adrian tried to control his fear and anger. It wasn't Brooke's fault, he thought. He was the one who risked the safety of his people by revealing himself to a human. Mak was his best friend, the one who knew everything. Adrian knew he could trust him with his life. He hoped human friends were the same.

Adrian relaxed and took a step back from Brooke. Mak and Zoe continued to glare at each other. Zoe held her knife up, strategically covering the boy's nether regions in her field of view.

"Do you mind getting some clothes on while we figure this out?" Zoe said, in a disgusted tone.

"I'll get you something of my dad's," Brooke said, hurrying from the room. She came back with a pair of swim trunks and some sweats. "Here," She handed them to the boys while trying to avert her eyes.

Mak pulled on the sweats begrudgingly. "Do you have food?" he growled.

"Sure!" Brooke said trying to act like everything was normal.

She went to the kitchen and spooned up some of the food Zoe brought from her mom.

Zoe frowned. "You are not giving him my mother's picadillo!" she protested, still hanging onto the butcher knife.

"Zoe!" Brooke said, through clenched teeth. She handed Mak the plate of food and looked at Adrian. "Do you want anything?"

Adrian looked into Brooke's eyes and then down at the seunach on her arm. It was so close, yet out of his reach. There was so much he wanted.

Being in Brooke's presence, he was once again torn by his desire to be close to Brooke and his desire to help his people. If he asked for the seunach and she said, no, what would he do? Keep pressuring her? Then she would become suspicious and realize the power of her amulet and keep it for herself. If she gave him the seunach, he would never see her again. At this moment he couldn't stand that thought.

"Nah," he said quietly. Brooke turned to go but Adrian grabbed her arm and pulled her close to him. "I want…" he whispered.

But Adrian was interrupted by two things, Mak, who had been shoveling the picadillo into his mouth as fast as he could suddenly felt the heat of the spicy food. He spat out what was left in his mouth and started choking, which of course made Zoe laugh out loud. The second thing was the door opened and Brooke's dad walked into the room.

"Hey girls! I'm home!" Tom yelled.

Luckily for Adrian and Mak, Tom immediately dropped the stack of papers he was holding. Tom kneeled to pick up the papers and in a flash the boys were in Brooke's room and diving out the window. Brooke and Zoe stood there frozen. Tom looked up, saw all the food on the floor and Zoe holding a butcher knife.

"Oh, you guys doing some cooking?" he asked.

Mrs. Kowalski, who spent all her time peering at her neighbors, saw the two boys run across the yard, rip off their clothes and jump into the canal.

"What is this world coming to?" she muttered to herself.

21 ONE MIND

Bronte had been meeting privately with the council members for weeks. He was handsome and naturally good at debating and with the power of his silver seanuch he was almost unstoppable.

It was true, the Builder had the respect of the entire colony, without him none of them could survive, but there was also something about him that the rest of the Athlanmara didn't trust. Clan lineage was very important to their race, relationships meant safety and power, and the Builder had never shared his family history.

There was also his disconcerting familiarity with all things human. The Athlanmara not only rejected human culture and technology because of fear but also because of pride. They were the mightiest creatures of the sea, ruling with the power of their minds and bodies unlike the gasping human's who couldn't survive without all their machines.

The Athlanmara of the colony had accepted the Builder's peculiarities because most of them had been victims of abuses from their tribes; they were looking for a better future and were willing to try something previously forbidden. But with the sickness spreading and the threat of the Guardians, Bronte saw his chance to undermine the Builder's influence.

Bronte's highest value was honor and in his eyes the Builder had none. His leadership had made the entire colony reliant on human machines. Bronte felt like their proud race was licking up the scraps the humans left behind. It was time for The Builder's rule to end.

As Bronte silently swam through the tunnels of the colony, he could feel the electricity rising. Every living creature in the world gives off a slight electrical current and the Athlanmara could feel and interpret the signals. Bronte knew there would be a colony wide aonachd.

He went to search for Kai, he wanted his son's support. How powerful I would be with two strong sons at my side, he thought, bitterly. But he knew that was never going to be a reality.

Bronte found Kai with the young male Athlanmara near the food stores. They weren't hard to track down, they were always either fighting or eating. Kai joined his father without a word. Adrian and Maksim entered the storeroom as they were leaving. Maksim nearly did a backflip to get out of Bronte's way. It was the first time he had seen Bronte since the council meeting when they were punished.

Bronte just glared at them. Adrian looked down ashamed. He knew what was about to happen, he could feel the tension in the colony and knew his father couldn't count on his support in the aonachd.

Maksim quickly recovered from his fright and started to stuff his face with food. *I hate seeing your father,* he said to Adrian. It was easy for Mak to talk and eat when he could send messages telepathically. *I always think he's going to read my mind and know what we've been doing!*

Adrian didn't answer, he was too busy thinking about the aonachd. He had heard the rumors about Bronte's plans to destroy the humans, but his father had talked that way his entire life, he never thought that he would actually do anything about it. And now, Brooke had changed everything. Adrian knew an actual human, he cared about her. Adrian swam quickly out of the storeroom, he had to find out what was going on.

Adrian! Maksim whined. He grabbed an armful of squid and followed him.

The entire colony was starting to gather in the open ocean near the domes. Their movements were chaotic and uncoordinated. Bronte and Kai joined the milling crowd, then the Builder swam up with a few of his supporters. They each started to swim in a distinct pattern.

One by one, the Athlanmara began to join with either Bronte or the Builder. Their respective groups got bigger and bigger. The patterns became more complicated and they swam faster and faster. The aonachd was a joining of minds, the coordinated movements were just the outward expression of the collective consciousness of the group.

Adrian stayed on the edges with the suire with young children, it was humiliating. He tried to listen, to figure out what was happening. Adrian could hear a cacophony of voices and was able to catch a word here and there but it was mostly just confusion to him.

Mak swam up next to Adrian. He saw his friend anxiously following the movements of the gathering but unable to join in.

I'll find out what's going on, Mak said, without looking at Adrian.

Adrian nodded and Mak swam off to join the milling bodies. Adrian so wished he could feel a connection with his people. His father had tried to help him, but he wasn't patient and had given up on Adrian. He had asked Mak about the aonachd and he had tried to explain it.

Mak said it wasn't so much about the words, but that he could feel everyone's feelings. Even more than that, Mak said he could see what everyone else was seeing, experience their life, become one with the group. That was why, even when the Athlanmara were making complicated movements at incredible speeds, no one bumped into anyone else, they moved as one unit.

Adrian could see that his father's group was getting larger. There was movement of bodies from one group to the next but the net movement seemed to favor Bronte. Mak joined with Bronte's group then went over to the Builder's. The movements started to speed up and even Adrian could feel anger rising. Suddenly, the greater part of the Builder's group joined Bronte. The Builder was left with only a small contingent of the Athlanmara, though most of the older council members were on his side.

The movements started to slow and the Athlanmara began to dissipate. Mak swam over to Adrian and motioned for him to follow him. They swam away from the colony.

What is it Mak? Adrian asked, nervously.

It's not good, Mak answered, he looked shaken. *Your father wants to cause a tsunami to drive the humans from the shores.*

Adrian felt like someone punched him in the gut. He felt sick. He knew with the help of the entire colony it would be possible.

Mak looked serious. *The Builder says it won't help and it would only put us all in danger,* Mak continued, *He wants us to stay hidden and be patient,*

191

he is trying to find a cure.

Adrian didn't need Mak to tell him who won the argument. He could feel the fear and anger of the Athlanmara well enough.

Adrian's body was as tense as a bow string. *When Mak?* Adrian asked.

Mak shook his head. *I don't know.*

Brooke, Adrian thought. He swam as fast as he could to find a bata.

Morning found Brooke and Zoe fast asleep on Brooke's bed. After Adrian and Mak had taken off they had stayed up for hours hashing through every syllable the boys had said and every move they had made, till their adrenaline had faded and they both fell asleep exhausted.

Brooke woke up as the summer sun pricked at her eyelids. She looked out at the beautiful sunshine, the white fluffy clouds, the palm trees swaying gently and for some reason Brooke felt scared. It wasn't the fear she was used to, the crushing, overwhelming fear of what people were thinking or fear of failure. This fear was very immediate, like she was in danger, like something was coming to get her.

Brooke carefully climbed out of bed, trying not to disturb Zoe. She walked over to the window and peered out almost expecting to see someone. She quickly got dressed and ran out to the dock.

Secretly, she hoped to find Adrian but all she found was her dad's clothes lying on the ground. She picked them up and started back towards the house but then she went back, neatly folded the clothes and laid them at the end of the dock.

"What do you think you're doing?"

Brooke nearly had a heart attack. She looked up, Zoe was standing on the dock with her arms folded, looking perturbed.

"Sheesh! You scared me half to death!" Brooke exclaimed.

"Well better half dead than all dead! I thought we talked about this last night," Zoe said.

"I know but...well, if they do come back we don't want them running around naked." Brooke smiled sweetly at Zoe.

"Oh my gosh!" Zoe exclaimed, plopping down next to Brooke, "You want them to come back!"

"No! Yes...Oh I don't know!" Brooke said. She started to chew her nails.

Zoe grabbed Brooke's hand. "Stop that! Now listen sweetie, I know you don't have a lot, ok any, experience with boys but boys that run around naked with long spears are not the boys you should be hanging out with," Zoe shook her head, "Take it from me!"

"I know, I know, you are totally right," Brooke sighed, "But Adrian rescued me, and he's so smart and gentle, and his eyes..."

Zoe groaned. "Yes, yes, they were totally amazing and hot," Zoe grinned, "Especially the big guy, I've never seen a guy with such great muscles..." She shook her head. "No! No, this is not some guy at school we are talking about!" She looked into Brooke's eyes. "These guys are dangerous Brooke! They aren't even human!"

Brooke shushed Zoe and quickly looked around to see if anyone had overheard them. "Zoe!" she whispered.

"Sorry, I just don't want to see you get hurt."

"I know," Brooke said, smiling at her friend. Brooke stood up and looked out over the water. She bit her lip nervously. "But something's coming Zoe, I feel it." She looked back at her friend sadly, "I think everyone's going to get hurt."

Blood spurted out of the fish's head as Raffe beat the helpless Mackerel that was flopping around on the DeLuca's yacht.

"Hey!" Chris yelled, as he got splattered.

Raffe cackled. "You better stay out of the spray zone bro! This fish just don't wanna die!" Chris backed away from Raffe who continued to pound on the poor fish.

Chris liked Raffe, he was a cool dude, but there were sometimes when he was really creepy. The main reason Chris liked to hang out with Raffe was because he knew his father didn't like it. He'd found out some unnerving things about his dad recently and it made him angry. Chris looked for any chance to get at him.

"Yeah, baby!" Raffe exclaimed, holding up the bloody carcass. He handed Chris his phone. "Bro, take a shot of me with this beauty!" Chris took a picture and handed the phone back to Raffe. He leaned on the rail and looked out over the ocean.

Raffe rolled his eyes. "Bro, are you still thinking about that broad?"

Chris glared at Raffe. "Don't call her that," he said, coldly.

Raffe held up his hands. "Okay, okay, no need to be so touchy, but bro, you have got to stop being her little backpack." Raffe found a towel and wiped the blood off his hands. "You gotta take control, get her where you want her." Raffe walked up to Chris. "You are Chris 'The Bomb' DeLuca! Every girl in this town should be dyin' just to have you look their way, am I right?"

Chris smiled. "Yeah," he said, sheepishly.

"Well, you can count on old Uncle Raffe," he said, slapping Chris on the back, "I'll make sure things work out right for you!"

On the starboard side of the boat a pod of dolphins swam by, the spray of their breath sparkling in the setting sun. Raffe's eyes lit up. He ran to the rail of the boat, pulled out his Ruger handgun and started firing into the peaceful group.

"What are you doing?" Chris yelled.

The air was filled with high pitched whistles and the thrashing of the terrified animals. Raffe was laughing maniacally.

Chris ran over to Raffe and knocked his arm down. "You can't shoot dolphins, you idiot, that's a Federal offense!" Chris cried.

Raffe stopped laughing, his face suddenly contorted in rage. "Did you just call me an idiot?" Raffe yelled. He started waving his gun in Chris' face. "I know you didn't just call me an idiot!"

Chris backed away from Raffe with his hands up. "Dude, sorry, I...I just don't want you to get in trouble, that's all!" Chris stammered.

"Okay then!" Raffe yelled. He stuck his gun into the waistband of his shorts, "Let's get out of here, fishing is lame," he said. Raffe plopped down on a chair, pouting.

Chris' hand was shaking as he started the engine. Maybe my dad is right, he thought.

22 "HUMANS SCARE ME!"

The sun was setting in another dramatic display over the Florida Keys. Adrian and Mak didn't notice the beauty however, they were in a somber mood after passing a number of dead dolphins out in the open ocean, all with bullet holes in them. They didn't have to guess what had happened. The incident made the boys extra careful as they approached Brooke's dock.

Adrian was afraid he would see Brooke's father at the end of the dock with a rifle in his hands. He poked his head out of the water tentatively and approached the dock. Adrian found the swim trunks and sweatpants neatly folded. He thought that was a good sign.

The boys cautiously got out of the water and put on the clothes. They hid their spears under the dock.

Mak tried to adjust the sweatpants, they kept sticking to his wet legs. "Why are we even here?" he growled, "You know they will just scream and run away."

Adrian just grinned. Even though he had a pit of fear in his stomach for Brooke's safety, he couldn't help but feel exhilarated about being on land and walking among humans. There was so much he wanted to experience.

"Come on Mak, it'll be brilliant!" Adrian said, cheerfully.

They started to walk towards Brooke's house. Adrian looked back at Mak, he was walking awkwardly, not bending his knees.

"Jeez, bend yer legs!" Adrian whispered, "Act human!" Mak just glared at him.

They walked up to Brooke's door under the watchful gaze of Mrs. Kowalski and stood there unsure of what to do. Should I push it open, Adrian wondered. Last time they just dove into a window. Adrian wasn't even sure how to get the door open. He was afraid to call Brooke's name, he knew there were other humans nearby and he didn't want to attract too much attention. Maybe we should just go in the other opening he thought.

Adrian walked around the side of the house, Mak following. He looked at Brooke's window, it was closed but he could see into her room, no one was there. They turned around to try the front door again and almost ran into Mrs. Kowalski coming around the corner.

"Excuse me!" she said, loudly.

The boys were terrified. They were face to face with a human that looked like an ancient walrus. Her face was saggy and wrinkled, she even had whiskers on her chin like a walrus. Her glasses made her eyes look enormous as she glared at the boys. But the most disturbing thing was her shocking bright orange hair. It reminded Adrian of the garish brain coral on the reef. Mak was about to bolt for his spear but Adrian grabbed his arm.

He took a deep breath. "Hello!" Adrian said, awkwardly.

"What do you boys think you're doing?" Mrs. Kowalski asked. She held up her cell phone, "I can call the police right now, you know!" Adrian and Mak had no idea who the police were but it sounded intimidating.

Adrian plastered a smile on his face hoping it would appease the woman. "I'm lookin' for Brooke," he said.

"What are you Scottish?" Mrs. Kowalski asked, suspiciously. Adrian was relieved, he remembered that seemed to explain things to Brooke.

"Aye! I'm Scottish and he's Russian!" Adrian said and nodded enthusiastically.

"Humph! Well, I guess that would explain a lot." Mrs. Kowalski knew those people from Europe were crazy nudists but she was disappointed about not being able to call the police. "What, are you exchange students?"

"Aye!" Adrian said, hoping that was the right answer.

Mrs. Kowalski frowned. "Well, Brooke and her father aren't here right now, they hardly ever are. If you ask me Tom does not spend enough time at home, what with Brooke running off and almost getting herself killed. But I guess that makes sense, her mother ran off years ago…"

Adrian and Mak just stood there as Mrs. Kowalski kept up her steady stream of gossip. They couldn't believe anyone could talk so much.

Finally, Adrian got up the courage to speak up. "Where's Brooke?" he asked, loudly.

Mrs. Kowalski looked irritated at being interrupted. "Well, I'm sure they're at that ramshackle warehouse her father calls a lab," she answered curtly.

"Where's that?" Adrian asked quickly before she could launch into another stream of non-stop gossip.

"You go down to 20th street then take a left, there's no street sign but you'll see a big lemon tree…" The boys just looked at her wide eyed. "Oh, here I'll draw you a map."

As Adrian walked down the street holding the map Mrs. Kowalski had drawn he could hardly contain his excitement. He had never been on such a wild adventure. At first he and Mak were terrified of the cars rushing by. They thought one of them might come crashing into them at any moment, but soon they realized that the cars only followed the line of the road.

They passed by buildings filled with amazing articles. Adrian stopped at every store window wanting to go inside and touch everything but he wasn't sure he was allowed to do that. Mak was more interested in the smells and sights of people in the restaurants eating food. The further they walked the more their feet hurt. The sidewalk was still hot from the heat of the day and Adrian and Mak didn't use their feet for walking very often.

Adrian looked around at the few people walking on the other side of the street and noticed they all had shoes on their feet. Up ahead he noticed a store that had bins out front on the sidewalk with flip flops in them.

"Look Mak, things for our feet!"

They walked up to the store and took some flip flops from the bin, sat down and tried to put them on their feet. In a few minutes they figured out how to make them stay on their feet and started to walk away from the store. .

"Hey!" called a man walking out of the store. Adrian and Mak stopped and turned around. The man looked angry. "You have to pay for those!" he yelled.

Adrian had no idea what the man was talking about so he tried his human greeting. "Hello!" he said, loudly.

"Those are five dollars each, buddy!" the man insisted.

"Aye!" It was all Adrian could think of and it seemed to work with the woman.

"Look, I don't care where you're from Scottie, you pay up or I'm calling the police."

Adrian wondered who this police was that everyone wanted to call. He was out of ideas and he could feel Mak getting ready for a fight. Suddenly, a red sports car with three girls in it pulled up right next to them, scaring the boys half to death.

"Oh my gosh!" said the driver, a blonde teen wearing sunglasses. She jumped out of the car and ignoring the store owner, ran up to Adrian and Mak.

"Hey, I'm Whitney, you guys visiting?" she gushed.

"Aye, I'm Adrian."

"Oh my gosh!" she turned to her friends, "Did you hear that accent?"

Whitney took her sunglasses off which was a relief to Adrian and Mak, they were wondering if she even had eyes. "So, where are you guys from?"

"Hey!" the store owner interrupted, "They were stealing my sandals."

"Oh brother!" Whitney scoffed. She pulled a twenty dollar bill out of her purse and handed it to the owner. Satisfied, he walked into the store. "Anyway, so where are you from?" she continued.

"I'm Scottish and he's Russian" Adrian said, pointing at Mak.

Whitney eyed them both up and down. "Mmmmm. So what's his name? Where are you staying? How long will you be here?"

Adrian wondered how humans could talk so much, he had only spoken to two of them and his head was already starting to hurt. "Uhhh…" he couldn't think of anything to say. "I'm, lookin for Brooke," he managed.

"Oh," Whitney said irritated, "Brooke Williams?" Adrian just nodded. "So, you're staying at her house?" The girls in the car giggled.

"Aye," Adrian said.

"What are you, like exchange students?" Whitney queried.

"Aye." Adrian just decided to stick with the answer that seemed to work.

Whitney smiled. "Well, I can't wait for school to start," she said touching Adrian's arm. Adrian pulled his arm away.

"Come on Whitney, let's go to Chris' party!" said a girl in the car.

Whitney whirled around angrily. "Shut up Courtney! I'm coming!" she yelled. Then she plastered on a smile as she turned back to the frightened boys, "Well, see you soon Adrian…and friend."

Whitney got in her car, blew them a kiss and took off, tires screeching.

"Humans scare me," Mak said. Adrian nodded.

The two alien visitors continued on their quest. It was getting dark but Adrian had no trouble reading the map with his primal eyes. As they walked down the gravel street towards the hulking warehouse, Adrian and Mak noticed two figures dressed in black sneaking up to the door.

The boys exchanged a quick glance and melted into the shadows. They knew what predators looked like, Adrian and Mak were hunters themselves. Without making a sound they followed the suspicious humans.

Brooke sat in her dad's lab absent mindedly eating her Thai noodles. Her mind was going a mile a minute but it wasn't chemical data she was thinking about. All she could think about was how it felt when Adrian pulled her close. Brooke took a deep breath and shook her head. I have got to concentrate on what's important, she chided herself. Lives are at stake!

Her dad was on the phone with one of the scientists at the Ocean Research and Conservation Association trying to get them to send him the latest Kilroy data. "Yes!" Tom said hanging up, "They will send it to us tomorrow. We are getting so close to pinpointing the source!"

Brooke couldn't remember when she had seen her dad so excited. It made her happy. She was also happy that they seemed to be making progress in the mystery of the killer crabs. Soon Adrian and his people will be safe, she thought.

She put her noodles down. "So, I was..."

Brooke was interrupted by the door flying open and two men in ski masks bursting into the lab. They pointed guns at Brooke and her father. Brooke was paralyzed with fear.

"Get down on the ground!" the leader yelled.

Brooke and her dad put up their hands and got down on the ground.

"We don't have any money or drug chemicals," Tom said trying to remain calm.

"Shut up!" one of the gunmen growled.

The two men started to smash everything in sight. Tom couldn't help himself, all of his research from the last two years was being destroyed. He jumped up. "No!" he yelled.

The leader hit Tom on the head with the butt of his gun. Tom fell to the floor bleeding.

Brooke screamed. "Dad!" She crawled over to him. "Dad, are you okay?" Brooke asked, sobbing.

The second attacker kept destroying the lab while the leader held his gun up to Brooke's head. "Shut up or I'll blow your head off!" he yelled.

The next second he went flying as a body slammed into him. Brooke couldn't believe her eyes. There was Adrian on top of her attacker hitting him in the face over and over. She heard the other man yell and looked over to see Maksim bludgeon him on the head with a microscope.

Adrian was choking his victim but the man grabbed a knife from his leg sheath and stabbed Adrian in the thigh. Adrian cried out, but didn't let go of the man's throat. Mak had the other assailant in a full Nelson wrestling hold completely incapacitating him and cutting off his air.

Brooke was frozen in shock. She looked at Adrian. He's going to kill him. That thought brought her back to reality.

She ran over to Adrian. "Adrian, no!" Brooke grabbed his arm, "You can't kill him!" Adrian looked up at Brooke, anger in his glowing eyes. "Adrian, I'll get in trouble if you kill him."

He immediately let go of his victim's neck. The man gasped for breath. Adrian was shaking.

He grabbed Brooke's hand. "He was gonna kill you! He should die!"

Brooke's heart was pounding more from being close to Adrian than from her fear. "It's more complicated than that," she said, quietly. She became aware of thrashing sounds and suddenly remembered Mak's victim. She whirled around. "Mak, no! Let him go!" she yelled.

Mak just glared at her and didn't let up. Adrian struggled to his feet on his wounded leg. He looked down at Brooke's pleading eyes. "Let him go, Mak," Adrian said. Mak grunted then threw the man to the floor.

Brooke smiled at Adrian. Then she saw blood running down his leg. "You're hurt!" she exclaimed, "Let me see."

She helped Adrian sit down in a chair and saw the deep stab wound in his thigh. She grabbed a towel to try to stop the bleeding. As soon as she touched his leg she felt the heat in her arm. She quickly glanced up at Adrian. His eyes glowed brightly then went back to normal. Brooke looked down at his leg, the wound was gone.

She jumped up, her mind reeling. "I...I...did you.." she stammered.

Suddenly, Brooke had a stabbing pain in her head. Adrian jumped up and grabbed Brooke as she almost fell to the floor. Behind her, Tom sat up groaning and holding his head. Brooke had totally forgotten about her dad.

He saw her grimacing in pain. "Brooke, honey, are you okay?" he asked groggily getting to his feet.

Her heart skipped a beat. He's going to see Adrian and Mak. What if he finds out what they are? The thought terrified her. Would he capture them and study them like his crabs?

Adrian saw the look of fear on Brooke's face. He got between Brooke and her dad. His experience with father's wasn't good and he wasn't taking any chances.

All Tom saw was his precious daughter standing next to a bloody, half naked man. "Get away from my daughter!" he yelled, going for Adrian.

Brooke quickly intervened. "Dad, no! These boys saved us!"

Tom wavered and almost fell down. She grabbed her dad's arm and helped him sit on a stool.

"Oh, sorry," he said "Brooke, honey, are you sure you're okay?"

She knelt down by her dad. Brooke breathed deeply, trying to relieve the stabbing pain in her head. "Yes, I'm fine daddy."

At that moment the two attackers ran out the door. Adrian and Mak moved to follow them but Brooke held up her hand to stop them. "Let them go! We're fine, the police will handle it," she said.

Who were these police Adrian wondered, they must be very powerful. Adrian came and stood beside Brooke. He saw that she had her hand on her father's arm. He looked at her father's head wound, it wasn't going away. Adrian was puzzled.

Three blocks away two figures stumbled up to a black Escalade and got in. Raffe pulled off his ski mask, still gasping from his encounter with Adrian.

He turned to his companion who was rubbing his sore head. "Where's your gun Anton?" Raffe asked, his voice cracking from his recent choking, "I swear, if you left it behind, I'll kill you myself!"

Anton glared at Raffe. "It's stolen anyway, no one can trace it back to me!" Anton argued, "And you said this job would be no trouble, it'd just be some lame scientist!"

Raffe started the car. He turned to Anton and rubbed his neck which was already bruising. "That's what it woulda' been if those two boneheads didn't show up." Raffe pulled out his knife and looked at the blood on the wicked blade. "I'll tell ya one thing Anton, I know two guys named Adrian and Mak that don't have long to live."

Bronte made another round of the colony looking for his sons. Well, no matter, he thought, they will show up sooner or later. He was too proud to ask anyone if they'd seen them. Gursel swam up to Bronte cautiously, trying to gauge his mood before interrupting him.

Bronte saw him hesitating. *What is it?* he asked, perturbed.

The Builder wishes to see you, Gursel said, quickly. Bronte didn't answer, he just swam in the direction of the workshop.

When he got to the workshop, the Builder was pouring over large maps spread on a table. He didn't look up when Bronte walked in.

"Well?" Bronte asked, rudely.

The Builder looked up and sighed when he saw Bronte. "You think you have won but you will only bring more suffering."

Bronte made a move towards the door. "If ya brought me here ta talk me outa the plan, save your breath old one."

"Wait," the Builder said. Bronte stopped. "When are you planning on implementing this folly?" the Builder asked, coolly.

Bronte turned to face him. "What does it matter to ya?"

"Well, if you must do this you should know that Feargach Doineann will work best when there is a natural storm." The Builder sighed again and rubbed his tired eyes. "You know this won't do any permanent damage to the humans." Bronte frowned, that was exactly what he was afraid of. The Builder continued, "There will be many humans that die, but more will come and they will rebuild again."

Bronte just turned and walked to the door. "I won't do nothing while my people are dyin," he said quietly, as he left.

Bronte swam out of the colony. He needed time to think. The Builder was right, they should wait for a storm to intensify their power and cover their tracks in case any humans got suspicious and came looking for them. His worry was that the others whom he convinced to join him would change their minds if he waited too long.

Deep in thought he didn't see or feel the lone figure that came up behind him. All at once, he felt the presence and in an instant Bronte pulled his knife and faced the intruder.

Good to see you, Bronte, the figure, chuckled.

Bronte tightened his grip on the knife. *Utari! So you've come ta kill me at last?*

Utari was large and muscular with dark eyes and long black hair. The last time Bronte saw his mother's lackey, he had barely escaped with his life. It was Utari that he could thank for the striking scar on his face. He wondered why his nemesis wasn't attacking, it made him nervous.

Why would I kill you? Utari said calmly swimming through the water, *We are on the same side.*

Bronte kept his distance holding his knife ready. *Are we?* Bronte asked. *I thought we were on the same side years ago during the revolt,* Bronte stopped swimming and glared at Utari, *Then ya tried ta kill me.*

Utari was unarmed. He swam in slow circles around Bronte doing his best to seem harmless. *That was Morgan's doing,* Utari said, *Her plans failed, time to move on.*

Bronte turned in circles never taking his eyes off of his foe. *What do ya want Utari?*

The same thing as you, death for all humans, Utari spat out.

Bronte continued to keep his distance. *What are ya doin here?*

Utari smiled. *I heard you have a plan, I know what it is but that won't be enough to kill the humans. I can help you succeed Bronte.*

How? Bronte asked.

Utari laughed. *Did you hear about the devastation in the east? Thousands of humans killed?*

Bronte kept moving to face Utari with his knife. *Aye.*

That was my people, Utari bragged.

Bronte relaxed a bit. *How?* he asked.

Utari swam closer. *I will tell you everything, but there's a price to pay,* he said menacingly. Bronte nodded, he was all too familiar with the high cost of his dreams.

23 BEST DAY, WORST DAY

The early morning sunlight filtered through the white curtains of the Williams kitchen window. Mak slammed another cupboard shut. He had been rummaging through Brooke's kitchen, eating everything he could get his hands on since sunrise.

Tom had found out after the attack that the boys were exchange students that didn't have a place to stay so he let them spend the night in his office. Mak had slept terribly. Everything on land was so hard. So, he did what he always did when he was irritable, or nervous, or scared, he found his comfort in food.

Suddenly, the kitchen door burst open and in walked Zoe. "Brook.." She was in mid yell when she saw Mak.

Zoe took in a breath to let out a scream but Mak was too quick for her. He grabbed her and had his hand over her mouth in half a second. This time he expected her to fight and he held her so tight she couldn't breathe.

"Don't scream!" he growled in her ear.

Zoe nodded her head. Mak slowly released his grip. They backed away from each other, glaring like prizefighters in a ring.

Quickly, Zoe whirled and ran towards Brooke's room. "Brooke!"

she screamed as loud as she could.

Mak ran after her but before he could catch up, Brooke, Adrian and Tom all ran into the living room terrified that there was another invasion. Zoe was shaking.

She pointed at Maksim. "If that animal ever touches me again, I will make sure he will never have offspring of any sort.." she ranted.

"Zoe!" Brooke cut her off, afraid of what she might say. Adrian was glaring at Mak. He glared right back as they had an argument telepathically.

Finally, Mak turned to Zoe. "Sorry," he grunted and walked off to the kitchen.

Tom stretched and yawned. "Okay, so we're all good?" he asked.

"Sure dad!" Brooke said, enthusiastically.

"Aye, brilliant!" Adrian added.

Brooke grabbed Zoe, hustled her to her room and slammed the door while Adrian stormed off to the kitchen after Mak.

Tom was left alone in the living room. "Okay. Well, I'm going to the lab to clean up!" he yelled for Brooke to hear.

"Fine dad! We'll just hang out here!" Brooke yelled from her room.

Tom sighed. "Teenagers, well, at least I know she'll be safe with those exchange students around," he said to himself.

After talking with the police last night and thinking more about it, the attack didn't seem like drug addicts looking for a fix. It seemed like someone was deliberately targeting his research. Tom was worried they might come back.

He also worried about what he was going to do now. All of his grant money was spent, his equipment destroyed and his research unfinished. I may have to get a job at the marina fixing boats again, he thought dejectedly. Tom grabbed his car keys and walked out the door.

Back in her bedroom, Brooke turned to Zoe. Before she could say a word Zoe started freaking out. "What are they doing here? I thought they were never coming back! And your dad knows? Are you crazy Brooke? You can't have a couple of fish people living in your house!"

Brooke grabbed Zoe's shoulders. "Calm down!" she said, then she took a deep breath, trying to remain calm herself. "My dad and I were attacked by gunman last night at the lab."

"What?" Zoe was back to hysterical, "What happened? Oh my gosh Brooke are you okay? Why didn't you call me last night?"

"Zoe!" Brooke tried to get her to focus, "Adrian and Mak saved our lives! If they hadn't shown up my dad and I would probably be dead. And no, he doesn't know anything, I told him they were exchange students."

Zoe suddenly looked like she was going to cry. She grabbed Brooke in a big hug. "Oh my gosh! Brooke, I'm so sorry," she cried. Zoe let Brooke go and looked in her eyes. "Are you really okay? You must have been terrified!"

Brooke couldn't help smiling. She remembered how Adrian had burst into the lab to save her, how powerful he was. "I was...till Adrian showed up."

Zoe rolled her eyes. "Oh my gosh!" Zoe exclaimed pacing the room, "Brooke, you have got to get over this!"

Brooke sat on the bed. "I know, I know, but Adrian said he wanted to stay a few days and learn about humans and…" Brooke trailed off knowing it sounded bad.

Zoe put her hands on her hips. "Brooke," she said sternly, "You remember when Steve rescued that baby seal and you fed it and it followed you around everywhere and you taught it how to fish like you were it's mom?"

Brooke sighed. "Yes."

"And then what happened?" Zoe asked.

"I had to let it go back to the wild," Brooke said, quietly.

Zoe sat down next to her on the bed. "And it took you months to recover! You were so depressed." Zoe put her arm around Brooke. "You can't keep him sweetie, and I don't want to see you get hurt again."

Brooke took a deep breath. "You're right! He can't stay here, he needs to go back!" she said, emphatically.

Zoe smothered Brooke in a hug. "That's my girl!"

The boys were sitting at the kitchen table glaring at each other.

Stop causing problems! Adrian yelled.

Mak stuffed a banana in his face, glaring defiantly at Adrian. *I can do what I want!* he said.

Adrian knocked the banana peel out of his hand. Mak looked up surprised. The two boys looked at each other for a moment then they both jumped up and started wrestling.

Mak threw Adrian to the floor. Adrian knocked Mak's feet out from under him. They both rolled around on the floor knocking over chairs. Adrian punched Mak in the face giving him a bloody nose. Mak grabbed Adrian around the neck choking him.

Brooke heard the ruckus from her room. "What is going on?" she asked Zoe. The girls ran into the kitchen to see the boys pummeling each other.

Zoe folded her arms. "Figures!" she said.

The boys saw the girls and jumped to their feet panting, Mak wiping the blood from his face.

"Hey!" Brooke yelled, "What's going on?" The boys looked at each other embarrassed.

"Nuthin," Adrian said.

"Well, we've had enough of this. Tell them Brooke," Zoe said, sneering at Maksim.

"Well…" Brooke said. She looked at Adrian and all her resolve melted, "Do you want to go sailing?" she asked. She quickly looked at the floor to avoid Zoe.

Zoe's jaw dropped. "Brooke!" she said.

Adrian quickly answered. "Aye! That's brilliant!" Mak elbowed Adrian in the side, Adrian elbowed him back.

Zoe grabbed Brooke's arm. "Hang on!" she said to the boys and she drug Brooke from the room.

"Ow, Zoe!" Brooke protested. In the living room, Zoe glared at Brooke with her arms folded.

Brooke looked up at Zoe, her big blue eyes pleading. "Please, Zoe, it's only for a few days," she said.

"Humph!" Zoe sighed, "Fine, but only a few days!" She glanced through the kitchen door at the boys, their hair and borrowed clothes were disheveled. "Ew, if they are going to hang out with us in public, I'm going shopping."

Brooke was ecstatic. "Yes! Go shopping! I will take them out on my boat. No one will see us out there." Brooke felt like jumping up and down, she was going to spend the whole day with Adrian.

What is wrong with you? Mak yelled in Adrian's head, *I thought we just came here to warn her and then go back!*

No worries Mak, Adrian assured him, *If I can get close to her, I can get her to give me the suenach. Then maybe I would have the power to stop my father.*

Mak looked at Adrian and narrowed his eyes. *You tried that before, it didn't work,* he said.

Adrian patted him on the back. *But I'll have more time now, I'll be...more convincing.* Mak shook his head. Adrian smiled at Mak. *You go back,* Adrian said, *See if ya can find out how much time we have before the doineann.*

Mak's jaw dropped. *By myself?* he asked, incredulous.

The Athlanmara never traveled alone, it was too dangerous, not to mention Mak and Adrian had been inseparable since Adrian saved his life two years ago.

Aye! Adrian said, impatiently, *The bata's not far.*

Fine! Mak growled. He was glad he could get back to the sea and out of all this human nonsense. The girls walked back into the kitchen.

Brooke's face was glowing. "Well, Zoe is going to go find you guys something to wear and I'll take you out on my sailboat,"

"Aye, but Mak...he has ta go get sumthin, so it'll just be me," Adrian said, smiling at Brooke. Zoe and Mak rolled their eyes simultaneously.

"Don't hurry back!" Zoe said, as Mak turned to go.

Mak snorted. "I won't!" he snarled and walked out the backdoor.

"Your friend is a real charmer," Zoe said to Adrian. Adrian and Brooke looked at each other uncomfortably.

"He's Russian," Adrian said. He and Brooke burst out laughing.

A flight of Pelicans flew low over the sparkling ocean. The warm summer breeze stirred the perfectly trimmed landscaping around the DeLuca estate. It was a beautiful morning but Paul Deluca was in no mood to drink in the tropical beauty. He sat brooding on his porch; he was missing a boat.

"How does a whole stinkin' fishing boat disappear?" he muttered to himself.

Things at the warehouse had finally been getting better. He had chartered a few more fishing boats, and with four boats moving barrels he was beginning to catch up with the overflow. But now one of his boats had gone out and never come back.

Paul cursed under his breath. He felt like he just couldn't get a break and he was sick of that punk Raffe always on his back. Paul saw Chris walk into the kitchen.

"Hey buddy," Paul called, "Come out here for a sec."

Chris stuck his head out of the french doors, bleary eyed. "What?" he asked, irritably.

"You didn't have anything to do with that incident at Tom Williams place did you?" Paul asked his son with trepidation.

"Geez, dad, no!" Chris said.

"Good, good," Paul smiled, "I didn't think so, it's just," Paul paused, "I just don't want you hanging out with that Raffe so much, he's bad news Chris."

Chris rolled his eyes and walked back into the kitchen.

Paul got up and followed. "I know I've been really distracted with work lately, but how bout I take a couple days off and we go to Atlantic City, just you and me?"

Chris stuck his head into the fridge. "Can't, Raffe and I are going to Miami tomorrow."

Paul was frustrated. "I don't know what you see in that loser, Chris," Paul said, trying to keep his cool, "You are better than that!"

Chris stood up and faced his dad. "Well, I guess that 'loser'," Chris made air quotes, "cares about my life and can actually remember my girlfriend's name." Chris slammed the fridge door shut and stormed out of the kitchen. Paul sighed. Oh, well, he thought, he's just an emotional teenager, he'll get over it.

Paul walked back out onto his expansive deck. He leaned on the railing and looked out over the ocean. Paul didn't condone Raffe trashing Tom's lab but he was cunning enough to seize the opportunity it offered. He pulled out his cell phone and started to dial.

The little boat cut through the turquoise water like a knife, leaving a foamy white trail in its wake. Adrian had never felt so free before. He was at the front of Brooke's sailboat leaning out over the water, the wind rushing through his hair. He had propelled himself at great speeds under the water and had ridden in the smooth and quiet bata but he had never had the feeling of effortless, wild motion.

Adrian looked back at Brooke. She had a huge smile on her face as she expertly maneuvered the craft into the wind. She moved the tiller to the side and the tiny sailboat slowed.

"That was brilliant!" Adrian exclaimed, moving back towards Brooke.

Brooke just smiled and aimed the boat towards a small metal tower sticking up out of the waves. As the craft slowed and approached the tower, Adrian looked down through the crystal clear water and saw hundreds of fish swimming around a shallow reef.

Brooke tied the boat up to a tiny buoy. "No one should bother us at this reef. Wanna go for a swim?" she asked with a grin.

Adrian smiled and dove into the cool water. Brooke stripped down to her bikini, grabbed her snorkel and fins and followed him.

Immediately, Brooke felt like a different person. The crowded, noisy, complicated world was left behind and she was alone in the silent beauty of the underwater universe. But she wasn't alone. She looked over at Adrian moving strongly and smoothly through the water, even without his tail.

Brooke realized that she had changed a lot since she had met Adrian. She had been through lots of things that should have sent her into a tailspin of panic but even though she had felt fearful at moments, she hadn't felt the overwhelming, uncontrollable terror that had plagued her since her mother left.

Adrian turned to Brooke, he smiled and held out his hand. Brooke swam up and took it. She let Adrian propel them through the beautiful nooks and crannies of one of the amazing reefs off the coast of the Keys. They saw barracuda, butterfly fish, angelfish and even some hawksbill turtles. It wasn't as beautiful as Adrian's magical island, but right now Brooke was more interested in the company rather than the scenery.

Brooke looked over at Adrian, his skin was glowing faintly. It was hard to even notice in the bright sunlight filtering down. Then she noticed her arm was glowing. Her heart skipped a beat as she realized they had been underwater for a long time and she hadn't surfaced once to breathe. Brooke choked into her snorkel. She pulled her hand away from Adrian and sped to the surface. Her head broke the surface of the water, she gasped for breath.

Adrian came up beside her. "What's wrong, lassie?" he asked concerned.

Brooke looked at him, her eyes wide with shock. "I..I wasn't breathing...my...arm…" she choked out. Adrian was confused, he tried to take her hand but Brooke backed away. "What did you do to me?"

"I didn't do anything…" Adrian trailed off. He avoided Brooke's gaze.

Brooke examined her arm in the sunlight, the gold bracelet flashed in the sun. Brooke may have been distracted by all the drama that had been going on lately, but she wasn't stupid.

She held the bracelet up in front of Adrian. "Is it this or is it you?" she asked him intently. Adrian said nothing and looked away.

Brooke's mind was racing. She remembered the heat in her hand when Adrian's foot healed and the same thing happened with his terrible leg wound, but not with her father's wound. She thought hard. She remembered touching her dad, if it had something to do with this bracelet then why didn't her dad's head get better, she wondered.

Adrian stared at Brooke. He began to get agitated. He grabbed Brooke and pulled her close to his body. "It's me," he said.

Brooke's heart was pounding, she could hardly breathe. Her face was inches from Adrian, she could feel his heart beating against her chest. He looked into her eyes then he leaned into her and put his lips on hers.

As they slowly sank in the water, Brooke felt a warmth go all through her body. It was different from the searing heat she felt when his wounds were healed. This sensation was a warm tingling that spread from her head all the way to her feet. Adrian pulled back, looked into Brooke's eyes and smiled his crooked grin. She looked down and saw that her entire body was glowing. Brooke had never felt so incredibly happy before.

Suddenly, she was overwhelmed by her senses, not sight or sound or even the sense of touch, it was something totally new to her. She could feel the electricity in the water. She could sense where every creature was by the electrical current they gave off. It was as if she had been in a dark room and someone switched on a light. She could feel Adrian, more than just knowing where he was in space, she could feel what he felt, like she was inside of his body. She could see herself through his eyes.

When he kissed Brooke, Adrian felt an intense oneness that he had never felt before. His loneliness and isolation were quenched and Brooke was the life giving water. Adrian had always felt the life force all around him, but suddenly he was experiencing how new it felt for Brooke. He could feel what she felt, look at himself through her eyes. All of the walls that he had built up around his heart came crashing down. It terrified him. He felt exposed.

Adrian released Brooke, swam away from her as fast as he could and jumped on the boat. The spell was broken, Brooke stopped glowing and followed Adrian. She pulled herself out of the water and found him huddled in a corner of the boat.

"Are you okay?" she asked him.

He nodded. The brief moment of intimacy with Brooke caused his normal feeling of isolation to come crashing in on him. All sorts of emotions that had been buried his whole life were welling up.

Sitting in the boat with his damp hair hanging over his forehead, Adrian looked like a lost child. Brooke reached out and touched his arm. She felt a stab of heat pulse through her hand. Instantly, she was transported in her mind to a dark rocky shore.

She was running, her heart was pounding, she was afraid. A tall man was holding her hand, dragging her along. She looked back and saw a beautiful woman running after them. She had raven black hair and she was holding a small child.

"Hurry!" the woman said, breathlessly. Brooke could feel hot tears running down her cheeks. "Mathair!" she cried out. Brooke gasped and pulled her hand away from Adrian's arm, the vision was so intense.

She was back on the boat in the hot Florida sunshine. She put her hands to her face, there were no tears. She looked at Adrian. He was crying. Shocked, she realized that what she had seen was his memory. It was his fear and pain that she had felt. She waited a moment for him to calm down.

"Was that your mother?" she asked, quietly.

He nodded and wiped his face. "Saltwater!" he laughed. Brooke chuckled too at their shared island memory.

Adrian was embarrassed. He never remembered crying before, in fact he had very few memories of his childhood. He had even forgotten what his mother looked like. She had become just a dull ache in his heart that he tried to ignore. Now he realized why he had shut down all of those memories. Adrian looked at the seunach on Brooke's arm and wondered at its power. Our people are right to fear it, he thought.

Brooke looked at Adrian with compassion in her eyes. She moved towards him. He backed away. Adrian didn't know what the seunach might bring up next. In a panic he dove over the side of the boat and disappeared from sight.

"Adrian!" Brooke yelled.

Brooke sat in the boat alone. She was in shock, Adrian was gone. She had felt the same deep connection she had felt with her mother and now he had abandoned her, just like her mom. Brooke felt like someone had kicked her in the gut. She had gone from the peak of happiness to the depths of despair in a space of twenty minutes. Brooke put her head in her hands and sobbed.

24 COVERT PLANS

The tropical sun flashed off the metal roof of the forlorn warehouse, turning the building into a ramshackle kiln. Tom dumped another dustpan of glass into the trash can and wiped off the sweat running down his face. It was worse than he thought. He knew the insurance would pay for some of his equipment but it wouldn't be nearly enough for him to start over.

He sighed thinking about all of the data he had compiled, some of it was on the cloud but most of the files were stored in his computer that was a pile of rubble. To retrieve the data would take time and money he just didn't have.

"Hey Tom." Paul DeLuca called out as he gingerly walked through the wreckage that used to be Tom's lab.

"Hey, Mayor DeLuca," Tom said, dejectedly.

"Now Tom, it's Paul, remember?" he said cheerfully. Tom nodded stooping to pick up a dead crab. Paul cleared his throat nervously. "I heard about what happened Tom, I'm real sorry about your lab. You sure you and Brooke are okay?" Paul asked, feigning concern.

"Yeah, but only because a couple of Brooke's friends stopped by just in time."

"Did you get a look at the guys who attacked you?" Paul asked, nervously wiping his hands on his pants.

Tom started to sweep again. "No, they were wearing masks."

Paul nodded, relieved. "Look Tom, I want to help you out as much as I can. I talked to the warehouse owners and they are willing for me to take over the lease." Tom stopped sweeping. "And I want you to move whatever you need to that office space I got on the other side of town. You can stay there for as long as you need, no charge," Paul said quickly. He waited breathlessly for Tom's answer.

"Wow," Tom said, "Mayor DeLuca...I mean Paul, I would really appreciate that."

Paul smiled, relieved. He walked over and shook Tom's hand. "Great Tom!" he said, "I'll have a couple of guys over here this afternoon with a truck to help you move whatever you need."

"Thanks...Paul, thanks again!" Tom turned back to sweeping.

Paul pulled some folded papers from his jacket. "Just a second Tom, I'll need you to sign these papers turning over the lease to me."

Tom took the papers, looked them over quickly then took the pen Paul was holding out to him and signed them. He handed the papers to Paul.

Paul smiled, pleased that his plan was accomplished. "You're doing the right thing Tom!" he said, patting him on the back.

Paul quickly left the warehouse, got into his air conditioned BMW and pulled out his phone. "You get some guys over here with a truck now!" Paul paused, "Don't give me your lame excuses! I have two shipments coming tonight and I can't have anymore mistakes!"

Paul hung up the phone and gripped the steering wheel. He took a deep breath then started the car. Things are looking up, he thought.

Mak was glad Adrian made it back to the colony in one piece but there was something different about him, like he wasn't really back at all. For weeks Adrian had swum around in a daze, staying away from everyone. Adrian avoiding the other Athlanmara wasn't a new thing, he had always been a loner, but now he also seemed to be distant from Mak and Mak didn't like it. The only thing Mak was happy about was they hadn't seen Bronte since they got back.

Things at the colony had become very tense. In the normal rhythm of the colony the Athlanmara would come and go constantly, night and day, hunting, playing and communing in the vastness of their ocean realm. Now, because of the danger, there were only a few select groups that left the safety of the colony. The tight quarters were putting the colonists on edge.

Mak was hunting through the tunnels for Adrian when he felt a stirring in the community. A security detail was returning, Mak knew Bronte was among them. He made a dash for Adrian's dome hoping he was there so he could warn him in time.

Mak entered the dome, he saw Adrian but before he could say anything he felt Bronte approaching from behind. Mak couldn't retreat so he dove into a corner and tried to remain unnoticed.

Bronte entered and was relieved to see his son in one piece, but he showed no outward emotion. *Where have you been?* he growled.

Around, Adrian mumbled.

Kai swam into the dome. *Is it true father?* he asked excitedly, *Did you really take out two human vessels?*

A rare smile spread over Bronte's face. *Yes Kai, we did,* he said with pride. Adrian felt sick. *Our hunting party will rest for a few days and then we will go out again, and you,* Bronte said turning to Adrian, *will come with me.*

Both boys looked at their father with consternation. Kai because he didn't want to be left out and Adrian because he didn't want to go.

No, Adrian said, quietly.

Bronte stopped in mid-stroke. *What did you say to me?* Bronte asked.

Adrian turned to face his father. *I'm not going with you to destroy the human boats.*

In a flash Bronte grabbed Adrian by the throat and slammed him against the wall of the dome. Mak cowered in the corner in fear.

I am your father and your commander, you will do as I say! Bronte spat out.

No, Adrian rasped.

Bronte released his grip and hit Adrian hard in the face with his tail. Adrian flew across the room. He righted himself, blood flowing from his mouth. Adrian glared at his father.

Bronte swam up to him. *You're a weak, insignificant, failure. The only reason you are still alive is because I am your father!* he yelled. Adrian held his ground, his eyes flashed but he made no answer. *You will not leave this colony until I give you permission!* Bronte continued. He put his face inches from Adrian. *If you do leave, don't ever come back.*

Bronte spun around and saw Mak huddling in the corner, their eyes met. Mak froze in terror but Bronte bolted out the door without a word. Kai glared at Adrian then followed his father.

Mak sighed with relief. He swam up to his friend. Adrian's lip was still bleeding and his left eye was getting puffy. *You okay?* he asked.

Adrian looked at Mak like he just noticed he existed. *Aye,* he said, absentmindedly. Adrian swam slowly around the dome thinking. He stopped and swam up to Mak. *You know, don't ya?* he asked, intently.

Mak knew exactly what he meant. He had known for a week that the Athlanmara were planning the doineann for the next big storm but he didn't want to tell Adrian. He knew exactly what Adrian would do when he found out.

What are you talking about? Mak asked with artificial perplexity. It was Adrian's turn to shove Mak against the side of the dome. Adrian glared at Mak until he relented. *Okay, okay,* Mak said. He knew Adrian would get it out of him eventually, *They said the next big storm, it's going to happen then.*

Adrian released Mak. *Come on,* he said, as he fled into the tunnels, *We have to warn Brooke.*

Mak groaned, I knew it, he said to himself.

Mak and Adrian made their way to the bata portals as stealthily as possible. Most of the colony was off celebrating the recent victory over the humans. Swimming through the empty tunnels, Adrian and Mak felt safe as they boarded a bata and set off.

However, two pairs of glowing eyes observed their escape. Bronte was no fool, he knew that his rebellious son wouldn't obey him, and he had his suspicions as to the reason. He and Kai had been hiding by the portals, lying in wait.

Bronte turned to Kai. *Follow them, see where they go and come back to report to me alone,* he said, quietly.

By myself? Kai whined. For all his bravado Kai was terrified to be alone in the treacherous ocean.

Bronte touched the silver band on his wrist. *This is your chance to prove your worth as a warrior of the Athlanmara,* he said, with a musical waver in his voice, *Don't you want that?*

Kai nodded, his eyes wide. *Yes, commander!* he answered bravely.

As Kai boarded a bata alone Bronte gave him one last warning. *Remember tell no one! Report to me only!*

Yes, father.

Bronte watched the near silent craft float up, following Adrian's path. He turned back and swam slowly through the oppressive tunnels. He clenched his jaw and hoped his suspicions were wrong. If he was right, if Adrian was consorting with a human girl, it would mean certain death. And I, Bronte mused, must be the one to kill him.

Raffe and Chris were laying out in the sun on the DeLuca balcony. Chris wasn't one to lounge around in the sun but Raffe insisted.

"Bro, you're killin me!" Raffe exclaimed as Chris finished another story about Zoe, "You have got to let that broad go! What about all the hot chicks I've been setting you up with?"

Chris just glared at Raffe. He hated all the girls that Raffe knew. They were cheap and loud and stupid, Zoe was smart and classy. Me and Zoe make the perfect couple, he thought, why was she being so stubborn about what I said to that loser friend of hers?

Raffe sat up and noticed Chris' pouty demeanor. "Okay, okay Bro, don't get all bent outta shape," Raffe cajoled. Chris folded his arms and stubbornly refused to look at Raffe. "Listen, if you want that broad so bad then go and get her!"

"It's not that easy," Chris whined, "I heard she already has a new boyfriend, some lame exchange student."

"Uncle Raffe will help you out okay?" Raffe patted Chris on the leg, "You take care of the girl and I'll take care of the competition, you got it?"

Chris glanced at Raffe, the look in his eyes made Chris uneasy but he just smiled. "Thanks, bro!"

25 KILTS IN THE KEYS

The afternoon sun beat down on the still water of the little inlet. Two heads rose up cautiously. Mak and Adrian looked around warily before pulling themselves out of the water onto Brooke's dock. Adrian searched and found a couple of swim trunks hidden under the dock. He handed the larger one to Mak who took it reluctantly.

Let's just get this over with quick, he said to Adrian.

Adrian didn't answer, he just trotted off down the dock towards Brooke's house. Mak was worried about Adrian. He had never seen him so happy, almost euphoric. He had also never seen Adrian make so many rash decisions, like defy his father and spend time with humans, on land!

Mak was beginning to be concerned that this wasn't just a passing fascination for Adrian. What if he commits the cronachd, Mak wondered, shuddering at the thought. If Adrian joined himself with a human girl he would be hunted down and killed, along with every Athlanmaran that sheltered him.

Mak wished for the hundredth time that he and Adrian had never seen that boat. He wanted nothing to do with humans and he was sick of all the seunach nonsense, the old magic scared him. He wished the thing had never been found. Mak sighed and stomped off down the dock, unaware of a dark head in the water watching him.

"How do I look?" Jackson asked.

He was standing in Brooke's living room wearing a red plaid kilt, a t-shirt with a Tardis on it and red high-top Converse shoes. Zoe and Brooke were sitting on the couch.

Zoe had her mouth open in shock. "There is no way I am going anywhere with anyone who looks like that," she said.

"What?" Jackson asked, "Is it the kilt or the Dr. Who t-shirt?"

"There is so much wrong I don't know where to start," Zoe said. She turned to Brooke. "Back me up on this Brooke!" Brooke just stared into space. Zoe snapped her fingers in Brooke's face. "Yo! Best friend! Snap out of it."

Brooke gazed at Zoe, confused. "Oh sorry," she said. She turned to Jackson, "You look fine."

Jackson grinned. "Yes! That's what I thought!" he cried, triumphantly. He walked over to the hall mirror to admire himself.

"Brooke! No! What is wrong with you!" Zoe cried. Brooke looked down at her hands. "I told you this would happen!" Zoe continued, "It's been two weeks, they are not coming back!"

Jackson turned to the girls. "Who's not coming back?" he asked.

"The baby seal," Zoe said, sarcastically.

"Huh?" Jackson said.

Before he could ask anymore questions he was interrupted by two tall, muscular, dripping wet men walking into the room. They all sat there staring at each other for a moment.

Well, at least Brooke left them swim trunks, thought Zoe, surprised that she didn't feel like screaming. Jackson did feel like screaming but he looked at Brooke and Zoe calmly sitting on the couch.

"Hey! Who are you?" he asked bravely, though his voice cracked. Mak walked towards Jackson threateningly which got the girls moving.

"Gigantor, cool it!" Zoe said, jumping up and standing in front of Jackson, "He's with us."

Brooke stood up, trying to stay calm. "This is Adrian and Maksim, they're the exchange students, we told you about," she said to Jackson, trying to act normal, while her heart was pounding out of her chest.

Jackson furrowed his brow. "What, are they from the country of swimsuit models?" he said, his heart sinking to his toes. Zoe laughed. Adrian tried his best to be human and avoid looking at Brooke.

He held out his hand to Jackson. "I'm, Adrian."

Jackson shook his hand. "So you're from Scotland or something," Jackson said, suspiciously.

"Aye," Adrian answered.

Jackson looked Mak up and down. The giant youth was standing with his arms folded, scowling at Jackson. "Where's he from?" Jackson asked, his voice wavering again.

"He's Russian!" Adrian said, cheerfully.

"Oh!" Jackson nodded.

Suddenly, there was awkward silence. Adrian and Brooke were both looking everywhere but at each other. The others could feel the tension in the room. Jackson looked around, feeling like everyone knew something that he didn't.

"So…" he said, wondering why the girls were so quiet. They never stop talking. What's wrong with them now, he thought. "Well, we were going to go to the Kilts in the Keys carnival this afternoon, you guys wanna come?" Jackson asked, just to have something to say.

He regretted it as soon as he said it. Why would I want Zoe hanging out with two guys who look like that, he asked himself. Dang it! Why am I so polite?

"Aye," Adrian said.

At the same moment Mak said, "No!"

The two boys glared at each other. Zoe burst out laughing relieving the tension. She grabbed Mak's arm and headed for Brooke's room. "Come on, Hercules, I got something decent for you to wear."

Jackson followed. "I could probably get another kilt if he wants to wear that," he said.

Brooke and Adrian were left alone in the living room. Brooke finally got up the courage to look at Adrian. She saw that his lip was bleeding and one eye was starting to bruise.

"Are you okay?" she asked, her concern overriding the awkwardness.

Adrian gave her his crooked grin. "Aye," he whispered, "It's nothin."

Brooke was bewitched by Adrian's eyes, her brain was having trouble functioning. "Adrian I'm..I'm sorry, if I scared you, I don't know what happened…" she stammered.

Adrian moved close to Brooke. He tenderly touched her arm, closed his eyes and breathed in her scent. Brooke instantly felt a connection with Adrian.

Adrian felt it too, he pulled Brooke into his arms and held her tight. The memories of his mother had opened a gaping wound in his heart. Being with Brooke was the only thing that seemed to make the pain go away. He felt like he wanted to pull Brooke inside of himself, to be one person with her. Is this what humans call love, he wondered.

Brooke felt as though the weight she had been carrying for weeks floated away, but then she sensed a deep fear in Adrian.

"What's wrong?" she asked.

He pulled away from Brooke. He knew he had to tell her about the coming tsunami, her life was in danger. But the thought of Brooke leaving, of never seeing her again, was physically painful for him. If we could just spend a few days together first, he argued with himself, then I can tell her.

Adrian smiled and leaned down towards Brooke. "I missed ya," he whispered.

Zoe, Mak and Jackson walked back into the room. Mak was wearing tan shorts and a black t-shirt Zoe had bought for him. Zoe had even convinced him to use some gel and comb his hair back.

"What do you think?" Zoe asked, rubbing her hands together and almost jumping up and down. Her favorite thing was makeovers.

Mak looked uncomfortable. "This shirt is too tight," he complained, pulling at the garment.

Brooke saw the shirt was very tight. It showed off his amazing muscles perfectly and with his hair combed back he did look like a model.

Zoe looked him up and down and smiled. "Nah, it's good," she said. Zoe looked at Adrian. "Come on, lover boy, you're next, when I'm done with you, no one will even recognize you."

"Oh...my...gosh!" Whitney screamed almost pushing Courtney into the street so she could run up to Adrian and Mak.

So far Brooke and Zoe hadn't made it three blocks without being stopped by someone they knew from school. Funny, Brooke thought, if it was just me and Zoe no one would have said a word to us, but when you walk down the street in Marathon with two gorgeous strangers you can't get anywhere.

Mak with his bulging muscles and Adrian in torn jeans and a green t-shirt that made his eyes pop were practically stopping traffic.

"Where have you guys been?" Whitney gushed, trying to grab Mak's arm. Mak backed away from her in circles.

The crowds were overwhelming to Adrian and Mak who were used to the open ocean. Even when large numbers of Athlanmara got together there was always limitless ocean to retreat to. But between a building and a highway, Mak felt trapped. Whitney finally gave up on Mak and turned to Adrian.

"Wow! You look great!" she raved, grabbing onto Adrian's arm. He tried to smile.

"Hey, Whitney!" Jackson said, loudly.

Whitney ignored Jackson and the girls. "We are having a bonfire tonight at Chris DeLuca's place, you should totally come!" Adrian just stared at her wide eyed.

"Hey, Whitney!" Jackson said, again.

Whitney glared at Jackson. "Hey, Fraction, nice skirt," she said with a sneer. Her friends laughed at the nickname they had given Jackson in the fifth grade. Jackson's face turned red.

Zoe had had enough. "Shut up Whitney!" she said pulling Whitney's arm off of Adrian, "Why don't you go eat a funnel cake and throw it up!" Whitney's friends grinned at each other but kept quiet. Whitney glared at them. Normally, she would have cussed out Zoe but she wanted to stay cool in front of the boys.

She snorted. "Looks like you've eaten all the funnel cake yourself Zoe," she said. Then she turned her thousand watt smile at Adrian and Mak, "Well, I hope to see you two," she said, pointedly excluding the others, "at the bonfire tonight!" Whitney and her posse strutted off down the street.

"Jerks!" Zoe said. She turned to her friends, "Come on, let's go have some fun!" Adrian looked down at Brooke. He grabbed her hand and grinned.

The Marathon carnival was like every other small town carnival in

America. There were rickety rides packed into the park, along with every imaginable greasy food truck. However, this event added a beer garden and drunk men in kilts. It was the perfect combination for a gastrointestinal and vertiginous assault on the body and Adrian loved it.

Mak was content to stick with the food trucks but Adrian wanted to go on every ride. Brooke had never been one to go on the scary rides, the merry-go-round was more her speed, but with Adrian at her side she felt like she could take on anything. They sat next to each other screaming and laughing for hours.

Brooke had fun on the rides but what she loved the most was walking around the carnival holding Adrian's hand. She never had a boyfriend before and she always envied the girls walking around holding hands with a boy, those girls looked so secure. Now here she was, in front of all the kids from school, holding hands with a guy so handsome he was turning heads wherever they went.

But *is* Adrian my boyfriend, Brooke wondered. They hadn't discussed anything about boyfriend, girlfriend labels. She had never had a boyfriend, she wasn't sure how it worked. Brooke looked up at Adrian, he smiled down at her.

Brooke felt her face glowing. She didn't care about labels, she didn't care what the kids from school thought. All Brooke cared about was what she saw in Adrian's eyes every time he looked at her. He made her feel like she was the only girl in the world. She felt accepted for who she was even with all of her imperfections. Brooke felt connected to another person in a way she hadn't been since her mother left. Her head was dizzy and giddy and it wasn't from the carnival rides. She wanted the evening to go on forever.

Zoe, who normally loved going on the rides with her latest boyfriend, actually had fun watching Mak experience all that carnival food had to offer. At every ethnic food truck Zoe explained the human culture where the food originated.

"Okay, now this is real food," Zoe said excitedly, as they stopped in front of the Carta Buena truck, "This is the food of my people!" She ordered Mak empanadillas and arroz con Gandulez. "Cuba has lots of cultural influences from Caribbean, to Spanish, French and Italian," Zoe explained. Mak took the food and looked at Zoe skeptically.

She laughed. "Don't worry, it won't hurt you, only my mom makes it spicy enough to melt paint."

He ate the delicious food while Zoe told him about Cuban history. Mak had never had much interest in human culture when Adrian would go on and on about it. But eating delicious food and staring at Zoe made it all seem more interesting.

He admired Zoe's curvaceous figure, her full lips, her dark wavy hair. Mak had been really annoyed with Adrian for risking everything for some human. However, looking at Zoe, he was beginning to understand his friend a little more.

Suddenly, someone bumped his arm from behind, causing Mak to drop his plate of food. He turned around to see Raffe and Chris cracking up.

"Yo, bro!" Raffe said, "You think with all those muscles you could hold onto a plate of food."

"Guess he's missing the brain part!" Chris added. The two boys laughed uproariously at their cleverness. Mak paid no attention to what the two stupid humans were saying, he just looked sadly at the food on the ground.

"Ha, ha, ha," Zoe laughed, sarcastically. She glared at Chris. "Come on Mak," she said grabbing Mak's arm, "Let's get out of the children's area."

Chris walked in front of them. "Zoe, just talk to me for a minute," Chris asked in his sweetest voice, "Please?"

Zoe rolled her eyes, but let go of Mak's arm and allowed Chris to lead her around the side of the food truck. Mak made a move to follow her but Raffe got in his way. He recognized Mak as one of the stupid teens who thwarted his attack on the lab. He would have liked to take Mak out right then but he wasn't crazy enough to do something like that in front of a huge crowd.

"Listen to me, bro," Raffe said, lowering his voice, "You're gonna stay away from Zoe, you hear me?" Mak's eyes narrowed, he didn't like to be bullied. Mak made a move to walk around the offending human. Raffe pushed him backwards. "I mean it, bro!" he said and lifted up his tank top revealing the 38 revolver shoved into his waistband.

Mak didn't know a lot about guns, but he knew enough to realize this puny human was threatening his life and when Mak was threatened, he attacked. Raffe was lucky that Zoe was sick of listening to Chris' excuses and came back at that moment. She glanced at Mak's face and knew she only had seconds to stop him from tearing Raffe in two.

Zoe lunged between the adversaries. "Okay, okay, that's enough, gentleman!" Zoe grabbed Mak's arm and pulled him away from his tormentors. "Let's go get more food!" she said with enthusiasm.

Jackson had been following Zoe and Mak around and he was getting annoyed at the way Mak was looking at Zoe.

He pushed himself between the pair. "Well, it's getting dark now so we better find Brooke and Adrian and get a spot to watch the fireworks," he said. Jackson hoped that Adrian and Mak would sit together and leave him a chance to get close to Zoe.

"Yeah, sure," Zoe said, texting Brooke.

They met up with Brooke and Adrian who were already sitting at the end of the pier looking out over Boot Key Harbor. Zoe was not happy seeing the two of them sitting as close as possible, holding hands.

"Well, you two look cozy," Zoe said, eyeing Brooke.

Brooke scowled back at Zoe shaking her head. The two girls had a silent glare conversation for a moment. Normally, Zoe could make Brooke do whatever she wanted, but Brooke had been a different person since her trauma at sea.

Frustrated, Zoe gave up and tried the direct approach. "Can I talk to you for a minute Brooke," she said, tensely.

"Sure," Brooke said, through gritted teeth.

As Zoe had a whispered conference with Brooke, Adrian pulled Mak aside. "Ya gotta keep Zoe away from Brooke," he glanced at the girls, "I'm real close ta gettin the seunach." Mak nodded. Adrian was surprised that Mak didn't argue with him.

Jackson stuck his head in between the boys. "What are you guys talking about?" he said, worried Mak was making some plan about Zoe.

"Uh, Mak, he's afraid of fireworks," Adrian said. Mak glared at him, even though he wasn't sure what fireworks were. The girls joined the group. "Zoe," Adrian smiled, "Could ya take Mak somewhere the fireworks won't bother him?"

Zoe looked at Mak confused. "Uh, sure, I guess." Zoe was more concerned with keeping Adrian and Brooke apart but then she thought about the look on Chris DeLuca's face if she showed up at the bonfire with Mak. "Yeah!" she said, cheerfully, "We'll go to the bonfire!"

Mak shrugged his shoulders. "Is there food?" he asked. Zoe laughed.

"The bonfire sounds like fun!" Jackson quickly chimed in, not wanting to get left out of what Zoe was doing. Zoe grabbed Jackson and pulled him away from the group. "Ow!" he yelped.

"You are not going!" Zoe whispered, "You have to stay here with Brooke and Adrian and keep the two of them apart!"

"What? Why?" he whined.

Zoe gripped his arm harder, Jackson grimaced. "Because, he is the baby seal!" she exclaimed.

Jackson was confused but he knew better than to argue with Zoe. "Okay, okay!" he said, "But who is going to keep you and Mr. Abs apart?"

"As if!" she said, laughing. But she glanced at Maksim with a gleam in her eye. The two conspirators rejoined the group. "Okay," Zoe announced, "So Mak and I will go to the bonfire and we will meet up with you later!" Zoe grabbed Mak and took off before Brooke could argue.

Jackson squeezed between Brooke and Adrian. He put an arm around each of them. "Yes! This'll be great!"

The Coast Guard defender class boat ploughed through the warm Florida waters. Master Chief Brian Hale was at the helm, he peered out into the gathering gloom. Their base had received a report of a suspicious vessel and he hoped they could locate the craft before dark.

Brian was having trouble concentrating on his mission. All he could think about was his son Jackson. Brian and his wife Lisa worried about all four of their children, but Jackson's actions over the last month had been really hard on them. A Coast Guard officer's son stealing a boat was not only embarrassing and threatening to his career, it terrified Brian to his core.

He and his wife Lisa had adopted Jackson through the foster care system when he was only three weeks old. They had nursed him through his drug withdrawal and had dealt with his ADHD and other health issues from his premature birth. Jackson had thrived and been successful in school, but deep down Brian's greatest fear was that Jackson would get in with the wrong crowd and have issues with drugs like his birth mother. He drummed his fingers on the arm of his chair mentally reviewing his parenting over the years wondering if he could have done more.

"Unmarked vessel, three points off the starboard bow!" a sailor cried out.

 Brian stood up and looked through his binoculars. He saw the same suspicious fishing vessel he had seen last month.

He turned to his crew. "I want a boarding party ready to go, now."

"Aye, sir!" they answered.

 Five minutes later, two armed sailors jumped onto Eddy's fishing boat. The nefarious captain stood on the deck relaxed and smoking a cigarette. He had been boarded by the Coast Guard many times during his drug running years.

"What is your name and nationality?" the first sailor asked.

Eddy blew out a cloud of smoke. "Eddy Figueroa, and I'm Dominican man," he said, smiling.

The sailors proceeded to search the vessel. They inspected the paperwork and the safety equipment.

One of the sailors radioed back to their vessel. "They seem to check out, sir,"

Brian sighed. "Swab them for drugs," he commanded.

The Coast Guard sailors lined up the crew and swabbed all of their hands for drug residue. But after analyzing the samples they came up negative. Brian had no choice but to let the vessel go.

As he watched the ramshackle craft move off he still couldn't shake his suspicions.

One of the boarding crew walked up to Brian. "Master Chief?"

"Yes, McConnell?"

"Well, those samples, they came up negative for drugs but…" he paused.

"What is it?" Brian asked.

"The entire crew had a really strong, sulfur type smell."

"Thank you, McConnell."

Brian stared out at the retreating fishing boat. He sighed and turned the Coast Guard boat back towards the base. There was something wrong. He wished he didn't have so many rules to follow, but that's what you deal with when your government is a democracy, he told himself.

The little park in Marathon was filled to overflowing with tourists and locals alike. People filled the thin beach, crowded onto the little pier and boats were beginning to line up in the protected bay. Everyone waited excitedly for the sun to finish its journey into the ocean so it would be dark enough for the fireworks to start.

Brooke and Adrian sat on the pier, their legs dangling over the edge. Jackson was standing next to them.

"This is no longer a democracy!" Jackson said, doing a perfect impression of Rick, the main character from The Walking Dead. "And then they see the prison!" he gushed, back to his normal voice.

Brooke and Adrian gave each other pained looks. They had been waiting for the fireworks to start for thirty minutes and Jackson, finding out that Adrian had never seen the Walking Dead, decided to fill him in on all six seasons.

The pier was getting crowded, Brooke was disappointed. All she wanted to do was be alone with Adrian. She looked around for a way out and noticed an old dinghy pulled up on the sand below the pier. She had an idea.

Jackson continued his performance. "So Season 3 starts with..."

"Hey, Jackson!" Jackson's friend Martin pushed through the crowd and joined them.

This was just the distraction that Brooke was hoping for. "Hey, don't you guys think the new Star Wars movies are better than the old ones?" she asked innocently. Jackson froze, his mouth open in shock.

Martin took the bait like a hungry swordfish. "Yes, the plots in the prequels were much more complicated and..." Martin continued his review, falling into Brooke's trap perfectly.

"Are you crazy!" Jackson interjected, his face turning red.

As Jackson turned to Martin and launched into the diatribe that Brooke had heard a thousand times, she motioned to Adrian. The two of them slipped off the edge of the pier and dropped to the sand below. Giggling, Brooke grabbed Adrian's hand and lead him to the overturned dinghy.

"I hope it floats," she said as they turned it over and pushed it out into the bay.

They had found an old wooden paddle under the boat and Brooke used it to maneuver their tiny craft out between the bigger boats lined up to watch the fireworks. The little boat continued to stay afloat so Brooke kept paddling until they got away from the noisy, crowded part of the bay. Brooke put the paddle down and they glided to a stop on the still water.

Adrian, careful not to unbalance the boat, slid closer to Brooke. "Aye," he said softly, "Tis grand out here." Adrian took Brooke's hand.

All at once, Brooke felt nervous and unsure of what to do. "So, how long can you stay on land?" she said quickly, before she lost her mind completely at Adrian's touch. Brooke had mostly seen Adrian in human form and her secret hope was that he could just stay that way forever.

He puckered his brows in thought. "I don't know for sure, no one talks about it," He looked down ashamed, "But, I know it's forbidden ta interact with humans." He looked into Brooke's eyes, sadly. "If they found out I was here, I could never go back, they'd kill me."

Brooke's chest tightened with fear. Adrian was risking his life, his whole world to be with her. She couldn't ask that of anyone. He was just like the baby seal, she couldn't let her selfish desires cause harm to someone she loved. She had to let him go.

Adrian knew the danger he was putting himself in but his life had been so bleak and lonely he was willing to risk anything to experience the tenderness and connection he felt with Brooke. Adrian leaned down towards Brooke. She moved toward Adrian, then pulled back.

"Tell me about your mom," she said, her cheeks turning scarlet.

Adrian's face clouded, that first memory of his mother had been a terrible shock to him. He had kept his feelings and memories buried for so long, he wasn't sure he wanted to try to remember more.

Brooke got a pained look on her face. "It's fine...I mean if you don't want to…" Brooke stammered.

"It's okay," he reassured her, "I don't remember much about her, and my father…" Adrian paused, "He won't talk about her." Adrian closed his eyes as if to search his mind for an elusive picture.

"I do remember my mum, sittin by a fire, she was holding my brother and singing a sweet song. My father came and took my sleeping brother from her arms and took him ta bed. Then my mum," Adrian paused, struggling with his emotions, "She looked at me and smiled, she held her arms out ta me and I crawled up in her lap."

Adrian took in a sharp breath as if he experienced a sudden pain. He glanced at Brooke ashamed of his feelings and bit his lip to keep from crying. Brooke had tears in her eyes, memories of being held in her own mother's arms flooded her mind.

"Do you remember the song she sang to your brother?" Brooke asked, intently.

Adrian wasn't sure he wanted to remember more but it seemed to mean a lot to Brooke so he closed his eyes and tried to conjure up the tune. Adrian never sang, only the suire sang in his culture, but he could hear the words and tune in his head so he tried his best to repeat the ancient Celtic lullaby.

Gu robh neart na cruinne leat

'S neart na grèine

'S neart an tairbh dhuibh

'S àirde leumas.

It was a beautiful, haunting melody but Brooke looked disappointed. "That's not the song my mom sang. What does it mean?" she asked.

"It means, may you have the strength of the universe, and the strength of the sun, and the strength of the black bull which jumps the highest." Adrian laughed and smiled his crooked grin.

All at once, there was a loud explosion and a brilliant light filled the night sky. Adrian would have jumped into the water if Brooke hadn't stopped him.

"It's the fireworks!" she said pointing up at the sparkling shower overhead.

Adrian chuckled at himself. The two of them sat in the still boat and watched the beautiful display. They could hear the crowd respond with "ooooo's" and "ahhhhh's" at each new blaze of light but Adrian was silent.

The fireworks were beautiful and something he had never seen before but what really grabbed his attention was the changing colors on Brooke's upturned face. Her delicate features disappearing in the darkness then reappearing in bright green, red and blue hues, enchanted him.

Brooke looked over at Adrian and saw the look on his face, her heart flipped in her chest. She smiled at Adrian. He put his arms around her and pulled her close to his warm body. All thoughts of the baby seal flew from her mind. He leaned down and kissed her. Once again she felt the strange unity they had felt before.

Brooke was transported, she felt a weight in her arms. She looked down and saw she was holding a crying, dark haired little boy. Brooke looked around. She was in a cold dark cave, the ocean came in and lapped at her feet. From her throat rose the haunting Celtic lullaby, Adrian had sung. The child stopped crying and looked at her with eyes filled with trust. Then a tall, severe man rose from the water in front of her, she saw a long red scar on his face.

"Eist do bheul!" he commanded.

Brooke's eyes flew open, she was back in the dinghy with Adrian.

"Your father!" she said, almost shaking in fear. The sight of Adrian's father brought back the terrible scene she witnessed on the island. Adrian nodded, solemnly. "Was that your brother?" she asked, timidly.

Brooke was afraid Adrian would jump over the side again and never come back but he hadn't let go of her which was a good sign. He seemed resigned to deal with his painful memories.

"Aye," he said, not looking at Brooke, "his name's Kai."

"Is he still...alive?" Brooke asked with trepidation. She had sensed how frail the child was.

Adrian looked at Brooke with pain in his eyes. "Aye," he said, quietly, "but not for long."

The love she had felt for the little boy in the vision brought tears to Brooke's eyes. If something was wrong with Kai she knew it would be terrible for Adrian.

"What's wrong with him?" Brooke asked, she wanted desperately to help.

"No one knows, he has...fits." Brooke looked confused. Adrian tried to explain. "He shakes and can't talk, his eyes roll back in his head."

"Oh!" Brooke finally understood, "He has seizures." Adrian just nodded, and seemed satisfied that Brooke understood him. Brooke grabbed Adrian's hands in excitement. "Maybe he has mercury poisoning, it makes sense with your diet, Steve's been doing lots of research on the dolphins and how high the level of mercury is in their systems!" Brooke was starting to get in her 'save the world' frantic state. "We have medicine that might be able to help Kai!" she said, "I could find a way to get you some!"

Adrian smiled as Brooke went on about her plans to save Kai, then he remembered that the Athlanmara were about to destroy the humans who lived by the sea. There would be no medicine for Kai. There would be no Brooke, unless he told her to go far away to safety. So far away, that he would never see her again. The pain of losing Brooke hit him like a ton of bricks.

He pulled Brooke against his body and stopped her in mid sentence with a passionate kiss. She was the only creature on earth he had ever connected with, how could he let her go?

A rush of feelings washed over Brooke. She felt safe, she felt peaceful and she felt something else she had never experienced before, a strong desire that almost scared her. For a moment, she pulled back. Brooke looked into Adrian's eyes they were glowing, she felt like a mouse hypnotized by a cobra, she was powerless. Brooke gave into her feelings and kissed Adrian recklessly.

All at once, Brooke realized water was lapping up her legs. Their dinghy had finally sprung a leak and had been slowly sinking while Brooke and Adrian had been busy kissing. They looked at each other, shocked at first, then they burst out laughing as they both started to tread water.

"There you are!" Jackson said, rowing a dinghy up beside them. He had been frantically locating a boat to go after the two as soon as he saw his charges escape. He knew he couldn't possibly face Zoe if he lost track of Brooke and Adrian.

He stood up in the boat. "Now get in here!" he chastised them.

Brooke looked up. "Ahhhh!" she cried, shielding her eyes from the unwanted view. "Jackson sit down! Why aren't you wearing anything under that kilt?"

Jackson quickly sat down as Brooke and Adrian pulled themselves into the little boat. "It wouldn't be authentic if I wore something under my kilt," Jackson said, petulantly.

26 A BIG MISTAKE

Forty feet long and encased in a silvery sheath, the oarfish glided like a prehistoric snake along the stygian subaquatic plain. Drawn by the faint bluish glow, the creatures highly sensitive eyes beheld Bronte, Nereus and Gursel. They were floating in the darkness like living skeletons, the weight of 250 atmospheres slowing their movements to a grisly dance.

As the oarfish moved on to smaller prey the Athlanmara connected the last section of pipe to the generator. Then they moved on to the other side where Bronte was starting the new line of pipe. He looked back over the pipeline stretching out of sight and smiled.

He knew they only had three more generators to connect and then he could implement Utari's plan. He had kept this plan to blow up the generators between himself and his trusted lieutenants knowing that he would find little support in the colony.

The Athlanmara of the colony had grown to depend on the comforts and protections the Builder's machines provided. However, Bronte was confident they would be able to rebuild once the human threat was taken care of. He only hoped this plan to start an earthquake would work.

Bronte certainly didn't trust Utari. He was the one who had

convinced his mother to overthrow the Murrigh council then was nowhere to be found when her plans came crashing down around her. The only thing he knew he could trust was that Utari hated the humans as much as he did. Death to the humans, he thought, for now that was enough.

Shadowy figures milled around in the orange glare of the flickering flames. Music pulsed out into the night, punctuated by screams of laughter. Zoe and Mak walked up to the group of teens gathered in the backyard of the DeLuca mansion and for a moment all eyes were on the beautiful couple.

Zoe glanced over at Chris, he looked furious which somehow gave her a warm glow inside. She smiled smugly and hung on Maksim's arm. She put her head on his shoulder, trying to really sell the deception. Mak pushed her off but she didn't think Chris noticed that. Mak of course, abandoned Zoe immediately in his search for food. Zoe found a few friends to talk to while Mak stood by a table eating whatever he could get his hands on completely surrounded by adoring high school girls.

The girls kept talking and talking at him which annoyed Mak. They seemed like a flock of babbling seagulls, but at least they didn't seem to require him to answer back. The blonde one is the worst, he thought, she keeps trying to touch me.

"Oh, my gosh!" Whitney gushed, "Look at these muscles! Do you like totally work out all the time?" she said, grabbing Mak's arm and almost elbowing a girl in the face.

"Jeez, Whitney" another girl said, pushing her way back into the group around Maksim, "Way to punch me in the face!" Whitney glared at the interloper.

"So tell us about Russia," Courtney said, seeing her chance to break into the conversation, "Are there beaches in Russia?"

"Oh my gosh, Courtney! You are so stupid!" Whitney said, "There's snow there, duh!"

Chris and his friends were getting tired of being ignored. Chris was used to getting all the attention from the girls and being rejected by Zoe Moreno, after all he did for her, infuriated him. He didn't know what to do to get Zoe's attention. He looked over at Raffe for help but his wingman was busy trying to impress the high school girls by doing a handstand while drinking a beer.

D'andre, his best friend, noticed Chris' sullen expression. "Dude! Lighten up!" he said, already half drunk, "I got some killer whiskey from my dad's place, let's see how the Russian likes it!"

Chris smiled, he was up for anything that might harm Mak, except for a fight. He realized he would have no chance against the Russian giant but he knew Raffe had a plan for that.

Chris took the cup from D'andre and pushed his way into the group of girls around Maksim. "Hey Ivan, I hear you Russians like to drink," Chris said, holding out a red cup to Maksim.

"Uh, his name's Maksim," Whitney corrected.

Chris ignored her. Mak took the cup always willing to try anything related to eating. He took a big gulp and immediately spewed it out, all over his adoring audience.

"Ewwwww!" all the girls screamed.

Zoe doubled over in laughter from a safe distance. D'andre gave Chris a high five as he and his cronies cackled at Mak's performance.

"What a pussy!" D'andre exclaimed. Mak glared at them. He didn't know what that word meant but he knew they were making fun of him.

He was about to grab the snickering human by the neck when Zoe intervened. "Let's dance!" she said grabbing Mak's hand and dragging him towards the fire.

Zoe loved to dance and she was very good at it. Mak understood what dancing was but he had no intention of joining in the human ritual. He just stood in front of Zoe like a statue while she danced around him.

The Latin music pulsed and Zoe's hips kept up with the beat. She noticed Chris watching out of the corner of her eye, so she ran her hands down Mak's chest, then turned her back to him and gyrated her body against the complicit youth. Zoe was a pro at manipulating boys. A huge smile started to spread over Mak's face, he was enjoying this dancing ritual.

Chris had had enough of Zoe's taunting. He threw his drink down, ran over and grabbed Zoe's arm. He pulled her away from Mak and they started to have a heated argument that Mak couldn't quite hear.

Chris roughly tried to kiss Zoe, she pushed him away. Chris came back at Zoe so hard he knocked her down. The next second Chris was pinned to the ground by what felt like a brick wall. He couldn't breathe as the steel grip of Mak's fingers were around his neck.

All the girls started screaming and the entire football team ran over to join in the fracas. Chris' ten friends managed to pull Mak off, mostly because Mak let them. There was nothing he loved more than a fight where he was outnumbered. He stood up grinning, as the lesser boys surrounded him. Mak couldn't wait for them to charge. They just stood there looking at each other, all hoping that some other boy would start the fight.

Mak was about to lunge at the nearest victim when he noticed Zoe sitting on the ground crying and holding her ankle. None of the girls were making a move to help her. Mak was disappointed at missing out on a good brawl, but he knew his first responsibility was to a fallen comrade. He ran over, scooped Zoe up into his arms and walked off into the dark away from the crowd. The football team was relieved.

"That's right!" D'andre yelled with false bravado, "Walk away!"

Raffe came out from the bushes where he had been puking. He saw Chris still sitting on the ground gasping for breath and rubbing his neck. "Bro, what happened?" he asked, helping Chris to his feet.

"That crazy Russian attacked me!" Chris spat out.

Raffe's face turned to stone. "Which way did he go?"

Zoe had stopped her crying by the time Mak found a deserted spot down the beach from Chris' house. He sat her down on the sand and stood there awkwardly as she sniffed and wiped her tears away. Zoe looked up at Mak.

"Thanks," she said, "That guy is such a jerk!" Zoe started to rub her twisted ankle.

Mak sat down next to her. "Are you injured?" he asked. Mak was surprised that he really cared if Zoe was okay.

"Oh, it's just a sprain, I'll be okay in a few days."

They sat in the moonlight looking at each other unaware that another, malevolent pair of eyes watched from the bushes behind them.

Zoe leaned into Mak, he was so warm and comforting. At the moment she felt scared and alone. She knew there was something that always made her feel better. Zoe lifted her face up to Mak and started kissing him.

Mak had seen other couples at the bonfire grappling and pressing their lips together, it had almost made him jealous. He wanted to be close to someone. But when Zoe pressed her lips to his the only feeling he experienced was fear. Mak jumped to his feet and stared wide eyed down at Zoe.

"What?" she giggled, "You never been kissed?"

Mak's face turned red. He knew she was mocking him. Normally, Mak never backed down from a dare but he knew how steep the consequences were for just talking to Zoe, not to mention anything else they might do.

He looked down at Zoe, his resolve wavered. The moonlight reflected off of her perfect features, her eyes were sparkling, her full lips slightly parted. Mak took a deep breath and sat down next to her.

Zoe took his arm and placed it around the small of her back, she pressed her chest into his and kissed him again. This time Mak felt a different sensation. He pulled Zoe closer, she ran her hands under his shirt and along his chest, regretting that she bought a shirt so small.

Mak copied her and ran his hands under Zoe's shirt, disappointed that he found more human coverings and confusing straps. Zoe laid back on the sand and Mak pressed his hips into hers, he ran his fingers through her hair.

Raffe pulled out his gun as quietly as he could. He saw the two bodies writhing on the sand. Between the darkness and his half drunken state he wasn't sure if he could determine which was Mak and which was Zoe. Who cares, he thought, they both deserve to die. It wasn't the first time he had pulled a gun on a cheating girlfriend. Raffe stood up stealthily and aimed.

"Oh...My...Gosh!" Whitney walked right into the line of fire with two of her cronies ruining his plan. "Zoe Moreno, you are such a slut!" she spat out. Whitney was jealous that Zoe was accomplishing her strategy for the night. Mak and Zoe sat up disheveled and panting.

Jackson ran up behind Whitney. "Here they are!" he called to Brooke and Adrian. Then he noticed Zoe pulling down her top and Mak wiping lipstick off his face. Jackson's face fell. "Zoe are you okay?" he asked, giving Mak an accusatory look.

Brooke and Adrian came up behind the others. Brooke figured out what was going on in an instant. She stood looking at Zoe, her mouth hanging open.

"What?" Zoe asked innocently, as Mak helped her to her feet.

Zoe took a step then winced. Mak easily picked her up in his arms and the four of them walked off. Mak refused to look at Adrian, knowing he would never hear the end of it from his friend.

"Zoe!" Tina Moreno yelled for her daughter again. "My niña, I don't know what is wrong with her!'"

It was late in the morning but Tina was bustling about her kitchen making another batch of her famous Puerto Rican cornmeal pancakes. Mak was sitting at the counter having no trouble finishing off the first batch.

Tina looked at the youth and smiled. "I like a man with a good appetite!" The family dog, Poncho, an elderly Chihuahua, sat on the floor and stared at Maksim with his one good eye and growled. "Callate! Poncho, you naughty dog!" Tina scolded.

Mak had come by the Moreno house earlier in the morning looking for Zoe. When he got to the door, he hesitated. He was mad at himself for being taken in by some human girl, but after what happened between them last night, he had to see her.

Poncho had spied his latest victim through the doggie door and launched his most ferocious attack. All Mak saw was a hair ball with yellow teeth coming for him making a terrifying sound. Tina had found Mak perched on the railing trying to fend off the beast and recognizing him as Zoe's protector from the night before. She of course invited him in for breakfast.

"Your family, they are in Russia?" she asked Mak, filling his plate with more pancakes.

"I don't have any family," he answered between mouthfuls.

"You have no family?" she asked horrified, "You are an orphan?" Mak nodded not quite sure what the word meant but following Adrian's plan of just saying 'yes' to everything. "Ay, you poor niñito!"

Tina was about to call for Zoe again when Jackson walked in the back door. "Hey, mama Moreno!" he said, cheerfully. Jackson stopped dead in his tracks when he saw Mak sitting at the counter.

"Jackson!" Tina said and gave him a big hug. Jackson and Mak glared at each other as he sat down at the counter.

Jackson sniffed. "Yum! Smells good!"

"Oh, I'm sorry Jackson but the pancakes, they are all gone."

Jackson looked at Mak like he had just murdered someone. "You ate all of Mama Moreno's pancakes!"

Tina walked over and pinched Jackson's cheek affectionately. "We have oatmeal, carino."

Jackson's mouth opened in shock. "Oatmeal?" he gasped.

Tina ignored him. "Zoe!" she yelled again.

Finally, Zoe shuffled into the kitchen in her jammies, her hair a tangled mess. She was wiping the sleep from her eyes.

"Ay! Momi! Why are you yelling?" she said. Then she saw the two boys sitting at the counter and froze in shock. They both looked at her with big grins on their faces.

Tina pointed at the boys with her spatula. "Your friends, they are here, niñita."

"You look beautiful this morning Zoe!" Jackson said quickly, making sure he made a good impression before Mak had a chance.

Mak jumped up and took Zoe's hand. "Are you okay?" he asked. He reached out his other hand to touch Zoe's hair.

Zoe ducked and grabbed her hand away from Mak. She ran from the room yelling at her mother in Spanish. Tina just waved her hand in Zoe's general direction and muttered in Spanish. Mak sat down at the counter looking confused.

Jackson slapped him on the back. "Girls, huh?" he said cheerfully, glad to see Mak rebuffed.

Mak had no idea what to do. He wasn't about to ask some human boy for advice and he certainly couldn't go to Adrian after all the grief he had given him about Brooke. He sat there morosely staring at the counter. Tina saw how downcast he looked.

She made a tsk, tsk, sound. "Don't look so sad niñito." Tina paused for a minute as if trying to think of a solution. She got a big smile on her face. "I make you some lunch!" she said.

Zoe slammed her bedroom door. She was furious with her mother for not telling her that Mak was at her house before she walked into the kitchen, all gross and with no makeup. She threw herself on her bed. After a moment, Zoe realized that she was more furious at herself for making out with Mak last night.

"What were you thinking!" she screamed into her pillow.

It wasn't like her usual mistakes, like making out with someone's boyfriend or a college guy she just met, this guy wasn't even human. Zoe shuddered thinking about what he must look like swimming around with sharp claws and a tail. She grabbed her phone and texted Brooke, '911 GET OVER HERE NOW!'

27 "911"

The skiff cut through the beautiful tropical waters like a knife. The sky mirrored the perfect blue of the ocean and a bank of clouds hovered on the horizon looking like dollops of whipped cream. Brooke couldn't help smiling as the warm breeze played with her ponytail.

She was having a great time teaching Adrian how to drive the boat and how to use the navigation equipment. Adrian was always interested in learning new things about humans and he was so smart he caught on quickly. Brooke gazed into Adrian's sparkling eyes, he flashed her his crooked grin. It would be perfect, she thought, if it wasn't for them.

Brooke looked back at Zoe and Mak sitting in the stern, arms folded, glaring out over the beautiful water, refusing to look at each other. After Zoe's continued coolness towards him, Mak's confusion turned to anger. He had wanted to storm off and never set foot on shore again but of course Adrian wanted to spend more precious time with Brooke.

He convinced Mak that this would be the day he would tell Brooke. Mak hearing it all before decided to come along and make sure Adrian followed through for once. Zoe, after her passionate debacle, was even more convinced that Brooke was a victim of some magical spell and needed to be protected. There was no way she was going to let Brooke out of her sight.

Brooke pulled back on the throttle. They were nearing some nice dive spots around Coffins Patch. No other boats were around, seeing as it was off-season in the Keys. Brooke looked at Adrian with a mischievous grin. She quickly pulled off her shorts and tank top, grabbed his hand and they jumped into the water before their respective chaperones could stop them.

Zoe jumped up. "Brooke!" she yelled at the departing shapes in the water. Mak stood up shaking his head in disgust. He pulled off his shirt. "You're just going to leave me here?" Zoe asked, irritated. She was used to untiring pursuits from boys and she felt that Mak had given up a little too easily. He gave her a nasty smirk then dove into the water. "Fine!" she yelled, "Who needs you!"

Zoe tied the little skiff to a buoy and sat down feeling sorry for herself and suddenly a little afraid. She felt like someone was watching her. She whirled around but saw nothing, aside from the endless ocean.

Brooke felt like she was swimming in a dream. She had always loved the ocean but now, holding Adrian's hand, her entire body glowing, she felt like she was a creature of the ocean herself.

Brooke and Adrian swam through the brilliant waters both of their bodies shimmering like the sun was shining inside of them. Adrian could hardly take his eyes off of Brooke. He had always been enamored by her beautiful innocence but now, as he saw her radiant body gliding through the water at his side, he realized there was nothing in the world he wanted more than Brooke.

Adrian stopped swimming. What if we could be together, he thought. After all, the seunach had given Brooke the power to breathe underwater, maybe they could live together with the Athlanmara. The thought filled him with hope.

Brooke looked quizzically at Adrian, wondering what made him stop. He drew her close to him and kissed her. Their shining bodies curved around each other in a beautiful, intimate dance, the two moving as one. Adrian pulled back from Brooke to look into her eyes, but it was as if he was looking through her eyes. He could see himself. This was what he had always longed for, to know another being fully and to be fully known himself.

Brooke too felt the strange oneness, she was looking through Adrian's eyes and seeing herself. Suddenly, looking past her own shoulder she saw a dark shape hurl a spear towards her back.

Duck! Adrian screamed in her head.

As one they threw themselves to the side. A spear grazed Adrian's broad shoulders. In a split second Adrian had transformed and was after the attacker. He made a sharp piercing cry and Brooke saw Maksim, also transformed, streak into the melee. She couldn't tell what was happening. To her it just looked like a silent tangle of tails and arms.

All at once, she realized she needed to breathe. She looked down at her body, the glow was fading. She swam as fast as she could for the surface.

Adrian knew it was Kai even before he saw his face. As he approached, Kai pulled out his long wicked knife from the sheath on his arm and struck at Adrian. Adrian ducked around Kai and hit his back with his powerful tail. In a flash, Mak was by his side.

Kai was no match for the two of them. Adrian disarmed Kai as Mak put him in a hold from behind.

Traitor! Kai screamed at Adrian, *Everyone will know what you've done! You'll both be fed to the Guardians!*

Who's gonna tell them? Mak said, tightening his grip.

Kai laughed. *Sevan's on his way ta the colony right now, lebnah!*

Adrian and Mak exchanged a terrified glance. Their worst fears had come true. At best, they would be banished, the worst...Adrian didn't want to contemplate that right now.

What are we going to do with him? Mak asked, angrily. He wanted to blame all of his troubles on Adrian but he realized he had made the choice to follow Adrian. And then there was Zoe, no one forced him to do that.

Adrian couldn't think. All he could see was his father's enraged face. Suddenly, Kai began to shake all over, his eyes rolled back into his head.

Mak, let him go! Adrian cried. He took his brother in his arms. *Kai!* he yelled. There was no response. Adrian had never seen him shake so badly. He was beside himself with fear, then he remembered Brooke. He took Kai in his arms and sped towards the boat.

Brooke swam as fast as she could to the little skiff. As she pulled herself into the boat Zoe could see something was wrong.

"What happened?" Zoe asked, grabbing her by the shoulders. Brooke was panting so hard she couldn't talk. "Did he attack you?" she yelled.

"No," Brooke got out, "Another one did."

"What!" Zoe cried, "There's another one!"

Just then a hand with sharp claws grabbed onto the side of the boat. Zoe screamed and fell back, terrified. Mak and Adrian's heads popped up out of the water and they threw Kai into the boat. He lay there shaking, in his full Athlanmaran form.

Adrian and Mak pulled themselves into the boat. Thankfully, they were in their human forms however, they had lost their new swim trunks in the process.

"Jeez!" Zoe cried out, covering her eyes. She didn't know where to look. Between a terrifying mythical creature and two naked boys there weren't a lot of options. Brooke took in the scene and realized that Kai was having a seizure.

She looked at Adrian. "Can't you heal him, like you did for your wounds?" she asked Adrian, panicked. Brooke hated to see any creature in pain, even though this one did just try to kill her. Mak looked at Adrian quizzically.

Adrian was ashamed, he wasn't used to lying. "I can't heal anyone," Adrian said, looking down at Kai.

"But on the island and when those guys attacked us, you healed yourself then," Brooke insisted. Adrian shook his head. "But...you told me...it was you..." Brooke trailed off.

"It's the seunach, the bracelet," Adrian said to Brooke barely able to look at her, "You healed me," he said.

Brooke was in shock. "Me?" she said. How can it be me, she wondered, Adrian's the one with the magical powers. It suddenly became clear to Brooke. She looked at Adrian with pain in her eyes. "You lied to me?" Brooke felt sick.

Kai was bouncing around in the boat, Adrian was frantic. "Please!" Adrian grabbed Brooke's hand, "Please, heal him, he's my brother!" he begged.

"That's Kai?" Brooke asked, astonished. Adrian nodded.

Brooke was scared, but she knew she had to do something. She got as close as she could to the tortured youth, put her hand on him and waited for the familiar rush of heat. Nothing happened. She looked at Adrian helplessly.

"Try harder!" he said.

"I don't know how to try harder!" Brooke said, almost starting to cry, "I don't know what any of this means!"

Adrian was confused. He was so sure that the seunach had the power to heal. Why wasn't it working?

Zoe had had enough of this bizarre drama. She decided to take charge, if there was a sea creature in trouble she knew where to take it. "We can take him to Steve, he'll know what to do," she said, emphatically. She threw a towel in Mak's direction hoping he would get the hint. "We're only three miles from the DRC."

Brooke shook her head. "Zoe, he's a merman, not a dolphin! We can't just drag him into the center, everyone will see!" she protested.

Zoe ignored her and started the engine. "It's after five, the center is closed and Steve won't say anything," she said, looking at Brooke intently, "Are you just going to let him die?"

Brooke and Adrian looked at each other. It was a huge risk for him, he had to be the one to make the decision. Adrian looked at Mak.

His faithful friend just shrugged. *We're dead anyway,* he said to Adrian.

"Do ya think your friend can help him?" Adrian asked Brooke. She nodded. "Alright," he said.

Zoe pointed the boat west towards the Dolphin Research Center while Brooke got Steve on the phone. In twenty minutes they ran the little skiff up onto the sand of Grassy Key and realized that they would have to carry Kai up a residential street and across the main highway to get to the center.

Brooke looked at Adrian. "Can't you get him to transform?" Adrian shook his head.

"Great!" Zoe exclaimed, "Two naked guys and a merman won't draw any attention!" she said.

Luckily, they had a few articles of clothing and a couple of towels. Between them all, they were able to cover up the important parts. They were a strange sight running down Third Street, two boys wearing tight girl shorts carrying an unconscious youth covered in beach towels.

When they got to the highway Zoe didn't even pause. She ran out into the street and stopped traffic while the boys hustled their burden across the four lanes. Brooke was barely able to keep the towels from falling off.

A man in a pickup truck ogled Zoe in her bikini. "Need a ride baby?" he yelled out his window.

Zoe just flipped him off and followed the others. They ran through the parking lot of the center, relieved that it was empty. Steve met them with a gurney. They tossed Kai on the stretcher, Brooke making sure the towels remained in place.

Steve knew Zoe well but he glanced suspiciously at the strange boys. "What's this all about Brooke?" he asked, as they all ran alongside the gurney.

"Is the staff gone like I asked?" she said, breathlessly.

"Yes, but Brooke, are these kids in trouble, what's going on?" Steve loved Brooke like a daughter and he didn't want her involved in anything illegal.

They finally rolled into the lab. Kai was barely moving now. Brooke was afraid he was dead. Steve pulled out his stethoscope and listened to Kai's heart. He started to examine the unconscious adolescent. The teens froze waiting for his reaction, but when he moved the towels they saw with relief that Kai had reverted to his human form.

Steve looked at Brooke. "Did he overdose on drugs?"

"I think he has mercury poisoning," she answered.

"Mercury poisoning?" Steve said, incredulous.

He reached for his little flashlight and shone it into Kai's eyes, the light reflected back in a rainbow of colors and he could see a second, clear eyelid. He paused, his hand shaking.

He looked hard at Mak and Adrian. "Is this your friend?" he asked them.

"He's my brother," Adrian said.

"He's an exchange student, so we can't take him to the hospital," Zoe lied, hoping Steve would ignore the odd situation. Steve looked at the youths gravely. He glanced at the shallow tank in the room.

He grabbed Kai under the arms. "Help me get him into the tank," he said to Adrian.

Shocked, Adrian did what he was told. As soon as Kai's body hit the water, the teens watched in horror as he transformed before their eyes into his Athlanmaran form. Steve didn't react at all. He just got a syringe, reached into the tank and took a blood sample from Kai, like he had done a million times on the dolphins. The friends stared at each other in shock.

"Steve...I...he's..." Brooke stammered, not knowing what to say.

Steve looked at Brooke sadly. "Honey, I know." Steve busied himself with the blood sample. "It's going to take a few minutes to see if his levels of mercury are high, but that's not going to matter much." Steve looked up from his microscope slides. "There's not much we can do for him once the mercury has reached his nervous system."

Brooke was stunned at Steve's reaction. He acted like he saw mermen every day. Adrian and Mak were relieved, they had made a plan to flee with Kai if Brooke's friend turned out to be dangerous, but for some reason the boys felt like they could trust him.

Steve attached some leads to Kai and switched on a monitor. They all listened to the slow beating of Kai's heart. Steve went back to check on the blood sample. As the teens waited for him to tell them the verdict, they all stood around the tank watching Kai and wishing they could do something to help. While they were distracted, Steve pulled out his phone and sent a text message.

Adrian looked at Brooke with tears in his eyes. She knew what he was feeling, she had felt it herself. She reached out and held his hand. Kai lay as still as death in the tank, the only way they could tell he was alive was the soft glow of his skin and the beeping of the monitor. Steve walked over and took his vitals again.

"Hand me that blood pressure thing, Zoe." He motioned at a counter filled with instruments.

Zoe grabbed a metal box with an antenna. "This?" she asked, walking by Mak to give it to Steve. As she passed Mak, the box made a beeping sound.

Steve looked up quickly. "That's my tracking receiver, Zoe," he said. He walked over and grabbed the box from Zoe. He ran it up and down Mak's body, it continued to beep. Mak backed away from him in fear.

Steve looked from one boy to another. "Have you been captured?" he asked them tensely. Adrian suddenly became uneasy. How does this human know everything about us, he wondered. Adrian looked around for a weapon.

Steve saw the boys getting defensive. "I don't mean you any harm," he said, holding up his hands, "but I think your friend here has a tracking beacon in him."

Mak was shocked. "What?" he exclaimed, feeling around on his back like he could rip it off.

Adrian moved toward Steve. "He was captured, I saved him," he said, cautiously.

"Crap!" Steve said under his breath. "This thing is sending a signal right now and someone is pinging back to it!" he cried. "We have to get rid of it!"

Adrian looked at Mak to reassure him, then he nodded to Steve. Steve ran the receiver over Mak's body again trying to pinpoint the source. He noticed a tiny scar on Mak's right hip.

"Yep!" he said. Steve grabbed a scalpel and moved towards Mak. The suspicious teen seized his hand in a grip of steel.

Adrian put a hand on his friend's arm. "Mak, it's okay." Mak let go of Steve.

Steve rubbed his wrist feeling like it was almost broken. "This might hurt a bit," Steve said, as he made an incision exactly where the scar was.

Mak didn't move a muscle. He looked over at Zoe hoping she noticed how brave he was. Steve had to dig a bit. He hoped the giant youth wouldn't suddenly pummel him. He finally reached the tiny transmitter and pulled it out.

Mak and Adrian looked at each other amazed that the little thing had been inside of Mak for two years. Steve examined it closely for a moment then dropped it on the ground and crushed it with his foot.

He looked at the boys. "That is not good," he said.

Steve had a lot of questions to ask Adrian and Mak but before he could interrogate them, Kai began to violently shake again, splashing water out of the shallow tank. The heart monitor started beeping like crazy. Kai was going into cardiac arrest.

Steve looked at Brooke helplessly, knowing there was nothing he could do. Adrian ran over to the tank and grabbed his brother's hand. He didn't want Kai to be alone when he died.

Zoe was close to tears. She walked up to Mak and leaned her head on his shoulder. Mak looked down at her and put his arm around her. Brooke had tears streaming down her face. She walked over to Adrian and took his hand.

He looked down at her with pain in his eyes. "Give me the seunach! It doesn't belong to you!" he said, angrily. Brooke looked at Adrian, her eyes wide with fear. She pulled her hand away from Adrian and backed away. Adrian was desperate. With one hand still clutching his afflicted brother he pulled Brooke towards him with his free arm and kissed her hard.

It was like an explosion went off inside of Brooke. Her entire body felt like it was on fire. Adrian could feel the intense heat travel down his arm and into his brother. Kai's shaking intensified but to the astonishment of the onlookers tiny silver bubbles seemed to be escaping from Kai's skin. The bubbles fell to the bottom of the tank and rolled together into one silvery, liquid mass.

The strange link between Brooke, Adrian and Kai lasted only a few minutes but to Brooke it seemed like an eternity. Adrian felt the heat stop, he released Brooke and removed his hand from Kai. He looked at Kai floating peacefully. The heart monitor let out a slow and steady beeping.

Adrian turned to Brooke ecstatic. Brooke was in a daze, her eyes rolled back into her head. She would have fallen to the floor if Adrian hadn't quickly caught her.

"Brooke!" he cried, his elation turning to dismay.

At that moment Tom burst into the lab. He took in the scene in an instant. There was his precious daughter, in the arms of a beast.

Steve could read the look on his face. "Now, Tom…" he began, trying to calm the storm he knew was coming.

"Get away from my daughter!" Tom yelled at Adrian in Gaelic.

Mak stood there with his mouth open. Zoe had no idea what was going on. Adrian gently placed Brooke on the floor and faced the irate father. Tom crossed the room in two paces and punched Adrian hard in the face. Adrian fell to the ground blood spurting from his nose. Mak flew to his friends defense, but Adrian managed to jump up and stop Mak from obliterating Tom.

Steve got in between the boys and the enraged father. "Tom!" he yelled, grabbing him by the shirt and pushing him back, "This is not the way to handle this!"

"Daddy?" Brooke said, sitting up groggily.

Tom immediately fell to his knees and pulled Brooke into his arms. "I got you baby girl," he said. He glared at Mak and Adrian. "What did you do to her?" he yelled. Mak was silent,

Adrian looked at the ground ashamed. "My brother...he was dyin...I'm sorry," he ended lamely.

Tom looked at Steve. "You let this happen?" he asked Steve, accusingly.

Steve was distraught. "I didn't know! It all happened so fast."

Tom picked Brooke up in his arms and carried her towards the door. "Come on, Zoe," he said. Zoe terrified, glanced at the two boys and hurried after Tom. He turned back to look at Adrian. "If you ever come near my daughter again...I'll kill you." Then he walked out of the room. Adrian could tell that Tom was deadly serious.

Steve looked at the downcast boys and sighed. "You guys can stay here for the night. I'll keep watch over your brother," he said, kindly.

28 LIES

Lightning flashed in the sky followed immediately by a thunderclap so loud it shook the SUV driving along Highway 1. Dr. James Gordon was sitting in the back seat. He tried to peer out into the blackness, but all he could see out the window was a river of water running down the glass.

"You're sure about the signal Malcolm?" he asked.

Malcolm was driving at breakneck speed down the almost deserted highway. "Yep, doc," he answered, glancing back at Gordon, "Yer eggheads said it was coming from somewhere in the Keys and it was real strong."

"Well, before it ceased completely," Gordon said with disappointment.

His hopes had been so high. The tracking beacon that had been placed in his specimen two years ago had suddenly come to life in the Atlantic Ocean near the East coast of America. The signal was too weak to pinpoint with accuracy so two months ago he sent a few of his scientists to Miami, Florida. They would get a clear signal, then it would disappear. This had gone on for weeks. Gordon had finally decided to investigate for himself. He couldn't stand the uncertainty.

When he landed in Miami he got the news that there was a strong signal in the Florida Keys but before he could charter a plane, a tropical storm had come in. No planes could take off and then the signal was lost completely. He immediately rented a car, he couldn't afford to waste any more time.

Gordon closed his eyes. He was exhausted, not only from the last two weeks he had spent in the hospital at the bedside of his wife Anne, but from the fifteen years they had been dealing with the relentless devastation of her disease; Anne suffered from multiple sclerosis. There were no words to describe the utter powerlessness he felt as he watched his beloved wife alter from a beautiful, vibrant woman into a trembling invalid who could barely speak. He had labored for years to come up with something that would stop the progression of the terrible death sentence over the woman he loved. So far he had been defeated.

His last hope was to capture one of the monstrous aberrations he knew existed and tear them apart until he discovered their secrets. Another thunderclap shook the vehicle.

Gordon leaned forward. "Drive faster."

The rain was pounding on the windows in sheets as Brooke lay on the couch in her living room pale and weak. Her dad had taken Zoe home with dire warnings not to tell anyone what she had seen. Brooke had come clean and told her dad a synopsis of everything that had happened between she and Adrian, though she had kept out a few of the more romantic details. She also hadn't told her father anything about healing Adrian or her suspicions about the bracelets power.

Tom was pacing back and forth in the living room. His worst fears were realized. Tom knew he had to reveal all of his long kept secrets to Brooke but he was terrified that if she knew the truth he would lose her, just like he lost Nina.

Brooke could tell he was struggling with something. "Daddy, I'm sorry I lied to you, say something," she begged. Tom looked at Brooke, she had tears in her eyes.

He sat down next to her on the couch and gave her a hug. "No, honey, I'm sorry. This is all my fault."

Brooke wiped her eyes. "Your fault?" she asked, confused.

Tom took a deep breath. "I have something to tell you, please don't be mad at me." Brooke nodded, she couldn't imagine what her dad could say to make her mad. "Your mom and I met in the Mediterranean, like Steve said, she'd been shot," he continued, "I found her on a remote beach naked and almost dead. I thought she had just been in some kind of terrible accident. We brought her on the boat and would have taken her to a hospital but she got really agitated so Steve took care of her as best he could." Brooke was fascinated, she had never heard any of this.

Tom got up and started pacing again. "We spent a lot of time together, her name was Sierna. I called her Nina." A smile spread across Tom's face as he remembered those carefree days of his youth. "She was so beautiful and full of life. We fell in love." Brooke had so many questions but she was afraid to interrupt.

"I bought this little ring at a flea market in Greece and one day while we were out swimming alone, I asked your mom to marry me. She said no!" he laughed. Then Tom got serious. "She told me she had to show me something that might change my mind." He took Brooke's hand. "Honey, your mom, she was one of the Athlanmara."

Brooke felt like her heart stopped. "No, she wasn't!" she said frantically, "She was my mom! She was human!"

Tom wished he never had to tell Brooke. "She loved you so much, honey!" he said, not sure how to make the truth hurt less.

"She left me," Brooke said, emotionless, "She left me."

"Honey, she wanted to go back to her people. We argued about it. She wanted to take you, she didn't want to leave you but...you couldn't breath under water."

Suddenly, the realization of what her dad was saying hit her like a bullet in the heart. Brooke felt like she was going to throw up. "I'm half mermaid?" she choked out. Just saying it out loud sounded utterly ridiculous. She looked at her dad. "You lied to me," she said, her eyes wide with shock, "You said she was a marine biologist."

"Well, your mom did know everything about the sea..." Tom paused, realizing he was getting off topic. He squeezed Brooke's hand. "Brooke, honey, I was trying to protect you."

Brooke pulled her hand away from her dad, a wave of anger and confusion washing over her. "You lied to me my whole life!" she yelled, tears pouring down her cheeks, "My mom left for a reason and you made me think she left because she didn't love me!"

"I never said that!" Tom cried, "I didn't want her to leave, I begged her to stay. She loved you but she chose them over us Brooke!" He tried to hug Brooke but she pushed him away. "That's why I don't want you to be around that boy!" Tom continued, "You'll give him your heart and then he'll leave you. That's just what they do, honey!"

Brooke looked at her dad, incredulous. "They? They, dad?" She jumped up off the couch, "I'm one of 'them'!" Brooke ran to her room and slammed the door. She threw herself on the bed and sobbed into her pillow. Her whole world had just come crashing down.

The tropical storm battered the Dolphin Research Center and whipped the palm trees into erratic gyrations. A palm branch fell on the metal roof of the center with a crash. Steve sat up and rubbed his eyes. He had been studying Kai's blood sample for hours. What he found was that Kai had red blood cells with nuclei in them and red blood cells without nuclei. This discovery was fascinating because the difference between human and animal blood is that human red blood cells have no nucleus.

It was something that of course had never been seen in the natural world. Steve couldn't wait to study Kai's DNA. He had been able to study Brooke's DNA over the years and it was incredible. Humans have a normal double helix, with two strands of DNA. Brooke had six strands. The ramifications of the exponential different expressions that her DNA was capable of were mind boggling.

Steve got up and stretched. He glanced out the window at the raging storm. Then he walked over to the tank to check on Kai. He seemed to be resting peacefully, floating in the water.

Steve was troubled, he had three Athlanmara in his center that had to be out of there before any of the staff came in at seven am. He took another look at Kai and wondered if he should take his vitals again.

Suddenly, Kai's eyes flew open. For a moment Steve and Kai stared at each other through the glass. Then in one swift motion Kai leaped out of the tank, transformed in mid air and knocked Steve to the ground.

Adrian and Mak heard the crash of Steve's body hitting the floor.

They jumped out of the cots they were sleeping in and ran into the next room to find Kai on top of Steve, choking him.

"Kai no!" Adrian yelled.

Mak and Adrian pulled Kai off of Steve. He was unconscious but Adrian was relieved that he was still breathing. For a moment the three boys stood looking at each other.

Adrian took a step towards Kai, he was overjoyed to see his brother looking so healthy. "Kai, yer healed!"

Kai backed away from him. "Ya turned me over ta the humans, ya traitor!" he yelled.

"No Kai, I brought ya here so you wouldn't die!" Adrian said, trying to calm Kai. Kai was suspicious, but he had never felt so good in his life. His mind was clear, his muscles strong, he had no tremors.

"What did they do to me?" he asked, backing away from Adrian.

"It wasn't the humans!" Mak said, irritated, "It was the seunach!" Adrian wished once again that Mak would keep his big mouth shut.

Kai looked hard at Adrian but he didn't perceive any magical amulet on him. "Where is it?" he asked.

Adrian glared at Mak, who finally realized he should shut up. "I have it somewhere safe," Adrian said, trying to keep Kai's attention while Mak was moving behind him. Kai noticed Mak out of the corner of his eye. Kai quickly looked around. He saw an open door and bolted from the room.

Adrian and Mak ran after him. When Kai exited the building he sighted open water. He ran as fast as he could and dove into the safety of his native domain. Adrian and Mak knew they were too late to stop him.

Mak turned to Adrian. "What are we gonna do now?" he yelled, "We can't go back to the colony and we can't stay here!" Mak groaned and sank to the ground.

Adrian knew he should be panicking but for some reason he felt as if a great weight had been lifted off his shoulders. Kai is going to live, he said to himself. For as long as he could remember the knowledge of Kai's sickness and impending death had been a huge burden he had carried, but now Brooke had healed him.

As soon as Adrian thought of Brooke, he remembered his father's plan and a wave of fear washed over him. "We have ta warn Brooke about the doineann!" Adrian exclaimed and started back towards the center.

"Ahhhh!" Mak yelled, "We should have done that days ago! Then none of this would have happened!" He watched Adrian walk away completely ignoring his outburst. Mak sighed, got up and followed.

Brooke looked around her bedroom, she saw her stuffed toy bear with the missing ear, her sailing trophies, her science fair awards, pictures on the wall of her friends. It was all fiction. I'm not even human. My whole life has been a deception, she said to herself.

Brooke got up and walked over to her dresser. She stared at herself in the mirror. She saw a girl with blonde hair, blue eyes and freckles. "You are a lie," she said, tears running down her cheeks.

Brooke desperately needed to remember her mother. She pulled out one of the few pictures she had of her. Brooke was four and she and her parents were sitting in front of their house. She studied her mother. She was a beautiful woman, her voluminous hair was golden brown, her skin tan, and her eyes were a brilliant shade of blue. Tiny, pale Brooke was sitting in her mother's lap, her dad had his arms around them. They looked like a normal family. Brooke knew her life would never seem normal again.

She lay down on her bed holding the picture and closed her eyes. As she tried to remember her mother's face, a warmth spread over her body. Brooke could see her mother, she was sitting at their kitchen table with her dad, they were fighting. They stopped when Brooke came into the room.

Her mother got up and walked over to Brooke, she smiled and brushed her tousled blonde hair out of her eyes. Brooke noticed the golden bracelet on her arm.

"Come on, koritsi mou, back to bed," her mother said, picking her up in her arms. Her mother put Brooke tenderly into bed. She held her hand and sang a lullaby to her, Brooke not quite catching the tune.

Then the vision changed. Brooke was under the water, her mother was transformed, her blue eyes and her whole body were glowing. She was holding Brooke's arms so she couldn't swim. Brooke was panicking, she couldn't breathe. She heard her mother's voice in her head.

Breathe, Brooke, relax, it's okay honey, just breathe. Brooke tried to scream but no noise came out. Her last breath floated up as bubbles.

Brooke sat up gasping. She was back in her bedroom. Brooke began to cry again. Why did you leave me? Brooke thought learning more about her mother would answer that painful question but she still couldn't understand. I guess I wasn't that important to her. The realization was like a knife in her heart.

But why would she leave her bracelet, she wondered. Brooke pondered everything she knew about the bracelet. It belonged to her mother, it had called to her on her sixteenth birthday, somehow it could heal wounds and illnesses, but not always. It could make her breathe underwater but not without Adrian. She realized the bracelet only seemed to work around Adrian, she wondered why.

"Adrian," Brooke whispered. Just saying his name made her feel like she was back under the water straining for breath. I can't live without him, she thought in a panic.

There was a knock on her window. Brooke looked up and saw Adrian and Mak staring at her. She froze, she could feel her heart pounding out of her chest. She walked slowly over to the window and opened it, motioning for the boys to be quiet as they climbed into her room.

They stood there for a moment dripping on her floor. She was glad they remembered to hang onto the swim trunks Steve found for them. A big bruise was already forming under Adrian's eye where her dad had punched him, his hair was falling over his eyes and he looked so sad, giving him that irresistible lost little boy look.

Adrian took a step towards Brooke, but she took a step back. Adrian looked confused. "Are ya ok, lassie?" he asked.

Brooke just nodded. She felt like she was looking at Adrian and Mak for the first time. She saw their scarred, taunt bodies, their shining savage eyes. She looked at them now like she was part of their alien tribe, and it terrified her. Adrian saw the fear in Brooke's eyes.

His face clouded. "Did your father hurt you?" he asked.

Brooke shook her head no, but in her mind she was saying yes. Her father's lies, or half truths, had hurt her deeper than she could grasp at the moment.

Just hurry up and tell her! Mak yelled at Adrian in his head, *I wish we had just killed her and taken the seunach when we had the chance!*

Eist do bheul! Adrian yelled back at him.

Brooke heard the entire conversation in her head. Her eyes got wide with terror and she backed away from the boys and sat on her bed. "You were going to...kill me?" she gasped, "For this?" Brooke held up her arm.

Adrian's eyes got wide with fear. "How...ya heard that?" he asked.

Memories flooded Brooke's mind. All the times on the island when Adrian lied to her. His interest in the bracelet. How he tracked her to her house. How he lied and said he was the one with the power. How he used her to heal his brother, even though he must have known how it would hurt her.

"All this time, you just wanted the bracelet," she said, almost to herself.

Brooke looked down at the delicate band on her wrist. She realized that the connection she felt with Adrian was a sham. I don't matter to him, he never loved me. A feeling of isolation washed over Brooke like an ice cold wave.

"Brooke, no…" Adrian whispered.

Adrian didn't know what to say, what Brooke said was partly true. He had just wanted the seunuch from her, but then so much had changed. Mak looked at Adrian waiting for him to tell Brooke what they came to tell her. Adrian just stood there, paralyzed with grief.

Mak couldn't take it anymore, he was sick of humans and sick of the all the lying. "Our people are going to make a big wave and destroy all of this land. You and Zoe need to go away or you're gonna die," Mak blurted out. He surprised himself, mentioning Zoe.

"What?" Brooke asked, confused. She looked at Adrian. "Is that true?"

Adrian looked at Brooke with pain in his eyes. "Aye," he said, "My father convinced them all that the humans are causin the Guardians to attack us and are makin us sick."

Brooke's scientific mind took over in her shock. "Yes, that's true!" she said, "My dad and I think that there's some sort of pollution being dumped in the water that's making them act like that. If we can track the source we can stop it!"

Adrian took her excitement as a good sign, he went over to Brooke and took her hand. "The seunach has givin ya powers. You can come with me, we can go far away from here. I can keep ya safe!" Mak groaned loudly. Brooke pulled her hand away from Adrian.

She stood up and pushed him. "You don't love me!" she cried, "You just want this!" She held up her arm. "If I can't do what you want, you'll just leave me behind!"

Adrian shook his head. "No, Brooke, I do…" it was hard for Adrian to even say the words. Fear gripped his heart. "I do love ya," he almost whispered.

"No you don't!" she sobbed, "You'll choose them over me, you'll always choose them!" Brooke put her face in her hands and cried. Adrian not sure what was going on tried to put his arms around her. Brooke pulled away. "Get away from me! You're a monster!"

she screamed. All of her self hatred pouring out on Adrian.

Tom had heard the crying from Brooke's room but figured he had better let the storm pass however, hearing Brooke's yell propelled him into action.

He ran to her bedroom and pounded on the locked door. "Brooke!" he yelled, "What's going on?" Mak was out the window in an instant, but Adrian paused. Tom broke the door open to find Adrian standing next to a sobbing Brooke. Adrian held up his hands in surrender.

"I told you to stay away from my daughter!" Tom yelled at him, wishing he was the kind of dad who owned a shotgun.

"I only came ta warn ya about the doineann!" Adrian said quickly, hoping to avoid more beatings. Adrian realized the human probably wouldn't even understand the meaning of the word but what he said stopped Tom in his tracks.

"A doineann?" Tom asked.

"Aye," Adrian answered, his eyes wide in surprise.

"When?" Tom asked, tensely.

"The first big storm," Adrian said. Brooke had stopped crying and was watching this bizarre exchange. "Ya need ta leave," Adrian said. Then looked at Brooke sadly.

Tom walked over to Brooke and put his arm around her protectively. "We will," he said, "Now leave and never come back!"

Adrian risked taking a step towards Brooke. "Brooke, I…" Adrian wanted to make Brooke understand how he felt about her but he didn't know where to start.

Brooke took a deep breath. "Go away," she said, coldly, "I don't ever want to see you again!" Adrian looked like someone had kicked him in the gut. He turned and climbed out the window.

29 HUNTERS

Bronte swam through the silent corridors of the colony. He had been to the surface and felt the pressure changing, he knew a storm was on the way, a big one. Bronte's lips curved in a cruel smile, his plans would finally be realized. He sensed Kai swim up behind him but something was different.

Bronte whirled around always ready for an attack. Kai stopped, unsure of his father. Bronte circled Kai suspiciously, something about him was altered.

Father, I'm healed, Kai said.

How? Bronte asked, still not trusting his senses. Kai was loathe to tell him all the details of his encounter with the humans. He didn't want to seem weak to his father and he knew Bronte would only be proud of him if he had destroyed his captors.

It was a seunach, he said, simply. Bronte was on Kai in a flash. He held Kai by the throat searching his body with his eyes. *I don't have it!* Kai exclaimed, his eyes wide with fear.

Bronte released him. *Where is it!* he yelled.

Adrian has it, Kai said, sullenly rubbing his neck. *And he's a traitor!*

Kai added, angry and disappointed at his father's reaction.

What do ya mean? Bronte asked, still circling Kai. He felt a pain in his heart. Bronte knew what Kai was going to say.

Kai faced his father squarely. *Adrian's been on land with the humans, he's...he's committed the cronachd!* Kai wasn't sure of Adrian's guilt but he had seen him swimming with the human female and he was tired of Adrian getting all the attention from their father. Bronte gripped his spear until his knuckles turned white. Kai could sense his fury.

What about the seunach? Bronte said, menacingly, *Did ya see it?*

No, Kai answered, *He said he had it somewhere safe.*

Bronte stared hard at Kai. He could see and feel that Kai was indeed healed, he had a new strength and vitality. Bronte struggled against the desire he felt to hold his son close. He hated when those emotions rose unbidden into his mind, they only brought with them images of his dead wife. Bronte renewed his grip on his spear.

If Kai really was healed, it changed everything. Bronte no longer had to depend on Adrian as an heir. Kai was loyal to his people, Adrian was a traitor, and now there was a chance for Bronte to acquire a mighty weapon. Bronte knew he would have to kill his son, but if he gained a powerful seunach from it he convinced himself it would justify his actions.

Take me to your brother, Bronte said, looking at Kai with eyes of steel, *He must die.*

Kai stared at his father in horror. He had always been jealous of Adrian but Adrian had also been the only person in his life to show him any kindness. He had known the penalty for Adrian's crime but he didn't think his father would really go through with it. Kai thought Bronte had sworn him to secrecy to protect Adrian.

Though his body was now strong Kai had a sick feeling inside. However, he knew better than to argue with his father. Kai nodded and swam slowly to the bata portals, Bronte following. As the two figures receded into the darkness, Utari watched from a side passage, a smile on his lips and his yellow eyes glowing.

Tom threw another box on the floor of the living room and started to rummage through it. Brooke came out of her bedroom carrying a small duffle bag. She put it down on the ground.

Tom looked up at Brooke. "Did you call Zoe?" he asked.

Brooke nodded. "I left her a message, but dad we can't just leave!" Brooke said, her lip trembling. Tom stood up.

He lifted Brooke's chin so she was looking into his eyes. "Honey, we've been over this, I just want to make sure you're safe, then I'll come back here and try to get people to leave." Tom went back to looking through his box. "Not that anyone will believe me," he mumbled.

Brooke crossed her arms. "I am not leaving without knowing my friends are safe!" she said. Tom sighed.

He ran his fingers through his hair. "Brooke…" he paused, then he looked at his hand, "What the…"

Brooke walked up to her dad. "Ew! What is that smell?" she said, wrinkling her nose.

Tom looked down at the box he had brought into the house. He turned it around and noticed the corner was soaked with some kind of fluid. Brooke knelt down and smelled the box.

She almost gagged. "It smells like some kind of sulfur compound..." Brooke said.

Tom and Brooke looked at each other in amazement. "The pollution!" they both said at once.

"Where was this box?" Brooke asked, excitedly.

"It's from my lab, but..." Tom thought for a moment, "The movers!" he exclaimed. "Those delinquent guys DeLuca got to move my stuff, it has to be them!"

Brooke jumped up. "Okay, we just have to find them and follow them to the source and we can stop it!" she said, ready to run out the door.

Tom grabbed her arm. "Wait a minute! You are going to get on the train to Uncle Jimmy, I'm going to do the investigating. It's too dangerous, you know what's coming."

Brooke pulled her arm away. "But dad, if we can stop the pollution we can tell the Athlanmara and then they won't have to make the storm!" Brooke said, starting to tear up, "Dad, we can help everyone!"

Tom folded his arms and raised his eyebrows. "And how do you think you're even going to contact the Athlanmara?" he asked, sternly.

Brooke looked down. "I can tell Adrian and Mak," she said.

"No! I don't want you anywhere near that...boy! That's out of the question!"

Brooke walked up and took her dad's hand. "Daddy, I know you want to protect me and I don't want to see him either, but this is not just about us. We have to try to help everyone!" she said, boldly.

Tom looked at Brooke in astonishment. When did his scared little girl grow up to be this confident young woman, he wondered. He wasn't sure he liked the new independent Brooke. It terrified him.

Tom sank onto the couch and put his head in his hands. "Brooke, I can't...I can't lose you like I lost your mom!" he looked up at Brooke with tears in his eyes, "I just couldn't take it!" Brooke sat down next to her dad and held his hand as he continued. "I know I should have taken you far away from here, we should have gone somewhere away from the sea, but..." Tom wiped his eyes, "I always hoped your mother would come back someday and..." he looked at Brooke, "I wanted her to be able to find us."

Brooke hugged her dad. "You aren't going to lose me, daddy," Brooke said smiling at her dad through her own tears, "We are going to find some low life polluters and put their butts in jail!" Brooke stood up. "And we are going to stop this wave thing, even if I have to ruin my incredible breakup speech and talk to some lying merman!"

Just off the coast of Boot Key, Utari piloted his bata as close as he could to Bronte's craft without getting near enough to raise his suspicion. Utari sensed that Bronte's bata had stopped. He powered down his engine and floated silently, listening and sensing. He felt nothing. Utari decided to open his hatch and investigate. He swam out into the ocean and was attacked from both sides.

Bronte and Kai had been waiting for him. They each had hold of his arms but Utari wasn't just strong, he was also clever. With a powerful swipe of his tail he pulled both of his attackers down, forcing them to slam into each other weakening their grip. He tore himself free and pulled out his knife.

Bronte and Kai circled the lone Athlanmaran. *Why are ya hunting me, Utari?* Bronte asked.

Hunting? Utari said, smiling, *I was only going to inquire if you needed my help on your quest.*

What quest? Bronte said, keeping his voice even, though he was raging inside.

You found what I've been searching for, surely you were going to tell me about it! Utari spat out. Bronte just glared at his adversary. *After all,* Utari continued, *That was our agreement, I help you destroy humans, you help me find the seunach.* Kai glared at his father.

Bronte paused. *I don't know where it is,* he said, reluctantly.

Utari smiled and put his knife away. *Come, come, Bronte, we are allies,* he said reassuringly, *You know if we work together we can accomplish so much more.*

That's what ya told my mother, Bronte spat out.

Utari chuckled. *It was a good try, but we should have waited to collect all four of the seunach,* Utari said. *And you remember what happened with Sierna, she abandoned us when we needed her.* How could Bronte forget, it was the day that changed his life.

He looked down at the silver band on his arm. Silver from the Murrigh, copper from the Salasku, gold from the Thalahassis, and the fourth, that had been a mystery to them. There were only the three clans of the Athlanmara but there was rumored to be a fourth seunach, one made of platinum.

Morgan, his mother, and a very powerful suire, had told them if all the seunach were joined together she would have the power to melt the great ice and turn the world back to the way it should have been, a world of water and peace.

Morgan had the band of silver, Utari was willing to support her, she almost had the power to take over her clan, but Sierna had backed out at the last minute and fled with the seunach of her tribe. All their plans had come crashing down.

Bronte looked at the copper band on Utari's arm. He knew that the seunach Adrian had found belonged to Sierna, it had to be, hers was the only one with healing powers. If I could get that one and then kill Utari and get the copper, he thought, then I wouldn't have to rely on anyone to help me.

Bronte saw Utari eyeing him. He knew the same thought was going through his rivals head. Bronte made a slight motion to Kai. He realized he may never have another chance to find Utari outnumbered. Bronte and Kai closed in, Utari pulled his knife.

Suddenly, an electric arc pulsed through the water around the combatants. All three of the Athlanmara knew the cause instantly.

It's here, Bronte announced.

They fled to the batas, their personal feud could wait, there were humans to kill.

30 THE COMING STORM

The harsh sun beat down on the little back road near Tom's old lab. The heat and stillness were stifling as he tried to scrunch down further in the front seat of his little red Honda.

He handed the binoculars to Brooke. "Yep, that is the same white truck, I'm sure of it!" Tom said, excitedly. He was all keyed up from their undercover sleuthing.

Brooke peered through the binoculars. "Well, there's no plates. We still have to figure out who's behind all this," she whispered.

Tom took the binoculars back. "Steve confirmed that the box was soaked with hexachlorobenzene, I could identify the movers...probably," he said. "We should just give the information to the EPA and let them handle it."

"Dad, we have to find out what is going on and stop it so the Athlanmara will stop their plan! You know how long it takes for all that bureaucratic red tape!" Brooke whined.

Tom sighed. "You're right," he said ducking down further as a car drove by, "We don't know how much time we have." The two sleuths sat in silence for a moment.

"Dad," Brooke whispered, "What's a doineann?"

Tom shifted uncomfortably in his seat. "It means hurricane or big storm in Gaelic, but to the Athlanmara it's more than that." He looked at Brooke, then he furrowed his brow and avoided her gaze. "The Athlanmara have some sort of, I don't know, magical powers. They can control some aspects of the weather and the sea."

Brooke felt like she was in a dream. Is any of this real, she wondered. Can my mother really be some sort of mermaid with magical powers?

Tom pulled out his phone, hoping Brooke wouldn't ask anymore questions. He checked the weather for the twentieth time. "Brooke!" Tom whispered loudly.

"What?" Brooke asked, terrified that they had been spotted. Tom handed her his phone. She glanced at it and looked at her dad, her eyes wide with fear.

"Hurricane."

Brian Hale sat in the Coast Guard station staring at the weather system on his monitor, it had to be at least a Category 3 hurricane. He slammed his notebook down in frustration.

He had seen a lot of strange weather in his twelve years in Florida, but this storm seemed to come out of nowhere. In the last eight hours it had gone from a Category 1 hurricane to a Category 3 hurricane with sustained winds of over 120 miles per hour.

Brian got on the phone with NOAA. He had been involved in the

Coast Guard response for hurricane Katrina and Sandy, he knew advanced planning was essential. He had just made his tenth call of the morning when Tom Williams burst into his office.

Brian looked up surprised. "Tom…" he began.

Tom interrupted him. "You have to evacuate the Keys immediately!" he said, breathing hard from his dash up the stairs.

"Uh, Tom, there's no need to worry. I've been on the phone all morning, it looks like this storm will head north before the…"

"No…" Tom tried to calm himself and catch his breath, "It's not just the storm, there's going to be a massive storm surge, the Keys will be underwater!"

Brian looked hard at Tom, he could tell he was extremely agitated. "How do you know, Tom?" he asked, calmly.

Tom knew this part would be awkward. "I just…" he racked his brain for a plausible explanation, "The sea creatures, they just know these things and they are all going deep, and that's a sure sign of a massive storm surge!" he ended emphatically.

Though they weren't close friends, Brian had known Tom for years. He had always considered him an absent minded professor sort, but not actually crazy. Brian wasn't sure how to respond to this outrageous suggestion.

"Well, Tom, you know I can't evacuate the entire population on your hunch," he said. Tom's face fell. Brian got up and put his hand on Tom's shoulder. "Look, I've been through a few hurricanes Tom. We have plenty of data on this storm and safety procedures in place," he looked Tom in the eyes reassuringly, "It's gonna be okay. If I hear anything about an evacuation, I'll call you right away on your cell."

Tom looked down at the floor. He thought of all the innocent people who were going to die, his neighbors and friends. Tom looked hard at Brian. "You're not gonna see this coming Brian," he said with an eerie calm, "At least get your family out, please, I'm begging you."

Tom turned and walked slowly from the room. Brian wasn't a superstitious sort like other sea captains, but the look of certainty in Tom's eyes sent chills up his spine.

He pulled out his cell phone and dialed. "Lisa honey, how bout you and the kids go visit your sister for a few days?"

"What?" Zoe yelled.

Brooke had finally tracked Zoe down at the local nail salon and was trying to explain the dire situation to her. "Keep your voice down!" Brooke whispered.

"So they are trying to kill everyone now, not just you?" Zoe asked. The manicurist looked up shocked.

Brooke and Zoe looked at her and smiled awkwardly. "It's just boyfriend trouble," Zoe said.

Brooke punched her arm. "Zoe!" she said through gritted teeth. "We're just talking about a movie," Brooke said to the manicurist. "We need to go!" she whispered loudly in Zoe's ear.

"But my nails aren't dry!" Zoe whined.

"Come on!" Brooke said, grabbing Zoe's arm and dragging her outside.

The girls walked down the street towards Zoe's house, Zoe walking like a duck in her flip flops trying to save her pedicure.

Brooke tried to get Zoe to move faster. "So you have to get your family out of here now, before the storm hits!" Brooke said, anxiously.

"Well, what are you going to do?" Zoe asked, trying not to panic.

"My dad and I are going to try to catch the polluters, then maybe the Athlanmara will stop their plan."

"Maybe?" Zoe exclaimed. "Even if you can stop the polluters, how are you going to tell the fish people?" Zoe could tell that Brooke didn't want to answer her, then she realized why. "No!" Zoe exclaimed, "Brooke, that is not a good idea!" Zoe stopped dead in her tracks. "You cannot talk to that lying creep! Remember what he did to you?"

"Well, how else am I going to get them the message? I don't know that many mermen!" Brooke yelled, exasperated. Brooke looked at Zoe with her big blue eyes. "Will you come with me?" she asked, timidly. Then she looked down at the ground. Brooke felt bad for getting Zoe involved in this mess.

Zoe put her arm around Brooke. "Of course! What are friends for but to be there when you have to talk to your hot, merman ex-boyfriend about not destroying the world?"

They looked at each other and laughed.

Adrian and Mak swam slowly through the brilliant Caribbean water, the beauty and sparkling sunlight mocking Adrian's dark thoughts. Adrian was thinking it would have been better if the shark back at the island had just finished him off. A few minutes of excruciating pain seemed better to him than the unending agony he was enduring now.

To have finally experienced a deep connection with another person and then have that taken away was too much for him to bear. Adrian knew that he and Mak had nowhere to go. They couldn't return to the colony, he was sure by now Kai had told everyone what they had done and he and Mak would be killed on sight.

Maybe it's for the best Adrian thought, I might as well just go back and get it over with. He looked over at Mak and felt a stab of guilt. He knew the only reason Mak was in trouble was because of his loyalty. He had to do what he could to keep Mak safe and stop feeling sorry for himself.

Without warning, Adrian saw Brooke, she was under the water by her dock, she looked scared.

Adrian! she called in his mind. Adrian froze.

Mak turned and looked at him surprised. *What's wrong?* Mak asked.

Adrian! Brooke called to him again.

Adrian looked at Mak, his eyes wide. *Did ya hear that?* Adrian asked him.

Mak narrowed his eyes in suspicion. *No,* he said.

Adrian took off, heading back the way they had come. *Brooke needs me!* he yelled to Mak.

Mak shook his head and followed. *Of course!* he muttered. Mak was angry that they never seemed to put this human fiasco behind them, but he secretly hoped to see Zoe.

The sun beat down on the water of the little bay. The normally placid water was getting rough. Zoe peered down at the motionless form in the shallows. Finally, Brooke pulled herself out of the water and threw her snorkel down on the dock.

"Well, did it work?" Zoe asked concerned, "You were down there like ten minutes! I was going to jump in after you!"

"I'm fine," Brooke sighed, drying her hair with a towel, "I think it might have worked," she added as she looked out over the water. "I saw him swimming with Mak and I called his name in my mind." She shook her head, "I don't know! I just don't know what else to do!"

Brooke sat on the dock, pulled her legs up close to her body and laid her head on her knees. She felt small and helpless in a world that had suddenly become crazy and unpredictable. Brooke remembered how upset she had been on the last day of school because kids had laughed at her. How trivial that seems right now, she thought.

"This is kind of freaking me out," Zoe said, "I don't get how you can see each other or how you made his brother get better."

Brooke avoided Zoe's gaze. She couldn't handle getting into her dad's revelation with Zoe right now. She had to focus on saving as many lives as possible.

Zoe snorted. "But I guess when you discover some mythical creature weird things start to happen!"

The girls sat in silence for what seemed to Zoe to be hours. They checked the weather a million times not seeing any change. However, the high winds, choppy water and advancing clouds foretold of the storm to come.

Zoe had distracted herself with her phone but now she felt like she couldn't take another second of the tense waiting. "I swear, if those characters don't show up in like two minutes I'll…"

"You'll what?" Mak asked, pulling himself up on the dock behind her.

"Ahhhhh!" Zoe screamed dropping her phone in the shallow water. She punched Mak in the arm. "My phone!" she yelled.

Mak grinned.

Adrian came up out of the water and handed Zoe her phone. He pulled himself up onto the dock and glanced at Brooke tentatively. Brooke kept her eyes on the dock as she handed them a couple of towels.

"Shoot!" Zoe exclaimed wiping her phone furiously on her shorts.

Adrian faced Brooke, she could barely look at him. She could sense his desire. "Are ya alright?" he asked, softly. Brooke nodded, being this close to Adrian unnerved her. All the things she had planned to say fled her mind. "Ya called me," Adrian stated. He looked at her strangely, "Only powerful suire can…" he trailed off looking at the shining band on her arm.

Brooke was trembling, it took all her self control not to reach out and take Adrian's hand. "There's a storm…" Brooke began, then she thought, duh, he already knows that, "I…I mean we…my dad and I have found where the pollution…well, we found out who is polluting…"

Mak started to edge closer to Zoe while she was trying to get her phone to work. He leaned down and smelled her hair.

Zoe looked up. "Get away from me, Lurch!" she said, pushing Mak back. She saw Brooke struggling and remembered she was supposed to be her wingman.

Zoe got up and walked over to Adrian. "Look, Aquaman," she said to Adrian, "We can stop the polluters which will stop the Guardians or whatever from attacking your people so you.." she poked Adrian in the chest, "Need to go call off your merman army from making this freaking giant wave. Got it?"

Adrian looked at Brooke, her face was red with embarrassment. She just nodded to confirm what Zoe said.

Mak snorted. "We are not going back! It's because of you they will kill us!" he said, angrily.

Adrian was torn, he knew Mak was right, going back was suicide, but he also knew trying to stop the Athlanmara was the right thing to do. He wouldn't mind facing his death if he could just make Brooke understand how he felt about her. Adrian took a step closer to Brooke, she backed away.

"Brooke, I…" he said.

Brooke took a deep breath. "Just please, please, try to stop them," she said. She reached out to touch Adrian's arm, then pulled her hand away.

Adrian looked into Brooke's eyes and saw her fear. He realized she didn't trust him. He knew Brooke had no reason to trust him after he had lied to her and used her to heal his brother. His heart felt like a lead weight. Maybe if I can save the humans she will believe that I care about her, he thought.

He clenched his fists. "I'll go. I'll try and stop them," he said.

"Adrian, no!" Mak exclaimed as Adrian dove into the water. Mak looked at Brooke with anger. "You just killed him!" Mak yelled.

Brooke's heart stopped. What have I done, she asked herself. Would his own people really kill him just for talking to me? She was mad at Adrian but she didn't want him dead. I love him.

The thought surprised her and scared her too. Loving someone gives them the power to hurt you, she thought. It's what Brooke had tried so hard to protect herself from all these years. Now Adrian is in danger. I could lose the person I love the most...again. The thought was suffocating.

Mak looked at Zoe with pain in his eyes. "They will kill us both and the wave will come anyway!" He dove into the water after Adrian.

Abruptly, Brooke's phone made a loud piercing, siren sound. It was her storm app. She looked at Zoe with terror. "It's here!"

31 VILLIANS

The silvery bata came to a stop in the dim depths of the North Atlantic. Adrian and Mak silently entered the sea and approached the outskirts of the colony cautiously. Adrian glanced at Mak. He had tried to persuade his friend to let him go alone but Mak had just glared at him and kept following. Adrian felt guilty for once again putting his friend in danger but he was also grateful, he didn't want to face death alone.

The boys could see that there was a lot of movement around the colony. Groups of Athlanmara were forming and splitting off and reforming but the bulk of the population was moving off to the West towards the land. Adrian had no idea how he was going to prevent the disaster that was already in motion. His only idea was to find the Builder and get his advice.

He turned to Mak. "You don't need ta come Mak, I can…" Mak suddenly shoved Adrian as hard as he could. A spear went whizzing past Adrian catching Mak in the side. They both spun around and saw Kai fleeing. Mak was after him in a flash, trailing blood. Adrian was about to follow when he was grabbed from behind.

Ya worthless traitor! Bronte said, tightening his grip on Adrian, *Where is it?* he yelled.

What? Adrian asked, knowing exactly what his father was after.

The seunach! I know ya have it!

Adrian's mind was reeling, if his father ever found out about Brooke and the seunach, she was as good as dead. For once Adrian was glad he wasn't part of the mental oneness of the Athlanmara. His father couldn't sense anything from him, his secret was safe.

I don't have it, Adrian said.

Who does? Bronte growled.

In one great effort Adrian twisted his body and sunk his sharp teeth into Bronte's shoulder. His involuntary pain reflex gave Adrian the opportunity to escape his grasp. The combatants were separated, circling each other, knives in hand.

Bronte was almost proud of his son for besting him, but that didn't change his objective, to find the seunach and kill Adrian. Adrian held his hands out, trying to make peace with his father.

Ya don't have ta do this, Adrian said, *I found out what is makin the Guardians attack and I stopped it!* He had total faith that Brooke would be able to do what she said, he just hoped his father would listen. Adrian knew he didn't have much chance of beating his father in a fight.

Bronte sneered and kept circling. *How did ya discover that, your precious humans tell ya?* Bronte dove left and slashed at Adrian. Adrian kicked back hard with his tail barely keeping out of his reach. *Was that before or after they captured your brother so they could cut him apart like an animal?* Bronte sneered.

No! They helped him. Adrian exclaimed, *Kai is healed!*

Bronte rushed at Adrian. Adrian blocked his knife hand but Bronte twisted quickly and drove his knife into the back of Adrian's left shoulder. The pain was excruciating. Adrian could barely move his left arm. He slashed at Bronte but his father had already darted out of reach.

Adrian's heart was pounding. He could feel the blood pouring out of the deep wound on his back. It was all he could do to keep out of Bronte's reach.

Mak came up behind Adrian, he had chased off Kai easily enough, but he hesitated to get in between Adrian and his father. Duels in Athlanmaran culture were a matter of honor and others were not allowed to interfere. Also, Mak had seen Bronte go after both of his sons many times but he knew that as soon as they submitted to their father he would relent.

Bronte slowed down and lowered his knife, trying another tactic. *Tell me where the seunach is and I won't tell the colony what you've done.*

Adrian slowed his swimming, though he didn't lower his knife. Mak felt relieved, *if no one in the colony knows maybe we won't have to die,* he thought.

Call off the doineann and I'll tell ya, Adrian said, cautiously.

Bronte laughed. *You still care about the humans?*

Quicker than lightning, Bronte dove at Adrian. Before he could react Bronte wrapped his strong tail around Adrian and had his knife at his neck. Adrian could feel the sharp blade pressing into his artery. In shock, he realized that this time his father was going to kill him.

Nothing will save them now, I made sure of that. My earthquake will make Utari's triumph look like nothing, Bronte crowed.

Adrian felt chills run up his back, he knew instantly what his father's plan was. He was going to blow up the generators. Brooke, Adrian said to himself. He wasn't afraid of his own death, all he could think about was that Brooke was in danger. Who will save her if I'm dead, he agonized.

It's on the land! Mak cried out. Mak hoped that Bronte would call off the disaster long enough to search for the seunach.

Mak! Adrian yelled.

Bronte glared at Mak, then he looked down at the band of silver on his own arm. Realization came over him, Adrian had given it to the human girl. He didn't have much time. Bronte released Adrian and fled. He knew he could deal with Adrian later. Finding the seunach was his priority now.

Mak! What were ya thinkin? Adrian cried. He was terrified for Brooke.

Well, it wouldn't help anyone if you were dead! Mak said, stubbornly, *And he doesn't even know who she is.*

Adrian knew that was true. They had known who Brooke was and even had her numbers and it had taken he and Mak days to find her. Now they had two potential disasters to deal with.

Adrian wanted to rush off to protect Brooke but he would have to trust that Brooke was safe from his father for the moment. He had to make sure Brooke was protected from the potential tsunami.

My father is going to blow up the generators, Adrian said to Mak.

What? Mak exclaimed, *That would destroy the entire colony!*

Adrian ignored Mak's outburst. *I'll stop the explosion, you go stop the doineann. Then we'll meet back at Brooke's place.* Adrian turned to go.

Wait! Mak cried, *How am I going to stop them?* he asked Adrian, his eyes wide with fear. Mak had just gone along as Adrian's back up, he didn't know what to do alone.

Adrian started to swim away. *You'll think of somethin!* he yelled over his shoulder as he disappeared into the depths.

Cac! Mak exclaimed. He would rather face a shark frenzy. He knew he needed help. He needed a leader, someone who always knew what to do, someone bossy. A smile spread across his face. Zoe, he said to himself. Mak took off back towards the land.

The wind was starting to pick up as Brooke and her dad drove down Highway 1 back to his old lab. There was no mistaking now that a storm was on the way, and it was a big one.

Brooke looked up at the darkening sky. "We don't have much time!" she yelled over the wind.

Tom nodded grimly. "We're gonna have to do more than just get some evidence if we're going to stop the doineann," he said, glancing at his backpack in the back seat.

Inside his backpack Tom had magnesium flash bombs and a few Molotov cocktails. Brooke had never seen this side of her dad before, this radical environmentalist, Indiana Jones type guy. She was a little scared but she also had never felt so close to her dad before. It was as if he could finally be himself with her, now that the big secret he had been keeping from her so long was out in the open.

They turned on the little back road in the warehouse district and pulled off a few yards from Tom's old lab. They got out and ran down the street and hid behind a dumpster. The warehouse looked deserted. They ran up to the door and Tom pulled out a bolt cutter and cut the lock on the door. They ducked inside.

In the gloom they could see that almost the entire warehouse was full of rank smelling barrels. Tom grabbed a few specimen containers and collected samples of the chemicals spilling from the barrels while Brooke got out her phone and took a video of the warehouse.

"Send that to Zoe and the EPA, right away," Tom said. Brooke nodded surprised at his composure. She had a feeling her dad had done stuff like this before.

She sent the video to Zoe then remembered her phone wasn't working. She sent it to Jackson with a text telling him to get it to Zoe.

Tom stuffed the samples in his backpack. "But how are they dumping it," he said, rubbing his temples.

In a flash, Brooke remembered what Jackson had said about the strange goings on at the DeLuca shipyard and how Mr. DeLuca had insisted that her dad leave this warehouse.

She pointed to the window. "Dad, the DeLuca shipyard."

Tom ran to the window and saw a fishing boat bobbing in the waves at the boatyard marina. "Of course!" he exclaimed, "Come on!"

They ducked out of the warehouse and ran across the street to DeLuca's shipyard. The office was closed. They ran through the boatyard and cautiously approached DeLuca's warehouse. They could hear voices inside the warehouse. Tom and Brooke hid behind a dry docked fishing boat to listen.

"Forget about the storm! I can't afford to let this crap build up around here. You dump this load today or else!" they heard DeLuca yell at an unseen hireling.

"I knew that guy was a crook!" Tom whispered to Brooke.

Brooke was in shock, she couldn't believe that someone she knew, Chris' dad, the mayor of her town, was so evil. She felt anger rise up inside of her thinking about all the poor sea creatures he had harmed, not to mention putting Adrian and his people in danger. Oh yeah, she thought, they're my people now too. The thought made her queasy. She took a deep breath. Focus, Brooke, she told herself.

Brooke took out her phone, panned DeLuca's shipyard and quickly sent the video to Jackson. Tom reached into his backpack carefully, taking out a flash bomb.

"I'm gonna go in there, surprise them and then disable the boat." He handed his backpack to Brooke. "You take the evidence and that video to the police and tell them what is going on. They will have to do something if you tell them I'm in danger."

Brooke looked at her dad, her eyes wide with fear. "No, dad! You can't go in there alone!" Tears started to run down Brooke's cheeks. "What if something happens to you?"

Brooke felt like she had just gotten her dad back. She couldn't lose him now. She would be absolutely alone without him.

Tom smiled and brushed a tear off her cheek. "Sweetie, it's fine. They're just low down polluters, they're not murderers. I've done stuff like this before." Brooke tried to be brave and stop crying.

"Now go!" Tom said.

Brooke stood up, turned around and ran straight into Raffe. He grabbed her and put a rough hand over her mouth before she could scream.

Tom jumped up. "Hey!" he yelled. But before he could take a step towards Brooke's abductor he was hit on the head from behind by one of DeLuca's men. He crumpled to the ground unconscious.

Paul DeLuca walked out of the warehouse and took in the scene. "What the...?" he exclaimed.

Raffe cackled in Brooke's ear. "Looks like we got a couple of trespassers!"

Paul walked over, picked up Tom's backpack and pulled out the containers full of chemicals. "Stupid meddling scientist!" he yelled at Tom's unconscious form.

Paul glanced at Brooke struggling in Raffe's arms. He sighed and ran his fingers nervously through his hair. This whole thing was getting out of control. He just wanted to make some extra money and now this. He knew Tom and Brooke couldn't be bought off. He ran through the scenario of letting them go in his head. He couldn't do it, he would lose everything.

Paul looked out at the ocean, the storm was getting worse. Well, people die in storms everyday, he said to himself.

"Take care of it, Raffe," Paul said, wearily.

Raffe laughed. "Sure thing, DeLuca," he said, "I know what to do."

Paul walked back to his car as two sailors picked up Tom's senseless form and drug him to the boat.

Raffe pulled Brooke's head around so he could look into her frightened eyes. "This isn't my first time dumping a body," he said, menacingly. "Don't worry, I make sure they stay down." Raffe laughed at her terrified reaction.

Brooke felt like she was going to faint. She couldn't believe what was happening. Not only had she and her dad failed in their mission, they were going to die.

Raffe started dragging her to the boat which was beginning to pitch wildly in the rough water. Brooke had to think fast. I have to leave some evidence, she thought.

Brooke started kicking her legs, trying to knock off her shoes. It worked, one shoe fell to the ground unnoticed by Raffe who was doing his best to keep her under his control. Her hope was that Zoe would come looking for them, find the shoe and know she was in trouble. At the end of the dock Brooke kicked off her other shoe hoping again that her kidnappers wouldn't notice, luckily they didn't.

Raffe threw Brook and her dad into the back of the boat next to the noxious barrels and duct taped their wrists, ankles and mouths.

Raffe rubbed his hand on Brooke's bare thigh. "Too bad we don't got more time," he sneered, "I coulda given you one more thrill before you died."

When Brooke desperately tried to get away from Raffe, he burst out laughing. Raffe started to run his hands over Brooke's shorts. Her heart was beating out of her chest with fear. But Raffe just pulled her cell phone out of her shorts pocket.

"You won't be needn' this," he said, and threw the phone overboard. He found Tom's phone and threw that in the water too. Raffe pulled Brooke's hair away from her face, he pursed his lips in a kiss, then he cackled again and walked away.

Brooke started to cry which made it very hard to breathe through her runny nose. She scooted closer to her dad and saw blood matted in his hair. She closed her eyes, she wanted to curl up in a ball and escape.

Come on Brooke, she chided herself, think! Suddenly, she knew what to do.

Adrian! she called in her mind, *Adrian!*

Brooke worried that she had to be underwater to make him hear her. A chill ran up her spine, as she realized that she and her dad would be underwater soon.

Adrian, help! she cried out again.

Brian Hale rubbed his tired eyes, he had been working frantically all day making preparations for the storm with his crew. He looked at his computer screen again. He still couldn't believe how crazy this weather system was. Normally, a storm would build up out at sea then make its way slowly towards the coast, usually heading up towards the Carolina's. But this storm seemed to stay in one place, off the Southern coast of Florida and just build and build. It was unnatural.

He looked out the window. The wind was whipping the palm trees into a frenzy, the waves were pounding the dock, he shuddered. This was only the edge of the storm. It wasn't like he hadn't been through some terrible storms before. It was Tom's words that kept echoing in his head. He knew he had to push harder for an evacuation order.

Brian sighed and picked up his radio again. "Commander, this is Master Chief Hale."

The bata ran slow and almost silent along the floor of the deep ocean. Adrian's sunken, glowing face peered out into the gloom looking for another generator. He knew his father's plan was to blow up the generators but he wasn't sure where he planned to begin the explosion. Adrian decided to start his search at the generators farthest from the colony. It seemed like the best bet as he knew his father was hiding his plan from the others.

Adrian had shut down four generators and unhooked pipes and he was following the pipe trail to the next one. In a few moments, a large structure appeared out of the darkness. Adrian stopped the bata and listened, all was deathly silent in the crushing depths. Adrian opened the hatch and approached the softly humming generator. He opened the control box and slowly began to pull the lever to shut off the power.

Suddenly, Adrian was hit from behind and smashed into the hard metal of the machine. He tried to turn around but his attacker held his neck in a vise like grip.

Traitor! Nereus spat out, *You deserve to die!*

Adrian sensed Nereus' arm swing back for a death blow. He had no time to think. Adrian felt a small metal latch under his hand. He pulled it open. A powerful stream of hot water hit Nereus in the face. He cried out and released his hold on Adrian.

Instantly, Adrian pulled out his knife and stabbed Nereus in the tail. Nereus slashed back viciously, catching Adrian in the back. Adrian whirled around as fast as he could, just in time to ward off Nereus' next attack. The two aquatic forms struggled slowly and silently in the pressure of the dark abyss.

The opponents were evenly matched, Nereus, though stronger

than Adrian, couldn't match the youth's agility and cleverness in battle. Nereus also couldn't anticipate his adversary's moves as Adrian had no mental connection with his race. The combatants each held the other's knife arm. Nereus head butted Adrian's injured shoulder causing him to flinch.

Nereus broke free of Adrian's grasp and stabbed downward towards his chest. Adrian managed to fling himself backwards to avoid certain death but his attacker's knife drove deeply into his tail. Adrian churned up the sediment temporarily blinding Nereus. Then he charged slashing Nereus from hip to shoulder. Nereus backed off for a moment, glowing brightly, trying to catch his breath.

Adrian was feeling light headed from blood loss. The pain from his wounds was trying to take over his mind. He looked down at his tail and saw blood slowly flowing into the frigid water. He knew that Nereus wasn't going to stop until he was dead. The notion of fleeing passed through his consciousness, but then he thought about Brooke. Adrian was the only one who could stop his father's deadly plan.

Adrian gritted his teeth, he would fight to the death for Brooke. He tightened his grip on his knife and charged. Adrian could see the light of anger in Nereus' eyes as he approached. All at once, there was a thump and Nereus went limp.

Adrian stopped. He saw Gursel behind Nereus holding a rock in his hand. Adrian tensed, ready to face this new threat but Gursel just dropped the rock and looked at Adrian with a face as gaunt as death. Inexplicably, Gursel moved towards the generator and pulled the lever to shut it off.

Still wary, Adrian kept his distance from Gursel. *What are ya doing?* Adrian asked, amazed at this turn of events.

Gursel looked at Adrian with sadness in his hollow eyes. *There are some I love that aren't part of this sphere,* he said.

Adrian was shocked, he thought he was the only traitor. The realization that other Athlanmara had dealings with humans gave him hope. There were so many questions he wanted to ask Gursel but he knew they would have to wait.

How many more generators are hooked up? Adrian asked tensely. He chafed at how long his mission was taking. He was worried that Mak wouldn't be able to stop the doineann and Brooke would still be in danger.

I will disable them all, Gursel said.

Adrian wondered if he could trust his father's lieutenant. He decided he should assist Gursel with the tedious operation. All at once, a vision of Brooke flashed into his mind.

Adrian!

He heard her terrified call in his mind. He saw through Brooke's eyes. Her legs were bound, her father was beside her, bound and unconscious. The wind was blowing rain and seawater in her face. He saw evil looking humans with guns on a boat.

Adrian was filled with fear. *Brooke!* he yelled. Gursel looked at Adrian strangely. *How do I find her?* Adrian asked without thinking.

He looked at Gursel helplessly, realizing that the Athlanmaran would never be able to aid him. Yet, it was almost as if Gursel could read Adrian's mind.

You will find her, he said, *Just clear your mind, reach out to her, your body will follow.*

Adrian looked at him again in wonder. He had known Gursel for years, how had he concealed this part of himself from the society? But Adrian had no time to ponder these revelations. He nodded his head at Gursel and fled towards the bata. He had only one thought in his mind: Save Brooke.

32 VIDEO GAMES PAY OFF

The wind rose in fury, whipping trees about like crazed pom poms. The rain came down on the tiny town of Marathon in horizontal sheets pelting Zoe as she took another box to the family car.

"Brooke!" Zoe yelled into her mother's phone, "This is the twentieth message I've left for you! You are freaking me out! There is an evacuation order, where are you?"

Zoe looked up to see a runaway lawn chair shooting towards her like a rocket. She screamed and braced for the blow, closing her eyes, but nothing happened. She opened her eyes cautiously and saw Maksim standing in front of her holding the lawn chair three inches from her face. He threw the chair on the ground and stood in front of Zoe, his black hair blowing in the wind, rain running down his bare chest.

As Zoe stood gaping at him, her big brother Luis, hearing her scream, came running around the side of the house with a hammer in his hand. Luis saw a naked stranger standing in front of his little sister.

He ran towards the intruder. "Get away from my sister!" he yelled.

Zoe dropped her box and dove in front of Mak. "No, Lou!" she yelled, "He's a friend!"

Luis stopped his rush but he glared at Mak. "What the heck is he doing out here naked?" he asked, suspiciously.

Zoe racked her brain for a plausible answer. "He's Russian," she said. She quickly pulled off her rain jacket and shoved it at Mak. Mak, knowing the drill by now, sighed and tied it around his waist.

Luis scowled. "Well, he better get his naked Russian butt out of here quick," he said.

Zoe pushed her brother toward the house. "Just go help mami and pop with the shutters, get out of here!" Zoe glared at Mak. Just what I don't need right now, she thought. "What are you doing here?" she yelled at him over the wind.

"I need your help," he yelled back. Zoe rolled her eyes, grabbed his hand and drug him into the storage shed by her house. She slammed the door behind them blocking out the wind.

She turned to Mak. "What's going on?" she asked.

Mak looked at Zoe, her wet hair pushed back from her beautiful face, her drenched t-shirt clinging to her curvy form, her huge brown eyes. He wanted to grab her and put his lips on hers one more time before he died.

"Well?" she asked.

"I have to stop the doineann and…" Mak hesitated, he hated to seem stupid in front of Zoe, "I...wanted to make sure you were safe," he ended lamely.

Zoe folded her arms. "I'm fine! Where's Adrian?" she asked.

"He's stopping Bronte from blowing up the generators."

"What?" Zoe exclaimed. She felt she couldn't take another crisis. "Well, how are you gonna stop the merman army?" she asked, anxiously. Mak just shrugged. "What kind of an answer is that?" Zoe asked, starting to get hysterical, "First the tidal wave, now generators blowing up. Brooke went after the polluters and I haven't heard from her for hours, everyone on the whole East coast could die and…"

Mak grabbed Zoe and kissed her. She pulled back and looked at Mak. She didn't know whether she wanted to slap him or kiss him back but she was so terrified and his strong arms felt good around her body. Zoe put her arms around Mak's neck and kissed him passionately. Jackson burst into the shed.

"Zoe!" he yelled, "Hey!" he said, seeing Zoe in Mak's arms.

Zoe pushed Mak away and looked at Jackson guiltily. "What are you doing here?" she asked.

Jackson pointed at Mak. "Me? What's he doing here?" he retorted. Mak glared at Jackson wishing him at the bottom of the ocean.

"We are trying to figure out how to stop the Athlanmara," Zoe said, without thinking.

"Yeah, I can really see you were 'putting your heads together' on that one," Jackson said, bitterly. Then he asked, "Who are the Athlanma-whose-its?"

Zoe realized her slip of the tongue and tried to invent an excuse but then she had an idea. Who would be better at battling mythical creatures than someone who played video games and D&D all the time?

She decided to take the risk. "The Athlanmara are merpeople," she began.

"Zoe!" Mak yelled.

"It's okay Mak, Jackson can help us," she reassured him. Mak glared at her and folded his arms. He looked Jackson up and down menacingly. I can kill him if I have to, he thought.

A light of understanding crossed Jackson's face. "Wait a minute, he's a merman?" he asked, pointing at Mak.

"Yes!" Zoe said, excitedly.

Jackson snorted. "Nice try," he said.

Zoe gave Mak a meaningful look. Mak stared at Jackson. His eyes started to glow with a greenish hue. Mak held up his hand and sharp claws appeared on the ends of his fingers.

"Uh...okay," Jackson said, his mouth suddenly going dry.

Zoe smiled at Mak then told Jackson the whole story in a lightning fast speech. "So, now we have to figure out how to stop the merman army before they make a tidal wave and kill everyone!" she concluded.

Throughout the briefing Jackson had nodded his head solemnly, taking it all in. "So, just to be clear, Mak there is a merman, so…" he took a step closer to Zoe, "It's not like you can date him or anything, right?" Jackson smiled at Zoe, she punched him in the arm. "Ow!" Jackson said rubbing his arm.

"That is all you can think about at a time like this?" she yelled.

"Sorry!" he said, "I'm just trying to figure things out." Jackson started pacing. "One more question, and this is important," he stopped and looked from Mak to Zoe, "Are there any zombies involved?"

"Oh my gosh!" Zoe yelled, "No!"

"Well, there's mermen, I'm just asking!" Jackson said, defensively.

Zoe grabbed Jackson by the shoulders. "Think about how to defeat mermen!" she exclaimed.

"Okay, okay!" Jackson cried. Zoe let him go and he started to pace back and forth.

"Don't worry," Jackson said, "I've been preparing for this type of scenario my whole life. What you have to do is find the creature's weakness." He looked at Mak. "What are mermen afraid of?" he asked.

"Nothing!" Mak retorted. He looked at Zoe smugly.

Zoe moaned. "Come on! Stop being so macho, what will make them run away, or swim away... whatever?" she asked Mak.

He looked down at the ground. "The Guardians," he admitted.

"Wait, those crab things that Brooke was talking about?" Zoe asked. Mak nodded. Zoe started pacing. "Of course!" she said, "That's why they're so riled up in the first place!" She grabbed Jackson. "You're brilliant!" she cried.

Jackson smiled. "I am?"

"Yes, now we just gotta get the crab things to attack the Athlanmara and stop them from doing the wave thing!"

"How..." Jackson began.

Zoe interrupted him. "The pollution! That's what Brooke said made the crabs crazy. If we just get a bunch of the pollution stuff and dump it by the mermen, the crabs will come and chase them away, right?" she asked, excited by her plan.

Mak just looked at Zoe with eyes full of fear. He didn't want anything to do with the Guardians.

"But where do we get the stuff?" Zoe muttered to herself.

Jackson smacked his forehead. "Duh!" he exclaimed, "I forgot! That's why I came over here. Brooke sent me this weird video and told me to give it to you." He pulled out his phone and showed the video to Zoe.

"Those are barrels of chemicals!" she said.

"And that's DeLuca's shipyard," Jackson said, gravely.

Zoe looked at the boys. "Now we just need a boat," she said. Zoe smiled, "And I know exactly where to find one!"

A huge wave crashed over the bow of Chris DeLuca's beautiful yacht. Zoe was having trouble maneuvering the craft in the violent seas.

"I think I'm gonna be sick!" Jackson yelled from the back of the cabin.

"Oh shut up! We're gonna be fine!" Zoe replied. But her knuckles were turning white as she grabbed the wheel tightly.

Even Mak, who was used to the sea in all her moods, was feeling like he wanted to jump overboard and escape the fragile craft that was being tossed about like a leaf in the wind. Finally, through the rain, they could see the dock at DeLuca's shipyard. Zoe slowed down as much as she could but the waves were pounding their craft into the shore. For a moment it looked like the yacht was going to smash into the dock.

"Look out!" Jackson yelled.

By some miracle, the craft twisted and they bumped up against the side of the dock safely.

Zoe let out a sigh of relief and pried her hands from the wheel. "Told you!" she said to the boys.

They all scrambled off the craft and cautiously made their way down the dock towards the warehouse, not sure of what they would find. The place however, seemed deserted. At the end of the dock Zoe looked down and saw Brooke's shoe. She picked it up and exchanged a terrified glance with Jackson. They both started to run towards the warehouse.

"Brooke!" Jackson yelled.

Zoe grabbed his arm and put her finger to her mouth to get him to be quiet. "They could be holding them hostage in there!" she whispered loudly to Jackson.

Zoe and Jackson crept up to the warehouse door. Mak followed behind at a safe distance, not sure what his companions were up to. They looked in the door and saw nothing but a warehouse full of smelly barrels.

"Huh," Zoe said, disappointed and relieved to not find her friend.

"Ew!" Jackson exclaimed, "That stuff smells nasty, we really have to touch it?" he whined. Zoe ignored him, she was too preoccupied with the shoe in her hand. She walked a few steps trying to figure out why Brooke's shoe was there. Or maybe it's not even her shoe, she thought. Then she looked down. On the ground was another shoe. There was no mistaking it, the matching shoes belonged to Brooke.

"Oh..my..gosh!" Zoe said, as she picked up the other shoe,

"Brooke's been kidnapped!" she screamed. She looked down the dock and put two and two together.

"What?" Jackson exclaimed, running up to Zoe.

"Those jerks have taken Brooke and probably her dad onto their nasty boat and they are going to kill them!" Zoe said, distraught. She looked at Mak. "We have to do something!"

Mak sighed, he wished Adrian was there to tell him what to do. Zoe looked at the boys, they just looked back at her expectantly.

She realized it was up to her to figure out what to do. "Great!" she muttered, "Okay, I'm gonna go for help. You guys have to stop the wave thing or none of this will matter anyway." Zoe pointed at Mak. "You and Jackson load up the barrels, find the Athlanmara and dump the stuff all over them and keep a look out for the polluters and Brooke." The boys just stood there staring at her.

"Well, move it!" she yelled and ran towards the road. Zoe didn't look back. She was frantic with worry. She dialed 911 as she ran, but the call wouldn't go through. "Crap!" she yelled. It was like she was in a nightmare.

Zoe got to the main road but she could hardly see through the wind and driving rain. Suddenly, out of the downpour a black SUV approached. She waved frantically and stepped almost into the path of the oncoming vehicle. The car slammed on the brakes narrowly missing her. Zoe ran to the passenger side and the occupant rolled down the window.

"What seems to be the trouble, young lady?" said a distinguished looking man with a British accent.

33 I NEED A HERO

Another huge wave swept across the decks of the decrepit fishing boat. Brooke was slammed back into a barrel. She was glad she'd been able to rub the duct tape off her mouth as she gasped for breath.

She crawled back towards her father and pulled the tape off of his mouth with her bound hands. "Dad!" she yelled over the howling wind.

Tom groaned and looked up at Brooke. "Honey, are you okay?" he asked groggily.

"Yes, I'm fine." Brooke tried to hold back her tears, "But they said they're going to kill us, daddy!" Brooke couldn't help letting out a sob. Tom took a deep breath to clear his head. He looked around taking in the situation and his heart sank.

He turned to Brooke with tears in his eyes. "I'm so sorry, baby, this is all my fault." Tom was devastated by their plight but he was no quitter. He immediately started to tear at the duct tape around his wrists with his teeth. "Come on Brooke!" he said, "Try to get your hands free." The two captives worked at their bonds unmolested by the crew whose attention was totally encompassed by the raging storm.

Raffe entered the bridge, water running off him like a river. "Who cares where we dump this stuff! Let's just get outta here!" he yelled at the captain. Raffe wasn't much of a sailor under normal circumstances but the raging tempest was making him frantic.

"We're not even out of U.S. waters!" Eddy yelled back at him. "We gotta dump more than barrels this time and I ain't takin no chances!"

Raffe pulled out his gun and pointed it at Eddy. "Stop this boat now!" he screamed, "We are dumping it all here!"

Between the crushing waves Tom had finally gotten through the duct tape on his hands. He scooted up to Brooke and pulled the tape off of her hands. He was working on her ankles when one of the guards turned around and noticed them.

"Hey!" the guard yelled and made his way over to the captives brandishing his weapon. He grabbed Brooke by the jacket and drug her away from Tom.

"Leave her alone!" Tom screamed, trying to get to his feet.

Suddenly, there was a shot from the bridge. Tom looked up to see Raffe step out onto the bridge deck and throw Eddy's body into the raging sea. Raffe looked down and saw that Tom was almost free.

He ran down the ladder and grabbed Brooke. "You shut up and stay put!" Raffe yelled, "Or I'll toss her over right now!"

Raffe was frightening to behold. He had Eddy's blood spattered all over his face and a wild look in his eyes. Tom held up his hands in surrender and sat down. Brooke tried to fight her attacker. She twisted around and hit him in the face. Raffe threw her to ground and slapped her hard.

Deep below the surface of the raging sea Adrian felt the slap and saw the evil look on the human's face as he bent down towards Brooke.

"No!" he yelled, the sound echoing in the bata.

Rage filled every part of Adrian's being. His eyes glowed so brightly they looked like they burned with green fire. He looked up through the glass and saw in the distance the outline of a boat being tossed on the waves. Adrian opened the hatch and entered the ocean. He shot towards the vessel like a glowing arrow.

Not far away another craft was struggling to stay afloat in the tempest. Mak lugged an oozing barrel to the side of the heaving boat, splashing chemicals all over Jackson's skinny legs.

"Hey!" Jackson yelled, "This is not the mythical adventure I had envisioned!" he said angrily, trying to wipe off the nasty muck. Mak just glared at him and dumped the barrel into the churning waves. Jackson stared out into the storm. "You're sure my dying of cancer at seventeen will be worth it, right?" Mak just ignored him and reached for another barrel.

Jackson tried to help but he mostly just got in Mak's way. "So, won't this stuff like kill your people, too?" he asked.

Mak grunted as he moved the barrel. "It hasn't killed anyone yet," he replied, "Zoe said it just draws the Guardians. They're the killers."

"How do we know where the Athlamawhatsits are anyway?" Jackson asked as he tried to help Mak roll the barrel over the edge. Mak pointed out to sea. Jackson looked where he was pointing. He could just make out a slight glow on the distant waves. "Oh," Jackson gulped, "Can they see us?" Mak nodded. "Let's dump the rest and get out of here!" Jackson said, his voice cracking.

Mak pulled another heavy barrel to the side of the boat. Jackson put his arms around a barrel and pulled with all his might but it didn't budge. He stood up his cheeks red with embarrassment. He was glad Zoe wasn't around.

Jackson nervously backed toward the bow. "I better check the navigation equipment," he said earnestly, trying to escape his humiliation. Jackson entered the cockpit of the cruiser and glanced at the controls. What he saw made his heart stop. The dials were spinning around and the lights were sputtering on and off.

"Mak!" he yelled, "I think we have a problem!"

Mak jumped up the ladder to the cockpit. "What?" he growled.

Jackson pointed to the controls. "This is not good," he said.

Mak looked from the controls to the ocean. The glow was getting brighter. "We have to get out of here," Mak said.

Mak jumped down the ladder and frantically threw the last two barrels overboard. Jackson frowned, he was annoyed that Mak was so strong and handsome. But how could Zoe possibly date a merman, he pondered.

"Let's go!" Mak yelled, seeing Jackson frozen on the deck.

"Yeah! Okay!" he yelled back. Jackson tried to start the engine, it turned over once then quit.

Mak came up next to him breathing hard from his exertion. "Make it go!" he yelled.

"I'm trying!" Jackson squeaked. Jackson kept turning over the engine to no avail.

Suddenly, the wind and rain stopped like someone closed a door. It was deathly quiet. Mak and Jackson looked at each other their eyes wide with fear. All around their craft the ocean glowed with an eerie light. Mak ran to the side of the boat. His intention was to abandon Jackson and make a run for it, but as he gazed into the water he saw something that terrified him more than the Athlanmara. The water was teeming with Guardians. Their plan had worked.

Jackson jumped down the ladder and joined Mak. "We did it!" he shouted.

He tried to hug Mak in his exuberance but Mak shoved him to the deck. The glow disappeared as quickly as it had come and their craft was hit with a huge gust of wind and rain.

"Let's go!" Mak yelled.

"Right!" Jackson said jumping to his feet, "We still have to find Brooke and her dad!" Jackson ran to the cockpit, punched the engine. It roared to life.

Mak stared out at the churning water. "And Adrian," he muttered to himself.

The wind was getting stronger, the ancient fishing boat was making very little headway against the formidable storm. The first mate, Charlie, had taken over the bridge when everyone had seen what Raffe did to Eddy. He wasn't happy about losing his captain and taking orders from a psychopath with a gun but he figured he and the crew could take care of Raffe when they got back to land. He was just as desperate as Raffe to dump their load and make it back alive.

Charlie pulled back on the throttle and was about to give orders to the crew when he saw a sight he had never seen in his twenty-seven years on the sea. A beast, half man, half fish, shot up out of the water on his starboard bow. In mid air he saw the creature transform into human shape and land on the deck. The crew, as shocked as Charlie, stood paralyzed.

Adrian took advantage of the human's surprise. He grabbed the closest sailor and threw him overboard. The hapless sailors scream propelled the crew into action. They ran from the intruder and hid behind anything they could find, blindly shooting in the general direction of the monster.

"Adrian!" Brooke screamed, terrified he would be shot.

Adrian had expected this reaction. He quickly dove behind some barrels and made his way towards Brooke.

Raffe was stunned. He recognized Adrian as his attacker in the warehouse and he had seen Adrian and Brooke at the carnival. He instantly realized that she was the object the creature was after. He grabbed her around the neck, using her as a human shield and stood up.

"Hold your fire!" he yelled at the crew. The hail of bullets stopped. "Come out or I'll put a bullet in her head!" he screamed.

Adrian had crawled to where Tom was and saw that Tom had managed to free his legs. They exchanged a look, each knowing that the other would have his back.

"Adrian, no!" Brooke yelled, sobbing.

Raffe tightened his grip on her throat. "Shut up!" he yelled.

Tom nodded at Adrian and they both stood up to make a rush at Brooke's captor. They were immediately thrown to the deck as a luxury cabin cruiser slammed into the fishing boat. Mak and Jackson had found Brooke.

Mak jumped onto the boat and slashed the throat of the nearest criminal with his sharp claws. Adrian quickly regained his feet. He saw Mak go for another astonished victim bellowing at the top of his lungs.

Adrian smiled but he had no time for reunions. Raffe had also got his footing and was dragging Brooke to the back of the boat, his gun still pointed at her head. Adrian rushed after the pair, Tom at his heels.

"Stay back!" Raffe yelled, pointing his gun at Adrian. His back was at the gunwale. He had nowhere to flee.

Adrian walked towards Raffe slowly. He looked terrifying. His form was halfway between human and Athlanmaran, his eyes were glowing, his hair was blowing in the savage wind, his hands were sharp claws, he was bleeding from his encounter with Nereus and his father.

"What...the...the hell... are you?" Raffe stuttered, his eyes wide with fear. Adrian kept advancing slowly. "Stay back, you freak, or I'll shoot!" Raffe aimed the gun at Adrian.

Adrian's only thought was to save Brooke. Heedless of his own danger he lunged at Raffe.

"Adrian!" Brooke screamed. She pushed backwards with all of her might as the gun went off.

In that split second, Tom shoved Adrian out of the way. The next moment Adrian saw Brooke and her captor plunge off the back of the boat and Tom fall to the deck bleeding from the abdomen.

Adrian looked down at Tom distraught.

"Go save her!" Tom gasped, barely able to breathe. Adrian nodded and dove into the sea after Brooke.

Jackson tried hopelessly to keep the yacht near the fishing boat but in the furious waves the vessels just kept slamming into each other over and over. He knew he had to make a choice, stay in the relative safety of the yacht or take a risk and be the hero who saves his friend. Jackson maneuvered the cruiser as close as he could, he let go of the wheel and took a flying leap towards the fishing boat.

"This is for you Zoe!" he yelled. Jackson landed smack on his stomach on the edge of the gunwale. He fell to the deck, the wind knocked out of him.

Jackson groaned. "Being a hero sucks!" he gasped. He looked up to see Charlie coming at him with an ax. "Ahhhhh!" he screamed, too terrified to move a muscle.

Jackson saw a metal line weight fly over his head, then Charlie was lying at his feet, blood pouring out of a gash on his temple. He turned around to see Mak pick up a heavy pulley and hurl it at the next sailor. Jackson flipped to his stomach and began to army crawl towards the back of the boat where he had last seen Brooke.

He heard terrifying screams and yells from the sailors, amidst bursts of gunfire. This is just like Call of Duty, except I can really die, Jackson thought. He made his way around a pile of barrels and saw Tom Williams lying in a pool of blood. Jackson felt like he was going to throw up.

He took a deep breath and crawled over to Tom. "Are you okay, Mr. Williams?" he asked, his voice wavering.

Tom looked at Jackson, his eyes glazed with shock. "What are you doin' here buddy?" he asked, like Jackson had just showed up at his door.

Jackson saw the bullet hole in Tom's abdomen. "Crap!" he exclaimed. Jackson pulled off his shirt and tried to stop the bleeding. He pulled out his cell and prayed that he could get reception. The number rang.

"Jackson, you better get your butt home right now!" Brian Hale yelled, "Your mother is worried sick!"

"Dad!" Jackson yelled back, "I'm on a fishing boat in the middle of a hurricane and Mr. Williams is shot!" That got his dad's attention.

Being in the military taught Brian not to waste time with useless questions. "What are your coordinates?" he asked, tersely. Jackson gave him the last coordinates he could remember from the cruiser. "Try to stop the bleeding Jackson, I'm on my way."

The wild sea engulfed Adrian. He looked up at the surface and saw that Brooke had escaped from Raffe when they plunged into the water. She was swimming away from him as fast as she could. Adrian quickly shot up beneath Raffe, grabbed his legs and pulled him down. He continued to pull the villain down into the depths, until there was no chance Raffe could make it back to the surface.

Adrian, who had transformed back into his aquatic state, grabbed the murderer by the throat and stared into his terrified eyes. Adrian had endured many violent conflicts with his father. He'd had fierce battles with his Athlanmaran rivals, but never before had he felt the murderous rage in his heart that he felt looking at the pathetic human that had almost destroyed the one he loved most in the world.

Raffe struggled in his executioners grasp but he was no match for Adrian in his element. Adrian stared at Raffe with his glowing eyes then he released him and shot towards the surface to locate Brooke.

To Adrian's horror he saw a form shoot up beneath Brooke and pull her down into the darkness. Adrian, his heart in his throat, swam after them swiftly. As he got closer to Brooke he recognized her abductor, it was his father. He was dragging Brooke down deeper and deeper.

Adrian knew Bronte's plan, he had just executed it. He swam with all his might. Adrian could see the terror in Brooke's huge eyes. She was reaching out her hands to him. He could tell she was running out of air. Adrian knew that if he could just touch her she would be able to breathe.

Yet, Adrian, still wounded from his earlier battles, was tiring. He made one more herculean effort and reached out. He grabbed Brooke's hand and flipped his tail downward, breaking Bronte's grip on her ankle. He pulled Brooke close and made for the surface. Adrian knew he wouldn't be able to escape from his father while dragging Brooke along but he had to try.

Suddenly, he was hit hard from the side. Brooke flew out of his arms, and for a moment Adrian was stunned. He couldn't get his bearings. When his vision cleared, he saw Nereus circling him, spear in hand, a cold sneer on his face.

Quickly, he looked for Brooke and saw her immobilized in his father's arms, choking for air. In the moment it took for Adrian to locate Brooke, Nereus was on him. He held Adrian in his vise like grip and tied his hands together behind his back. Bronte swam leisurely up to Adrian, his prize struggling in his arms.

You may have stopped my plans today, but with this seunach there will be an end to all humans forever! Bronte gloated. Brooke could hear every word in her mind. It terrified her.

Adrian struggled fiercely against his bonds. *Brooke!* Adrian yelled, helplessly.

Bronte smiled, he could feel the prey in his arms getting weaker. *Don't ya want ta save your own people?* Bronte asked Adrian. *With the humans gone we'll rule the whole earth!* Bronte changed to his most charismatic voice. *Everything will be put back in order, like it was in the beginning!*

Ya can't just kill everyone! Adrian cried.

Bronte's face contorted in rage. *I will do whatever it takes ta save my people! I will sacrifice anything!* he yelled, looking hard at Adrian.

Brooke heard them arguing, but it was like she was hearing them from far away. As her oxygen ran out, her mind was floating away from her body. She heard a woman's voice singing.

> *The wind and waves, they call to me*
>
> *I see your face above the sea*
>
> *Below is life and company*
>
> *I'll leave it all to be with thee*

Brooke saw her mother's face. *Just breathe, Brooke, just breathe,* she said, smiling. Brooke's eyes rolled back in her head and she became as still as death.

Brooke, no! Adrian screamed.

Bronte let her go and she floated in the water, her beautiful hair spread around her head like a halo. In that moment Adrian realized he would do anything for Brooke. He would sacrifice anything for her, his family, his people, his life.

Adrian ripped his hands free from his bonds and lunged at Bronte. The two locked in mortal combat, Nereus circling the battle. Bronte hit Adrian hard in the back with his tail and clawed his chest with his free hand. Adrian's hold weakened.

Bronte reached for his knife. *You have betrayed your people*, Bronte rasped, *You are no longer my son.*

He stabbed Adrian in the chest with his wicked knife. Adrian backed away from Bronte blood spilling from his mouth. Bronte watched impassively for a moment, then he turned to Brooke. He reached out to take the seunach from her still body.

All at once, Brooke's eyes flew open. Starting from where the bracelet rested on her arm, her body began to glow brightly. Bronte and Nereus froze in shock.

Adrian! Brooke screamed loudly in their heads.

Bronte's face contorted in anger. He lifted his spear but before he could hurl it at Brooke, he heard a noise that brought terror to his heart, a loud clicking sound. The Guardians were almost upon them. Bronte and Nereus fled for their lives as Brooke swam to Adrian and held him in her arms.

Lassie, Adrian said weakly, *You're alive!*

Brooke choked out a laugh. *I guess so.* She grabbed Adrian tightly, *Hang on, I can heal you.*

No! Adrian exclaimed, *Swim, Brooke! Save yourself!*

Brooke just shook her head, though her heart was pounding with fear. *I'm not going to leave you, I won't run away this time,* she said. She closed her eyes. Her body began to glow even more brightly.

Adrian felt an intense heat course through his entire body. Strength flowed into Adrian as it left Brooke. It was over in a moment. Adrian's wounds were healed. He was glowing brightly but Brooke's light had almost faded.

Brooke! Adrian exclaimed, as he held Brooke's limp body, *Why did ya do that?*

She smiled weakly. *Because, I love you.* The clicking noises grew louder, the Guardians surrounded them. *Swim,* Brooke said, almost losing consciousness, *You can outrun them now.*

No! Adrian cried, his chest tight with anguish.

Adrian pulled Brooke close. In a moment the Guardians attacked. Adrian could feel their sharp claws dig into his tail. He tried to cover Brooke's body with his own but he knew he couldn't protect her. At least it will be over quickly, he thought.

Ironically, Adrian felt a deep peace. So this is what love is, he thought. It's not the yearning desire he felt for Brooke, it's about giving all you have to someone else. All the pain that Adrian had been through was worth knowing that love.

Through the screaming pain in his head, Adrian remembered a line he had read in a human book, 'It is a far, far better rest that I go to than I have ever known'. He knew his death was near. He looked into Brooke's serene face and kissed her.

Adrian felt a searing heat pulse through his body. There was a blinding flash and a sonic pulse so strong, he was momentarily stunned. Adrian shook his head to stop the ringing in his ears.

Everything was quiet. He looked around and saw lifeless crabs being swept away by the current. Adrian looked down at Brooke, she was unconscious but still glowing faintly. *Brooke, ya did it,* Adrian said, softly. Then he fled toward the surface with Brooke in his arms.

34 AFTER THE RAIN HAS FALLEN

The hot August sun beat down on the chaos the storm had produced. Palm branches were lying about like mammoth green snowflakes. Signal lights were dangling like derelict piñatas. Sand had been brought up from the ocean and deposited on every surface imaginable. But overall Marathon was in one piece, thanks to the little group ensconced in Brooke Williams house.

Brooke opened her eyes. She was lying in her bed. The sun was filtering through the curtains that were swaying gently in the warm breeze. She sighed and stretched. Every muscle in her body ached. Why am I so tired she wondered. In a flash, her memories came flooding back.

Brooke sat up. "Adrian!" she exclaimed, not even knowing if anyone was near.

Adrian jumped up from where he had been lying on the floor by her bed. "Brooke! I'm here." He kneeled by the bed and took her hand. "Are ya alright?" he asked, intensely searching her face.

"What happened?" she asked, holding her aching head, "How long have I been asleep?"

"Two days," he answered, "We were so worried for ya."

Zoe burst into the room. "Brooke!" She jumped on the bed and gave her friend a huge hug, "You're awake!" Steve, Jackson, Mr. and Mrs. Moreno and Mak came into the room. Steve sat on the edge of the bed and took her pulse.

"Where's my dad?" Brooke asked him fearfully.

"Brooke honey, your dad is gonna be fine," he said, patting her hand.

"What do you mean? Where is he?" she asked, looking from one face to the next.

Tina Moreno pushed Zoe aside. She sat on the bed and put her arm around Brooke. "Those low down dirty pirates, they shot him, but don't you worry niña, the doctors, they have fixed him up. He will be healthier than a pear in no time!"

"What? My dad was shot?" Brooke started to get out of bed, "I have to go see him!"

Everyone in the room, except Mak, yelled "No!"

Tina gave Brooke another squeeze. "You just stay here in bed niña. I will go fix you some food. You will feel better, then you can go see your daddy!"

Tina got up and she and Mr. Moreno left the room. With Zoe's parents gone the others began to fill Brooke in on all the details she missed.

"I saved your dad!" Jackson said, proudly, "Well, the Coast Guard did, but I helped!"

"I battled a whole army of humans by myself!" Mak chimed in.

"Well, remember boys, I was the one who came up with the idea that basically saved the entire world," Zoe boasted. Brooke looked at her quizzically. "The pollution Brooke!" she said, "Your video showed us where to find it and we dumped it on the Athlanmara and stopped the wave thing!"

"Oh, and you know what else?" Jackson interjected, "Mr. DeLuca got arrested and they confiscated his house and his yacht," Jackson looked at Mak, "Well, what's left of it."

Mak scowled at Jackson. "It was your fault!" he exclaimed to Jackson, "You showed me how to make it go, not how to make it stop!"

"It's not that hard dude," Jackson said, he mimed pushing a throttle up and back, "Go and stop." Mak's face turned red in embarrassment. "He just aimed the boat at the dock and ran right into it!" Jackson cackled.

"At least I was the one who found Adrian and Brooke!" Mak exclaimed. Brooke laughed.

Zoe ignored the boys. "And Brooke," she said, "We did more than just stop DeLuca, it turns out what was happening here was going on all along the East coast! Sweetie, you saved an entire ocean of creatures!" Brooke's face beamed.

She looked around at her friends. "We did it together," she said. Brooke took Adrian's hand and looked into his eyes. "And you saved me," she said.

Adrian looked down, ashamed. "I tried to save ya," he looked up at Brooke, "but I couldn't." He fingered the seunach on her arm. "It was you who saved us both from the Guardians," he said.

Brooke was astonished. She looked down at the seunach on her arm. The power that it contained frightened her. Maybe it would be better if I gave it to Adrian, she thought. After all, it did belong to his people.

Then Brooke thought about her mother. I guess they're my people too. The seunach was somehow connecting her to her mother, to her past and to her future. She looked at Adrian. What will he think when he finds out what I am, she wondered.

Brooke felt the old fear of rejection rise up in her mind. For a moment she wanted to run away again and not let anyone in. Brooke took a deep breath and decided to take a risk.

She looked intently at Adrian. "I have to tell you something," she said, quietly.

Zoe saw the serious look in Brooke's eyes. "Do you want us to leave?" she asked.

"No," Brooke said, as she looked around at her friends who had risked everything to save others, "I want you all to hear this." Adrian took her hand. "This bracelet, or seunach as you call it...it belonged to...my mother," Brooke looked at Steve, he nodded encouragingly, "Her name was Sierna. She was an Athlanmaran." Adrian's eyes got wide as he realized the significance of what Brooke just said.

"Wait, what?" Zoe yelled, "My best friend is a mermaid?" she exclaimed.

A huge smile spread over Jackson's face. "Cool!" he said.

Mak just stood in the corner of the room scowling. In Athlanmaran culture a half-breed was worse than a human. A confession of that sort in his world meant instant death. Mak left the room without a word. Adrian saw him go and guessed what he was thinking.

Brooke looked at Adrian waiting for a response, her heart pounding. Fear started to wash over her like a tidal wave. He's going to leave me, he's going to leave me, the thought pounded in her brain. Adrian let go of Brooke's hand. Her heart stopped. He leaned over and kissed her. A feeling of peace coursed through Brooke's body.

Adrian pulled back and looked into Brooke's blue eyes. He gave her a crooked grin. "I always knew there was somthin special about ya, lassie," he said.

The morning breeze was warm and gentle as it played with Brooke's hair. She and Adrian were sitting on the edge of Brooke's dock dangling their feet in the water. The sun sparkled off the tiny waves made by their movements.

Brooke's dad had been able to come home yesterday, the town was getting back to normal and she and Adrian had spent every moment of the last few days together. Everything felt...perfect. However, with Brooke's overactive brain, that feeling didn't last long.

Brooke looked down at her tiny feet and Adrian's large ones. What would it feel like to have a tail, she wondered. Even though it had been some time since she found out about her bizarre heritage she still didn't feel like it was real.

What's going to happen to me? Will I just randomly turn into fish shape? Will it change my personality? Will I abandon the people who love me, like my mother did? Brooke started to chew her nails.

Adrian noticed the nervous frown on her face. He tilted her chin up so she was looking into his eyes. Brooke sighed as she lost herself in the luminous green depths. He leaned down and kissed her, warmth spread from his body to hers. Brooke had never felt so happy. Mak walked up, he gave Adrian a meaningful look.

Adrian nodded. "Brooke, I have ta leave," he said.

Brooke's heart stopped. "No!" she cried, "You can't go, I need you!"

Adrian took her small hands in his. "I have to find out what happened to my people," he paused, "My father and my brother."

"But your father tried to kill you!" Brooke said, "What if he tries again?"

Adrian brushed a tear off of Brooke's cheek and grinned. "That's enough of leaking saltwater," he joked.

Brooke couldn't breathe. I took a risk. I opened myself up to another person. I gave Adrian my heart and now he's leaving me, just like my mother. The thought was like a piercing blade in her chest.

Brooke looked at the ground. "Are you ever coming back?" she whispered.

Adrian pulled her close. *Brooke,* Adrian said in her head, *Nothing can keep me away from you. Not a fleet of sharks or a hurricane or even a death sentence over my head.* He tipped her chin up to look in his eyes. *I love you, Brooke. And the Athlanmara mate for life,* he said, grinning.

Zoe and Jackson walked out onto the pier.

Zoe folded her arms and sneered at Maksim. "Well, don't hurry back," she said smugly, "It's not like I'll miss either of you, no offense Brooke, it's just that I think I've had enough adventures for a while." Mak took a step towards Zoe. He paused, then turned and dove into the sea. Jackson smiled as he watched his competition disappear.

Adrian couldn't let go of Brooke. "I'll be back, I promise," he said.

He leaned down and kissed her again. They both felt the intense connection. Peace washed over Brooke and her fears faded away like the early morning fog.

Adrian pulled back and looked into Brooke's eyes, they were glowing. He walked backwards, his arm outstretched, touching Brooke's fingers until the moment he leapt into the sea that was his home.

35 NEW BEGINNINGS

Deep under the surface of the Bermuda Triangle, the bata circled above the colony. Adrian and Mak had trouble getting their bearings. The domes that had been Adrian's home for over a decade were as dark as the sea floor below. The youths could sense other Athlanmara in the general area but It was hard for them to figure out what was going on. They were loathe to leave the relative safety of the bata for the vulnerability of the open sea.

Adrian.

Both boys heard the voice. It startled them, the speaker was close. Adrian recognized the voice as the Builder. He opened the hatch and entered the open water, Mak following reluctantly.

The Builder was floating behind their bata serenely. He silently motioned to the boys. They followed him away from the colony. The Builder stopped and turned his powerful gaze on the young Athlanmara.

A slight smile crossed his ancient features. *You did well,* he said. Both boys had the feeling that he knew every detail of their recent adventures. *You helped to save their world and your own,* he went on, *But at a high cost.* His face grew serious. *You may never return to the colony.*

The hope that had been building in Mak's heart burst like a bubble. We're doomed, he thought. The word of their traitorous deeds will get out and no Athlanmaran will shelter them.

The Builder observed their dejected appearance. *Do you still want to serve your people?* he asked with all seriousness.

Aye, Adrian answered fearlessly.

The Builder swam in a slow circle around the youths. *The world is getting smaller,* he mused, *in my day you could live many lifetimes without seeing a single human.* The Builder sighed. *But no longer.* He looked at the boys thoughtfully. *You have made allies in the other world, haven't you?* Adrian froze in panic. Was the Builder going to harm Brooke, he wondered.

The Builder saw the look on Adrian's face and guessed his thoughts. *Don't worry, I mean no harm to your friends, in fact,* he paused, *that is how you can help your people.*

The whole conversation was mind boggling to Mak. Were they in trouble or were they being commended?

I don't understand, Adrian said. Mak was relieved he wasn't the only one who was confused.

The Builder smiled at the boys. *For our people to survive in this new era,* he explained, *we are going to have to live in communion with the humans. We have run out of places to hide. I want you and Mak to live among the humans and learn their ways to find out how our people can survive in this age.*

The Builder chuckled. *I am too old for this new world,* he said looking earnestly at Adrian and Mak, *our people need young, fearless Athlanmara to lead them into the future.*

Adrian's mind was reeling. Here was the leader of the colony asking him to break the oldest and most severe law of their culture, to go live on land with humans, with Brooke. Am I dreaming this? Is this possible, he wondered. Then he remembered how his father had tried to kill Brooke.

What about my father? Adrian asked.

The Builders eyes grew steely. *Your father committed treason against the colony, he and his accomplices have fled,* he said, *If they return, they will be executed.*

Adrian and Mak looked at each other wide eyed. They had expected to be the ones fleeing for their lives. This was not the reception they had predicted.

Will you take on this mission, the Builder asked, *for your people?*

A smile spread across Adrian's face. *Aye.* He almost spun in circles for joy. *We'll do it!*

The tiny yellow house baked in the late August sun. Inside, the Mario Kart menu was playing on the T.V. over and over. Brooke, Zoe and Jackson were sitting on the floor with Nintendo controllers in their hands staring at the screen. Tom was lying on the couch with his laptop open trying to find another grant to apply for.

"Uh, kids," he said, "That song is driving me crazy, are you playing or not?" The three teens didn't respond. "Brooke!" Tom yelled.

Brooke jumped. "What?" She looked up like she didn't know where she was.

"Just wondering if you guys are playing your game," Tom said. He tried to sound cheerful but he was extremely stressed.

He was injured, which meant he had astronomical hospital bills to pay and now he had no job. Tom was trying hard to hide his worry from Brooke, she had been through enough trauma lately, but he was at the end of his rope.

Brooke leaned forward and turned off the television. Zoe and Jackson didn't react. Brooke sat staring at the blank T.V. screen. All she could see was Adrian's dad stabbing a knife into his chest. Blood poured out of Adrian as the light left his eyes. He could die and I would never even know what happened to him, Brooke agonized. A shark could attack him, some random crabs might be floating around, who knows? Brooke started to chew her nails. Zoe sighed.

Jackson looked at Zoe and realized with his biggest competition gone he needed to step up his game. "So, school starts in two weeks, you guys excited?" he asked, "It's our senior year!" Brooke and Zoe just looked at Jackson sorrowfully. "Come on you guys!" Jackson continued, "I've worked my whole life to be a senior, it's gonna be the best year ever!"

There was a knock on the door. Brooke perked up until she remembered that Adrian and Mak never knocked. The two girls sighed again.

"Come in!" Tom yelled.

Steve walked into the living room. "Oh, hey!" Steve said, cheerfully, "Glad to see you're all here. I wanted you to meet some new exchange students that are going to be staying at my house."

Adrian and Mak walked into the room, fully clothed for once, with huge grins on their faces. Brooke and Zoe screamed at the top of their lungs and flung themselves at the boys knocking them to the ground.

Jackson put his hands over his ears. "Ahhhh! My ears!" he yelled.

Another tropical storm rolled in over the Florida Keys. The tempest earlier in the month made the current storm feel like a gentle spring rain. Dr. Gordon stood on the pier at the Marathon boat club, his mood as dark as the lowering clouds.

Once again, his quest had been thwarted. The tracking signal had never come on again. He had searched all over the Keys but had found no trace of anything unusual except for the freak hurricane that had interrupted his investigation. He wanted to leave the scene of his failure so desperately that he couldn't wait anymore for the roads or airports to reopen. He had sent Malcolm off to charter a boat to Miami.

On the other hand he couldn't stand the thought of once again going home empty handed, looking into the hollow eyes of the woman he loved, helpless to do anything to save her. All of his money and all of his miracle drugs could never repair her damaged nerves. Multiple Sclerosis would be her death sentence.

He looked around at the landscape so foreign from his native Scotland, the palm trees, the brilliant blue water, the white sands. He hated this place. If he hadn't of stopped to help that bloody girl he might have made it out of this backwater jungle before the hurricane struck.

That girl. Suddenly, Gordon remembered that she had been yelling crazy things. At the time he had been too focused on his own hunt to heed the ravings of the deranged teen. But there was something that she said that stuck in his mind. He tried to remember the girl's words.

She had gone on to the police about her friend being kidnapped by polluters and that they needed to hurry and stop the storm. Gordon mulled over the events of the last few days, the beacon going dead, the freakish hurricane, the distraught girl trying to stop a storm. Who could stop a hurricane, he wondered.

The answer hit Gordon like a slap in the face. It could be stopped if someone or something was responsible for starting it. Gordon knew just the kind of creature which possessed that power.

Malcolm floated up to him in the powerful cruiser he had just acquired. He looked at his employer standing on the dock. Dr. Gordon was staring off into the distance as if he'd been turned to stone.

"Ay, doc," he yelled, "Ya comin?"

A slow smile spread over Gordon's face. "No," he stated, "In fact, I've become so fond of this place I'm going to build a new research facility here, in Marathon, Florida.

EPILOGUE

The moon reflected off the rocky beach of the tiny island nestled on the northern coast of Scotland. The black pebbles were slick from the waves that had rolled over their shores for eons. Two figures rose out of the icy waters, spears in their hands.

An old woman appeared on the hill above the beach, her white hair blowing in the wild wind from the sea. She was beautiful, though wrinkled from enduring the elements of her remote domain. She looked down at the two fierce Athlanmarans and her green eyes sparkled.

Bronte and Utari approached the woman. "Hail, Morgan," Utari said bowing with one hand on his chest, the customary Athlanmaran greeting. Morgan returned the greeting.

"You've recovered my son, Utari," she said, smiling, "I'm grateful to ya."

Morgan pulled out a knife quick as a striking cobra and stabbed Utari in the gut. Bronte grabbed him from behind and sliced open his neck with his wicked claws. Morgan knelt down and removed the copper seunach from Utari's still twitching arm. She placed it on her own arm and laughed. The sound of her laughter was lovely and terrifying.

She turned to Bronte. "I see ya received my message," she said. Bronte nodded, stone faced. She walked up to Bronte and gently touched his arm. "And now yours," she whispered in his ear.

He felt like he was in a nightmare. The humans murdered his wife, poisoned his son and turned his other son against him. His heart was filled with hatred. He had only one thing to live for now, the deliverance of his race.

Bronte was loathe to part with his last shred of dignity and power but he had nowhere else to turn to accomplish his goals. He removed the silver band on his arm, his fingers trembling. Morgan snatched it quickly and placed it on her own arm next to the copper seunach. The two bands glowed momentarily, then they wound around each other becoming one.

Morgan closed her eyes and breathed deeply. She could feel the power course through her body. Bronte watched in horror as her skin became youthful and her hair returned to its former auburn splendor. Her eyes flew open. The light was so piercing, Bronte had to look away.

Morgan ran her fingers through her hair, admiring her own beauty. She laughed again, then turned her gaze back to Bronte.

She saw his look of terror and sensed the sadness in his heart. "Don't worry, my heart," she said, softly, "When I have collected the four seunach all your pain will be washed away and the world will be made new."

Morgan fingered the intertwined bands on her arm. "Wait till I have the band of gold," she sighed. Then she turned her penetrating gaze onto Bronte. "And you know where it tis, don't ya?"

"Aye," Bronte answered, "I know where it tis."

Morgan ran her finger along the scar on Bronte's face. Then she put her hands on his cheeks. "Let's see what else ya know." She dug her nails into the flesh of Bronte's temples. His eyes rolled back into his head, blood trickled down his face. "Ah, I have two grandsons," Morgan said, smiling, "You were wise ta hide them from me."

She dug her nails in deeper, "Now, show me everything."

A NOTE TO MY READERS

This book is about a group of young friends who, by working together and crossing barriers, were able to impact the world around them. You too, dear reader, can make a difference in this world. There are many organizations that are working hard to clean up our environment. I have included some links to get you started. But don't forget, there are other young people just like youself in other countries, China, Indonesia, the Phillipines, that are just as concerned about making a difference as you. Cross those barriers, start a non-profit yourself, educate others around you, find friends who want to help. You can change the world!

www.4ocean.com

www.theoceancleanup.com

www.oceanconservancy.org

www.surfrider.org